Praise for *The*

"Tautly paced, *The Byways* has aspects of both *The Lightning Thief* and *Alice in Wonderland* with a protagonist who must learn the language and laws of another realm in order to find herself and her way home. This lush, well-written YA fantasy tale follows CeeCee as she overcomes her feelings of being an outsider by courageously embracing herself through a series of trials rife with humor and action—all within a gorgeous paranormal universe."

—**Susan Wands,** author of *Magician and Fool*

"From the first page, Mary Pascual captivates and enchants with this modern, edgy take on *Alice in Wonderland*. Her rich and complex characters shine brightly in the dark world she paints in *The Byways*. The tension and the twists will keep you reading until the very end. A true delight—wildly original!"

—**Stacey L. Tucker,** author of The Equal Night Trilogy

"The agility and caliber of imagination Mary Pascual exhibits in this book are impressive. Move over, Lewis Carroll!"

—**Maki Morris,** author of *Blood and Brume*

"CeeCee is a worthy and powerful heroine, filled with grit and determination. Readers will root for her from beginning to end as she combats weird, dangerous, and frightening challenges in the Byways."

—**Fatima R. Henson,** author of *Love in the Age of Dragons*

"*The Byways* is a fast-paced fantasy ideal for readers craving a perfectly mysterious adventure through a magical and unknown realm. For both the young and young at heart, this urban retelling of *Alice in Wonderland* guarantees gasps, laughter, chills, and excitement—and will leave you dreaming of a new self to discover."

—**Yodassa Williams,** author of *The Goddess Twins*

THE
BYWAYS

THE BYWAYS

A
NOVEL

MARY PASCUAL

SPARKPRESS

Published by SparkPress, a BookSparks imprint,
A division of SparkPoint Studio, LLC
Phoenix, Arizona, USA, 85007
www.gosparkpress.com

Published 2023
Printed in the United States of America
Print ISBN: 978-1-68463-190-2
E-ISBN: 978-1-68463-191-9
Library of Congress Control Number: 2022917179

Interior design by Katherine Lloyd, The DESK

for lucky Chance
and Jake the Magical Kitty
(pugs and pisses)

"Who am I, then? Tell me that first, and then, if I like being that person, I'll come up: if not, I'll stay down here till I'm somebody else."

—*Alice*

ONE

This Is Not the First Time You Tried to Get Away

In the drop of blue, everything was fine—or maybe richer or deeper or more significant. CeeCee pushed around the ink on her desk, mesmerized by the way it moved. She imagined swimming through the blue ink. It looked like what she imagined smoky jazz nightclubs must feel like.

"Detention!" Mr. Beauchamp slapped a hand on her desk and smiled, tight and mean.

CeeCee threw herself back against her chair. Her temper flared, and she wrestled it under control. She took her time digging a tissue from her backpack, snapping it open, and with exaggerated movements cleaning up the ink, because it didn't matter. Mr. Beauchamp would still tell the principal she was defacing school property.

He was smirking at her, and she glared back mutinously. She swore he lived for these moments. Normally, she'd challenge him—occasionally, she even won a few rounds. But today . . .

today she just wanted to get the school day over with. Instead of arguing with him, CeeCee stared stubbornly at the clock. They were the only numbers in math class that stayed sane. Every other number frolicked about and blew raspberries at her. If Mr. Beauchamp would only explain the problems in words, she thought she'd be all right. But he never did, especially for her. He'd just point to the board every time she asked a question.

"It's right here," he'd say. "Right here. You're just not paying attention."

The bell went off with a screech. She scooted past Mr. Beauchamp, grabbing the detention slip he waved at her. She looked at the slip, and sure enough, it said, "Graffiti" in the spot marked "Reason for Detention." Not that it mattered. Once he had given her detention for "Sitting."

Crumpling the slip into a ball, she shoved it into her bag. She pulled a Jolly Rancher out of her pocket and crunched it. The force of the candy breaking against her teeth felt good, giving her a focus that wasn't Mr. Beauchamp's stupid smirk. With each bite, her anger dissipated. Chewing candy or gum was one of the techniques she had learned in therapy. It was supposed to help center her when she felt overwhelmed or her body felt antsy. But it worked well for managing her temper with idiots too—at least sometimes.

She hurried down the crowded hall to the cafeteria. Her best friend, Trudy, was a grade ahead and had lunch scheduled a period earlier than CeeCee's, but sometimes she could catch Trudy on the way to class. The rows of lockers stretched on forever, gray lockers against light gray walls. She knew it was an illusion, but occasionally it gave her vertigo. Rumor had it that someone in the district had screwed up the paint order, and they ran out of money before they could repaint the lockers to whatever cheerful, contrasting color they were supposed to be. She doubted it, though. Institutional gray was so much more mind-numbing. It kept the sheep docile but only by so much.

Down the hall, Corey, that stupid jerk, was harassing one of the freshmen again. She hated bullies. The kid looked petrified, scrunched against a locker while Corey towered over him. On instinct, CeeCee slowed down and banged her fist hard on the locker behind Corey. He jumped, whirling around to scowl at her, and the freshman bolted. She grinned at the escaping kid's back. Then she bared her teeth wolfishly at Corey, daring him to say something as she sailed by.

He didn't, of course. Sometimes bad reputations had their benefits.

Inside the cafeteria, Trudy stood next to a table talking with the Committee Crew. That's what CeeCee called them in her head anyway. The girls were organized and active and intense in their leadership responsibilities, and every one of them looked the part of an honor roll student, down to the extra notebooks they carried. God forbid one of them ever got their hands on a clipboard. Trudy, efficient and serene, her dark hair draped over one shoulder, projected so much confidence. She seemed taller than the rest of them, even though she was half a head shorter than CeeCee.

Today, they looked very serious. CeeCee fleetingly considered not interrupting them, but this was really her only chance to catch Trudy at school. Besides, they always had some drama or other going on.

"Hey, True!" The girls fell silent as she walked over, the clomping of her boots intrusive and loud.

Trudy had her head bent over a notebook but raised her head and smiled briefly. "Hey, CeeCee! Hold on a sec, I've got to get this down before I forget." She scribbled furiously.

Trudy's friends stared at CeeCee. One of the girls she recognized from the numerous groups Trudy tended to join, but she didn't know her name. She knew the other two girls, Kate and Marlowe, but she was never sure what type of reception she was going to get. Sometimes they were friendly, like when they were all at Trudy's house, and sometimes they were . . . well, not. But they were never outright mean either, these "almost friends," which CeeCee ironically appreciated. She tried for a smile, but the three girls continued to give her the side-eye. She let her face go blank and refused to leave, no matter how uncomfortable it felt. She ran her fingers along her left arm, counting the raised bumps of freckles and moles over and over in her mind.

"Okay, done!" Trudy jabbed her pen at the notebook. "Kate, I'll have those notes typed up tonight, and we can probably order the rest of the supplies tomorrow."

Then she turned and gave CeeCee a hug.

Something inside CeeCee loosened. "So . . . tonight?" She hoped the answer was still yes.

"Definitely. We're on!" Trudy beamed and grabbed a book bag off the table. "It has been way too long! I've got to run to class, but I'll call you later."

"Meow!" said CeeCee.

"Meow ciao, babe." Trudy winked a brown eye at her and laughed.

CeeCee gave a vague wave in the other girls' direction. "See you later!"

"She's such a weirdo," she heard behind her. "I don't know why you hang out with her."

"Because weird is awesome," Trudy shot back. "Better than being afraid."

CeeCee grinned. Trudy was one of those rare individuals who could rule a clique if she wanted to and do it without being a bitch . . . but that didn't mean she'd put up with any crap. Besides having extra college prep work, Trudy also participated on so many committees that CeeCee hadn't seen her in a while. But they'd been planning a sleepover for weeks for just the two of them. It had gotten delayed three times, but now it was finally happening. Most days, 80 percent of CeeCee's time felt like an exercise in self-control. She needed a good brain-dump session with her best friend.

With a happy spring in her step, she ducked out of the packed cafeteria into the bathroom. CeeCee stood in front of the mirror and shook her head so her blonde hair flew out around her, like she was shaking off the noise of the hall. She smoothed it back, then squinted at her reflection.

The mirror looked funny. She frowned at it. It was sort of blurry around the edges . . . but not. She put her hand out slowly, in case someone had smeared something gross on it. Just before she touched the surface, a buzz met her fingertips, like an electric current had jumped the gap. She gasped, yanking her hand back.

The door swung open while she gaped at the mirror, waiting for it to do something.

"Hey, trailer."

CeeCee forgot about the mirror as her hands curled into fists. That amused, snarling voice was a hot coal on her nerves. Taylor Blake and four of her closest thugs appeared behind CeeCee, smirking as if their lives depended on it.

"What kind of name is CeeCee anyway, trailer trash?" Taylor flicked her long Hollywood hair over one shoulder. Taylor and her friends were clad in their usual armor of perfectly groomed superiority. Behind her, Ashley—Taylor's number one crony and chief muscle—applied lip gloss while glaring at CeeCee. Somehow, the girls always looked polished even when they were vigorously bullying people.

Taylor also never seemed to grasp that "trailer" and "Taylor" were a perfect rhyme.

"It's better than being named after your future career." Cee-Cee turned slowly and crossed her arms. "I see your parents had high hopes for you. What's your middle name? Dog groomer? Sewage engineer?"

One of the girls behind her made a squashed choking sound. CeeCee smiled as Taylor's eyes narrowed.

"Did you remember your medication today, trailer trash?" Taylor snapped. "We wouldn't want you to forget your me-di-ca-tion."

Immediately, CeeCee's face heated up. She stepped toward Taylor before she could stop herself. She knew she should try to leave—it was the basis of every anti-bullying campaign. But no matter how many times she walked away, the girls always followed her.

"How's your nose, Taylor?" she said between gritted teeth. "Did you get the work done yet? It's looking a little crooked."

Taylor blanched. The bathroom door swung open, and half a dozen girls poured in. A few of them stopped short and looked warily at Taylor and CeeCee. But a beefy senior from the varsity basketball team casually body checked Taylor to the side on her way to the mirror without even an "excuse me."

Taylor flailed before catching her balance. Face red with outrage, she stormed out of the bathroom, her cronies in tow. CeeCee took a shaky breath and leaned on the wall, anger swirling inside her like a storm. Taylor used to only pick on her occasionally, with CeeCee just one of several victims in Taylor's regularly scheduled bitch rotations. But Taylor had underestimated the rumors about her temper. CeeCee had already gotten into a fight with her once, and if it happened again, she'd probably get kicked out of school. The only reason she was saved from expulsion last time was because the security cameras caught Taylor and her friends throwing trash at her. When one of them had picked up the garbage can to pour it over CeeCee's head, she had snapped and decked Taylor with a right hook. It had broken Taylor's nose, and ever since then, she and her friends had been relentless—but also a little afraid. It was a strange power struggle they were caught in, one that CeeCee couldn't help feel like she was going to eventually lose.

"If you keep rising to the bait, they're not going to stop. They've learned all your buttons." Mr. Reyes rubbed the space between his eyes.

The counselor's office was small and messy and much too familiar, and Mr. Reyes looked more tired than usual.

"If you know what they're doing, why am I the one who keeps getting in trouble?" CeeCee slumped in the chair, her arms crossed.

She had gotten tossed out of history class after Ashley began antagonizing her. Again! Her teacher knew she hadn't started it, but she had insisted CeeCee leave anyway. Frustration clawed at her throat. She was doubly annoyed because it was her favorite class and she had wanted to talk over her paper with the teacher.

"You're not in trouble . . ."

"Yeah, right."

"This is just a break. Your IEP allows you to take breaks. I wish you would ask for them instead of letting it get to this point."

"See? Even when I'm not in trouble, I'm in trouble!" Her stupid IEP—her stupid IEP and all the damn labels: sensory processing disorder, ADHD, impulse-control issues. The list went on. Different therapists had given her different labels over the years. But really it came down to that she was a girl and had a temper. It didn't matter how many superhero movies there were with women kicking ass, the truth was that no one wants that girl in their classroom or at their party or acting out when the sensory issues became too much. The therapies, the techniques she learned—they did help. But not one of those labels told her how she was supposed to anticipate when other people would be assholes. The injustice rankled, as it always did. "Maybe I don't want to be defined by my IEP."

"Well, that's the world you live in. You need to change some of your patterns. If you can keep a cool head and ignore the behavior, they'll get bored." Mr. Reyes patted around on the top of his desk as he talked.

"Why don't *they* change *their* patterns? Why aren't *they* in this damn office?"

"Hey!"

CeeCee took a deep breath and let it out all in a rush. She reached under a stack of papers and pulled out his glasses. "Here."

"Thanks." He peered at her over the tops of the lenses. "What about a new strategy? Have you ever tried a punching bag or hitting a pillow? It can be really effective. Whenever you feel tension build up, you can burn off energy in a harmless way."

She gaped at him. "Seriously? Where am I supposed to find a pillow at school? 'Excuse me, Mr. Beauchamp, your anal-retentive face is making me want to hit something. Can I go to my locker?'"

Mr. Reyes snorted in amusement, then gave her a stern look. He continued rifling through the papers on his desk.

It wasn't a bad idea, actually, similar to other techniques she had learned in therapy. It was just . . . impractical. People already thought she was weird. What would they say if she started punching a pillow stuffed in her locker?

"Do *you* use that strategy?" she asked.

"With this job? Three times a week at the gym."

"Hmmm." CeeCee sat in silence while Mr. Reyes half-heartedly organized folders.

It *was* calm in his office, more than any other place on campus. And she liked Mr. Reyes. He never talked down to her, even when she was in trouble. There were worse places to take a "break," but she was still pissed that she was sent out of class. She pulled a composition book and her favorite pencil out of her bag. It had a fuzzy pencil grip on it that she loved. When too many other sounds, like the buzzing light, were irritating, the pencil or other fidgets helped. It was ironic, using one sensory input to beat other sensory distractions, but it worked. She rolled the pencil between her fingers, using the soft feel to center herself, before she started writing out the lyrics to "Round Here" by Counting Crows. The words flowed as easy as water onto the page.

She felt herself unwind just a teeny bit in the quiet. Just to spite her, the fluorescent light overhead started flickering and the ever-present hum ratcheted up to a grating buzz. It felt like a chain saw in her ears.

CeeCee winced. "Are they ever going to fix that?"

Mr. Reyes groaned. "It's been doing that on and off all day." He rubbed his eyes again.

"No wonder you want to punch something." She smirked at him. "Do you really think advocating violence will alleviate the problem?"

"Well, you're just extra smart today, aren't you?" he snapped back.

Remorse twisted inside her. "No," she grumped, "I just always feel set up. Why do I have so many more rules than anybody else?" And the worst thing, her private fear—what if that never changed? She swallowed a sudden lump in her throat.

"Because, CeeCee, you get more . . . emotionally charged than other people. You need to be mindful of those triggers to keep yourself under control."

She gritted her teeth. She was fully sick of hearing about

control. It's not like she was jumping people in the halls, like Corey did. Boys got away with that crap all the time. She wasn't mean. She just had a lot of energy. And it spilled out sometimes. Exuberant, her mom called it. Her mom seemed to be the only one who thought her spirit was a good thing.

"Just wait," her mom would say. "You've got drive. It'll take you far in this world."

But the drive to do what, exactly? CeeCee felt like she was floundering. She'd like to do something with music, but she didn't play an instrument and she wasn't planning on learning one. Sound bothered her often; it was overwhelming and unexpected. But not when she could control it.

The light screeched louder overhead, and she beat her pencil rapidly against the notebook. On top of everything, people gossiped about her all the time, inflating her reputation, twisting the truth. The stories had gotten so bad, sometimes even she couldn't tell when it was her fault or when it was other people. It was already hard to handle the day-to-day sensory overload without being constantly reminded that she was too loud, too surly, and a troublemaker to boot. The world was just too much.

"Maybe it's all the excessive demands that make me lose control. If people would just leave me alone, I would be fine."

"You and I both know that isn't completely true. There are always going to be people or situations that irritate you." Mr. Reyes opened up drawers while he talked and rifled through more folders. "People who are jerks just because they can be. Lights that are possessed by demons." He jabbed an accusing finger at the flickering light above them. "Your job is to learn how to deal with that. And until you figure that out, things are going to be tough."

"I thought my job was to get an education," she said sourly. "My file is on the second stack on top of your filing cabinet, by the way." She pointed behind him.

"Thanks again." He turned and grabbed the folder. "Speaking of education . . ." Mr. Reyes stopped and sighed.

CeeCee's whole body went tense.

"I'm recommending that you retake your math class in summer school."

"What?! Why?" Her whole summer, ruined!

"Given how things have been going this year, I think you and I both know that you're hardly excelling."

"I'm getting a C!"

"You're one point away from a D."

"That's not failing! He tortures me every day, and I'm still managing to get a C!"

"He is not purposely torturing you, CeeCee."

"Sure he isn't. Anyway, a C is good enough!"

"No, CeeCee, you can do better."

"Really?" she demanded. "What if I can't?"

She left his office angry all over again. She couldn't bear the idea of sitting in a classroom with Mr. Beauchamp a second time. No matter what other trouble she got in, she'd always managed to keep her grades decent, in every subject except math. Even then, she had never been sent to summer school. School was a cage that triggered all her issues, without any chance for release. It was always too loud, or too quiet, or too rigid at the wrong time, and then people got in her face—don't fidget, don't touch, don't space out—when she needed to take a moment. Everything she'd do to help herself was wrong, and she kept the overload bottled up as much as she could until the end of the day. Even then, by the end of the year she felt like she would claw the roof off. Summers were her break—away from the bullies, away from the classrooms, and away from the rules that seemed tailor-made for her to inadvertently break.

Whatever, CeeCee thought. *I'll deal with it later.* Maybe she could pull up her grade enough to get out of it. Maybe Beauchamp didn't even teach summer school. Maybe she could just refuse to go.

The hallway was busy with kids and too loud. CeeCee staggered, unfocused. The noise overwhelmed her and made it hard to think. She could feel a headache building as bodies pushed past her. Everyone seemed excited that the week was almost over as they rushed to lockers before their next class. Each door crash and shout pinged through her head like a bullet.

She'd been so distracted by the idea of summer school that she'd walked in the wrong direction. She spun around and headed for her own locker, passing a knot of girls shouting at each other in front of the admin office.

"CeeCee!"

She turned to see Trudy break away from the group. She was walking too quickly. Her usually sleek hair was flying about her face, and her knuckles were white where they clenched her notebooks. CeeCee's stomach sank. She'd seen that flustered look before.

Not today, she thought. *Not today.*

"CeeCee!" Trudy reached out for a hug. As her arms went around her, Trudy's breath hitched. "It's bad."

She realized that Trudy was more frantic than school drama usually commanded. Trudy's hands trembled where they touched her back. When she finally pulled away, her face was pale and strained. CeeCee felt a flutter of panic. Her body went cold as terrible thoughts raced through her mind.

"Are you okay?"

"No." Tears welled up in Trudy's eyes. "No, I'm not. It's just awful."

"What happened?"

Trudy looked over at the knot of girls and put a hand over her mouth. She didn't seem to be listening. CeeCee's panic grew.

"Oh god, is someone hurt?"

"I think I'm going to be sick."

"Is it your parents? Or your brothers? True?!" She grabbed her by the shoulders, forcing Trudy to look her in the eye.

Trudy drew a deep, wobbly breath. "No, it's. . . ." She leaned in close to CeeCee. "I'm screwed if I don't fix it. The caterer called three times, but I just got the message."

"Wait . . . the caterer?"

"They're saying they don't have the deposit. I don't know what happened—I could have sworn I gave them the money when I solidified the menu with them. I have to go down to the place right now and get it paid, or we won't have any food for the dance. Then I have to figure out what happened to that money. It was all the fundraising cash from the carwash. I'm so screwed, CeeCee."

"Okay, whoa . . ." She felt sucker punched with relief. "This is about the dance. God, Trudy! I thought something really bad had happened!"

"This is bad, CeeCee! Money is missing, and everybody is pissed!"

"No, this is a problem, but it isn't bad."

Trudy looked stricken. "What if they think I stole it?"

Without CeeCee meaning it to, a laugh bubbled up. She knew, *she knew*, Trudy was upset. She even knew that losing money was serious, but it had been too long of a day already. "No one is going to think *you* stole it, True. You're not the delinquent, remember? I am."

"But I was still in charge! It was still my responsibility!"

"You need to calm down. It's just a stupid dance!"

"It's not stupid! People are counting on me!"

CeeCee took a deep breath and reined in her giggles. "Okay, what can I do to help?"

The panicky look crawled over Trudy's face again. "I don't think there's anything you can do. I'm getting excused early to run to the caterer right now. The counselor has cut me a check that we'll have to pay back somehow. Then . . ."

"Then I'll help you go over your checklists tonight, and we'll figure out what happened. The money is probably in one of your folders or marked on a note or something."

"No, CeeCee, I don't think we can do it tonight."

"Of course we can! Look, I don't mind if the other girls stop by. We'll figure out the problem because you always do, and then you'll feel better and we'll have the rest of the night!"

"No, no, you can't come tonight." Trudy shook her head, frazzled and distracted. "It's not a good idea. The other girls *are* coming to go through our records. If you're there, they might think . . ." She stopped guiltily.

"You're canceling on me." Slowly the words registered in her mind. "Wait, they might think what? That I had something to do with it?"

"Some of those girls . . . some of them might look for someone to blame."

"But I'm not even on the committee!"

"Yeah, but you were there."

"I was *where?*" CeeCee's volume rose with every word.

"You were over at my house a few weeks ago when we counted the money from the carwash and went over the budget."

"I didn't know that was what you were doing! I was working on my homework while you had your meeting, remember?" She gaped at her. "Trudy . . . you don't think . . . I had anything to do with it, do you?"

"*No!*" Trudy looked abashed. "But I don't know what other people will think."

CeeCee felt the whole world crash down on her heart. "Because I'm a delinquent. I'm a fucking criminal mastermind who lies in wait until I can steal money from a *dance committee?*"

Frustration flashed across Trudy's face, and her voice rose. "I can't do this right now! You have no idea what kind of pressure I'm under."

"I don't know about pressure? Are you kidding me? You just accused me of stealing!"

"I did *not* accuse you of stealing!"

"Yeah, but one of the other prom robots is going to, right? I'm the obvious choice?" Out of the corner of her eye, CeeCee could see people watching them, hanging on every word like they were prime-time drama. She would be mortified if she wasn't already so upset. She and Trudy never fought like this, especially at school. "I can't fucking believe this!"

"This doesn't even matter! It's not like it's happened!"

"It does matter!" CeeCee yelled. "And if *you* didn't join so many committees, maybe you wouldn't have lost track of the money! I mean, it was going to happen eventually!"

Trudy stared at her, wounded and angry and guilty. She pulled out her phone and checked the time. "Yeah, well, I've got to take care of this. Thanks for not being a baby."

She turned and walked away.

CeeCee felt the dismissal like a slap.

The hall had finally emptied, but it still felt like everything in it was staring. The drinking fountain pointed a finger; the silence sneered at her. CeeCee wanted nothing more than to curl up into a ball on the floor. Instead, she stumbled to her locker, her hands shaking as she opened it for her favorite hoodie. She still had two more classes to get through. Her stomach curdled in dread.

She wasn't cold, but she pulled the hoodie on. It blocked out everything for a moment, and CeeCee paused with it over her face, relishing the break. She stared at a fuzzy world through the red fabric, trying to figure out what had just happened.

Then her head popped through the hoodie. Directly across from her, a Spring Fling prom poster glared at her balefully.

Everything became a swirl and rush of heat. She ripped the poster off the wall, the paper tearing violently. But she still felt awful and helpless. She tripped against an abandoned desk in the hallway. CeeCee gripped the edge of the desk and threw it with all her weight. It crashed to the floor and skidded a measly three feet.

"Aaargh!" she screamed into the empty hall. That wasn't far enough; that wasn't nearly far enough.

"Principal's office *now*!" Mr. Beauchamp stood in the doorway of a classroom. He didn't even look smug, for once—he just looked pissed.

But not as mad as CeeCee.

"*No!*" She snatched up her backpack and ran out of school.

TWO

Happenstance Has Fallen

CeeCee stomped down the sidewalk, anger eating a yawning hole in her stomach. She thought she might fall into that hole and never come out.

How could Trudy say that? CeeCee knew things were said about her . . . that she was trailer trash, that she got in fights all the time, that she'd end up in juvie. Somehow it had never mattered that there were people who thought the worst of her because Trudy had always seen the best. She had always assumed Trudy had never heard the nastier rumors—or that she disregarded them . . . or something. Well, clearly she not only knew about them but also wanted to prevent CeeCee's bad reputation from dragging her down too. Somehow that hurt worse than actually accusing her of stealing.

She was so mad, she felt like crying. That made her even angrier. She kicked the pole of a bus-stop sign so hard, it bonged in the still street. Her headache rang with the impact.

CeeCee wandered aimlessly away from school. The streets were almost empty in the middle of the day. The neighborhood quickly changed from residential to storefronts as the buildings grew toward downtown office buildings. A few stay-at-home types and elderly people dawdled in small boutiques and vintage stores. Farther down the street, business people hurried between buildings or went into restaurants for a late lunch.

It was just so unfair! She hadn't done half the stuff people said she had, yet everyone immediately suspected her whenever something went wrong. The missing money was probably just a mistake. It wasn't her fault that Trudy constantly loaded up her schedule. She shouldn't be blamed for being in the area of a meeting she didn't have anything to do with!

Now she'd get in trouble for cutting class too. CeeCee wondered how far she could get if she just kept walking. Her anger faded into a dull depression.

She stared into the window of an import store. She and Trudy always stopped at this shop to look through the rack of Japanese T-shirts and blouses. Last time, she had picked out a cute Buddha cat T-shirt for Trudy. She loved it so much, she had changed into it right then and there and wore it home. Trudy swore CeeCee had lucky magic. "You always find the best stuff," she had said. "It could be under three boxes and a pile of jockstraps, and you'd still find it." And CeeCee *did* feel lucky . . . whenever she was with True.

Maybe that had been the last time. If Trudy really thought CeeCee's reputation was that bad, maybe she wouldn't want to be friends anymore. CeeCee stared morosely at the tchotchke table set up on the sidewalk. Stuffed animals swayed from key chains, smiling their stitched grins. Solar-powered figurines waved their arms or played on miniature swings in the afternoon sun.

No one saw who she really was. Well, True had, but that

seemed to be over now. She felt her eyes grow heavy and wet. The toys continued to swing in cheerful disinterest.

It doesn't even matter, CeeCee thought. *No matter what I do, they all think I'm trash anyway.* She flushed with anger all over again, and it pushed the tears away. Why even bother trying?

She was so tired of being on guard all the time. If she were exactly who they thought she was, would they be happy then? Would they be smug? She imagined herself stomping down the hallway at school as kids scurried out of the way. Rebellion flared around her like a nimbus. She could be a criminal if she wanted to. She could be a bitch, worse than a hundred Taylors.

"They'd be really scared," she whispered. "Then they wouldn't mess with me at all."

The toys on the table cowered.

She grinned miserably. "Fuck it."

Her hand shot out and closed around one of the hanging animals on the display table. Then she took off down a side street at a run.

The image of herself as a badass outlaw disappeared forty steps later. Instead, the look on her mom's face, if she had to open the door to a police officer, flashed through her mind. Her brief elation evaporated, and a sudden pang in her stomach matched the pain in her head. She slowed to a walk.

"It doesn't matter; it's just something small."

But she knew it did. It mattered just as much as words.

CeeCee didn't even know what she had grabbed. She looked at the warm lump in her hand. It was a rabbit, but . . . she peered more closely. There seemed to be something wrong with it. All the regular rabbit bits were there, the ears, the feet, soft fur against her thumb, but the expression . . . she couldn't decide if it looked terrified or outraged. Its eyes bugged out, one brow beetled down, and the mouth was stitched into a grimace. There were splatters of red paint on its fur, and one paw jutted out at a crooked angle. The key chain it dangled from was, in contrast, a cheerful pink plastic. It was probably the most deranged rabbit she had ever seen.

CeeCee shuddered and looked around. She was in an alley of gray bricks, with litter blown into grungy corners, a couple of dumpsters, and a few doors. The sick-sweet smell of fading garbage overlaid everything. Clouds blew across the sky past the buildings' edges, blue and gray and white. There was a quick-as-a-snake rustle behind her, and in a panic, she bolted.

She flew past the first dumpster, then the second. Right behind it, hidden from view, was a side alley. CeeCee darted right and ended up in a skinny passage of brick walls. She kept running, trying to put distance between her and whoever had seen her shoplift. She was sure it was the shopkeeper or a customer ready to call her out, and the adrenaline hit, as it always did, *after* she had done something.

I'll just cut through the alleys instead of the main street, she thought. Except now, she was going the wrong direction, and she was too pumped up to slow down. She coughed, her throat tight and hot, and tried to muffle the sound. The alley opened up on a right turn and gave a glimpse of the main street ahead. She zipped left into another side alley before she paused and listened hard. It didn't sound like anyone was coming down the passage after her. She rubbed her thumb over and over across the rabbit. Touching something soft usually eased her anxiety, but this time, it just made her feel worse.

That was so stupid, she thought. Nausea flared. Her stomach in coils, she turned and trudged down the alley, the lines of old brick stretching out like bars. She needed to get to the next road over. If she could just get home, maybe she could pretend nothing had happened. She would call True and apologize for yelling. Or she could offer to help again. Maybe make cookies for her? Her plans sounded dismal, just another pathetic evening at home after she had fucked up the day. The urge to cry welled up again, and she squashed it down. CeeCee shoved the rabbit into a pocket and trailed her hand along the brick wall, wiping the feel of fur from her skin.

She was so stupid.

An alley branched off, and she turned left. A building blocked the street from view, but another alley ran along it. She turned again, the gray cement reminding her of the school hallways. Broken clouds skittered across the sun, and the light dimmed and brightened the alley indecisively. Her head felt like it was throbbing in time. The image of a police officer popped into her head again, and she forced it away. A fluffy pink bunny replaced it instead.

"Not that either!" she barked—and jumped at the sound of her own voice.

Maybe she would take a nap when she got home. Her stomach hurt anyway; she was probably coming down with the flu. It was good her sleepover with True was canceled after all.

Really, maybe she was just useless.

"Useless," she whispered, and a ghost of the sound seemed to echo back at her. Her mom would be so disappointed in her. No wonder Trudy didn't want her around. She wasn't good for anybody.

The street traffic suddenly sounded farther away. CeeCee stopped. Gray cement bricks stretched out in either direction, and that same sense of vertigo she got at school washed over her. She realized she didn't know how many turns she'd made. How do you lose track of a street?

She tried counting the turns in her head, but they slipped away with each throb of her headache. She settled for staring at the dimming sky until she was reasonably sure she was facing the right direction.

She kept moving, hurrying to reach the street. Except the walls seemed to be getting awfully close. She glanced behind her, but the way back looked just as narrow. *That's odd*, she thought, and then, *I don't* have *to be useless*, even though some small part of her disagreed. *When I get home, I can clean the kitchen, then do math—which punishes me unfairly every day anyway—then reading.* CeeCee held her arm out in front of her and tapped the wall as she ticked off her list. She shifted her shoulders sideways so her hoodie didn't drag against the coarse brick. The alley was getting narrower, the walls crowding so close that the sky seemed very far away. But she could see the end of the passage, and there was plenty of room to walk through. The smack of her boots sounded muffled in the still, gray channel.

Her arm looked strange. CeeCee stopped, confused, and it felt too claustrophobic all of a sudden. She kept walking, shaking off the vertigo. Her backpack snagged on the stone, so she slipped it off and held it with her other hand. The walls squeezed in, brushing against her body, and she slowed down automatically. Her fingers crept along the wall like a daddy longlegs. She inched forward. It was almost like she was being squished, but she didn't feel anything, so that couldn't be right. Being squished was not even possible. The alley must have been narrower than she'd noticed, that's all. Her headache was distracting her. She shuffled forward three more steps, and her arm flattened against the sides of the alley almost exactly like she had been rolled by a giant rolling pin.

She gaped at her arm, at the alley. Now she could see it—the walls were moving silently in on either side of her, pinning her flat. But wouldn't that hurt? Shouldn't she feel that? CeeCee tried to turn and realized she could no longer move her head to look back. She panicked, the fear wild and sharp and unthinking. Her feet scuttled backward against the pavement, but she felt wedged in from behind. Her hand scrabbled at the wall, and she wrenched forward. She managed to jerk her chin down. Her torso seemed intolerably thin, and the ground looked farther away, as if she was taller now that she was rolled. Part of her mind started screaming then, while the other part refused to process anything but movement. She focused on the end of the alley where it looked marginally wider and willed her feet forward.

"Out," she hissed. "Out, out!" Tiny cracks in the brick caught at her hair as the walls pressed against her cheeks. She was pulled thinner than she thought she could possibly survive.

Then she popped out the end of the alley, like a cork from a bottle.

CeeCee dropped her backpack, bent over, and threw up. She gaped at her arms and grabbed her stomach. But everything looked normal. She was her regular size, not flat at all. She turned to stare at the alley behind her and gagged again. It was barely wide enough to let a cat walk through.

"What's happening?" Her voice was a bare shred of sound. The passage in front of her looked just like all the others. It smelled like old cement and billboard posters and vomit. The space was darker than it should have been at that time of afternoon, but it was still light enough to see.

"It's just an alley," she whispered. "It's just an alley."

She crouched over her ankles and breathed in and out very carefully. *I must have come down a different way—I'm just not paying attention again*, she thought. She stared at a spot of pavement with a torn flyer plastered to the ground. CeeCee couldn't see any other alley entrances out of the corners of her eyes, but that didn't mean they weren't there. She refused to lift her head to check. She breathed deeply until her hands stopped shaking and stared at the flyer. It read "Dead Hea . . ." before the tear, the ragged feathered edge almost pretty. It took a long time for the shaking to stop. She couldn't be sure, you see, what happened while she wasn't paying attention. That was always the problem—she couldn't be sure.

But she did know that she wanted to get to a regular street very badly.

She closed her eyes and forced herself to stand, settling her backpack on her shoulders. With a deep breath, she turned right, back toward the street where the shop was, opened her eyes, and trudged forward. The buildings towered above her as if she were at the bottom of a well.

She'd been walking too long.

I bet, she told herself, *I need to eat something. I bet my blood sugar is too low, and I'm imagining crap that didn't really happen.* She didn't feel particularly hungry, but that always happened when she was on her medication. She often skipped meals at school, but on the weekends ate like a horse to make up for it. And she'd gotten light-headed before. *Or maybe*, she continued in her mind, *the skinny alley did sort of happen, but I'm confusing the details.* She patted her arms for the hundredth time. She wished she had a mirror just to make sure she didn't look squished.

The alley seemed to stretch on forever, repeating trash cans, litter, and the occasional door into unending gray. *Stop being paranoid*, she thought sternly. *I'll hit the street at any moment. There's probably just a dumpster blocking the light at the end.* But her heart pounded as much as her feet did in the too-quiet space.

There was something up ahead. No, there was some*one* up ahead. She bit her lip and slowed down, the walls beckoning her with dubious safety until she shrank toward one side, while staring down the alley. Whoever it was looked bulky and shapeless and yet a little small. As she drew closer, she could see too many clothes and shabby ones at that.

CeeCee paused. This was the first person she had seen since

running into the alleys. *Not all homeless people are dangerous*, she thought. Old Oscar at the park told the best jokes, and he always shared a bit of his food with the pigeons. She was highly aware that being alone and female was not the safest position to be in. But since it had always just been her mom and her, CeeCee often had to manage getting herself to and from school and anywhere else she needed to go. She walked all over their part of the city while her mom was at work. She knew the streets better than most, just not this particular alley.

I can handle this, she continued in her head. *I've dealt with creepy guys before. It doesn't have to be a guy, even. It could be a woman. A nice, maternal homeless woman who would be happy to help me find the right street.*

She shook her head. Really it came down to two options: move forward or go back. The thought of going back to that impossibly skinny crack made her nauseated again. She edged closer. The person squatted next to an abandoned garbage can.

"Excuse me," CeeCee mumbled.

The person poured something back and forth between two cups, muttering.

She coughed. "Excuse me," she said louder. "Can you help me?"

The person looked up, revealing a man's small face. Black eyes peered at her above round red cheekbones and an almost crimson nose. The man broke into a smile that made his cheeks stand out even more. His whole appearance reminded CeeCee of a particularly cheery apple.

"Help?" the man chirped.

"I'm . . . I'm sorry to bother you. I just got a little turned around."

"Hello, dear! Hello!" He tipped a hat he wasn't wearing.

She could tell he was a little off, but at least he was friendly. Just in case, she kept several feet between them. "Hello. Please, I just need to know which direction to go in. Do you know where the highway is?"

"Yes, yes. You're on the way. This is the byway."

"The what?" CeeCee spoke slowly. "I'm looking for the highway. By Tenth Street?"

"Yes, dear. This is the byway. These are the byways and the bypassed and the letpasses and the letdowns."

"Um." She wasn't sure how to respond. "So is this the right way?" Frustrated, she waved in front of her toward more of the ceaseless alley.

"Of course, you're on the way."

"To the highway?"

"Every way is the right way, dear. Throughway, downway, byway."

"No *no*! The *high*way!" She slapped her hands to her head. "You're not helping!"

The man stood up abruptly, and the smell of urine and Darjeeling tea floated over her. She stumbled back, her hands curling into fists, but the man only smiled cheerfully.

"You could try a door?" he said tentatively. "Doors are very helpful. When they're not arguing with you."

"Um . . . okay, thank you," said CeeCee firmly and stepped past him. It was always best to be polite. Especially when people acted strange. You never knew what type of mental illness or drugs were involved

"Welcome, dear," he tipped his non-hat again. "Just remember, don't stop."

"What? Why shouldn't I stop?"

"Well, if you stop, they can catch you. Isn't that right, dear?"

"Oh god." She couldn't stomach asking him who "they" were. She hurried down the alley. *Probably no one anyway*, she thought. And then, wildly: *Where would he get Darjeeling?*

He was just another odd homeless person, but at least Apple Cheeks didn't try to grab at her or anything. And he did suggest a door. It hadn't occurred to her to try any of the doors that were randomly scattered throughout the alley. A window, even—maybe she could tap on one and get directions from somebody. CeeCee had the oddest sensation that she was walking in a curve, tilting farther to one side than the other. But that couldn't be right. She'd have heard about a neighborhood that was designed in a circle. She looked up along the line of the alley, and it was straight as an arrow.

She pulled up short. There was suddenly more color than the dimness should allow. She could have sworn it was just the same old blah dinginess a second ago. The outline of a door was tinged red for a moment, and the ground seemed to flash green, then blue, like neon was playing across the surfaces. She couldn't see any lighted signs, but that didn't mean a reflection couldn't pop up from a car or window somewhere. She looked behind her and saw Apple Cheeks staring. He jumped up, far quicker than she expected him to, waved at her, then scurried down the opposite way, quiet as a mouse.

She turned back, walking slowly as she studied the colors. Refraction, that was what it was called. She remembered getting detention in science class for breaking one of the mirrors. The colors were sporadic at first, but the farther she walked, the darker it got and the steadier and more pronounced the colors became, like jewels against the walls. There were more now too, like a disco ball reflecting light, but bigger. Each block of color was five or six inches across. That must mean she was close to a street. She craned her neck, trying to see where they were coming from, but the colors kept drawing her eyes. She didn't want to look away.

CeeCee knew her story, her bits of life, like most teenagers, centered a lot in the classroom—or in the hall or on the bus or after school doing homework. That was the routine, one she rarely escaped. It pained her because it was boring cliché bullshit. But the fact remained that a cliché was a cliché because it highlighted that certain things happen to work in a certain way, most certainly most of the time.

She would give a lot for the certainty of cliché at the moment.

In the drop of blue, everything had been fine. She didn't know what kind of color she was looking at now.

The colors were behaving oddly. CeeCee was positive she had never seen some of these colors before. Not in a flower, or a paint chip, or on TV—not even in a sunset. In fact, she was almost certain some of these colors didn't exist at all. Also, they were moving. She had a sneaking suspicion it was not refraction after all. The colors moved along the walls and lintels of doorframes, along the cement paving underfoot. They stretched to pace the lines of the building, almost creeping, almost soft. But then one would just . . . shift and suddenly be in another place. The colors were beautiful and much more mesmerizing than the drop of ink had been. Iridescence swirled across the surface of some, while others seemed lit from within.

She suddenly thought it would be a very bad idea to get too close. She leaned over toward the wall as far as she dared, staring at an almost-yellow block that had shifted from the ground. It pulsed quietly as it oozed along. Was it light, or was it a liquid or a slime mold of some sort? A detached part of her brain scientifically suggested that she should brush it gently with her fingertips, but instinct made her throat close up at the thought of touching it. She squeezed her arms tight across her stomach. They had surrounded her now. It was a miracle she hadn't stepped on one of the colors already with the way they jumped around, like a spider pouncing on a fly. Squinting at the wall, she noticed she could see the lines of the building through the not-yellow glow.

A chill shook her. It didn't seem to have any substance at all. It was just . . . color. Yet she couldn't help feeling like it was alive.

The colors didn't go on forever. She could clearly see where they ended just a short way down the alley. She crept quietly through them, her footsteps silent, freezing whenever one of the colors moved. She knew it was irrational; color couldn't hurt her. But color also shouldn't hold her attention so absolutely, either. A block of not-coral in front of her skittered to the side, and suddenly the way was open.

She bolted.

Ten feet later, she looked behind her to see an almost-peacock blue pulsing where she had been standing. It was so, so pretty. Everything else seemed dim and blurry in comparison. CeeCee realized she was staring again. She had also stopped moving. She shook her head and hurried on, spying a glimmer of light and shadow playing ahead of her, like cars passing by the mouth of the alley. *Finally*, she thought, breaking into a jog. She felt that sensation of curving again, and spots danced in her eyes. She stopped short in utter disbelief. In front of her was a brick wall.

An overwhelming urge to smash her fists against it welled up. A scream clawed its way out of her throat instead. Her voice bounced useless and loud off the concrete. CeeCee clapped her hands over her face and spun to lean against the brick, shutting out the ridiculous, impossible alley. Her breath shuddered painfully in her chest.

When she looked up, she was shocked to see the colors were closer than they had been. She peered at them, still trying to see where they were coming from. It had to be refraction, right? She was just being silly before. Suddenly several of them jumped in her direction, and a jolt of alarm coursed through her. The colors, whatever they were, were definitely moving toward her.

CeeCee twisted around, her eyes everywhere, and spied a

gray metal door. She yanked at the handle, but it was locked. Six feet away was another door—six feet closer to those creepy colors that were still slinking toward her, more rapidly than she could have imagined. She leaped for the handle. It swung open, fast and silent. She dove inside, and the door clicked quietly, firmly shutting behind her.

THREE

Starting Conversations

A cavernous room lay beyond the door, at least three stories high, with brick walls and wood beams that crosshatched the ceiling. CeeCee's nose itched from the smell of mildew and old fried food. A few odd pieces of industrial equipment were bolted to the floor, and remnants of cables hung from the roof beams, but otherwise the space was empty. Near the ceiling, dingy windows let in early evening light. She was shocked to realize how late it had gotten. CeeCee turned toward the street-side wall, looking for a door or a loading gate, any way out—at this point, she'd break a lock if she had to—but it was blank brick. She scanned the rest of the warehouse. Half-hidden in gloom was a door in the far wall.

Her heart sank, looking at the shadowy door. She was not having the best luck wandering into parts unknown today, but she didn't see any other options. *There had to be a street-side door somewhere in this building*, she thought. *Otherwise, what was the point in it being a building at all?*

The entrance led to a hallway that branched off into more doors, which sprouted into dark offices. Dim emergency lights lit the hall every few feet. The hallway was warmer than the warehouse, the low ceiling trapping humid air. Her skin prickled at the temperature change. She passed the glimmer of a security camera and wondered how many others she might have missed. She hoped whoever was on the other end didn't call the cops on her for breaking and entering. She just wanted to get home! If she could find someone, she could explain. A glow came from one of the rooms, and she made a beeline toward it.

Inside, rows of tall metal shelves filled a room of electronic equipment. Computers, circuit boards, stereos, and televisions were piled haphazardly on the racks. Old, outdated technology lay jumbled next to sleek new devices. Wires of all sizes and colors were looped up through the ceiling panels until it formed a canopy. The room felt hot, dense almost, like there was weight to the air, and underlying it was a persistent buzz. A pile of flip phones next to an antique rotary phone caught her eye.

Hope pinged through her. *A repair shop*, she thought. *This is a repair shop, which means it has to have a front door somewhere.* She shuffled forward eagerly.

In the center of the room, the shelves opened up to an island of desks arranged in a lopsided square. Several working computers and monitors lined the desks. Tablets, video equipment, and other devices were shoved in between the computers. Videos, websites, and games played on different screens. A mushroom hill of take-out cartons was growing under one of the desks. All of it gave the impression of a cluttered fort built out of electronic gadgets. Somehow, the heat and humidity increased, and her hoodie felt uncomfortably heavy. On the shelves behind the desks, more banks of live computer monitors glared at her.

CeeCee felt like she had stumbled into someone's secret space.

Something shifted behind the desks, and she jumped. Someone was hidden behind the mountains of equipment. She hesitated, wary, in the shadow's edge of the shelves. On the shelf next to her was a small screwdriver, its head as sharp as a nail. *Stinking thief*, she berated herself as she palmed it. But she felt better holding the scanty weapon. The point protruded neatly between the fingers of her closed left fist, just like using keys in self-defense. She took two steps forward into the open until she could just see a man's head and jowly neck as he stared intently at the monitors in front of him. The rest of his shape was blocked from view.

It's a store; he has to expect customers. She took a deep breath.

"Excuse me, sir? I was wondering if you could help me," Cee-Cee called.

Slowly, the man's head appeared around a monitor. He had a pale, round face, and thin brown hair lay in streaks across his skull. Sweat slicked his skin, dripping onto a grubby T-shirt. He was incredibly overweight. *Probably too big to move very quickly*, she thought, and she relaxed a tiny bit. His eyes met hers, and they were the shocking green color of cut grass.

"Little girl," he said and smiled.

CeeCee felt slightly insulted. She was young, but she certainly wasn't a little girl. She lifted her chin. "Is this your store? I'm sorry if I came in the back door. . . ."

"Yes, I saw you come in," he said, nodding toward a screen that showed a live feed of the warehouse. He seemed, strangely, both bored and interested at the same time. "Are you . . . lost?"

"No, no, I know where I am," she lied. "I'm just running late, and I saw your light. I was wondering if you had a phone I could use?"

"You don't have your own phone?"

"I did, but I don't have it at the moment." She clenched her jaw before forcing herself to relax. She was currently banned from owning a phone. She couldn't seem to resist jumping into pools with her clothes on, always forgetting about the phone in her pocket. After the second time, her mother refused to buy her a new one. She smiled her best smile. "You do repairs, right? Maybe I should bring my phone to you. It looks like you get a lot of customers."

The man kept smiling at her.

"So," CeeCee continued, "as I said before, I'm running late . . . can I use your phone for just a minute?" She casually looked around the shop, but there didn't seem to be a front door.

"Sure, little girl, I have a phone." He cocked his head. "You're a little tall for a little girl, aren't you? You should be smaller."

She started to scoff and bit it back. "I can't really control how tall I am," she said, laughing.

"Can't you? I think you could if you tried. You could be littler."

She wasn't sure if he was teasing her or not. "How would I possibly do that?"

"You could pretend until it came true," he said.

What? she thought. "Is that what you do?"

"Sometimes."

"Are you *pretending* to have a phone?" she asked flippantly.

"No, I have a phone. What will you give me for it?" His grin was like a slash across his face. "Oh, I'm just kidding. Come here, and I'll find it for you." His hands pawed around on his desk, but his eyes never left her.

Unease trickled down her back. She glanced at the monitors behind him, trying to spot a feed of the front door in the maze of hallways.

He licked his lips. "Why don't you come closer?"

"Why don't *you* come closer?" she challenged back.

"I don't know if you're worth the effort." His brow furrowed and then smoothed. "Oh, I'm just kidding. But I might need your help finding it. Things do tend to pile up."

CeeCee edged just a tiny bit closer. He was weird, but she needed a phone. She was sure she could move faster than him.

"That's the way." He grinned again.

Now that she was nearer, she saw he was even larger than she thought. His body seemed to have swallowed his chair. Sweat trickled down her neck. *I'll just grab the phone*, she thought, *I'll grab it and jump back.* She hid the hand clenching the screwdriver behind her thigh and scanned the desk for a phone.

"I think you're already pretending."

"What?" She dragged her attention back to the man.

"I think you're lost, little girl. I don't think anyone knows where you are."

"I know where I am," said CeeCee defiantly. "Other people know where I am too. I'm just late." Really, she wasn't even late yet. The plan had been to go from school directly to Trudy's, so her mom wasn't expecting her, but she would worry if she didn't make a check-in call. If she had a phone, she could pull up a map, too, or call for a ride. It was worth putting up with his strange questions.

"It would be okay if you were. I was lost once too. In fact, it would be wonderful."

He was creepy when he talked, in a way she couldn't place. She blurted, "What do you mean?"

"I was lost, and now I am completely free." His fingers wiggled like caterpillars along the desk. "Would you like to be free?"

"Really, I'm not lost."

"Sure, little girl."

But the more he talked, the more unnerved and impatient she got. "Maybe it's just the phone that's lost. Maybe I should try another shop." She turned halfway.

His eyes widened. "Oh look, here it is," he said, plucking up a cell phone and waving it at her. "Come here, little girl."

Three big steps took her to the desk. He held the phone just out of reach. On the screen directly in front of him she could see writhing naked bodies. She didn't want to, but she couldn't help staring.

"Do you want to watch?" he asked, his eyes too bright, and he tilted the screen toward her.

With a start, CeeCee realized that half the naked bodies belonged to children—young children. Her body flashed cold and then hot; rage and fear swirled together. Her vision tunneled into a fine point.

"Do you want to pretend with me?"

"No," she said, flat and fast.

"I think . . ." he said slowly, ". . . you don't know what you want. I can show you." Sweat dripped off his chin in a steady rhythm.

Her revulsion settled into furious defiance. How dare he? The disgusting pervert—screw him and his games! She lunged and snagged the phone out of his hand.

His arm shot out, quicker than she expected, and caught her sleeve. CeeCee jerked her arm, but he only clenched the fabric harder. He heaved toward her, straining against his own weight. There was something wrong with his body.

"Let go," she hissed at him, spitting mad.

His frame was much larger than it should be, and she couldn't see his legs. His stomach just went on and on, bare skin below the edge of his ratty T-shirt, until it disappeared in rolls under the desk. He lurched slowly forward in a strange sliding motion.

"Little girl." He sounded hurt. "Don't you want to make your call? I'm not going to hurt you." Then he laughed. "Oh, I'm just kidding."

A yank on her sleeve jerked her toward him. He made that strange undulating motion again, backward this time, and her chest dragged across the desk. He was so much stronger than she expected, but he wasn't fast. And CeeCee was more pissed off than she was afraid.

"You goddamn creep." She whipped her other arm overhand and buried the screwdriver tip into his hand.

He bellowed and yanked his hand back, letting go of her sleeve. The screwdriver tore through his skin as he pulled back, leaving a jagged tear. Blood welled up sluggishly. In the light of the monitors, it looked strange and brackish. She jumped backward, clutching the phone and screwdriver, grinning triumphantly. The man snarled at her and heaved forward again, this time pushing the desk forward with the force of his body. Now CeeCee could see. There were no legs at all . . . but nothing ended. His body just continued. It swelled bigger and bigger, bigger even than his enormous stomach. Then it began tapering off. There were little bumps at regular intervals. She didn't understand. It was like a bug's or a worm's. That couldn't be right. His body moved in a rolling motion, and the bumps gripped the edge of the desk to help pull him forward. She jerked her gaze up to his face, and his eyes stared at her, mad and hungry.

Her stomach heaved. She staggered back, almost falling. But she couldn't get caught there—she couldn't. CeeCee ran in a blind panic, rushing past the shelves and into the hall. Where was the front door? She was in another hallway, lined with offices again. The glow of security cameras followed her like eyes. She shoved the phone into her pocket and grabbed doorknobs at random. They opened into rooms filled with more electronic crap. Wires clutched at her hair as she ran. The warm air was suffocating, sucking at her face like a wet towel. She fled down the hall, and the corridor abruptly ended in a T shape.

Facing CeeCee were three heavy metal doors, laid flush in the brick wall—an outside wall. She ran to the farthest door, the farthest away she could get.

"Please, oh please," she gasped as she turned the handle . . . and stumbled into an alley. The door clanged shut behind her with a final sounding boom.

CeeCee stood in the alley, gulping air as if she had been drowning. The screwdriver in her hand was sticky with blood from whatever that thing was. She thought she had been over-imaginative with the too-skinny alley and those strange colors moving toward her, but now . . . was she hallucinating? *No*, she thought. No matter how ADHD distracted or light-headed she got, there was no way she had just made up a pedophile slug man.

Pedophile. Slug.

A cry strangled her throat. It was much darker than it had been when she went into the warehouse. The sky seemed full of more stars than she could normally see on a city night, and it was too quiet. Panic rose in her chest, and she shook from adrenaline. She was back in an alley. Back to an alley. This alley was new, and it was the same, and it was cold, and she felt like she was losing her mind. She fumbled for the phone in her pocket. In the dim starlight, she pushed every button she could find, but the phone refused to turn on.

She couldn't even pretend to know where she was anymore.

CeeCee stumbled down the alley, sobbing.

FOUR

Dressed Up
in Their Clothes

There was a light. There was a light down there. It flickered.
CeeCee had been walking awhile, enough time to stop crying but not enough for the strange hazy feeling in her head to go away.

There was that light again. It looked warm.

But things could look like all sorts of things here, she thought sluggishly. She had no idea what to do anymore. Her feet shuffled forward automatically.

A dark shape stepped out from a side alley in front of her. CeeCee yelped and crouched next to the wall before she even realized she had moved. One hand fumbled for the screwdriver and the other scrabbled at the bricks as the shape turned.

"Why hello, dear, hello!" It was the homeless man with the apple cheeks. His cheerful face scrunched up in a grin. "Oh, I'm so glad to see you again! I was awfully afraid . . . well, you know, the jib jab and all that. But here you are!"

She was confused. He seemed genuinely happy to see her. She wondered if he was really there.

"Some things were other things," she whispered. "Other things were nothing."

"Oh, I know, dear," agreed Apple Cheeks, nodding sagely. He looked sad for a moment and then brightened. "Are you going to the park?"

He leaned toward her, and the smell of urine drifted close.

"The park?" CeeCee felt the world start to sharpen around her. She knew almost every park in this part of the city. At any one of them, she could figure out where she was and find a pay phone or a bus line.

She edged her way up the wall until she was standing and looked over Apple Cheeks carefully. It was a little hard to tell with all the baggy clothes, but he looked normal. She was taller than he was; she hadn't noticed that before. She couldn't tell how old he was or even the real color of his skin and hair, under the layers of dirt, but there wasn't anything extra that she could see. He smiled at her vaguely.

"And look, dear!" He dug something out of a pocket. "Soup!"

Somehow, CeeCee just couldn't find a man with a can of soup threatening.

"I'm still a little lost," she confessed. "Can you show me where the park is?"

"Oh yes, dear! Just down the way." He trundled along with her beside him.

"There was this man," she whispered, "but he was also like a worm . . ."

"Oh, him who likes the metal talking bits? I wouldn't go near him," Apple Cheeks said. "Nasty one, he is."

Half a sob choked out of her throat. He was real, then. The slug man was real. She never wanted to see him again.

Apple Cheeks pulled a filthy handkerchief out of a pocket and handed it to her. He seemed to have a lot of pockets. She took the handkerchief and pretended to dab at her face before handing it back.

"Don't worry, dear, we're on the byways now."

The alley broadened until it was wide enough for two good-size trucks to fit side by side. At the same time, the walls on either side of the alley changed. On the right side were raised platforms in front of dock doors, the type of doors that slide up into the ceiling so boxes could be unloaded from trucks. The light she had seen was a fire inside an oil drum on one of the platforms. All of the metal doors were rolled up. The metal gleamed from light inside the building, and voices bounced off the walls. On the left side of the passage was a wall that looked like it had collapsed ages ago, a great gaping hole opening into darkness. Crumbling bricks piled at the bottom were worn smooth, while an arch of brick still hung above like jagged teeth. A muted susurrus crept out of the broken wall. CeeCee thought the two sides of the alley looked like they belonged to different places, like two streets torn out of a magazine and pasted together for a child's school project.

Men stood around the fire, and her heart rate picked up. Before she could cringe, Apple Cheeks gently took her hand and ushered her up a set of steps onto the platform.

"This is where we park," he said genially. "When we're in the mood, you know. It's a good place to stop and wait."

"Oh," she whispered. She eyed the men on the platform as they glanced over. One looked especially drunk, and they were all various degrees of dirty, but they looked like regular men. Still, CeeCee crept a hand into her hoodie pocket and clutched the sticky screwdriver. Regular men could be just as dangerous. The drunk man was leaning heavily on the guy next to him and seemed to be having an intense conversation with him, all in grunts.

"What's that on the other side?" She turned to gaze at the gaping hole across from them.

"Oh, we don't go in there, but the view is nice." Apple Cheeks tugged her toward the doorway.

CeeCee stood on the line where the loading dock door would come crashing down. She peered inside.

The space bloomed with color, but not the weird moving colors she had seen earlier. Walls, where they could be seen, were covered in artwork and graffiti in equal measure. Flowers, animals, people, landscapes, swear words, and abstract designs, layered over each other until the paint peeling in places made its own strange patterns. Scaffolding was anchored to the walls, built from old pallets with the splinters painted over. They ended in makeshift platforms, creating multiple levels in the large warehouse. Patchwork canopies were hooked to beams and draped into tents. Cardboard was mixed with fabric and old boards until they resembled strange little houses. People were clearly living here, crafting their homes and a bit of privacy out of nothing but reclaimed garbage. Everything from large oil drums to small metal trash cans held fires, lighting the place up like a carnival. It was like she had walked into an exotic marketplace, except the smell of unwashed people and urine rolled over her like a wave. Apparently, a flushing toilet couldn't be built out of scraps.

There were a lot of men in the room, of all ages, but there were also women. That made CeeCee feel a little better. She mentally picked out one woman, middle-aged and wearing multiple skirts and a kind expression, to go running to if things got weird. Then the woman picked up a small potbellied pig and set it on her head like a turban.

Apple Cheeks led CeeCee over to one of the huts. It was made of layers of cardboard held together with zip ties until the walls were thick and durable. Red squares were painted on it, making it red-and-brown checkered, like a game board. A battered card table sat in front of a cloth door. Apple Cheeks ducked inside and emerged again with two apple crates, stacked one on top of the other.

Ha, she thought dully, *Apple Cheeks has apple crates.*

He set them both down, then pulled an old pot and a metal grill out of one of the boxes, before setting the crates up fussily. She watched as he dragged over a small metal trash bin from behind the door and lit the paper scraps and wood inside with a flint and steel knife that he pulled out of another pocket. The pocket knife was rather big for such a small man. It looked very sharp. CeeCee swayed where she stood, suddenly queasy.

Apple Cheeks noticed. "Oh, my dear! Sit down, sit down! We'll have soup in a jiffy."

She fell heavily onto the apple crate farthest from the knife. Apple Cheeks smiled at her and flipped open a can opener from the pocket knife. He emptied the soup into the pan, set the grill over the trash bin fire, and proceeded to cook. It smelled wonderful, and she was suddenly famished. He pulled small jars out of his pockets and added bits from them to the soup now and then. It was the strangest domestic setting CeeCee had ever been in.

She warily watched the warehouse as he fussed with the fire. Where was she? At the house next to them, a worn-out man stared vacantly into space, singing. A few people were staring into space, actually—stoned or mentally checked out, she couldn't tell which. Others seemed terribly busy with activities she didn't quite understand. A man muttered to himself as he painted a cityscape made of flowers on an open space of wall. He seemed particularly offended by a painted heart. He stabbed at it fiercely as he turned it into a tulip/parking garage. It was very strange but also sort of brilliant. Two levels above her, a raucous game of cards was going on, the men tottering on their seats, dangerously close to

THE BYWAYS

falling from the skinny platform. The woman with the pig turban was intent on hanging up yards of wet diapers on a clothesline, then taking them down and starting over again. A young teen boy was catching the water dripping from the linens in a bucket, and she kept swatting him away. The pig was very good at keeping its balance.

CeeCee realized that they were all a little mad, in their different ways. She wondered if she was going crazy too.

As the smell of soup grew stronger, another man approached the table. Apple Cheeks's smile fell. He looked at the man, sharp and shrewd.

"How about a nibble, eh?" said the stranger. He smiled insincerely, spread his hands wide, and shuffled a little two-step. He wore wide-legged brown pants that looked like they were from the Depression era, topped by a Rolling Stones T-shirt and suspenders.

"What do you got?" Apple Cheeks demanded.

"I don't see her with nothing." The man waved a hand at CeeCee.

"She's a guest!"

The man grumbled but pulled out a bottle from his pants pocket and thumped it on the table.

Apple Cheeks was all smiles again. "Well, all right then."

CeeCee dug into her backpack and pulled out a granola bar. She always had a couple stashed for after school. She laid it quietly on the table. Apple Cheeks positively beamed.

"Such a sweet dear!" He darted back into the house and emerged with a metal teapot and another crate. He thrust the teapot at the suspendered man. "Tea biscuits!"

Suspenders muttered but took the teapot. "That better be here when I get back!" He pointed at the bottle before hurrying off.

"We'll have proper biscuits with our tea, won't we, dear?"

It was only a couple of minutes later that Suspenders stomped back and set down the full pot, water sloshing onto the grill. "You know," he grumbled, "I don't like people telling me what to do!"

"Do you want biscuits or not?!"

"The shovel was always so bossy. Not sweet and chirping, like the hose was."

"You don't get out of working, no how, nowhere, no what!"

"The cement was the worst, heavy and mean." He squinted at Apple Cheeks angrily. "Are you becoming cement?!"

"Cement!" Apple Cheeks laughed so hard he wheezed. "Oh ho, I think I'd know if I was turning into cement." His laughter eased off. "Soup!" He pulled three spoons out of a pocket and handed one each to CeeCee and Suspenders.

The two men leaned over the pan and began scooping up soup. Eating out of one pot was disturbing, especially given how dirty both men were, but her stomach overruled her squeamishness. CeeCee decided not to look too closely at how clean the spoon was, or the pot, or anything else, really. She leaned toward the pot and dipped in her spoon.

It tasted amazing.

For a while they sat in silence as they ate. The last of the haziness drifted away as she slurped up soup.

The problem with the fog lifting was that her mind sped up and frantically ping-ponged between memories that were unbelievable. Denial warred with dismay. And as friendly as Apple Cheeks seemed, her nerves were on high alert that she was sitting in an abandoned warehouse full of questionable people, which she should reasonably leave as soon as possible.

"I thought," she finally ventured carefully, "you meant a regular park. How do I get to a regular park?"

"This is the park! Time for a sit-down-a-spell and a nibble."

Apple Cheeks checked the teapot and added three large tea bags to the kettle.

"No, I mean . . . one with grass and, you know, benches and um . . ." Her voice faltered.

"She means out there," grumped Suspenders.

"Oh, my dear." Apple Cheeks shook his head sadly. "Once you're here, you can't go there."

"You mean in the alleys? What's so different about an alley? They're part of the city." She noticed Suspenders scooped up soup twice as fast whenever she and Apple Cheeks paused to talk. CeeCee doubled her eating speed.

"These are the byways and the bypassed."

"You said that before, but what does it mean?" They almost made it sound like she was in an entirely different place. But that didn't make any sense. On her hand was a splatter of brackish blood. She shuddered and wiped it across her jeans.

"You by and you let, until you're here. It moves one way and not the other," said Apple Cheeks.

"But getting out of an alley is simple," she said stubbornly. "It's just walking. You walk in, and then you walk out again."

But she remembered the too skinny, impossible alley, and her heart sank as she said it.

"Once you're in the byways, there's no other way to go," said Suspenders.

"So I'm stuck here?" she whispered, stricken. Had she screwed up again without even knowing how?

"Well, you can't be here and there at the same time, can you?"

"That's mostly true, but it's not completely true," said a voice. "Sometimes you can be here and there at the same time."

CeeCee twisted around on her crate. A young man was leaning against a beam, half in shadow.

"Maybe for you," said Apple Cheeks.

"Not for us," agreed Suspenders petulantly.

"Who are you?" she asked.

He smiled rakishly in the gloom. "I'm Jesse."

He stepped away from the beam and sauntered closer. He had dark brown hair and a lean frame but prowled with wiry grace, and although his jeans and T-shirt looked well-worn, he was cleaner than anybody she had seen in the alleys so far. He met her eyes, and his were a tawny hazel, almost gold in the firelight. He grinned again. CeeCee thought he might only be a couple of years older than she was.

"You seem new." He tilted his head to one side. "Are you new?"

"I got lost today, if that's what you mean."

"Now don't play any games with her!" Apple Cheeks scolded. "Poor dear has been through a lot already!"

Jesse studied her. "You don't look like the usual type we get here."

She glanced incredulously at the woman with the pig on her head. "Do you have a usual type?"

Jesse laughed. "Touché."

"Dear ran into the jib jab, you know! She ran right through it!" said Apple Cheeks proudly.

"No!" Suspenders narrowed his eyes at her.

"Right through! I saw her!"

"Really?" Jesse asked.

"Is that the worm man?" She looked from one to the other.

"The worm man? Oh. No, he's . . ." Jesse answered. He'd lost his smile. "Just unpleasant."

Suspenders snorted scornfully and took a long pull on the bottle.

She looked back at the young man helplessly. "I still don't understand where I am."

He was smiling again, but his gaze looked more serious. "How did you get lost?"

"I don't know really. I got turned around."

"No," he said, his golden eyes staring into hers. "How did you get lost?"

CeeCee thought about the rabbit that was still in her pocket, and guilt stabbed at her. She suddenly wanted to pour out her whole day to him, the whole awful mess of it, to this guy who was almost her age and looked normal and clean and didn't seem quite as mad as everyone else.

"I made a mistake," she said. "I made a mistake, and then I got lost. I didn't mean to."

"Then there is still time."

A weight felt like it lifted off her lungs. Somehow, he was telling the truth. She wasn't stuck yet. She could fix this.

"It might be hard," he continued. "But there are ways out. If you really want them."

"Yes," she said. She needed to see her mom again. "Yes, I really want one."

"You need to find one of the halfway places. You need to find a door."

"Yes, doors can be helpful," agreed Apple Cheeks.

"If you stay here too long," Jesse said, nodding at the warehouse, "it'll be like you belong here. Keep moving."

Her mouth opened to ask the first hundred obvious questions, but before she could settle on one, something caused a stir on the other side of the park. Suspenders looked up at the bustle.

"Finally!" he said. "Doc M is making his rounds!" He jumped off the crate and hurried toward the noise, joining a group of people around a new stranger. CeeCee could barely see through the crowd, but she could hear a man talking in a booming, jovial voice.

"Isn't it a perfectly lovely evening tonight? Come now, don't be shy, I can ease your awful. How are we feeling, Frank? You know I can make you feel better. Here's a bit to take the edge off. No one deserves to suffer."

Jesse hissed, "*He* is not a way out." His hand shot out, brushed her arm, and withdrew just as fast. "If I were you, I wouldn't even let him know you were here."

Then he spun on his heel and slinked into a shadow.

CeeCee blinked rapidly. He had disappeared. Her arm felt warm where he had touched it.

"Oh, my dear, I do believe he's right," Apple Cheeks said, fretting.

She turned back to see who this new guy was. He wandered through the warehouse, the crowd following him as he bent over one person or stopped next to another.

"Who is he?" she asked.

"That's Doc M."

"Is he . . . is he like . . ." Her hand clenched around the spoon she was still holding.

"He's not the worst person you could meet, but he's not the best either. No, no, not the best. Now hurry," said Apple Cheeks, pointing to a door in the back of the warehouse and away from the crowd moving toward them. "That way."

She peered between the makeshift houses and scooped up her backpack from the floor. She stood to walk away, then paused.

"Thank you for the soup," she said sincerely.

Apple Cheek's face lit up into a smile. "Such a sweet dear! I hope to see you again." He tipped his imaginary hat at her.

She couldn't wish him the same, as grateful as she was. Cee-Cee squeezed around the side of the shack and wove her way toward the dim doorway she could see behind the dwellings. In the shadow of a beam and a crooked tent, she stopped to look back. The crowd had thinned, each person drifting away as they got whatever it was they were getting from the man. Now she could see him clearly.

Doc M wore a purple velvet coat, crisp dark pants, and a gray shirt, and he held an old-fashioned doctor's bag that looked new. He was tall and broad in the shoulders, and all of him was sharply tailored, all creases and lines that seemed to stand out against the darkness instead of blending with it. His eyes moved constantly, sweeping over every face, watching the room and the people and even the shadows moving. CeeCee stood transfixed. And then, without meaning to, before she could turn, his gaze found hers. He had slate gray eyes that were surrounded by a ring of black— except the gray was too gray, and the black was too black, and those eyes looked right through to the startled heart of her. Then he smiled.

A chill raced through CeeCee. She bolted and didn't look back.

FIVE

Ripped My Life Away

It was so cold. Her hoodie just wasn't up to the kind of cold that crept in on a spring night when it was far past time to be home and in bed. It was how CeeCee knew it was much later—that, and the dark. It was also how she knew she was screwed. It wasn't just past her curfew or past the time when she should have checked in. She wasn't staying out all night for kicks. She was fucking *lost*.

There's no way, she told herself whenever the panic fluttered in her throat, that she was permanently stuck in some weird labyrinth of alleys. Apple Cheeks and those people in the warehouse were just too drunk or drugged out to know where they were half the time. That guy Jesse was probably a street kid who was messing with her for fun. Soon, she whispered over and over, she would find a street entrance or a back patio to a restaurant or a door to a shop, and it would be all right. There was no logical reason why she couldn't walk back to a regular street and figure out where she was in the city.

But the more she walked, the more her beliefs crumbled away into something else.

It was subtle at first. Doors faded away by the time she reached them, or she'd hear cars clear as day, but the alley would turn and it would be suddenly quiet again. Blank walls appeared where it looked like a clear path a moment before. Once, she'd seen a door actually *open*, electric light blazing within, but the people moving in and out were strangely shaped, their shadows more animal than they should be, and she couldn't bear to face that again.

It was so dark, CeeCee couldn't even tell if she was walking in circles. She was freaked out, and tired, and her feet hurt, and the cold made it all seem so much *more*.

The path felt uneven underfoot, like bricks or stone instead of pavement. The alley widened, and dim starlight trickled down into an open space. Weariness dragged at her. She squinted into the dark and listened as hard as she could. It was quiet, but there were shifting shadows everywhere. She reached her hand out cautiously and brushed her fingers across the nearest shadow. The cool curl of a leaf glided gently across her knuckles. CeeCee sighed in relief. It was a garden. It was someone's courtyard garden. Now that she had identified the plant, she could also smell earth, freshly turned and rich. There was a square-looking shadow off to the side, and she walked over gingerly, trying not to step on any of the plants. She patted the air with her hands until she felt the side of a plastic shed, and she followed it around its edges to a small gap between the shed and the corner of a wall.

She slid down and curled herself into a ball, cradling her head on her backpack. *It'll lighten up soon*, she thought. *It'll be easier when it's lighter.* Then she remembered the worm man in the light, sweat glinting as he grabbed her, and she shuddered. Right now the dark was easier; no one could see her. *I'll just rest for a tiny bit*, she thought. She buried her nose into her hoodie and drew the shadows around her like a shield.

I'll just rest for a little tiny bit.

CeeCee was surrounded by flowers. They were gorgeous, bigger than she'd even seen. Daisies in yellow and white nodded on stalks as thick as her wrist. Red and pink tulips looked like they could be used as goblets. Each petal was perfect and full of life. A fiery orange rose climbed two stories high against the side of the building. Poppies were bigger than her head, and fuchsias clustered into bells so thick, she could swear she heard ringing.

She almost didn't believe she was awake. Sunlight flooded the garden, and the colors dappled into spots in her eyes. CeeCee lay dazed and sleepy, drinking in the vibrant textures. She wasn't ready to think about anything yet. Someone had pried up most of the bricks in the widened courtyard and planted flowers directly in the rich and loamy soil. A few pots here and there held herbs and vegetables. Everywhere she looked, the plants were beautiful and lush, better than any nursery she had ever seen. An arched entrance on either end of the garden led away into narrow alleyways.

She sat up, stretching the kinks out of her knees, and scooted forward to brush the leaves of a lavender bush, the purple-blue heads swarming with bees. CeeCee leaned into the scent as it swirled around her. She concentrated on nothing but the smell of it. Then she spotted a green-speckled water faucet protruding from the wall on the other side of the bush. She scrambled over, turning the faucet to release a gush of clear, cold water. She tilted her head underneath the stream and drank until her stomach ached. Her sleeves had gotten wet in the process, and she scooched around for a dry spot to sit on as she inspected them.

Then she heard a small sound and froze.

Someone else was in the garden. Her hand grabbed for the screwdriver in her pocket, clumsy through the wet fabric.

"I was wondering when you'd wake up."

Standing in the shadow of tall cornstalks was a girl not much older than herself. She held a hand over her mouth as she talked, muffling her voice. Even with her hand blocking her lower face, CeeCee could see she was beautiful. Her complexion shone like it was lit from under her skin. She had long dark hair that curled and waved like the nodding flower heads. The tension in Cee-Cee's shoulders eased.

"Thank you for not stepping on my plants." The girl narrowed her eyes at her. "Or stealing anything."

"Oh, um." CeeCee wasn't sure how to explain why she was there. "I'm sorry, I must have fallen asleep. I didn't mean . . . I only meant to rest for a moment."

"It's okay, I get it," the girl mumbled. "Were you walking the alleys all night?"

"Yeah," said CeeCee.

She suddenly felt sure the girl really did get it. But the girl was also suspicious of her, and CeeCee felt unexpectedly ashamed for sleeping out in the open.

"You weren't *planning* on stealing anything, were you?"

"No. Well, I guess I stole some water."

The girl's eyes creased like she was smirking, but she kept her hand over her mouth. "That's okay—I'm stealing it too. At least, I've never gotten a utility bill." She fell silent, studying her.

CeeCee tried to fill the silence awkwardly. "I got lost. And I don't understand where I am. This is going to sound crazy . . ."

"You're not crazy."

"I'm trying to get out—of the alleys, I mean. I can't seem to find a street. Do you know the way?"

"Well, that's kind of complicated." Then, as if she had made up her mind about something, she offered, "I'm Kelly."

"I'm CeeCee."

Relief hit her hard. Kelly seemed so very ordinary. Even her name was ordinary. She was different and a little distant, but in the way an older sister or friend might have gone off to college and come back for the weekend full of a life you didn't know anything about. Kelly looked bohemian chic in a long, flowy vest over a short, light-blue dress and sturdy mud-splattered boots on her feet. Her eyes were a beautiful cornflower blue. She kept her hand over her mouth, and CeeCee wondered if she had bad teeth or a scar she was covering up.

"You know, don't you? About this place?" CeeCee stood up, and the words poured out of her in a rush. "Everything has been so strange. The alleys kept moving around and changing sizes. I saw things, creatures—not normal people, not normal at all! This man who had a worm body tried to grab me. There were these freaky creatures going in a door. Or they look okay, but they don't say anything that makes sense. There's something wrong here. Really, really wrong." She felt better finally saying it out loud.

"Look, I don't know if I can answer all of your questions . . ."

"Tell me anything." The desperation leaked into her voice. "I just need to get out of this place and away from these weird-ass monsters."

Kelly's eyes hardened, and she took a step into the light. "I can tell you how I got here. That might help . . ."

"Yes! Please!"

"But you should know something before I tell you." Kelly pulled her hand away from her mouth. "I'm not normal, either." As she spoke, dirt poured out of her mouth in a light but steady stream. It stopped as soon as she stopped talking. Her lips were full and formed a pretty bow, red as the roses. Kelly brushed her hand across her skirt, shaking the dirt into the flower bed.

"Oh shit." CeeCee backed up involuntarily.

"Are you going to run away screaming?" Kelly said sarcastically, her voice still muffled but clearer than before.

A blaze of embarrassment heated CeeCee's cheeks, and her spine stiffened. "Should I run away?" she asked defiantly instead.

Kelly laughed bitterly. "No." Dirt trickled off her chin. "Maybe. We're not all monsters. Sometimes people change when they get here. Other times they're already different, and this is where they run to. I ran here, but I didn't start off like this."

CeeCee's heart was beating fast, but she desperately wanted answers. What was this place, and why would anyone run here? She looked at this girl with dirt smudged on her cheek, who could have been a senior at her high school. She was even prettier without her hand in front of her face. Kelly swiped at her chin, annoyed but also a little vulnerable.

Finally, CeeCee asked, "What happened?"

Kelly fixed her in place with her eyes. "I'm telling you this so you understand—the way you get here is important," she said intensely. "I know that much. Before, back when I was out in the regular world, I used to steal boyfriends. For fun. It was especially fun if I didn't like the girl, but I often didn't even think about the girlfriends at all. I just did it because I could.

"I did it all through high school and then at college. I stole boys away from their girlfriends during parties or dorm mixers. I was old enough to know better," she said, her voice full of guilt. "I stole this boy once. He was funny, he made me laugh without trying. He wasn't putting the moves on me either, and those boys were always the best ones to take. The ones that weren't looking. His girlfriend was in one of my classes, and he'd wait for her in the quad. I could see she was head over heels for him, but I did it anyway. He was so cute. She fought hard for him, but I kept going back until I had him. She really loved him, and I think he loved her."

CeeCee was confused. What did this have to do with the alleys?

Kelly paused, remembering. "There's this park with a rose garden near campus . . ."

"I know it," CeeCee said.

"After I stole him, I was walking with him in the garden, and she caught up to us there. She tried to get him to look at her, to remember what they had, but he wouldn't even answer. He only looked at me. I was so proud of myself . . . and I wasn't nice about it. So she cursed me. She said, 'When you take love instead of letting it grow, you will reap what you sow.'

"And I laughed at her. I said, 'Okay, Granny, what does that even mean?'

"She said, 'It means you're full of bullshit, and I hope you choke on it.'

"It didn't even start for a few days. I remember sitting with him at a café, and he'd told one of his jokes. I laughed and felt something in my mouth. I spit into my napkin, and there was dirt. I thought they had given me a dirty cup, and I threw a fit at the counter. The next day, it happened again, and I thought, *Oh, it must be the wind blowing dust around.*" Kelly stopped for a long moment, her eyes distant. "She didn't know she was a witch. I didn't know, either."

CeeCee blurted, "Witches aren't real." But she wanted to take the words back as soon as she said them.

Kelly gave her a sad, measuring look.

"We both are, in our way," she continued. "The powers we don't know we have. They really were in love. I shouldn't have been able to pull him to me like that if I didn't have a witch power of my own. Not that it does me any good now."

As she talked, she leaned over the flower beds and the dirt fell from her mouth to the plants. "It's good for growing things. Natural fertilizer."

"What happened then?" Fascination had slowed CeeCee's heart rate, but dread was building underneath it.

"The dirt started falling more often. I went to doctors, and they all thought I had pica, this condition where you eat dirt because you need more vitamins, but mainly they thought I was a hypochondriac or had OCD. I stopped going to school or any-place I had to speak. I broke up with that boy, but it didn't stop. It kept getting thicker, until it was falling out all the time. Eventually, I figured out it wasn't going to stop.

"I hid in my apartment for a semester. I thought I'd choke to death on it in my sleep, but I didn't. I figured out pretty quick that I could breathe around it. When I felt like I was going insane from being inside, I'd walk to the rose garden at night and talk to myself, where the dirt wasn't so noticeable. Nobody bothers you much when you're talking to yourself.

"One of those nights, I noticed two rose bushes, hedges really, that I hadn't noticed before. I thought maybe they had just planted them, even though they were already tall. I started walk-ing down the path between them, and the next thing I know, I'm in the alleys."

"What about your parents? Didn't they look for you?" Cee-Cee had started fidgeting while Kelly talked. She had drunk too much water and her bladder screamed at her, but she didn't want to interrupt the story.

"I saw my mother once when the dirt first started, when it was still sporadic." Kelly's voice was tight. "She came to visit my apart-ment and drop off money for school. She was disgusted to say the least. Thought I was crazy too. She's kind of . . . particular. Every-thing has to be just so. And I was . . . they don't want me like this."

Horror swirled ugly in CeeCee's stomach. Even now, with her stealing and staying out all night, she couldn't imagine her mother giving up on her. Sure, she'd be in trouble, but her mother would still want her home, even if she punched Taylor a million times—even if she changed into something different.

Then she thought about the slug man, and her blood chilled.

To distract herself, she asked, "How do you eat around it?"

"It stops when I swallow. Funny thing, I don't seem to need to eat as much as I used to." Kelly looked at her narrowly. "I don't think I'm human any longer."

CeeCee was still turning that over in her head when Kelly continued.

"You have to pee, don't you? You're all twitchy. You can go inside." Kelly stepped over to a door hidden behind cascading wisteria vines and opened it. "There's a bucket in the corner."

CeeCee hesitated, then walked into a small windowless room that looked like it might have once been a utility closet. Now it had a small cot along one wall and a narrow table and bench along the other. The table held gardening tools, a few books, and a battered radio. The floor was covered in a layer of fine dirt and moss. She found the bucket and squatted over it, and thought about living here, like this, away from her family and friends. The metal rim of the bucket was cold against her thighs.

When she stepped back outside, she found Kelly kneeling between some gardenias, pushing a small mound of dirt around the base of the plants. Her hair shone in the sunlight, curling among the flower heads and leaves, another exotic species in the garden. The flowers seemed to whisper in Kelly's ear. If she listened closely enough, CeeCee thought she could almost understand them.

"I'm sorry for what I said before—how I acted."

"It's okay. If I wasn't already changed when I got here, I would have felt the same way." Kelly's lips twisted wryly.

CeeCee worriedly bit her lip. She should know better than anyone about judging people, since she was always on the wrong end of rumors. But the idea that someone could change that way freaked her out. What if it happened to her? She pushed the thought away frantically.

"This garden really is beautiful," she said instead. "When I woke up I . . . didn't think it was real. I didn't think anything this beautiful could be real."

"Thank you." Kelly sounded like she meant it. "I've always loved flowers. Probably more than I loved all those boys put together."

She looked up from the flowers and fixed CeeCee with an intense stare, her face full of sun. "The truth is, I don't know how to get out. I never tried. I'm not even sure which way to go. I know some people can't leave at all. But there are also others who can go back and forth. I know there are ways, but I never wanted to go back after I came here."

"Oh." CeeCee felt herself deflate.

She stood awkwardly in the garden. She knew she should keep going, now more than ever after hearing Kelly's tale. She'd find a way to get out as long as she kept moving, she told herself stubbornly. But it was hard to leave this bit of sun and color and almost normalcy, like her and True having lemonade in her back-yard during the summer.

"Do you need help?" CeeCee asked hesitantly.

Kelly looked at her sympathetically. "Are you hungry?" she asked, leaning back over her heels.

"Yes."

"Can you water these beds, while I pick some veggies? There's a watering can in the shed." Kelly stretched as she stood up. "I don't eat much, but I grow a lot of edibles for trade at the market."

"Sure." CeeCee hurried over to the shed. "But I don't have very much money on me."

"That's okay," said Kelly as she moved around the garden. "I remember when I first got here."

CeeCee filled the watering can and carefully walked from bed to bed. Most of the plants came up to her waist, and some of the plants were taller than she was. A soft breeze blew in through the alley entrances and made the flowers sway, caressing her skin. She could see how someone would want to stay in this peaceful place.

"Here." Kelly handed her a bowl and a water bottle. "I don't have dressing, but the peas are sweet." She sat down against the wall.

CeeCee put away the watering can and sat next to her, eating a breakfast of lettuce, snap peas, and sunflower seeds. After a short hesitation, Kelly peppered her with questions about where CeeCee went to school and about her family, if such and such band had put out a new album yet, or what was happening on a TV show. The dirt dribbled down while she talked, and she periodically brushed it into the beds. Once she got used to it, the dirt didn't bother CeeCee at all. In fact, she found she liked her. Kelly was charming and funny, even if she was a little sad. She got the impression it was a treat for Kelly to just sit and chat.

But underneath, CeeCee was anxious to move on. Jesse and Apple Cheeks both had said not to stop. She didn't know what would happen or when, but it felt like a deadline was looming. As if she could sense it, Kelly took the empty bowl from her and stood up. "I know you should get going."

"Yeah." CeeCee threw her arms around her and hugged her hard. "Thank you." Then she stepped back, embarrassed.

Kelly smiled like the sun. "Hey, if you stay, come back and visit sometime."

CeeCee barely managed a smile back.

six

Words Like Angels Crush Inside

Past Kelly's garden, an archway of brick spanned the walls over a narrow, cramped alley. CeeCee went under the arch and up a short set of stairs before the path widened. The building flanking the path was old and embellished, with fancy stonework and patterned bricks set over domed windows above her. Another flight of steps brought her head level with the first-floor windows.

She peered into the building as she passed. Inside were file cabinets and shelves full of ledgers and long wooden tables. Almost all of the rooms were empty, but when CeeCee saw one with people working, she paused. There were three men and a woman, all in suits, with files and notebooks scattered among them on a table. Her heart lifted. If they would let her in to use the phone, she could call her mom. She tapped gently on the glass. She wanted to be polite about it, but she wasn't sure how you could interrupt and be polite at the same time.

No one looked up. She tapped the glass a little harder and

waved for good measure, trying to catch the eye of the man facing her. She leaned into the glass pane just in case it was tinted on the inside, although she'd never heard of that before.

"Excuse me," she called. "Hello? I'm outside. I really need your help." She rapped harder.

Out of the corner of her eye, she saw a cat saunter down the alley and jump into a recessed alcove. The cat watched her with unblinking eyes.

"Hello? Could you please let me in?"

The business meeting continued.

"Is the glass soundproof?" She knocked long and loudly, then pounded on the window in frustration.

"Hey!" she yelled, waving both arms over her head. "*Hey!*"

One of the men stood up. Her heart soared. But he only refilled his glass of water before returning to the table.

She wanted to tear her hair out. You'd think they would at least look at her and threaten to call security or something. *Security—that's an idea.* CeeCee took a step back and looked around the alley. The cat twitched his ears at her. She ran down the way and grabbed a dented, metal garbage can lid. She stood to the side of the window and swung the lid.

It bonged loudly against the glass. No one in the room moved.

CeeCee couldn't believe it. She swung the lid at the window over and over again, faster each time, harder, yelling at the top of her lungs. She knew she looked like a crazy person, like the mad people at the park, like Don Quixote tilting at windmills, but she couldn't help herself. The glass didn't break, the people didn't react; it was like she was doing nothing.

The cat, however, seemed highly entertained.

"Oh my god!" She slowed down, gasping for air. "Oh my god! What the fuck?"

It was one thing to be trapped in this strange place, it was

altogether another to *see* the other side and not be able to do anything about it. CeeCee threw the garbage can lid at the window
one last time. It hit the glass and clattered down until it teetered,
squeaking against the edge of the sill, like it was snickering spitefully. The cat jumped down from his perch and followed her as
she stomped away.

"I hate this crazy place!" she vented to the cat. "No wonder
everyone is nuts."

"Meow," the cat agreed.

"I don't care what happens, I don't care what it takes, I'm getting out of here!"

"*Merreow!*"

She stopped and looked at the animal following her. It had a
brown coat the color of chocolate, and it seemed to blink its gold
eyes sympathetically.

"And now I'm talking to a cat," she said.

The cat halted, then spun and walked stiffly away. CeeCee
had the distinct impression it was turning its nose up at her. She
bit back an apology.

What do I do now? She'd thought that if she could just get to a
phone, that would solve everything.

Past the older building, ugly mid-century high-rises reared
up on either side, fire escapes and air conditioning units sprouting
from the walls like cankers. The way widened gradually. Graffiti peppered the walls, strange symbols that looked like code,
but unlike any hobo markings she'd seen before. Someone had
strung a line between the buildings, hung with raggedy pennants
and a banner with a heart on it, like the ones housewives hung
outside their doors for Valentine's Day. CeeCee heard a noise. It
sounded like the muted rumble of a crowd, and she slowed down
cautiously. *Was that coming from in here or out there?* she wondered.

Would she be able to hear people on the outside, while they wouldn't hear her at all?

She drifted to the side of the alley, creeping forward between ladders and AC units. The noise grew, and she glimpsed movement through the bars of fire escapes. She poked her head around the side of an electrical box and peered down the alley.

At a crossroad of alleyways, the high-rise ended on one side and a low green building took its place. A set of double doors were propped open, and people streamed in and out of the building. Several mats and rugs were set up on the ground in front, spread with items. People wandered between the mats as their owners haggled over prices or tried to lure patrons. It looked like a swap meet or farmers market, but most of the business was clearly going on inside.

She hunched into the shoulders of her hoodie. Much of the crowd looked like the people at the park; some of them were dirty, some were odd, but basically they looked human. But there were some that didn't look human at all. At one of the rugs sat a furry man with longer-than-normal ears. A very tiny lady with a gray tail peeking from under her skirt stood on a chair and excitedly beckoned people over to look at her baskets. Another man, tall, his shoulders and neck bristling with too many whiskers and muscles, ducked through the doors of the building, cheerfully calling out to someone inside.

CeeCee leaned her cheek against the cool metal of the electrical box and thought about Kelly. She thought about the slug man and the people at the park. And lastly, she thought about herself. At least she knew she wasn't going mad. She was just . . . someplace else. She needed information if she was going to figure out where this was and how to get back home, but she wasn't sure she could face up to a market full of strange. Her body was still zinging with adrenaline from attacking the window. She'd only gotten a little sleep the night before. And worst of all, her medication had finally run its course. She felt scattered, her brain jumping from one idea to the next, her eyes skipping all over the place trying to see everything at once. CeeCee was never quite sure if she was better like this or on her meds. Her mind moved faster off meds, and her reaction times were quicker. But she also knew from experience that sometimes she missed things, especially if there were distractions, and this place was nothing but distractions.

She turned to go.

Then the smell of coffee drifted strong and beckoning out the door. Her head spun at the scent. She had been bugging her mom for a few months to let her go off her meds and try drinking coffee instead, like she did on the weekends. Now she was just plain addicted to coffee, especially if it was strong and sweet. And just like her meds, coffee made her feel calmer, more focused. It dialed down her emotional reactions to sensory overload. The need pulled at her. CeeCee debated leaving the safety of her electrical box. Then she thought about how sad it was that she considered crouching behind an electrical box covered in crudely drawn sexual graffiti as "safety."

She clenched her jaw, shoved her hands in her pockets until her hoodie pulled tight against her shoulders, and stepped out from behind her sanctuary. She tried looking like she belonged as she walked up to the swap meet. She tried to project confidence. She was pretty sure she was failing.

She weaved stiffly between the rugs. Most of the wares looked either homemade or more beat up than most of the farmers markets she'd been to. These items looked like they had been, and were meant to be, used, not just cute shabby-chic décor. The lady with the tail waved to her as she went past, tottering on her chair in excitement.

"Baskets! Fine baskets for all your shopping needs!"

Up close, she looked more mouse than human, with soft gray fur and round ears. She was also adorably cute, like a character out of *An American Tail*, and CeeCee was mortified at how much she wanted to pat the woman on the head. She moved quickly to the doors and stepped into cool dimness.

Inside was an old bowling alley. Tables were set up as stalls along the lanes and at the bowling stations. The sharp smell of sizzling meat came from behind the shoe counter. Half the fluorescent bulbs overhead were burnt out, and the ones that were lit flickered over avocado-green carpeting and worn wood panels. Beat up lamps had been set up where there were working outlets and oil lanterns where there weren't. The protective eyes of stall owners watched their wares while a gang of young men, skinny and dirty, slunk around the edges of the market. People shouted and haggled and gossiped with neighbors. It was much louder inside than outside, the voices bouncing sharply off the lanes straight through her skull. The cacophony was almost overwhelming. Her nervousness ratcheted up. There was too much to see, too much to hear, too much to smell.

CeeCee took a deep, shaky breath, bracing herself, and scanned the tables for coffee. Halfway down one of the lanes near the door was a metal cart with a simple camp stove and coffeepot on top. A few people stood waiting as the pot brewed, holding cups of different sizes and types.

The coffee vendor had a sharp fox face, and his shoulder-length hair was red with a white streak right in the front. Long red hair covered his hands in a soft-looking pelt. He wore a motorcycle jacket like an old rocker, all weary experience and too many long nights coming off of him in waves. But the shrewd gold-brown eyes that met CeeCee's were kind enough.

She thought about what was in her wallet, maybe seven

bucks and some change. She wondered how long that would last here.

"How much?" she asked tentatively. "Do you have any cups?"

"I have a few cups, but it's all barter here. What do you have to trade?" He waved to the next person in line. A lady in too many hats stepped up, swooping the stack off her head and presenting them to him. The fox man looked them over carefully before choosing a blue felt one with pink flowers. He wrote something down in a little notebook on top of his cart. "Five days," he said as he poured coffee into her outstretched metal mug. "First day."

CeeCee stepped aside, into the space between his cart and the next stall. She slipped off her backpack and crouched over it as voices and the smell of coffee flew overhead.

She had two more granola bars and a pack of gum in her backpack, plus her folders, a binder full of notes, and her composition books. What else? The bloody screwdriver and the cell phone, which she should probably ditch as incriminating evidence. Pens, pencils, a calculator, the plastic water bottle Kelly had given her, her makeup case and some toiletries . . . not much that she thought was worth trading. She took out the calculator.

"Would this do?" she asked.

"All my math is up here," he said, tapping his head. He filled the last customer's cup with coffee.

CeeCee looked at the box he'd put the hat in. It was full of mainly clothes and a few houseware odds and ends. That gave her an idea. The spring mornings had been so chilly, she dressed in layers. She was wearing her red hoodie that she'd never give up—even for coffee—and a plain gray T-shirt, but underneath that was a tank top. Sure, she was really cold last night, and three layers hadn't been enough. But if she got out of here today, she really wouldn't need three layers, would she?

Holding her backpack firmly between her legs, she slipped

her arms into the sleeves of her hoodie and T-shirt. A few careful maneuvers later, her arm reemerged holding a cream-colored tank top with gray seagulls printed on it. She sniffed it surreptitiously. It was remarkably clean after a night spent sleeping outside and only a little smelly around the armpits, but still better smelling than half the people she had met.

"What about this?" She held up her top. "It's nice, right?"

He took the top and held it up to the flickering light. "Cute," he said. "Two days."

"And a mug! It's practically new, and look at this detail work." She pointed to the satin ribbon around the neckline.

He looked at her and barked a laugh.

"Well, well—when you first walked up, I thought you were new to the byways, but obviously you catch on quick. Two days and a mug. You're under the name Blondie." He made a mark in his notebook.

"Why thank you, Red the Coffee Man."

He barked that laugh again, then opened a sliding door in the cart and fished out a green metallic travel mug. He filled her cup, and she took a sip. The dark roast swirled like hot velvet in her mouth, and her shoulders relaxed.

"Oh, this is good!" she gasped.

"Thanks." He made a face at her. It wasn't quite a human smile, but it was still a smile just the same.

She grinned back. "It's all about the water, right?"

"Exactly!" he said, pouring a cup for the next customer. "Temp control and good water are key."

CeeCee took another sip, enjoying the warmth as it poured down her throat. She felt more centered just having it in her hands, and her anxiety eased. She loitered next to the coffee cart and watched the bustle of the market, voices bouncing off the walls of the bowling alley. It hadn't occurred to her at the park to look for familiar faces. If she had found this place, maybe others had too—maybe a homeless person that she actually knew, like old Oscar, who was more lucid than the rest. She inspected the crowd carefully. Some of the people looked strange, but they acted just like people did at any market. The man with too many muscles she'd seen earlier was earnestly negotiating over a trombone at a nearby stall. A twitchy teenager backed into a rack of pans, and the stall owner yelled at him to move on. She did the same thing once, tripping over a flower bucket at a fair with her mom last summer, and got the same reaction. She was suddenly curious about everything.

"So what do you do with the clothes?" she asked the fox man.

"I sell them to a thrift store. Sometimes my wife adds embroidery or other touches. Then I buy coffee and whatever supplies I need and start over." He shrugged and started setting up a new pot of coffee to brew. "It's a life."

She was so startled by the idea that he had a wife—*Is she a fox too? Do they have kids? Do fox kids go to school?*—that she almost missed what he said. "A thrift store? You mean, besides here? Outside?"

"Yes, at one of the halfway shops."

Halfway sounded promising, whatever that meant. "Maybe you can help me," she said. "When you said I was new . . . well, you're right. I am. Someone else said there were halfway places. What are those?"

He turned his full attention on her and looked at her intently. "They're like passages or gates. Places that sit halfway here and halfway there, for those who travel back and forth. Not everyone can. Or wants to."

"I want to. I'm trying to get back home. Can you tell me where the shop is?"

The fox opened his mouth, but before he could speak, a hand gripped her elbow.

"There you are, poppet!"

Startled, CeeCee stumbled a step away from the cart and looked up. Doc M's silver eyes were boring into her own.

"I've been looking all over for you," he announced.

"Hey!" The coffee proprietor reached his hand toward her.

Doc M turned his head and stared at the fox. He smiled the whole time, but the fox backed up a step and finally turned away.

"Come back for your second day," he muttered.

"Put another day on her account, my treat."

Doc M tried to steer her into the lane as the fox reluctantly made a note. Alarmed, CeeCee planted her feet.

"Excuse me," she said. "I don't know you. What do you want?"

"Well, I'm just being friendly, of course! I saw you at the park, and I always make it a point to meet anyone new. You could say I'm the welcoming committee around here." He smiled gregariously, patting her arm that he still held. "Let me introduce myself. I'm Doctor M. Awful-Ease. And you are?"

She felt trapped by the strictures of politeness. She really didn't want to tell him her name, but her mind blanked and she couldn't think of a way around it, especially after he bought her a cup of coffee. Her skin itched around the grip of his fingers.

"I'm CeeCee."

"CeeCee! A pretty name for a pretty girl. It's very nice to meet you. Never be afraid to meet someone new, I always say. People are our greatest resource. You never know when it might turn into a beneficial relationship."

He turned as he chattered, and without realizing it, CeeCee took a step to follow him, caught in his orbit. Doc M seemed bigger than everyone around him, brighter and crisper at the edges, like he was HD TV and the rest of the world was just fuzzy video. CeeCee could feel herself gaping. He drank up the attention, and the purple velvet of his coat glowed like a jewel. She fell into step beside him, drawn by his charisma.

"So . . . what brings you to our fair corner of the city?" He watched her sharply. "Did you run away from home? Don't worry! I understand if you did! I see it all the time. Sometimes a home isn't really a home. Sometimes people are better off in a new environment." He patted her arm again.

"No, nothing like that," she denied, even though part of her wondered if she had run away, just a little.

"Or perhaps you heard rumors about the byways, and you just had to come see for yourself! Wondrous, isn't it? And I bet you haven't even gotten a proper tour yet."

He talked fast and confidently, and it made all the words dry up in her mouth. It was intimidating and dazzling both. He seemed like a man in charge. She was suddenly certain Doc M knew more about this place than anyone. Maybe he could help her! She wondered why Jesse had warned her off him. *What was it Apple Cheeks had said? "Not the worst, but not the best either"?* She gulped at her coffee, trying to still her frazzled thoughts, trying to think of the right words to ask about halfway places.

"Or maybe . . . something happened? Something illegal?" His too-gray eyes caught her attention the same way the jumping colors had.

CeeCee stiffened, shame and guilt crashing over her. It chased all the questions out of her head. The noise of the market dimmed. She shouldn't have taken the rabbit. How could she have been so stupid?

"Whatever it was, I'm sure it wasn't your fault," he crooned. "People just push and push, don't they? Push us into corners. Make us feel awful about ourselves."

"Coming here was a mistake. I'm leaving today," she choked out.

He looked at her sympathetically. "Are you sure? I bet you haven't seen half the magic this place can offer, and I assure you, it is magical." He leaned in close like he was sharing a secret. "Besides, sometimes people come here for a reason. They don't fit in, and no one understands why. It's because they don't really belong out there."

His words hit hard, almost painfully so. Doubt and guilt curled in her stomach like a snake. She tried to fit in—she did. She tried for her mom and for Trudy and for a little bit of peace. But then she thought about Mr. Beauchamp and Taylor and the Committee Crew, and a little flicker of anger joined in. The snake coiled and coiled until it ate its own head. She wanted to bolt away from it all, but Doc M was still talking.

"This is their true home. I bet you try, and it doesn't work, does it? They just keep pushing. It's not your fault, you know. You're such a pretty thing; I bet they're all green with envy."

He was watching her too closely. She felt both flattered and cornered by his eyes.

"I can help you, you know."

"How?" She wanted to believe him.

"I can show you around, help you find your place. I know the byways can be . . . confusing."

"Can you help me get out?"

"Oh, poppet, I don't think that's the right question. I think the real question is, what would make you feel better?"

"What do you mean?"

"All those bad thoughts other people put in your head, all the times they pushed, it just goes round and round in circles, doesn't it? And who wants that when they're starting new?"

He was right; she didn't want those thoughts. She was sick of them. For a moment, she desperately wanted him to make it all better. He sounded so understanding. She tore her eyes from his confident smile. They had walked all the way to the end of the flea market, steering away from the front doors. They faced the back of the bowling alley, full of shadows where the lights had burnt out completely, and CeeCee thought she could see another door in the dimness. Doc M continued his unhurried pace as if they were out for a stroll. Some of the patrons watched him warily. Then a shopper gave her a concerned look behind Doc M's back.

Why is she looking at me that way? CeeCee realized she had missed what he just said.

"Excuse me, what was that?"

The skin around his eyes tightened. "I said, I could help you feel better," he said smoothly. "I specialize in treating people's reactions to life's stresses. I'm a doctor and a psychiatrist all in one. Whatever stress, whatever pain you feel, I can ease your awful."

A spark went up CeeCee's spine. She planted her feet again. He took a half step before stopping too. He turned and beamed at her.

"Huh, Doctor M. Awful-Ease, ease your awful," she said slowly. "That's clever."

"Isn't it just? A bit of marketing flair on my part."

She cocked her head at him. "So are you offering therapy? Medication?"

"Certainly, I can lend an ear to all that bothers you. I'm quite the skilled counselor. And if . . . medication . . . is what you need, well . . ." He patted her arm with the hand that didn't have a firm hold on her. "There's never a need to suffer. Ask anyone—I offer the most comprehensive selection than anyone in the byways. And there's more options here than you could ever find out there." He waved a hand lazily.

There it was, the same condescending tone masquerading as sympathy she'd heard all her life. Never mind that she knew he wasn't offering her anything as simple as Adderall.

"I think I've had my fill of medications."

"I can do more. Maybe you're looking for employment? I could use someone like you in my organization." His eyes never stopped watching her.

"Someone like me? You don't know anything about me," she said, startled.

"Oh, I think I do. As I told you, I've seen it all. I know promise when I see it—someone who thinks on their feet, who has a passion for life even if other people don't understand it. Maybe you don't fit in out there, but that doesn't mean you can't fit in here. Yes, I could use someone like you."

"How?" She was curious despite herself. What if everything he was saying were true? Maybe he was really trying to help, and she was just being suspicious, letting impulse get the better of her again.

"I have just the position for you, pretty poppet. Entry level, you understand, while we assess your . . . talents. Then once you got your feet wet, we could move on to more creative endeavors, where your strengths would shine. I think we could work well together."

Well, that didn't tell her anything at all. He hadn't offered up a job title or even a business description, just vague flattery. Did he think she was that dumb? Her temper flared, and impulse won out.

"I don't need that kind of help," she said belligerently. "I don't need anything you're selling."

He had a knuckle ring on his pinkie that ended in a metal claw. He tightened his grip on her arm, and it bit into her flesh.

She hissed and jerked back, peering at her arm. The cut was shallow, but blood dripped crisply off her wrist like a warning.

"Oh, poppet, I'm so sorry!" Doc M threw up his arms in dismay. "But never fear, I have just the thing for that." He smiled, wolfish and too large.

"I've got to go."

"But we've only just started," he said reaching for her again. "Let me get you a Band-Aid."

Shouts were moving in their direction. A pig was running loose in the crowd. People were jumping out of the way or trying to chase it down or frantically waving it away from their wares. Doc M took his weird gray eyes off her, finally, and turned his head as it passed. CeeCee took three big steps toward the front door and kicked over a wheelbarrow full of rusty metal at the head of a bowling lane. It fell clattering across the lane, and Doc M jumped back, sneering, then brushing the hem of his trousers. He looked at her over the heap of bulky metal between them.

"Oops!" CeeCee said insincerely. She backed hurriedly toward the door.

"Oh, don't worry, poppet. We'll meet again. I promise."

SEVEN

Whatever
Proper People Do

O utside the doors, she turned down a street at random. Then, for good measure, she took another corner just in case Doc M tried to follow her.

Her hands were shaking. CeeCee couldn't tell if she was angry or if she was scared or if she was just frustrated. A chill shook her as she remembered Doc M's probing eyes, which ferreted out every little secret. She wasn't sure if she had just run from a threat or the only person who could help her. He obviously peddled drugs . . . could he be a pimp too? Her thoughts stumbled then because how would she know? The slug man, clearly, was a disgusting pervert. But Doc M wasn't like *that*. He hadn't hit on her like other skeevy guys had tried. He seemed . . . professional. He radiated authority and reassurance.

But she hated being managed. CeeCee stomped her frustration into the pavement. All her life, people had tried to settle her down, curb her energy, muzzle her mouth, like she was an animal that needed to be tamed. Doc M hadn't been quite doing that. But he was doing *something*, even if she wasn't sure what it was.

She could still vaguely hear the echo of the crowd behind her. She slurped her coffee and turned at random until it grew quiet. She was so lost at this point, she might as well. The coffee was cooling, but it still tasted great, and she felt her mind focus with every sip.

She walked along the back of an aging, one-story building, the type they used for mini strip malls, and wondered what the halfway places looked like. Would there be a fee, like a toll charge, to use them? She rattled a locked door handle as she went by. Would they have signs? Or arrows pointing toward them, made out of magical pixie dust? In retrospect, she was irritated by Doc M's interruption. The fox man had been about to tell her where to go! Now she didn't want to go back, in case Doc M was still at the market.

The guilt he stirred up added a new, biting coil in her stomach. If Kelly's story was any indication, then stealing the rabbit had triggered this whole mess. CeeCee hadn't accidentally gotten stuck here; it was her fault.

She finished the last of her coffee and stowed the cup carefully away in her backpack.

I won't need it. I won't be here tomorrow. She clenched her jaw. All she had to do was find one of those halfway places.

A broken window beckoned her, light glinting off a bit of metal framing, and she peered inside. It was dusty and quiet, and the building looked abandoned. It had sounded like the halfway places that the fox talked about had people, but maybe some of them were empty. Maybe . . . the front door led to a street! She boosted herself up and over the sill.

The building wasn't very deep. It looked exactly like you'd expect an empty strip mall store to look like, too, except for the mice scurrying around. She crossed the musty shop, avoiding droppings where she could. There were an awful *lot* of mice. Maybe it used to be a pet shop, and all the mice had banded together to overthrow the owners. The thought would be more amusing if the mice weren't giving her the eye as she walked. They seemed utterly without fear.

"Hello," she said. "Just trying to find my way home. Sorry for the intrusion."

The inside door was also locked without a latch in sight, but next to it was another window. It was too dingy to see through, but she slid it open and boosted herself up again.

CeeCee landed on the other side in another alley. She sighed heavily.

There was a small sound behind her, and she jerked back around. A mouse stood on the windowsill. It looked at her a moment before it chittered at her quite seriously. Then, she swore it turned and pointed its paw down the alley.

She really wasn't sure if she should be following directions from a mouse. It's not that she had anything against mice, but she'd never considered them as particularly knowledgeable or anything. Although, when one considered how often mice had to run from danger, they probably would be good at sussing out every available path.

A thought struck her: If she went back to the market, could she find a guide there? Or at least get a map? She trudged forward, frowning. She didn't have much left to trade.

She wondered how much cheese a mouse would charge. Maybe it could ride her shoulder as it pointed the way. In a flash, an image of the mouse on one shoulder and the demented rabbit on the other came to her: her personal devil and angel rodents. She'd have laughed if she were anywhere but here.

She turned a corner, and a sculpture rose in front of her against a building, its elaborate height startling. Grocery carts made up the bulk of it, decorated and twisted and melded together, painted a dozen colors. But there were also ramps running through it and levers and pulleys turned by wheels attached to ropes. Other wheels spun, trailing ribbons. It was strange and gorgeous.

It was also dangerous as hell. Bits of broken metal stuck out at random places. There were sections clearly meant for climbing or sitting that also looked like they would collapse. This was an art installation that would never get approved back home.

CeeCee ducked under a beam and sat down, looking up through the center. It was beautiful inside—as beautiful as a song, except it didn't end. The light caught on the colors and the spinning metal. She caught her breath, and the world went very still for a moment.

A loud screech cut through the calm. CeeCee craned her head to find the sound. From a decrepit building across the alley, two older women and five children stepped onto a long patio balcony. They all looked strange, their hair and skin too brightly colored to be completely normal—blue and green and pink, like tropical birds. A little girl ran around the patio, spinning her arms. She was the one making all the noise. Her hair stood around her head, bright orange and yellow, like flames. The little girl climbed up and over an older boy, laughing the whole time.

CeeCee waited for the mom to tell her to stop, for the other children to yell at her.

No one pulled her aside; no one made her sit down. One of the women held a small board and pointed to it as she talked while the kids listened, even the little girl. CeeCee could tell the little girl was listening, even from where she sat, even though the girl never stopped moving.

Her throat grew hot and tight. *What if Doc M was right? What if I do belong here?*

She didn't fit in at home; she knew she didn't. She was always causing trouble. It didn't bother her so much when it only affected her . . . spacing out on a test or getting distracted in the morning so she missed the bus and had to walk. But her trouble seemed to spill out and splash everyone she cared about.

She wondered what was waiting for her at home. Her mom angry and yelling, ready to ground her, maybe for a long time, and then her own room, her own bed, her own *place*. That wasn't so bad. It wasn't like she had meant to get lost. Her mom would understand. But what if school had called and she was expelled—or accused of taking the damn catering money? What if someone had seen her stealing the rabbit, and there were cops at her door? She didn't think they could afford a lawyer.

She knew her mom loved her. She knew that. But even to her mind, she sounded like more trouble than she was worth. Her stomach swirled with shame and guilt.

Maybe she would never fit in. Maybe it would be better if she just disappeared.

The little girl's laugh sang free and treacherous. CeeCee imagined being allowed to run around the back of the classroom during a lesson. Being able to fidget without getting detention or called strange. Being in a place where being too loud and too energetic didn't bother anybody. Eyes stinging, she climbed out of the sculpture and left its beauty behind.

She was still sniffling when she spotted someone maneuvering a rolling bag backward through a door. She hastily scrubbed tear streaks away. He looked, somehow, familiar.

"Hey, you're that guy," she blurted.

The guy looked slyly over his shoulder, like he knew she'd been there the whole time.

CeeCee was already flushed, but she felt another wave of heat through her cheeks.

"Jesse." He grinned at her. "What's your name? I didn't catch it before."

"I'm CeeCee." She squinted at him. He looked . . . more disreputable in daylight, but maybe that was just his bag. It was overly large and an awkward shape, and there was an air of furtiveness about the scene. Jesse's hair fell in his eyes and he was sweating as he struggled, but he seemed suspiciously pleased.

"CeeCee," he said, like he was rolling it around in his mouth. "CeeCee."

"Don't be weird," she snapped. Now why could she say that out loud to him and not to Doc M? *Because* you're *weird*, she thought reproachfully to herself.

In contrast, his smile grew even wider. He wiggled the bag through the door, then, with a triumphant smirk, pivoted sharply.

"What is that?"

"A delivery," he said. "I'd love to stay, but I'm on a deadline." He rolled up to a fence and heaved the bag over it. Then he pulled himself up and over.

"O . . . kay," she said dubiously.

He winked at her before his head disappeared over the side.

CeeCee stomped across the concrete and berated herself for not asking him for directions. While she brooded, the path widened, and the texture of the buildings flickered. Shadows played against the walls in long lines and crisscrossing branches, then disappeared. Under her feet, the cement blurred into cobblestones, and dirt appeared along either side, getting thicker and wider until the cobblestones became a narrow path flanked by soil. Then a bush appeared, then two and three. Suddenly real trees, oak and maple, rose up on either side of her, like she was walking a path in a park. But all around, the steel skyscrapers towered above, hedging in the miniature forest like it wasn't even there.

The trees thinned out, then stopped as a lawn appeared, lush and overgrown, sweeping gently uphill toward a white, antebellum house. She froze at the edge of the lawn and gaped. It was bewildering how quickly everything had changed. The house was skinny and tall, at least three or four stories, with columns gracing the porch spanning the front. The grass was trampled down in places, and discarded sports equipment lay scattered across it. A bat and ball lying here, a broken wooden hoop leaned against a tree there. It all looked so terribly old-fashioned, like a slice of yesteryear had been squashed in and left here while the city had grown up around it without noticing.

Her shoulders set resolutely. This time she would make sure to ask for directions. She waded through the thick grass.

A boy came around the side of the house, stomping and beating the tall grass out of his way. He stopped short when he saw CeeCee.

"Oh hello!" he said. "Were we expecting you?"

Another boy followed him, exactly like the first. The twins had neatly combed dark hair and layers of grass stains on their light-colored breeches. The one coming around the corner was wiping mud onto his white polo shirt.

"No," CeeCee said, "I was just walking and found your house."

The boys began a rapid dialog.

"We haven't had visitors in a while."

"What a treat."

"I'm Ted."

"I'm Tom."

"We're brothers."

"Couldn't you tell?"

They spoke very fast, but they held peculiarly still. Then they both swooped into motion, one brother scooping up balls that lay hidden in the grass and the other retrieving a baseball bat, before they settled into stillness again and looked at her expectantly.

"Hi, I'm CeeCee," she said after a startled pause. "Do you live here?"

"Yes," they said together.

"All alone? You don't look very old."

"It's because we're not," said one proudly. She thought it might be Tom.

"Our parents died in an accident before we were quite ready, you see," said the other.

"Our parents left us everything, so we own the house."

"But all these awful people kept coming."

"They kept trying to make us grow up. School and numbers and business," said the one.

"How to dress, how to behave, how to pay bills," said the other.

"Responsibilities."

"And accountabilities."

That was a lot of information in one go. CeeCee didn't know what to say. It was dizzying how quickly they ran into the backs of each other's sentences, and she felt like she had to catch her breath.

Finally she offered, "I don't like school much, either."

The twins beamed at her. "It was all terribly boring!"

"And took so much time!"

"We didn't want to grow up," said the one.

"So we decided not to," grinned the other, showing too-sharp teeth.

They were so pale in the sunshine, washed out and without

a wrinkle. CeeCee peered at them, trying to guess at their age. They looked young and somehow not young at all.

"How long have you been here?"

"Oh, long enough," said maybe Ted.

"Long enough for all the toys to get broken," said maybe Tom, glaring at the other.

"It gets dreadfully boring."

"But you're here now! Would you like some lemonade?"

"Sure," said CeeCee.

"Good! You know how to make lemonade, of course?"

"Um . . . of course."

"Then it won't be hard at all!"

They burst into movement again, running up the front porch steps, clearly expecting her to follow.

She hurried after them into the house. For a brief moment, she was glad to be inside a regular house, after spending the night crouched in an alley. But upon stepping inside, she realized it wasn't quite what she was used to. The hallway was cluttered with toys and towers of dirty clothes. The paint was peeling on the staircase banister; there were smudgy fingerprints all along the walls and even some on the ceiling. They walked through a dining room scattered with plates of crackers and paper airplanes and board games, which looked played halfway through then abandoned. Another door led into the kitchen. Dishes were piled everywhere, and CeeCee noticed almost all of them were dirty.

"Here we are!" said Tom.

"I'll get the lemons; you find the glasses," said Ted, and he ran out a back door.

"No, I'll get the lemons!" said Tom, running after him.

"Hey!" CeeCee protested too late.

She felt like she did at Trudy's house when one of her younger brothers conned her into helping with his chores. She was annoyed, except . . . lemonade did sound good, and she was starting to get hungry. The kitchen was overwhelming in its clutter, and her eyes couldn't focus on anything in the jumbled chaos. She stared hard at a broken plate until the mess resolved back into individual objects. She was really glad she'd had that coffee; otherwise, this kitchen would make her scream. She picked out a grimy pitcher and three mismatched cups, then cleared a few dishes out of the sink and ran the water faucet until it was hot. The kitchen was antiquated, yet there was a bottle of Dawn dish soap on the ledge of the sink. It didn't seem to go with the rest of the house, but she was glad of it anyway. There were no dish towels, though. Fuming a little, she washed the dishes as best as she could with only her hands and set them on the table. Then she found a canister full of sugar and a packet of crackers after poking around on the shelves. One of the cabinets revealed an old-fashioned icebox, complete with a large block of ice. CeeCee had no idea how to get ice cubes from a large block of ice.

The back door banged open, and in ran Ted and Tom, their arms full of lemons. Some of them still had leaves and branches attached to them. She moved dishes out of the way so they could put them down on the table. She grabbed a filthy knife and held it under the hot water until the grime started to melt off.

"Oh, you're good at this!" said maybe Tom.

"Very clever!" agreed maybe Ted.

"Don't you ever clean?" she asked, exasperated.

"Oh, that's something grownups do."

"We're not grownups."

"Well, neither am I! Not quite," CeeCee grumbled as she cut up lemons. But compared to the boys, she felt ages older.

Could they really be living out here on their own? They weren't living well in her opinion, but they were managing. *If they can do it*, she thought with a pang, *I can too*. She didn't *think* she belonged in the alleys, but what if she were wrong? If she stayed here, she wouldn't be a burden on anyone any longer. Her mom would have more money. Trudy wouldn't have to defend her at school. She wouldn't be an embarrassment. CeeCee tasted acid at the back of her throat. She choked it down and concentrated fiercely on the lemons in front of her.

The lemonade, when it was finally done, was actually kind of pretty. It wasn't very cold, and it came out full of more seeds and chunks of pulp than she would have liked, but it was sweet enough, and she had cut one of the leftover lemons so the slices floated in the juice. She had to slap away Tom and Ted's hands the whole time she was making it. Finally, she ordered them to wash up, simply to keep their grimy fingers out of the sugar. She only had a moment to admire the pitcher before one of the twins grabbed it and ran out onto the front porch. The other one grabbed the cups and the packet of crackers and sprinted after him.

CeeCee had the distinct impression that if she wanted any lemonade, she'd better move.

Ted and Tom were happily sitting on a swing, each devouring a cup of lemonade and a handful of crackers. She perched on a rickety wicker chair near them and helped herself. The crackers were surprisingly tasty, and she unabashedly ate her fill. It was nice out on the porch. The air was warm, and sunlight reached the house despite the tall buildings on either side. It felt more wide-open here than in the alleys, with the lawn sloping away and birds flitting between the not too distant trees. The sun winking on the windows of the skyscrapers were like dozens of golden lights above them.

"How do they not see you?" she asked, waving to the skyscrapers.

"Well, it's not convenient. More convenient not to see, isn't it?" said one of the brothers, pouring himself another glass.

"This is a whole house!" CeeCee protested.

"Well, they noticed at first. Thought us a couple of real odd ducks!" said the other.

"They'd knock on the door and try to get us to come out! Oh, we had a good laugh about that!"

"But then we made them feel funny, after the years went on . . ."

"And us refusing to grow up . . ."

"So it became more convenient not to see."

She was thoroughly confused by this reasoning. *How is it convenient not to see?* Then she thought about how often people just walked right past old Oscar at the park or those neighbors who always looked a little angry and had funny smells coming out of their apartment. People whispered about them as they were getting mail, but no one really wanted to approach them about what was going on. Or even at school, how everyone overlooked Taylor's constant bullying. Her teeth clenched. They were right. Some things were easier to ignore.

"This is very good lemonade."

"Yes, very clever!"

"Maybe you could come work for us! Making lemonade, helping with the house," said Ted magnanimously.

"Oh, but then we'd have to pay her. That's bills," pointed out Tom.

Ted frowned. "And we'd have to keep track. Don't you have to keep track to pay bills?"

"Yes, isn't that one of the things they tried to teach us?"

"Who can remember? It was terribly boring!"

"Dreadfully!"

CeeCee thought boredom may have gnawed them clean from the inside out. She'd always thought living on her own would be cool, but there was something about the boys that had gone funny.

"You know, the one thing about learning new things," she said carefully, "is that you never get bored."

"Seems like a bother to me."

"I thought you didn't like school," said Tom, peering at her.

"Well, I don't really. The people bug me, and I hate math," she said. "But I don't mind reading; there are so many interesting things in books."

"Like what?"

"Oh, different places around the world, new discoveries, new ideas." She felt like she was explaining a basic concept to much younger children.

"But why would you want to do that?"

"I think it's fun. I guess I'm just curious," she said thoughtfully. "I wouldn't miss school, but I'd miss learning."

"They're just trying to change you, you know. It's a conspiracy," said Tom.

"A plot," said Ted.

"Maybe. But what if I changed for the better? You liked how I made lemonade—I had to learn that. Besides, who wants to stay the same all the time?"

"We do," they said together.

CeeCee laughed despite herself. "Well, what about all the new games?" she said. "That's something you have to learn."

"New games?" said Tom. He turned and looked at Ted.

Ted looked back at him. "What kind of new games?"

"New video games." It suddenly occurred to her that they might not know what a video game was; everything in the house was so old-fashioned. There might not be video games at all here in the alleys. But then she remembered the slug man's shop and his jungle of devices. "Do you have a TV? Or a computer? There's tons of games on electronics. You know, like on phones and for TV and tablets? Everyone plays them. And they make up new games all the time."

"I've seen a TV before," said Tom, speaking slowly for the first time.

"At one of the parties. It had all those buttons," said Ted.

"It was terribly confusing."

"Oh, but remember those funny cartoons?" Ted's speech sped up again.

"Yes, those weren't boring at all!" Tom brightened up.

CeeCee was beginning to think they had been around much longer than she thought. Maybe they had changed, like Kelly, but you just couldn't tell. What if they had stopped aging?

"See?" she said triumphantly. "Some things are worth learning."

They both turned and gazed at her, going preternaturally still again.

"Maybe."

"Maybe not."

"We will take it under consideration," said one cheekily.

"And get back to you at a later date," said the other. They seemed enormously pleased with themselves at this response, and CeeCee had a glimpse of what all those tutors and advisors had to deal with years ago. Irritation stirred just under her skin.

She shrugged instead. "You don't know what you're missing." The twins exchanged alarmed looks, and she suppressed a twinge of smugness. "Well," she said, "it was nice visiting with you, but I should get going." She stood up and brushed crumbs off her jeans.

"We're always happy to provide refreshments," said Ted grandly.

The hint hung in the air a moment before CeeCee managed a polite, "Yes, thank you," around gritted teeth.

"You are very welcome," said Tom. "Where are you going now?"

"I'm trying to get back to the city. Do you know the way?"

"Where they'll make you go to school? How dreadful!"

"I know you don't want to—it's not the thing for you—but yes." She added airily, "I miss my games. They're so much fun."

"Hmmm," said Tom thoughtfully.

"You could try the Queen," suggested Ted.

"The Queen? Who's that?"

"The *Queen*, silly! She's in charge," said Tom.

"Yes, you could try her. We're friends with her, you know."

"We get invited to *all* her parties."

"If we don't show up, she gets terribly upset."

"Yes," said Ted. He frowned at his brother.

"Responsibilities," Tom said, frowning back.

"Accountabilities."

"Sounds dreadful," agreed CeeCee as she settled her backpack on her shoulders. "How do I find her?"

"Take the back path, and keep going straight in that direction."

"Everyone knows the Queen. You can ask anyone."

"Stop by for lemonade any time!"

EIGHT

The Darkness in Their Minds

This alley wasn't straight, and it was darker than usual, despite the hour. Tall, cramped buildings were squashed in next to each other, creating a crooked path. The buildings leaned over the narrow passage, crowding out the light as if they were jealously guarding the darkness. CeeCee took a wary step in and was hit by a rank wave of smell. She gagged and staggered back. Garbage was scattered as far as she could see—rags, rotting food, rusty appliances—before a jutting wall cut off her line of sight, twisting the alley in another direction. The walls were smeared with refuse and who knew what else, thick enough that giant mushrooms as big as her head were growing out of them. They looked slimy and pale in the dim light. It was disgusting, but the twins had said this was the direction to find the Queen.

She wasn't sure if the Queen was an actual ruler of the alleys or just another weird character, but she was taking all the tips she could get from now on. In her experience, people who threw parties usually had some influence or at least knew a lot of people. It was strange how friendly and normal Red the Coffee Man had been, just like any barista, even if he looked different. The twins, however . . . well, the twins looked like they could be in a cereal commercial, but there was definitely something odd about them, almost eerie. She wondered if this place had changed them or if they had started off like that.

What if the alleys changed her into something awful? The rabbit in her pocket dug into her thigh. She remembered her fight with Trudy, the accusing eyes staring at her in the hall.

What if I already am someone awful?

Her fists clenched, and she forced them open. She tried plotting a course through the garbage. She wondered how long the alley was. Could she hold her breath until the end? She adjusted her backpack and took a deep breath.

A hand clutched her elbow and spun her around. Her stomach leaped into her throat, and she shrieked. Jesse stood there, looking half-concerned and half like he wanted to laugh. She yanked her elbow out of his hand. "What's with people grabbing my arm?!" she yelled. "And where did you fricking come from? Are you following me?"

"Don't travel down that way," he said seriously.

"Don't sneak up on me!" she snapped back. "Why not? Besides the smell."

"Pretend like you're walking away." He moved just to the side, out of sight of the alley and waved her over.

CeeCee still felt like hitting him. "What? Why?"

"You'll see." He grinned at her, but there was caution in his expression.

He stared at her, unblinking, looking altogether too sure of himself. She didn't know why he expected her to do anything he said. He curved his tall frame against the side of the wall so that he could look around the corner down the alley and still leave room for her to see. He patted the wall and waited, smiling that annoying smile. Then again, she thought grudgingly, he had warned her about Doc M.

She moved next to him and pressed her cheek against the wall. He was taller than she was but not by much. She could feel her hair shift with his breath.

"Now watch." He pointed. "It'll take a moment."

They stood hidden against the wall and spied down the alley. At first there was nothing to see but the twisting lane of stink and garbage. CeeCee jittered her leg up and down impatiently. Then a pile of old clothes moved, shifting in place and settling down again. A hand crept out from inside a box and grabbed a mushroom from the ground. A shadow crept very slowly across a broken fire escape and up another ladder. A chill skittered down CeeCee's spine. It was eerily quiet, but all along the passage, small bits of the scenery jerked and twitched.

"They wait for people," Jesse said. "They'll take everything you have. Not everyone makes it back out."

"What are they?" she whispered.

"Just people. Sort of like the people at the park but . . . worse. This is what happens when they go too far, so drunk or drugged out they give up and crawl in there." He shrugged. "The mushrooms keep them going."

CeeCee looked at the twitching people, horrified. "Will they chase us out here?" She'd thought the slug man was disgusting, but this was worse. Did the twins know about this when they pointed her in this direction?

Jesse stepped back and smirked at her confidently. "No, like I said, they've given up. And they don't really like the light anymore." He paused. "I wouldn't hang around this area at night, though."

She decided to forgive him slightly for scaring her—but only just.

She shifted from foot to foot. "I need to go that direction. Was that the only way through?"

"No, come on, I'll show you." He strolled down the alley without waiting for an answer.

She glared at his back. There he went, expecting her to follow him again. She stomped to his side just so he would know she was annoyed.

She glanced at him sidelong. The sun peeked in and out between the buildings as they walked and made his dark hair gleam in the light. She wondered what his story was . . . he didn't seem like a runaway or someone stuck in this place. He was cute, with high cheekbones and warm golden-brown skin. But his cocky air also made it seem like he might get into trouble. She usually avoided people like that because she always got the blame. He turned and caught her watching him.

"So . . . what do the mushrooms do? Do they eat them? Are they another drug?"

"Both. It changes them, makes them stronger when they should get weaker. There's a lot of drugs in the byways, but the mushrooms are the worst. Highly addictive. Sustainable as food, if you're willing to live like that." He pointed behind him. "It makes them different." He said it lightly, but his face was thoughtful.

She wasn't sure if he was serious or not. "Are you different?" she asked. "Are you one of the ones who changed?"

"I'm exactly as I always am." He waved grandly. "Sometimes I am this, and sometimes I am that."

CeeCee's temper flared. "That tells me . . . exactly . . . nothing." She sarcastically waved.

Jesse laughed as if she surprised him into it. He looked at her with a new light in his eyes.

"You're . . . unexpected."

"You're . . . a little annoying." She knew it was rude, but he seemed to enjoy rankling her.

He laughed again, as if to prove her point, and stared at her unblinking. "How do you like it here so far?"

"You know I'm trying to get out." *Are you though?* a voice whispered inside her.

"A shock, isn't it? Not quite what you expected?" he needled.

"I didn't expect anything because I didn't expect to get lost!" she said hotly.

She took a deep breath and wrestled her temper under control. She didn't know why she was reacting to him so intensely. The twins had been annoying, and it hadn't bothered her like this.

"It just seems like there are a lot of changed people here," she muttered.

He was watching her again. He changed the subject. "Where are you trying to go?"

"I met these twins. They told me I could find the Queen if I went in that direction."

The grin dropped off his face. "You're going to see the Queen?" he asked. His voice sounded funny.

"They said she could help me get out," she explained, nonplussed. She waited, half expecting him to tease her again.

"Oh." He stopped in the alley and stared toward the sky. Cee-Cee followed his gaze. Birds danced around the chimney of a building, swooping and diving at some game she couldn't guess at. She looked at him again. He stood perfectly still. She couldn't tell if he was going to pounce or was trying to blend into the wall. She had a feeling he was avoiding her eyes.

"What does that mean? 'Oh'?"

"The Queen can probably help you, but that doesn't mean she will," he said carefully. "Everything comes with a price."

She bristled at his tone of voice, like he thought she couldn't handle herself. "Maybe I'm willing to pay."

"Are you?" he asked. "There are other ways to get out. The Queen's more for . . . last resorts." He started walking again.

She trailed after him. "If you have any suggestions, I'm more than happy to hear them." It came out sounding more belligerent than she meant. She wanted help. He just kept working her nerves.

They came to a section where five paths branched off. Cee-Cee had that feeling again that they all belonged to different streets and were somehow pasted together.

Jesse jumped up onto a low wall and waved down one of the passages. "If you go that way, you'll find the Queen, or someone who works for her." He waved to another passage. "If you go that way, you'll hit some halfway shops. If I were you, I'd try that first."

He meandered along the wall until he suddenly hopped down out of view on the other side. She was unexpectedly crestfallen at his disappearance.

She wavered at the crossroads, feeling very alone all of a sudden, the different paths echoing empty bricks and pavement and concrete. Then, for reasons she couldn't say, she turned down the path toward the halfway shops.

"Hey, you—girly!"

It was Suspenders, the man who had hogged all of Apple Cheeks's soup. He leaned heavily against a wall and waved Cee-Cee over with one hand. She'd been trudging along for a while, and her feet were starting to ache. It was a relief to stop, even for him.

He was terribly drunk, the kind of drunk that warned her to keep out of arm's reach but also told her that he was likely to fall over if he staggered too far away from that wall. Her grandmother

and other relatives would get like that at family holidays sometimes. She remembered the tight look on her mom's face as she
held CeeCee back. Her mom always cut the visit short, holiday
or not, and they'd go back to the apartment and eat ice cream and
watch movies instead.

CeeCee tried to keep the disdain off her face as Suspenders
plastered on a sloppy smile.

"Girly!" he called again and kept waving long after she had
stopped walking toward him.

"Hi," she said cautiously. "How are you doing?"

"Peachy! Peachy keen, girly, thanks for asking!" His words
were slurred and slow, but he stared at her intently as he swayed
gently next to the wall. "You know," he said, "Doc M is looking
for you. He put out the word to keep an eye open."

"He what?" Alarm and surprise warred for dominance inside
her. Why would he do that? She was just another teenager; there
had to be plenty of more interesting people around, especially
here.

"He wants to find you. So you can talk again."

"How many people has he told?"

"Oh, everyone now. Everyone at the park, the guard boys, all
the usuals; he knows everyone, you know."

Holy crap! It had only been a couple of hours since she saw
Doc M at the market. Had he really started talking to people
about her? CeeCee hadn't been sure what to think about Doc M,
with his big energy and smooth assurance and pushy questions. It
was hard not to be drawn to him. But his eyes saw too much, and
it scared her more than she wanted to admit. And this—looking
for her—this definitely felt like a threat.

Suspenders was still talking. "He's a great guy, you know. A
real pillar of the community. I think you should go find him. He's
probably got something important to tell you."

"I'm not going to go find him," she huffed.

"Oh, but you should! It's Doc M!"

"So?"

"So?! He's a very important person!"

"Well, tough shit!"

Suspenders straightened up, just enough that he was taller than she was, and squared his shoulders. "Maybe . . ." He stared at her blearily. "Maybe I should keep ahold of you for him, until he comes round again."

CeeCee stiffened where she stood. She felt sparks of anger start at her head and cascade all the way down her spine. She stared at him hard as she fought down the instinct to start swinging something. That didn't seem to work very well in this place, if the window was any indication, and she knew it didn't always work with drunks either.

"I thought you didn't like people telling you what to do?" she asked innocuously. "You know, like the cement?"

Suspenders's jaw worked as he thought that through. "I don't!"

"But isn't Doc M telling you what to do?"

"That's different. He must think you're special, and he gives out rewards for special things."

"I'm not special; I'm just regular." She leaned toward him a little and whispered, "You know what I think?"

He tried leaning toward her too before falling back against the wall. "No, what?"

"I think he's getting bossy. Do you think he's the boss of you?"

"No one's the boss of me, girly!"

"Well, I know that!" CeeCee threw her hands into the air, getting into the drama of the moment. "But does Doc M know that?"

"Doc M knows!" he said loudly.

"Are you sure? Because it sounds to me like he thinks he's the boss of you."

"Well, he's not! We have a mutually beneficial relationship is all!"

"Maybe you should make sure. So there are no misunderstandings. So he doesn't start *thinking* things."

"You're right. I'm going to go tell him! Make sure everything is on the up and up!"

"You do that!"

He lurched away from the wall. She stepped quickly back out of arm's reach, then he pivoted sloppily away from her. "I'll tell him I passed on his message, though, just so he knows I did," he muttered, as he stumbled down the alley. Then he said louder, "But I'll make sure he knows he's not the boss of me!"

"Damn right—no one's the boss of you!" She congratulated herself on being so clever.

"Hey, girly! Do you want me to pass on a message, since I'm going to see him?"

"Sure. Tell him I'm going to see the Queen," she said flippantly. That should throw him off her trail for a while.

"The Queen?" Suspenders peered at her over his shoulder. "Oh, then you'll see him soon enough, I reckon."

CeeCee's blood chilled. If Doc M and the Queen were friendly, maybe the Queen was a last resort kind of lady after all.

NINE

The Hurting Grounds

I t was a dead end. At least, CeeCee thought it was. The alley
she had been following widened and then ended abruptly a
short block later in the back of a building. On one side were several doors that were clearly the back exits of retail stores. Could
these be the halfway shops? One had a stack of cardboard boxes,
marked with clothing sizes, piled next to the door. Another had a
bin full of broken toys. An old stool was pushed against the wall
halfway between two of the shops, the ground surrounding it littered with cigarette butts.

Something about those cigarettes made her pause. She didn't
think Jesse would send her this way for nothing. He had no reason to help her, maybe, but as annoying as his teasing was, she still
thought he was trying to help.

The first door she tried was locked. It looked unused and a
little sad, with dirt and debris blown up against the doorjamb.
She wondered if it was out of business. She knocked, and a faint
echo bounced back at her from inside.

The second one was the door with the broken toys. This time

she knocked first, as loudly but politely as she could. It didn't echo like it was empty; that was a good sign. She thought she could even hear someone moving around inside. CeeCee waited an interminable moment, twisting her hands together, before she grabbed the handle. The knob turned, and she heard the click of the lock disengaging, but the door refused to open. She tugged at it, even though a sinking part of her knew it was going to be like the window at the business meeting earlier.

The third and fourth doors were locked as well. Their handles didn't even turn.

The fifth and last doorknob turned just like the toy door had. She crouched down and stared through the gap in the doorjamb. This time she could actually *see* the latch moving, in and out of the lock, but the door seemed stuck fast, like it wasn't even a door at all.

Was there a secret knock she was supposed to know? She leaned her head against the warm metal and whispered, "Please. Please, what do I do?" She heard a tiny rattle, like sand skittering against metal, and jerked her head back. In the shadow cast by her body, something sparkled. Faint against the metal, a heart had been scratched into the door. She brushed her fingers lightly over the etching.

CeeCee heard the sandy rattle again, coming from the scratched figure. Her heart soared wildly—had the door decided to let her in? She tugged at the handle, but it still wouldn't move.

She walked morosely over to sit on the lonely stool and wondered how long it would be before whoever took smoke breaks came out here again. She fidgeted restlessly. On a good day, she hated waiting; now it made her whole body itch. She pulled out her comp book and fuzzy pencil but only stared at the blank page. Her mind kept cycling through worst-case scenarios. What if she couldn't get out? What if she were arrested when she got home?

What if she started to change into something else? Only one song played in her head, and it was making her feel worse. "Look right through me," she sang under her breath. Her stomach clenched with anxiety.

Then she thought about Doc M and his supposed horde of derelict minions looking for her, and a wave of clean anger washed it all away. She clung to it fiercely. She wasn't about to let a back-alley drug doctor, or whatever he was, get in her way, but maybe being out in the open wasn't such a good idea. She scanned the alley for likely hiding spots. There was nothing except a particularly smelly garbage can, which she didn't feel much like crawling into, near the dead end.

CeeCee craned her head. On the building across from the shops was a fire escape that went nowhere. There were no windows, and the striped metal fire escape climbed up the blank brick wall until it reached the roof. It seemed pointless and unnecessary, and she felt a little sorry for it, as if the lonely fire escape desperately wanted someone to climb it. CeeCee grinned. Good thing she was there.

She practically skipped over to the building. The lowest rung of the ladder was just above her head. She grabbed the ladder, and it slid happily down. CeeCee scaled up the fire escape without looking back.

At the top, a low parapet of brick ran around the edge of the roof. She hopped over it and settled herself on the gravelly surface. The roof was deserted, except for a few windblown leaves. She could sit on the roof and still see over the parapet to watch the doors. Her head was poking up a bit, but she didn't think anyone would notice if she sat really quietly—or maybe even if she screamed at the top of her lungs. Who could tell in this place?

It was quiet up there and hot, and a little breeze blew her hair around her face as she waited. She still felt twitchy, but the sun was hitting her fully for the first time since she'd entered the alleys. The warmth went right through to her bones and melted them into something pretending to be patience. The scenarios started cycling in her head again, so she pressed her hand into the gravel roof until indentations formed on her palm with tiny bites of pain. Distracted, she watched as the little red marks faded slowly in the sunshine.

From below, there was a scuff on the pavement, and she ducked her head automatically. The footsteps sounded loud but not like they were in a hurry. CeeCee peeked over the edge and saw, of all things, a guy she knew. Well, not really, but she recognized him from the market earlier that day. It was the bristly man who was too big with too many muscles. He had the same trombone tucked under his arm. He strolled up to the toy shop. Instead of knocking, he turned in place three times and placed his palm flat on the door. Then he grabbed the handle and swung it wide open.

CeeCee scooted down the fire escape as fast as she could, making far too much racket, and ran like a flash to the door. She scrabbled at the handle, but it had already closed, clicking behind him.

"Damnit!" She kicked the door, but the boom sounded muffled. *I should have called out*, she raged internally. *Screw Doc M and his people; I should have asked him to hold the door.*

She knocked again, hoping someone would answer, but even that sounded quiet, like it was being hushed against her hope. She looked closely at the door. A heart was scratched into this one, too, and some more of that strange code she'd thought was graffiti. That couldn't be a coincidence. Maybe that little dance he'd done was part of it too. She turned around three times, Hokey Pokey style, pressed her hand to the door, and yanked on the handle. Nothing.

"That's what it's all about," she whispered.

She stomped to the stool and slumped on it, this time determined not to leave until someone came out of the shops.

Instead, a man limped into view around a corner, clearly moving toward the shop doors. He was better dressed than some of the park residents, and he was big—not quite as big as the bristly man, but big enough. He stared at her from down the street.

CeeCee watched him warily as he drew closer, the hair on the back of her neck prickling. He might be her chance to get through a door.

"Hey!" he called abruptly. "You're that girl!"

She bolted for the fire escape. Despite the limp, the big man lurched forward into greater speed. She swarmed up the first ladder, then yanked it up behind her. By the time she got to the top of the building, he was just starting to pull it down awkwardly.

She didn't stay to watch. Her pulse beating loud in her ears, she ran across the roof, looking for another set of stairs or a window. Someone must need that fire escape to be here. On the opposite side was another lower roof. CeeCee jumped down, and suddenly she had options. To the right was a low roof across a skinny gap that she could easily jump. Farther away on the left, a fire escape poked up, probably leading to the street. In front of her was a taller brick building, at least three stories, with another ladder that went nowhere. Or, more accurately, it went to the roof again, which was funny because this building *did* have windows the ladder could reach if it had been built with concern of the inhabitants in mind. But it rose straight and relentlessly between them without a landing in sight, until it curved up over the edge of the roof's balustrade.

She paused and listened. It sounded, from the scuffling and cursing, like the big man was having trouble getting up the fire escape. The fastest and most obvious route off the roof would be the fire escape going down, so CeeCee ran to the other ladder and climbed up.

At the top, she heaved herself over the edge and flopped down, farther than she expected, into a messy heap, her air going out in a gush. When she stood and staggered away from the edge, she didn't think anyone would be able to see her. She scanned her surroundings while she caught her breath. This building was old; she could see it in the details. The balustrade was graceful wrought iron painted black, chipping in places but still pretty. A long ornamental section rose up in the center, covered in multipaned windows that were angled on the sides and flat on top, like a greenhouse plopped onto the building. It stretched all down the length of the roof.

CeeCee darted to the closest window. Humming vibrated through her hand as she cupped it against the glass, squinting to see inside. Through a layer of dust, she saw a series of catwalks underneath the windows. The highest catwalk didn't look as if it was more than six or seven feet below her. She listened for the man following her. The silent breeze grabbed fitfully at her hair. Maybe she had outrun him. But then . . . if he was a customer of Doc M's, drugs could be a motivator to keep following her, despite his limp. She hurried along the stretch of roof.

She found a window ajar. It was only open by a couple of inches, but it had a catwalk right underneath it. She curled her fingers into the splintery gap and tugged. It was stiff, but it moved an inch with each pull until she had enough room to squeeze through. CeeCee wiggled her legs in first and kept scooting until she dangled over the catwalk. As she let go, it flashed through her mind that the old walkway might not be stable.

She hit the catwalk with a yelp, sprawling forward to clutch at the metal grid. The world reeled, but it wasn't from the catwalk crashing to the ground. It was just her pounding heart making her dizzy. She breathed hard, staring through the flaking metal grid below her. Farther down were more catwalks and metal pipes and other machinery she couldn't name. There was a constant whooshing sound, and she felt a hum against her skin.

She pushed herself up unsteadily and grabbed the rail, casting one last cautious look at the windows above just in case the man had caught up with her. CeeCee doubted it, with his leg, but you never knew. She scurried toward the walkway along the wall and a set of stairs leading down.

At the next level, she paused to get her bearings. Pipes of different sizes filled the warm, damp room, with valves and levers and gauges attached to them, and catwalks under and alongside the major joints. Walking slowly and quietly, CeeCee wondered who maintained them. Twice now, someone had run after her, and that was twice enough for a healthy paranoia. Was it unfair to hope the racket she made breaking and entering had gone unnoticed? She listened carefully for something other than the white noise buzzing.

The pipes were soothing in their way. They ran through the room this way and that but always in right turns and precise curves. Some were old, part of the original building. Some looked newer, attached at different times over the years, for unknown reasons, by unknown hands. They looked like they would be here forever, in their wild geometric order. Then through the tangle of pipes, she glimpsed something bright and soft.

She stole down the walkway until she could see—a tapestry?—hanging among the pipes and valves. It was a muted scene, like a watercolor, but it depicted a forest of birch trees, each leaf of green or silver, waving against the white bark.

No, not a traditional tapestry. CeeCee leaned over the rail to see, then moved to a closer crosswalk. It was strips of fabric, cleverly hung so from a certain angle it looked solid. There were more pieces of fabric tied to each strip to make up the colors in the picture. There were even pieces that looked like birds fluttering between the trees.

She gawked. It was brilliant—and so out of place, she couldn't quite believe it was real, almost like it had a catch. Was there a catch? She crept a little farther and then retreated back to the wall, hesitant. It could just be art. People made art all the time, such as that shopping cart sculpture. This art just looked more high-end, like it would sell for a lot of money in a gallery. Maybe she was in one of those halfway places and would finally be able to go home! Maybe she was already in the regular city! Her heart beat fast, and she quickened down the walkway, scanning the pipes for color and movement.

Another tapestry appeared, one of sky and birds and streams of air, like jets had just passed by. A little past that was one full of red and orange people. They were dancing or fighting, but Cee-Cee couldn't tell which. There were still more, different sizes and colors, all made from strips of fabric or rope or ribbon floating from the pipes. A small one hung across the walkway in front of her, all in greens and blues and shiny bits of Mylar. The tapestry waved gently as she moved through it. It was like swimming through a kelp bed. A stray sunbeam from the windows caught the colors and dappled her skin with shadows. She paused for a moment, spread her arms wide, and turned slowly, feeling the soft material slide and stream against her body.

Past it, a break in the pipes made an open space. Only one large pipe ran across the floor, the sound of water whooshing through it. Above it hung an absolutely huge tapestry, so complex she couldn't see what it was for a moment. Something about it tugged at her, and she stared until it came into focus. Her hopes plummeted. The tapestry was of a garden party, and CeeCee suddenly knew for sure that she wasn't in the regular city. It was a scene you could only see here in these strange alleys. There were regular people and animal people and people in rags and people in fancy clothes. There was a table loaded with food and another table loaded with junk, and there were mushrooms and mounds of roses and even something that looked a bit like blood gushing out of one of the partygoers. His fluttering fabric form seemed intent on keeping a tight smile while a woman near him laughed.

"Crap on a stick," she whispered.

Just beyond the murderous garden party, she noticed a clothesline strung along the pipes, dripping water. As CeeCee walked, the tapestries tapered off and were replaced by rows and rows of laundry. Whoever had hung them was surely the same person responsible for the art. Most of the colors and fabrics were too similar to be coincidence, as if someone was snipping out bits of cloth from inside the clothes as they washed them.

That also meant someone was probably here. She stopped, wiping moisture off her face. She didn't think she could reach the window she had squeezed through. Even if she did, that guy might be waiting for her. She couldn't go back, so she had to keep going forward. She pushed past a small tapestry blocking the catwalk. Another tangle of pipes rose up and then abruptly ended, each pipe running into the floor or ending in a valve. The catwalk ended, too, at a set of stairs leading unceremoniously to the open floor. CeeCee stood exposed with nowhere to go but down.

On the floor, a woman stood next to a long basin, running water into it from a valve. A mountain of clothes waited by her feet and more lay in the bottom of the basin. Steam hung twisting in the air. CeeCee snuck a look over her shoulder and back again. With shock, she realized that, despite the amount of it all, none of the hung-up laundry or the intricate fabric strips actually blocked the woman's view of the catwalks. In fact, she suspected the woman could see a good deal farther along the building from her vantage point than CeeCee could.

It was with little surprise then when the woman looked up and grunted, "Oy, you got laundry for me or not?"

CeeCee debated what to say. She was glad to see a woman, but instinct warned her not to relax just yet. The woman's eyes were flat, like all the emotion had been squished out of her until only a worn blankness was left. She wore a gray jumpsuit and there were several colorful scarves tied limply around her waist, but she wore them more like tools than any form of decoration. Although the woman's face was blank, CeeCee sensed a simmering tension in her brisk movements.

Play it straight, then. "I'm sorry; I don't have any laundry," she said, staying at the top of the stairs.

"What you want, then?" The woman pushed a strand of graying hair out of her eyes.

"There's a man following me."

"Men are always following," she sniffed dismissively. "What they want you for?"

"I don't know," CeeCee lied.

"Well, I can imagine. I mind my own business around here; as long as they stay out of mine, I stay out of theirs." She looked sidelong at CeeCee before turning back to the laundry. "Men are always following, always want the same thing."

"Yeah . . ." CeeCee fidgeted uncertainly. She scanned the room beyond the woman looking for a way out.

"None of my business." The woman squinted into the distance. "Of course, I'm not of a mind to help them, either."

"Thank you." She drifted carefully down the steps. If the woman wasn't willing to turn her in, maybe she'd answer some questions too. "So . . . is this a water station?"

"I mind the pipes. I do the washing here too. For all the

lords and ladies and hoity-toities." She picked up a garment and smacked the wet fabric violently against the side of the basin over and over. "The hoity-toities don't like to mess up their hands with laundry. I do the work that needs to be done."

"Oh."

She looked sidelong at CeeCee again. "You look like you could be a hoity-toity. If you dressed fancy."

CeeCee barked a laugh. "I do too many dishes to be hoity-toity."

That seemed to set the woman at ease, although the anger never left the quick movement in her hands. CeeCee thought it might be a part of her, like another set of veins running under her skin.

The woman nodded. "We got our place; they got theirs."

CeeCee instinctively rebelled at the word "place," even while doubt picked at her and whispered *maybe*. Maybe they were right; maybe she would be happier here. Stay down, stay down, stay down.

She shook her head angrily. "Screw them."

"Ha!" The woman nodded approvingly and smacked the clothes with force.

"I'm really just . . ." she started.

"The hoity-toities have their parties, and they like to play their games," the laundress continued. She turned on a faucet, and steam boiled around her. "The lot of them wouldn't know real work if it hit them in the face."

"I'm really just looking for a door out . . ." she tried again.

"You can't always run, you know." The woman fished a knife from the bottom of the basin. "Sometimes you gotta face what's following you."

CeeCee froze. The knife was huge! She wondered if she should bolt back the way she came. Sweat prickled her skin. The woman picked the stitches out of a shirt seam.

"A man follows me, I stick 'em." She ran her knife through a long strip of fabric, cutting through steam and ire. "You stuck anyone?"

"No, ma'am," she said, surprised, before she remembered guiltily that she had stabbed the slug man.

"Sometimes a man needs to be stuck." The laundress scowled at the fabric. "I do the work that needs to be done."

CeeCee felt, uneasily, that she knew that anger—not just knee-jerk irritation, which she experienced a lot, but a deeper fury. It was how she felt sometimes, when things got really bad— pissed and shaking and nowhere to aim it. But she wasn't angry *all* the time.

"I mean, I'm trying to get *out* out," she said. "Like, away from the men following me, away from all of it. Away from . . ." What was it Apple Cheeks had said? "The byways."

"The Queen can get you out." The woman turned to face CeeCee fully for the first time. The knife glinted with water in her hand. "But she's the most hoity-toity of them all. I wash all her clothes for all those parties. People dance and dance and dance to be one of them."

"I'm not like them." The denial came out fast, on gut instinct.

"You sure?"

"Yes." Hoity-toity sounded a lot like Taylor and her friends— the popular crowd, the snobby crowd. She was just trailer trash according to them, CeeCee thought defiantly. Then she caught herself. If the Queen could really help her . . . wouldn't she put up with a little snobbishness? "What about the Queen? How can she get me out of here?"

"She holds onto all the keys. But she'll give them out if you earn her favor. You have one of them, you can open any door you like." She jerked her head toward the far end of the pump house. "There's an exit that way."

"Thank you." CeeCee edged past her. She was grateful for the help, but she didn't want to turn her back on those flat, angry eyes.

"Don't thank me." The washer woman turned back to her laundry. "They'll stick you too, you know. They'll just do it up hoity-toity-like."

CeeCee walked through the laundry, brushing past velvets and silk and cotton soft as clouds. "Maybe I'll just stick them back," she muttered.

"Ha!" Laughter echoed loudly behind her.

TEN

Undone

CeeCee pretended she was moving in the right direction. After the water station, she had lost track of which way the Queen was and the halfway shops, but she didn't want to admit it yet. This alley, more of a back road really, was lined with gates along a metal spike fence. It was strangely hazy on the other side of the fence, as if a fog was swirling on that side but not this side. She could vaguely make out weedy grass alternating with wet pavement. It was too high to climb, but she rattled each gate as she went by, just in case. She wondered, if she managed to get over it, if she would end up in an entirely different city, one where it was foggy and damp but whose forgotten alleys ended up here just the same.

Scratched into a few of the gates were hearts like the ones on the doors of the halfway shops. They caught the light even in the gloom, now that she knew to look for them. She slapped her fingers on each one as if it were a drumbeat.

The washer woman had rattled her, in an entirely different way than the men had. The isolation was starting to make her feel jumpy. She missed normal conversation, like her talk with Kelly or even Jesse's teasing. Every other conversation had been decidedly weird. She was alone a lot in her real life. The crowds at school would wear her out; the constant sounds and chatter of stores or restaurants grated, and she'd need a break. Or, when she did go somewhere she wanted to be, she'd do something wrong, and the awkwardness would drive her away. She often got home before her mom finished work, and she would relax in her own space. But that type of alone and this type of alone were two different things. At home by herself, she could play music, read, or putz around the web, where the environment was perfectly controlled, never too loud or too quiet. She could dance or fidget or move any way she wanted. Self-imposed anything was always preferable, even isolation. Then again, the washer woman seemed alone by choice too, and she apparently stabbed people.

CeeCee wondered when she would start stabbing people.

Oh crap, that's right—she already had. Plus, if she were being honest, there probably wasn't much difference between punching and stabbing someone, besides the bleedy bits.

It was hard to tell with the swirly fog what time it was, but it felt like afternoon. She was hungry again. She wondered dismally if she should dig into her bag for a granola bar or keep hoarding it.

The fence ended, and a tall corrugated metal building took its place. It was covered in graffiti, a mix of random tags and messages and street art. She'd seen a lot of graffiti around town, but some of the marks in the byways were symbols she'd only seen here, its own strange language. That was intriguing, but she didn't want to be around long enough to learn it. The street art was beautiful and just as strange as the walls she'd seen at the park with Apple Cheeks. She felt like she could study them forever and not see all the details.

Without thinking, she followed the graffiti around a corner. A knot of men stood at a gaping warehouse door half a block down. She froze and then eased back, watching them the whole time around the edge of the building.

She debated whether she could cross to the next building without being seen. Most of them were talking—or arguing, it was hard to tell at this distance—to one passionate degree or another. One man had a humped back that bulged up like a bison's, his arms beefy with muscles. Small puffs of flame were shooting out of another man's mouth as he spoke. The men shuffled their feet aggressively and waved their arms as they talked, seeming absorbed in the conversation. But one guy lounged against the wall looking utterly bored. He was the danger, the one most likely to let his eyes drift up and down the street.

The trouble was, she didn't know the rules in this place. She had absolutely no idea who worked for Doc M and who didn't. The fox selling coffee had been perfectly nice and so had Kelly and Apple Cheeks and even Jesse. The guy with the limp and Suspenders had been jerks. The washer woman had been helpful but also scary, so CeeCee put her in the neutral category. She sensed the fuzzy outlines of those rules on the farthest edge of her understanding. If she could learn just a bit more, she might be able to figure this place out.

Of course, her track record with rules was another issue entirely.

Damn it.

She looked back the way she had come and saw an alley opening on the other side of the street. She wasn't certain it had been there before. She might not have been paying attention again. But—funny thing—in this place, with or without meds, she felt like she was paying attention *a lot*.

She backtracked to the maybe-new-maybe-not alley. It was

gray and brown and not very distinct from the other paths she had walked. It was much narrower than the back road, and the world contracted down to a gray tunnel and a strip of sky. For a brief, dizzying moment, CeeCee flashed back to when she first entered the byways. Her hands flew out, all on their own, and slapped each wall beside her as if she could keep the alley from shrinking.

The alley kept perfectly still. She had to stop then and rest her head on her knees a moment.

It was too quiet, that was all. Too much noise overwhelmed her, but she missed music. With music, you always knew what was coming next.

The ground felt really nice, and CeeCee realized she had been moving almost constantly for the past twenty-four hours. Tears squeezed out of the corners of her eyes before she could catch them. She pulled her notebook out and furiously wrote out every line of dada's "Dizz Knee Land," even the repetitive ones. She felt better by the time she finished, the words neat and ordered on the page, but she still felt fragile behind her eyes.

She forced herself up. The passage ended a little way down, as if it were merely a shortcut to nowhere. The way looked familiar. She clenched her teeth, frustrated that this place had spun her around again. She flipped a random turn and met a branch where two slanting alleys met in a V. Down one way was a long strip of gaping doors and abandoned buildings, like failed strip malls had been thrown into the sea and just happened to wash up there. Little whirlwinds of dust and torn paper swirled between the walls. At least she didn't see any creepy men loitering around.

The other alley looked more put together. It was still covered in weird graffiti, still strange in that unspoken way, but it felt more used somehow and less neglected. It was short and ended in a wall, and there were a few doors at the end that almost looked like someone could live there. She waffled between knocking and moving on before her bladder decided it was too full of coffee.

She crouched behind a smelly dumpster, trying not to touch anything. Layers of gooey-looking gunk were spattered across its surface, but the blue metal underneath still had a newish sheen to it, like if someone scrubbed it hard enough it would be a perfectly nice dumpster. *Maybe I could move in*, she joked to herself and was appalled at her own humor. A petrified turd lay near one corner, proving she wasn't the only one who had used this particular spot.

A wave of fear and unreality washed over her. How did she get here, staring at someone else's shit? Why her? How did she go from being in class to being trapped in an endless maze of alleys, behind the dirty ass ends of buildings? She thought back to Mr. Beauchamp's room. In the drop of blue, everything had been fine. Everything had been fine. She'd give a lot to go back to thinking a fight at school was the worst that could happen. She'd give a lot to be in detention, for that matter. CeeCee wondered at what point she could have done something, anything, differently.

But deep down, she already knew. There were lots of points really—cutting school, stealing, letting her temper take over . . . being trouble for everyone around her.

These are the letpasses and the letdowns.

She stewed in remorse until the anxiety of being exposed drove her to put herself back together and stand up. She eyed the doors and wondered which one would be most likely to have some charmingly helpful non-stabby woman running a halfway shop on the other side.

While she hesitated, one of the doors opened.

Standing at the end of the alley was Doc M.

He narrowed his eyes at her and smiled. Rage flared through CeeCee. She bolted away from him down the alley, her anger pulsing in time with her pounding footsteps. Who did he think he was, stalking her? And what did he *want*? She spied a half-open door and ducked through it. She raced through the building, dodging collapsed drywall, the ceiling sagging perilously close to her head. Doc M followed on her heels, quick and relentless.

CeeCee ran furiously. Part of her knew she should be taking this more seriously, but she was way more pissed off than she was scared. Even while her brain thought *somewhere safe, somewhere safe*, her eyes searched for a chair to hit him with.

She spilled out into an alley of cobblestone bricks, and when she walked up a few steps and down a few more, she suddenly knew where she was. She practically flew into the hidden garden.

"Jesus! CeeCee!" Kelly jumped up from a flower bed, one hand dropping a trowel. Startled, she forgot to cover her mouth, pressing a hand to her dirt-covered chest instead.

"That guy, Doc M, is following me!" CeeCee gasped. She looked around for the watering can to swing at his head.

A moment later, Doc M was framed in the brick entry. He must have thought he had her trapped because he was moving at a slower pace than he had a moment before. Kelly slapped a hand back over her mouth. For a second, he stopped, sizing up the garden in a glance before strolling casually forward.

"Poppet! I thought that was you!"

"What do you want?" CeeCee demanded.

Doc M feigned hurt and surprise.

"Why, I just want to finish our conversation. We were so rudely interrupted before."

"We don't have anything left to discuss," she said hotly. "Wait, yes we do. Why are you sending people to look for me?"

"Poppet! I only mean the best! I was worried about you—a new citizen in a strange place. I thought it best to lend a helping hand."

He slinked a foot closer, and CeeCee stepped back, putting a row of tulips between them.

"I just know we'll be great friends. I can help you, you know. I can help you find home."

He was still as charismatic and polished as before. His words sounded right—she needed help—but she was much too wound up to trust him now. And he was in Kelly's garden, which felt wrong somehow. Still, doubt nagged at her as she frantically cast about for a way to make him go away.

"You said find home, not get home," she said.

"I want what will ultimately be best for you," he said smoothly. "I have a lot of experience knowing what people need."

"And you think you know what that is?"

"Yes, I think I do. I'm sure your past experiences have made it hard to trust people, but none of that matters here. All your past is behind you. If you give me a little faith, you'll see it was all worth it."

She felt herself wavering. She was tired, and hungry, and getting desperate. Anger layered it all into automatic self-defense. Maybe she was letting her temper, her impulsiveness, mess things up again. Maybe she did need to trust someone. On top of that, she was dragging trouble into Kelly's special place. What was wrong with her? She dropped her stare to the dirt. Doc M was half crushing a tomato vine.

Kelly reached out her free hand and drew CeeCee behind her.

"She doesn't want to talk to you," Kelly said firmly, suddenly seeming much older to CeeCee. She took down the hand still covering her mouth. "It's time for you to leave."

Doc M turned that smiling stare on her, full of weight and genial menace. "This really is none of your concern," he said, clearly waiting for her to back down.

Kelly stood straighter and neatly stepped through a row of plants so she was closer to Doc M. "This is my garden. And you're trampling all over my plants."

"I only want to talk with our young friend here. I don't think you know who you're dealing with."

"I don't think you know who *you're* dealing with."

He broke into a wider smile and gave Kelly his full attention. "You're quite right. I've never properly introduced myself. But rest assured, I've heard of you. You have quite the talent for gardening, I hear. Not one of the talents I usually foster, but now that I see you in the flesh . . ." He poured on the charm and took another step into the garden, bending the stem of a giant dahlia. "Maybe we could come to a mutually beneficial understanding."

Kelly couldn't keep the contempt off her face. "I don't think you've heard everything about me. But I've certainly heard enough about you."

She opened her mouth and screamed. It was loud and piercing, louder than CeeCee could ever scream or had ever heard before. The scream shot through her skull, and her thoughts scattered. She ducked instinctively and covered her ears. Dirt shot out of Kelly's mouth as she screamed, and it hit Doc M squarely in the chest. He reared back, disgusted, and swiped at the dirt, like he could smack it away or stop it from coming, but he plainly didn't want to leave. It started piling up around his feet, and where it touched, something happened to the fabric. CeeCee couldn't tell what it was at first. The fabric seemed to crumple. And then it faded, as if it were worn out and thin, the way old fabric looks before it starts disintegrating. Then it actually disintegrated.

When the first hole appeared, Doc M's eyes bugged out of his head. He backed up four big steps until he was out of range and inspected his clothes, affront written in every gesture. Kelly stopped screaming, and he glowered at her.

"Well, now you're just being unreasonable. I'm here to help." He said it lightly, like he thought he could still turn the conversation in his favor, but his eyes were burning with anger.

"I asked you once. I won't ask you again," Kelly said.

"Don't be difficult. That never works out for anyone." He bared his teeth at her. "Your little trick is cute, but clothes can always be replaced."

He stepped forward aggressively.

"Can you replace your skin?" Kelly asked.

She charged at him, screaming. This time, the stream of dirt hit him like a fire hose, flying into his face. It piled up on his shoulders and clung to his skin and hair. At first, he tried to just back up out of the way again, but Kelly followed, keeping up an unrelenting torrent. CeeCee had the feeling she had some practice using her curse this way. She was impressed. Doc M kept wiping at his face, trying to bluster angrily through it. It must have started to hurt because he suddenly looked alarmed, then panicked. He brushed frantically at the dirt clinging to his skin. He spun around and stumbled away. Kelly fell quiet but followed him up the path out of view. CeeCee heard one last short scream before Kelly came back again.

"You should stay here for a while, in case he's waiting," she said.

"Holy crap! What was that?"

Kelly looked down and brushed her mouth demurely. "Grave dirt composts everything."

CeeCee gaped at her. "That was badass!"

Kelly looked surprised and pleased. She shrugged one shoulder. "Thanks."

CeeCee walked to a bare patch of wall and slid down until she was sitting. "No—thank you! I didn't know what I was going to do if he caught up to me, besides start swinging." She dropped her head into her hands. "I don't know what I'm doing at all. I just want to go home."

Kelly was quiet, but she walked over and sat next to her

against the wall. "It's not so bad here—I mean, if you get stuck. You're welcome to visit any time."

"Thanks." CeeCee smiled wanly at her.

"It's nice having a friend. I'd kind of forgotten."

"I have to keep trying. Besides, beyond Doc M, I . . . I don't think this place is good for me."

"What do you mean?"

"Do you know the washer woman?"

"I've heard of her," said Kelly carefully.

"Yeah, well she's real stabby, but you probably know that. If I stay here, I'm afraid I'll turn into her. I don't have a superpower like you do." She whispered, "And I don't want to be angry all the time. Even when the world pisses me off, I don't want it to take over."

Kelly smiled sadly. "For some of us, this is the only place left."

CeeCee shifted so she could give her a half hug across her shoulders. Kelly felt very normal next to her, and she was so grateful for her help. The garden was just as beautiful as it was before, and gazing at it, her stomach sank. She'd never say it out loud, but she was terrified this might end up being the only place left for her too.

ELEVEN

Leave the Lights On

CeeCee left the garden, and it was like she was starting all over again from that morning. Kelly had fed her more veggies so at least she wasn't hungry, but paranoia curled in place of her empty stomach. She wandered aimlessly through alleys, trying to make progress but sneaking from one hiding place to another in case she ran into anyone else. Most of the pathways were eerily quiet. The times she could hear traffic, she pulled at every door and window she could find. At one point, she climbed a dumpster to look over a low wall, only to come face to face with a dog the size of a prehistoric wolf. He snarled and jumped higher than the dumpster. She had the feeling he wasn't even trying that hard, either—like if he really wanted a CeeCee snack, she couldn't do anything about it.

Frustration and hot tears curled in the back of her throat as she jogged hastily away. Her mom must have called the police by now. Not that she'd seen any cops in this strange place. She hated the idea of her mother worrying. How did she make such a mess of things?

She turned around the corner of an ugly '60s building, all avant-garde cement and sharp angles. On the other side was a high stone wall that looked ancient. It had ivy growing over it, and birds flew back and forth along the top, chirping loud and joyfully. Bird poop was everywhere. She was so absorbed with avoiding the droppings that she forgot she was supposed to be sneaking.

When the birds went silent, she looked up.

Facing her in the odd two-sided alley was a cat. She thought it might be the same one she had offended earlier. It was brown and glossy and looked surprised. It planted its feet and meowed loudly at her several times, then ran around a corner.

That was strangely urgent, she thought. *Does it want me to follow?* But since her feet were already moving, the question was rhetorical. She turned the corner and smacked into someone she knew.

"Jesse!" Without thinking, she said in a rush, "Doc M is looking for me. I don't know what he wants."

"I know; it's why I came looking for you." His tawny eyes bored into hers. "No matter what he says, don't go with him."

Heat rushed to her face in relief. She knew Doc M was wrong—she could feel it.

"Do you still want to go to the Queen?"

She hesitated, torn between desperation and foreboding. Maybe she should keep the Queen in her back pocket. "You said there was a price?"

"Yeah," he said. "Usually, those who are like her are the ones willing to pay."

"I have a feeling I'm not like her. I've been trying to find a halfway place first."

"And?"

"I think I found some, but I couldn't get through the doors. Will you help me?"

"I have another idea—not a halfway place but similar. I can take you there." He looked at her intently, waiting for permission.

It occurred to her that she didn't know him at all, besides the fact that he teased and was obnoxiously confident. He could work for Doc M or someone worse. He could be working his own angle. In real life, this was the beginning of a hundred cautionary tales of girls attacked in alleys. Except she had already been in a hundred alleys. Except he seemed very real in this unreal place. Except, somehow, none of what she didn't know mattered because in her gut, bone-deep, she knew she could trust him. Just like she knew she couldn't trust Doc M.

"Yes. Please."

He smiled and turned back the way she had come.

"I went this way already," she told his back. "I keep getting turned around. Even though I'm only walking in straight lines."

"It helps to think about where you want to go." He avoided the bird poop with the grace of a dancer.

"Wait, what?"

"Think about where you want to go. Then start walking in the general direction." He smirked. "Or follow, as the case may be."

She paused to take that in for a moment. She thought about the way the alleys seemed to curve, how entrances faded away or suddenly appeared.

"That actually makes sense." She hadn't known where she was going or what she was doing, so the alleys just moved in circles. And when she needed someplace safe, it took her to Kelly.

"You're getting used to this place." He turned on his heel and spoke over his shoulder. "We have to get you out faster than I thought. Don't get too used to the byways."

He led her through a maze of alleys. Every so often, he would pause at a crossroads as if to orient himself. After several blocks, he turned down a brick lane that ended in a small courtyard. A heart-shaped padlock and chain held an ornate door shut. Jesse reached for the chain and jiggled it until part of the length swung free. He grinned wickedly and held up a single chain link to show CeeCee. The link had been neatly sawn so a gap would let it slip out of the rings on either side, then hidden in the shadow of the lock so you couldn't see the breach.

"This was closed up by the Queen's men," he explained quietly. "But they rarely double-check their work."

"Did you do it?" She felt unexpectedly hushed, like she shouldn't make too much noise or the Queen's men would catch them, whoever they were.

"No, but I watched the man who did. It took him weeks."

He lifted the chain out of the way and opened the door.

They walked into a long room with a high ceiling, like an art gallery. Instead of pictures, there were mirrors hung on the walls.

"There are others around the city, but this place has the most gathered in one spot."

"What are they?" CeeCee asked.

Jesse looked at her sideways. "They're . . . mirrors," he said slowly, like he suddenly doubted her intelligence.

"I can see that," she huffed, exasperated. "I mean, what are they here? Are they going to talk? Are they going to enslave my soul and make spaghetti? What do they do?"

The amused gleam was back in his eyes. "Ah." He walked over to a foot-high, oval-shaped mirror. "Take a look."

She leaned toward the glass, the silver sheen of it throwing light in her eyes, and peered into the mirror. Instead of her reflection, she saw a living room. A couch with a toile slipcover faced a high-end TV. Next to it sat a comfortable leather recliner. In the background, a door provided a glimpse of a kitchen. There were lace doilies and expensive-looking knickknacks on side tables.

Everything was cream and black and mauve. It was very posh but a little outdated.

She was confused. Why would you put a random picture behind a mirror?

An older woman appeared in the doorway and crossed to the TV. Then it clicked. CeeCee was looking at a living room in *someone's house.*

She leaned away from the mirror and looked at Jesse. "What the fuck is this?"

He laughed, delighted at her expression. "It's a window."

"Are all mirrors like this?" She heard her voice rising. "Where someone can *see you?*"

"No, not all. Just a few." He paused. "I think it happens more when people want to be seen. Or if they're open to other sides."

"This is totally creepy." She looked around for mirrors looking into bathrooms. That would be even worse. "You know that, right?"

"Agreed. Creepy but useful." He looked pleased with himself. "Watch."

He moved to a mirror that was easily seven feet tall. CeeCee stepped up behind him and saw a shadowed nursery on the other side of the glass, full of cluttered tools and ailing potted plants. It looked like the dusty corner where someone put the stuff they didn't need right away.

Jesse went very still. Then he stepped *through* the mirror, the glass rippling like water around the edges of his body, into the nursery. He turned around to face her direction and grinned, smug and triumphant.

"Holy crap," CeeCee whispered.

He glided back through the glass again like it wasn't there.

"See? They can be used as doors. You can get back home, or close enough. It'll put you on the other side at least. Not all of the mirrors come out in our city, but I know the ones that do."

CeeCee felt her spirits soar. She took a trembling step forward and laid her hand on the glass. It felt cool and solid against her palm. "How do I do it?" she breathed.

"You have to believe it. Picture yourself there instead of here, then step through."

She took a breath and visualized herself on the other side. Part of her brain was screaming skepticism at her. But she had just *seen* Jesse step through, so she hollered at the voice to shut up. She made a move toward the mirror and stopped.

She looked at Jesse. "Thank you for bringing me here."

He only nodded, eyes narrow.

CeeCee stepped as confidently as she could toward the mirror . . . and hit glass. She rolled her eyes toward Jesse. "You knew that would happen, didn't you?"

"Try again; it takes a bit of practice."

She faced the mirror. She tried thinking about how glass is a liquid, not a solid. She thought about silver water and that drop of blue ink on her desk that she could push with a finger. This time, she led with her shoulder, like she could slide in sideways. She banged the glass so hard, the mirror shifted on the wall.

"Ugh! Why isn't it working?"

"Really feel it. Believe you are there, in that room."

"I'm trying. I thought I believed it. I told my brain the glass isn't solid."

"Deciding to believe isn't enough," Jesse explained. "It's more like . . . it never occurred to you for it to be any other way. Like when you fly, you just take a little hop and then decide not to come back down. Being on the ground doesn't occur to you anymore."

CeeCee blinked. "That's the trick to flying?"

"That's the trick to everything."

"Can you fly then too?"

Jesse ducked his head and looked at her from under his bangs, his grin wicked and a little rueful. "I can do other things."

She snorted, and he laughed. He seemed delighted that she saw right through him.

"Try again," he said. "It never occurred to you to be anywhere else. Think about the details: the way the dirt smells, the feel of the floor, how many mice are hiding in the tools."

"Um, that's a weird detail, but okay, I get it."

She breathed in deeply and imagined the dusty smell of dirt, the way the light was shadowed in the room, the brush of dry leaves. Very cautiously, trying to hold the image in her mind, she crept forward. As her body came within a hair's breadth of the mirror, she closed her eyes. She concentrated fiercely on terra-cotta pots and gardening gloves. For the briefest moment, the glass felt fuzzy against her skin, the barest tingle and give. Her heart sped up, and she pushed. It felt, suddenly, like there was no glass at all. Her eyes flew open in time to see the tips of her fingers sink through the mirror. She couldn't believe it! It was terrifying and weird, but it was working! Then her brain switched from screaming at her about physics to playing a slideshow of her worst fears at home: her mom scared and angry, the police at her house, the stares at school when word got out, expulsion, court time, juvie, the sneers of everyone who thought they were right about her . . . and her being able to do nothing, nothing, nothing about it.

The glass snapped back to solid. Her hand bounced off the mirror as if it had never gone through.

CeeCee rested her head against the cool, very hard glass. She shrieked loudly.

In the mirror's reflection, she saw Jesse jump two feet into the air. He looked at her with wide eyes, and then she could see him quite clearly pretend it had never happened.

She asked quietly so her voice wouldn't tremble, "Why can you do it and I can't?"

"Well, it's about believing but . . . it's also about belonging."

"What do you mean?"

"This side—the byways—sometimes they hold onto people because they belong here." He seemed worried as he said it, and he watched her carefully. "Where do you belong? Here or there?"

She felt a jolt of panic. "I don't belong here. I don't. I just . . . I don't know what I'm going back to. I fucked up bad back home, and I . . ." CeeCee stopped, ashamed and confused.

"One mistake doesn't mean you belong here," Jesse said. "It's not that simple."

"What did you mean about not staying too long? Is that part of it?"

"Yes. Every once in a while someone will come here as if it's a vacation. They might not really belong here, but if they stay too long, the byways will decide they do anyway, and then they can't get out."

CeeCee couldn't imagine coming here on "vacation." But if people were traveling here, as misguided as that sounded, then she could get out. She straightened her spine and frowned at the mirror. She just had to figure out how.

"Where do you belong?" she asked, curious about his tricks.

"I belong nowhere, and so I can go anywhere." He smiled with all his teeth. "Do you want to try again?"

"Yes," she said, jaw set stubbornly.

She seemed to get worse at it as time went on, as if the mirrors or the byways or something else was actively repelling her now. After an hour, she was ready to admit defeat. She swallowed her frustration with difficulty.

"I'm sorry it didn't work." Jesse seemed genuinely regretful.

She went over the options in her head. "Can you take me to a halfway place?" she asked. "Do you know how to get through?"

"I can take you but . . ." He shrugged and looked frustrated. "I don't have a key. I've never needed one."

Before she could form a response, her stomach rumbled loudly.

Jesse looked amused again. "When was the last time you ate?"

"I don't know—what time is it?"

"Probably later than you think. Come on." He turned toward the door. "I know a place."

"I am getting out of here." She scowled back at the mirrors. "And when I do, I'm covering up my bedroom mirror."

"Aw," he said in mock disappointment and ducked laughing when she tried to slug him.

TWELVE

My Heart Is Beating

When they got outside, CeeCee realized he was right; the sky was already shadowing toward evening, streaks of faint pink showing in the sky above them.

How did a whole day go by so fast? She thought about spending another night on the street and shivered.

Jesse noticed. He didn't say anything at first but set a quick pace down the alley.

Finally, he offered, "Don't worry; we'll get you out. There are ways—that was just one of the more likely ones."

"And if none of them work, I can still try the Queen."

He looked at her sidelong. "Avoid that if you can."

She thought about that. "What's she like?"

"The Queen?" He moved his head slightly, more of a twitch than a shake. "She's . . . very smart, focused, driven . . . but temperamental. Very temperamental. If you catch her on a good day, she can be generous." He said it reluctantly.

"And on a bad day?" She wanted to know everything he knew.

"You don't want to catch her on a bad day. I try to stay out of her sights." He fell silent a moment. "But she's also entrepreneurial. If you offer her a deal, something she's interested in, she'll work with you."

"What type of things is she interested in?"

"Ah, that's the trick. Sometimes it's products, sometimes it's promises, sometimes it's flattery."

CeeCee snorted.

He laughed. "I'm not kidding. Once I worked a deal by complimenting her hair's natural shine."

"Ugh." She thought about the type of person who would trade on compliments. An unflattering image was beginning to form. She knew she was being judgmental; it's not like she had met the woman, and Jesse did say she could be generous. But she also knew she didn't do well when she was expected to kiss ass. She usually remembered too late that's what she was supposed to be doing.

"Last resorts, right?"

"Last resorts." He smiled at her in the fading light.

For the first time, CeeCee didn't feel quite so out of her depth. Jesse was sane and solid beside her. They had something of a plan in motion or at least a few options to check out. He knew this place, and she wasn't alone. She tried working some of the tension out of her neck. It was still but not quiet. She could hear faint sounds of stirring, like the night creatures were waking up. The air felt softly warm in that way it does before the chill of evening really sets in.

She caught Jesse studying her without blinking.

"What?"

"How did you get here?" he asked suddenly.

"You asked me that before. I stole something," she said, ashamed.

"Was that really it?" Jesse looked thoughtful.

"What do you mean?"

"People steal all the time out there." He waved a hand. "And worse. If they all ended up here for stealing, we'd be our own city instead of an in-between one."

"Well, what else could it have been? I got stuck here right after." She fingered the rabbit in her pocket, guilt stabbing at her.

"Something else—something in your head maybe. Or how you felt."

CeeCee remembered Kelly's story about her mother's disgust, of hiding in her apartment and then walking in the gardens at night. She thought about her own mom, and anxiety jangled inside her.

What if she changed and her mom didn't want her anymore? "How did you get here?" she asked instead.

"Oh, I didn't . . . my people have always been here."

"Your family was born here?"

"It's more like my people have always been able to go between."

CeeCee was intrigued. "So you grew up here? Do you live with your parents?"

"Sometimes I live with them. I wander in from time to time."

"What are they like?"

He shrugged. "They're parents."

Was he stonewalling her? "Are they nice?" she pushed.

"Sure."

"Did you have a house?"

"Something similar."

"What was it like growing up here?" She practically snarled it.

"It was, you know, interesting." His teeth gleamed in the gloom.

Now she knew he was teasing—telling her less than nothing.

"You're, you know, inscrutable," she said, scowling. "No, wait, there's a better word for it . . . infuriating! That's it!"

He laughed.

Down the alley, lights gleamed from scattered windows as the sky darkened.

"Here we are." He stopped in front of a door.

A low wall ran under a nearby window. Jesse hopped onto the wall but kept his head below the window's level. He snuck a quick peek and then tapped on the window gently until it popped ajar. He jumped down again.

"This might take a little work. Just hang back."

He knocked briskly, and after a moment, a man opened the door. He wore a grease-spattered T-shirt and baggy jeans. His shoulders were so high and rounded it was as if he didn't have a neck. Dark hair covered his skin, and white streaks on his head made him look like a badger. He scowled the moment he spied Jesse.

"Hey, Tito, what's cooking?" Jesse said.

"Nothing for you," growled Tito. He went to shut the door.

Jesse stuck his foot in the jamb. He managed to look casual about it. "It's not for me; it's for my friend."

"I don't care who it's for! Piss off!"

"Yeah, yeah, no problem. Hey, Tito, I saw your daughter." He said it earnestly, like that was what he really wanted to talk about all along. "She's so grown up now! Is she seeing anyone?"

"You stay away from my daughter!" Tito kicked Jesse's foot viciously out of the door and slammed it shut.

Jesse grinned wickedly at her. She goggled at him, nonplussed. She wondered vaguely if she should feel insulted that he was asking about another girl while he was with her. Wait—this wasn't a date, for crying out loud! From inside, she heard Tito's raised voice and slamming pots and pans.

Jesse jumped gracefully back onto the wall and watched through the open window. Then he carefully eased a hand down into the building. When it emerged, he was holding a burger. He waved her over, and CeeCee leaped to take it. It was hot and dripping, and she was much hungrier than she thought. She shoved it in her mouth without thinking. It was delicious. She stopped guiltily when it occurred to her that Jesse might have meant for them to share it. But when she looked, he had already grabbed another one for himself.

He leapt off the wall, and they ran down the path and around a corner. He stopped next to a dripping spigot and leaned against the wall to eat his burger. He looked inordinately pleased with himself.

"Oh my god! This is so good!" CeeCee gasped around mouthfuls. "How did you know that would work?" She was stealing again, she distantly noted.

"Every time someone mentions his daughter, Tito throws a fit. He moves toward the front of the restaurant to complain to his friends." Jesse laughed. "He really should give it up, though—his daughter is thirty-seven."

At that, she struggled not to choke on her burger. What a scammer! And a funny one at that.

They finished their food and washed it down with water. She took some time to refill her water bottle and clean up as best she could. She was getting pretty grimy and hoped she didn't smell too bad.

She felt his grin before she saw it. She scowled a little as she looked up, trying to think what she had done for him to be laughing at her.

He stood with his hands in his pockets, poised and posed like the alley was a fashion runway, but not in a conscious way. It was the way of someone who was confident in his surroundings, no matter where he was. That, coupled with the smile, sent a burst of discomfort shooting through her. He grinned wider when he saw her watching him.

"You moved fast. That was good."

"Oh . . ." she said, the angst trying to dissipate and having nowhere to go. "Um, thanks."

"I've got a halfway shop in mind that might be just right for you." He pivoted on his runway and loped down the alley.

Despite the fact that he had just given her a hamburger in a fairly badass way, she couldn't help but roll her eyes behind his back as she followed. She put on a burst of speed to catch up to him.

He took her through another maze of alleys, throwing a grin at her every so often, like they were out for a jog. His smile seemed to catch all the light left and hang in the air. She couldn't help grinning back. These alleys seemed smaller and more tucked away than the ones they had walked before, as if he was trying to avoid people like she had earlier that day. Except he knew where he was going and was a lot more graceful about it. He didn't seem like he was sneaking around at all. What had he said? Think about where you're going, and the byways would take you there?

There was a lot of trash and garbage cans in their path. Jesse glided in between and around them without making a sound, and soon she was outpaced. He paused at the end of the alley to wait for her. CeeCee picked her way around them as best she could, but she just couldn't match Jesse's grace. He moved like a dancer or an athlete, and his balance was uncanny. After loudly stumbling over a loose bottle for the third time, she kicked a trash can in frustration. The empty can flew through the air and ricocheted off two others, suddenly clearing a path in front of her. She stomped, cheerfully defiant, to his side.

Jesse looked impressed. "That was accurate."

She blinked. Another compliment—that was twice now. At least, they felt like compliments. She was so used to people thinking she was too much, it was a shock to receive approval for being her normal, unrestrained self. Abashed, she looked around the alley instead.

Off to one side was a large bulky pile, like a plastic bag full of garbage. Except it didn't look quite right, and she couldn't pinpoint why.

"Wait, what's that?"

She stepped closer to see in the dimming light.

It was a man's body. His cold face was shriveled and used up, like another piece of crumpled trash. He seemed very small. A chill went through her, and the grin fell off Jesse's face. She already knew, but she touched him hesitantly to be sure. "He's dead," she breathed.

Jesse went still and then crouched down next to the body. "Take his shoes," he said.

"What? You're stealing his shoes?"

"No," he said shortly. "But they will get stolen if we don't take them now. Trust me."

They each pulled off a shoe, and he loped down the path. CeeCee followed him, clutching the poor man's worn oxford to her chest.

She followed him, not really paying full attention to her surroundings. It hadn't sunk in that she had just seen a dead body. It was like they had found a large doll that might get back up again as soon as they were gone. Except she had the man's shoe now, and it seemed terribly threadbare. There was a hole in one side already and another about to wear through on the other, and she couldn't help wondering how uncomfortable it must have been to wear them like that. She could never stand holes in her socks or scratchy tags.

The brick and cement of the alley flew past as they ran, and she remembered losing the left heel cap on a pair of boots. She had to get rid of them because of the uneven clacking sound it made when she walked, which only she could hear.

Jesse slowed, and she came to herself with a start, back to this strange world where she was carrying a dead man's shoe. Maybe she should have stayed lost in her thoughts.

In the double wide alley, thick wire cables crisscrossed the passage, and on the wires hung a million pairs of shoes. Chuck All Stars, and dress shoes, and ratty sandals, some of them strangely shaped and some too large and some smaller than a child's—they all dangled out of reach from their strings and straps. Jesse took the old man's shoes and knotted the laces together. With a quick, practiced movement, he sent the oxfords sailing through the air to arch over a wire before catching on it, bouncing from the momentum. The last crimson of sunset painted the shoes in stark relief.

"It's to remember them," he said. "Otherwise there would be nothing left."

The sky darkened, and little lights came on . . . no, not on, not like anything electric. The lights were like fireflies, just much bigger than she thought they should be.

"We try to write their names on the soles, if we know them," he explained reverently. "And we bring them here where you can always see."

"Who's 'we'?" she asked, although she already knew. They were the ones who cared, in this place where people went when no one cared. She gazed up at the shoes—so, so many of them— and CeeCee felt overwhelmingly sad. What had those people's lives been like to end up here? Her worry mingled with grief and threatened to drown her.

"I know we should go . . ." Her voice sounded far away. "But can we sit for a minute?"

"Sure." He pointed to a fire escape.

They climbed up almost to the roofline and sat with their backs against the brick building. The shoes dangled just above eye level, and the giant fireflies flitted around like stars.

"It's so beautiful," CeeCee said and was suddenly tired down to her bones, her eyes prickling with unshed tears. Fatigue sucked at her, and she was too overwhelmed to fight it, too overwhelmed to do anything but sit there. Heat radiated off of Jesse next to her. His head was tilted up toward the darkening sky. She closed her eyes and heard him whisper.

"This is the only place in the byways where there is always light."

CeeCee jerked awake, her head slumped against the wall behind her.

"Shit! How long was I asleep?" She straightened up and looked at the sky as if it could tell her the time. She felt embarrassed and slightly exposed. She had never fallen asleep in front of a stranger before. She had no idea if she snored or not.

"Not long. Just a catnap." Jesse smiled faintly. "You looked like you could use it."

"Have I screwed up again? Am I going to be stuck here?"

"There's time. As I said, it wasn't long."

"I guess we should get going." She stood reluctantly. She felt better after the nap, but she could tell she'd need to catch up on sleep. Another night out here was going to wreck her, coffee or no coffee. She moved toward the fire escape, and he caught her arm.

"No, this way." He grinned, then he turned and climbed up instead of down.

She followed him onto the roof, still a little groggy. The sudden space woke her up. After the narrowness of the alleys, everything felt free and wide open. It was like another world. The sky was full of stars that she could swear she never saw in the city normally. For a moment, she stood blinking at all that deep blue, scattered with a million white gems. Their glow was brighter than the city lights. The fireflies followed and surrounded her briefly, and she felt like she expanded until she was as big as the sky. She spread her arms out and knew she could reach forever.

She suddenly remembered Jesse was there.

She dropped her arms and said sheepishly, "Do you feel that? When the sky is big?"

His golden eyes looked at her unblinking in the starlight, solemn and wondering. "Yeah, I do. I like being up high."

She smiled as fiercely as he did.

They crossed over the rooftops, Jesse leading the way. They used fire escapes to move to new buildings or simply jumped if the gap was narrow enough. CeeCee suspected he could jump a lot farther than she could, but he kept the route easy and safe. There were even a few ladder-like bridges hung between some of the buildings.

They weren't the only ones up there. It was different than the other places she had seen in the byways. There were no garbage can fires or large groups huddled together. Almost everyone was solitary or in pairs. Jesse called out to a few as they passed. They seemed like him, full of grace and easy confidence. Other people kept their distance. Once, she saw a lot of people and lights on a high-rise rooftop, a few blocks away. It seemed raucous and overly gaudy in the shimmering hush.

"That's one of the Queen's parties," he explained when she pointed it out.

Hoity-toity, she thought.

A few more roofs and Jesse stopped, keeping well back from the building's edge. He motioned for her to stay quiet.

"There is a little store down there," he said softly. "The shopkeeper is more sympathetic than most; she helps people cross through if they have a good reason. She never put a lock on her door like some of the others."

"Will she think I have a good reason?" Hope rose in her, and she tried to keep it in check, just in case.

"A girl here by accident? Yeah, she will."

They crept to the edge and peered over the rooftop. Across and below them was the back door of a shop. It had a bench next to it and cheerful pots of flowers, as if the people who worked there came out all the time. A high window next to the door showed a light on inside. Maybe the shop was still open.

There were also a number of men loitering a few feet on either side of the door—grimy-looking men she recognized from the park. One was half sitting on a pot, crushing the flowers. Another one was burning a small heap of trash in the middle of the path.

"Damnit! Do you think they're looking for me?" she asked.

"Yes, I do." Jesse sighed. "A lot of people want to be on Doc M's good side."

"I don't get it. Why is he so interested in me?"

"He supplies things. Pretty girls are always high demand. Maybe he's thinking he can supply you." He looked pissed as he said it.

Fear and rage swirled inside her, exactly like when she saw the slug man's porn. "So he's a pimp." Her gut knew not to trust him, but somehow she was disappointed. For someone with so much charisma and authority, Doc M seemed like someone you could look up to, a role model, but instead he was just another sleazy perv. She'd expected . . . better.

"It's more complicated than that. He has his fingers on a lot of strings," he said. "Maybe he thinks he can use you in some other way. Use you in one of his businesses, foist you into the Queen's court for political reasons. He's done it before. But the main thing, the most important, is he likes to win. You've slipped away from him twice—that makes you unpredictable, a challenge."

"So if I'd gone with him and been dumb or boring, he'd have cut me loose?"

He looked at her like she was terribly naïve.

"That wasn't a real question," she huffed at him. "I may be a troublemaker, but that doesn't make me stupid."

"Are you now?"

"Am I what?" She was only half listening, staring at the men below. She could feel her face heating up in the way it did before she usually blew. Mr. Reyes would be so proud of her for recognizing a trigger.

"A troublemaker?" His eyes gleamed.

"That's what people say."

"But what do *you* say?"

"I don't know." She shrugged, uncomfortable. "It's not like I'm trying to start trouble or anything. It just seems to happen around me."

"Oh."

She was baffled. "Why . . . why do you sound disappointed?"

"Maybe I like bad girls."

He was teasing her—again. "Oh, shut up." Her anger lightened a little, but her frustration was still the same.

"Anyway, we can't sneak past them," he said, turning back to the men in the alley. "I can try to lead them away," he offered.

"They might not all go. Can we signal the shopkeeper somehow?" Her fists clenched and unclenched.

"We don't want to draw her into the middle of that. She'd lock up tight."

"Damn Doc M." She stared over the roof and counted. "We can drop some garbage cans on their heads. Two heads per can should do it. Some nice heavy ones."

He choked back a guffaw. "You do seem deadly with a garbage can. But let me try drawing them away before we launch an assault."

"I thought you liked bad girls? Full frontal assaults are our specialty."

Now he struggled not to laugh out loud. "Stop, they're going to hear us. Besides, sneak attacks are mine."

She didn't want him to leave, but in the end, she couldn't see a way around it. They sketched rough plans and climbed down a fire escape to an alley out of view. CeeCee would wait around the corner of the building closest to the shop. Jesse would circle around and try to draw them off from the opposite direction while she dashed for the door.

Jesse sauntered down the alley like he didn't have a care in the world. He nodded to one or two of the men and then stopped just outside of the group.

"There's a lot of you out tonight," he said amiably. From where she hid, she could just hear the conversation.

"So what if there is?"

"So . . . I heard Doc M is looking for someone."

"Yeah, a young lady. Blonde, pretty, about so high."

The man raised his hand to a level that was a good eight inches below CeeCee's actual height. She hunched against the side of the building, simultaneously pleased and insulted.

"You know what he's offering for her?" Jesse said it like he was feigning disinterest.

"Why? You seen her?"

"No, no, nothing like that," he said quickly. "But I can keep an eye out. What's she worth?"

CeeCee was impressed. Jesse made it seem like he was lying but not very good at it. She could practically see the ears perk up on the men in front of the shop. It was the perfect double con.

"Oh, you got it wrong, pal. She's not worth anything," said one man.

"Yeah, we're just helping Doc M out," said another. "He just needs to find her, is all."

"Oh, okay. Well, see you around." Jesse pivoted around and walked off like he was trying not to hurry. Despite the circumstances, she was enjoying his performance. He seemed like he was enjoying himself too.

The men nudged each other, whispering. Several of them drifted after him up the street. CeeCee tensed, ready to run to the door as soon as they were far enough away.

One man, a big guy, shot out an arm and stopped his smaller buddy from following.

"That one's a crafty cat, I wouldn't trust him," he said, and two other men heard him and stopped as well.

Jesse reached the corner and glanced over his shoulder. Then he looked down the other alley like he saw something interesting.

"Hey you!" he yelled. "Wait up!"

He sprinted around the side of the building. The men following him broke into a run, and even the two who had stopped took off. CeeCee held her breath waiting for the big guy and his buddy to leave, but the big man only planted his feet in front of the door.

For an agonizing five minutes, she waited, but they didn't move. Neither did the other men come back, so she hoped Jesse was leading them on a merry chase and hadn't gotten caught. Finally she retreated a few steps to stand beside a garbage can. She hefted the metal lid in her hands and seriously considered the full-frontal attack again. There were only two of them. If she got lucky with the first shot, maybe she could knock them out. She'd never knocked anyone unconscious before, but it couldn't be that hard, right? She saw it on YouTube all the time. *Okay*, she thought and took a deep breath, *go for the big guy first.*

Before she could take a step, she heard a sound behind her. She spun around to see Jesse running full steam toward her.

"Nope," he said, grabbing her hand as he passed so she had to drop the lid. It clanged loudly on the ground. He yanked her forward, into the alley facing the shop. She heard a shout behind her, and then he was pulling her, even faster, toward another side lane. He stopped abruptly at a broken window and grabbed her around the waist to boost her through before she knew what was happening.

Inside, they ran across the dark building and up a staircase. Adrenaline pushed her to go faster. Then he practically soared out another window onto a fire escape. She scrambled up after him, and even from below, she could see him grinning.

When she reached the top, she saw why he chose this building. It was close enough to jump to at least three other buildings, and all them were studded with rooftop sheds, chimney flues, and even a pigeon hutch to hide behind. Jesse pulled her across the roof. They jumped to a new building, and then he whipped her around the corner of a woodshed.

CeeCee slumped against the splintery wall and tried to catch her breath. They were standing close to the pigeon hutch. She'd never seen a pigeon cage in real life before. She had a feeling that in the byways, it held something different than pigeons. She could hear rustling inside it, even over the sound of her labored breathing.

By contrast, Jesse looked hardly winded. He also looked like he was having the time of his life. His mouth was hanging open in a silent laugh, and his eyes were sparkling.

"Are you having fun yet?" she gasped. "You're crazy, you know that?"

"Were you actually going to hit them with that lid?"

She shrugged. It had seemed like a good idea at the time. "Fine. Point taken."

They stared at each other and then burst into muffled laughter.

"Holy crap," she breathed.

They contained their giggles and listened for sounds of pursuit. Besides some faint scuffling from the streets below, it seemed quiet.

"Come on, let's take a look."

They tiptoed over to the low parapet surrounding the roof and gazed below. Two stories down, a man scurried through the alley like a rat. They walked to the other side of the roof, and on that side, two men were furtively looking under a pile of cardboard.

"Do you see what they're doing?" Jesse whispered.

"Looking for me?" she whispered back.

"Yeah, but they're trying to be quiet about it. They all think you're close by, and if they can get to you first, they'll get the reward and not the others."

"What, they think I'll just be huddling somewhere, scared?" The anger was rising in her again. She knew she should feel afraid that she was being hunted as a trophy, but she just felt affronted to her core.

He flashed her a grin. "You? Never."

CeeCee blinked. She wasn't used to being admired, especially for the tendencies that were always getting her in trouble. Her anger disintegrated under a wave of giddiness. She grinned back at him, and for once, the voices in her head shut up.

"This is good anyway; it's much easier to slip past a mob when they're all split up," he said.

She laughed. "Why do you sound like you have experience with that?"

THIRTEEN

Dance

The hey kept to the roofs until they were out of the area.
CeeCee noticed, on their overhead trip, that many of the
buildings were old and beat up, the type that were waiting to be
torn down instead of renovated. They felt left behind. Which,
she realized with a shock, was what some of the people she'd met
felt like, too—like that poor man with the shoes, all alone in an
alley. One of the buildings, though, was clearly part of the outside
world. They had crossed over from an abandoned warehouse to
the fire escape, and she could see people working inside brightly
lit offices as they climbed. The offices looked modern and clean
and full of electronics. She rapped on the windows as they passed,
and not a single person glanced up.

"I still don't understand. How can all of this be here, and no
one knows?" she said to Jesse as they moved to the roof of a broken-
down garage.

"People see what they want to see."

The twins' comments popped into her head, but she pushed
on stubbornly. "But people must wander in all the time! Doesn't

anyone notice that if people walk down a certain alley, they don't come back out?"

"It's harder to get here than you think. Remember what I said about belonging? People expect what they expect. First, they have to be in the alleys already or very close to a halfway point. Then, if they believe that they are lost or they think they don't belong out there *and* they are close, then sometimes the byways pull them in." He shrugged as the wind kicked up, ruffling his bangs. The air smelled like old brick and too-cold mornings.

She pushed her own hair out of her eyes. "And the buildings?"

"The magics that bind the byways together are strange. The places that are halfway to forgotten sometimes end up here. But some of this has always been around—people and places and ideas that were forgotten so long ago that this became the only place for them."

"What do you mean?"

"Well, just because something is forgotten doesn't mean it stops living," he said. "Some of the people here might have lived out there once, but they were too different, and it was easier not to see them."

"You mean like the ones who changed?" She thought of Kelly. She could hear the worry in her voice that it might happen to her.

"Not all of them changed. Some of them just were." He looked at her, suddenly serious. "Do you mind difference?"

"No," she said, abashed. "I'm different too. But maybe not as different as I thought. It seems kind of silly now." She scuffled her feet across the rooftop's crumbling concrete. "How do the halfway points work?"

"They are spaces that sit in between, halfway here and halfway there, doors or shops or mirrors," he explained. "Sometimes an alley that opens up and then closes. The stable ones have people who control who can come and go. If you belong here or you're halfway like me, you can see them."

"People can be halfway?"

"Yes. If you learn to master the mirrors, you'll be halfway too."

So her choices were to either convince someone to let her through a door or to become halfway herself? CeeCee wasn't sure how she felt about that—half belonging here, half belonging home, still not fitting in anywhere.

"It's a fuzzy line, what ends up here and what doesn't." He pointed out the roofline of an apartment building. It had scorch marks around the windows from a past fire. "That building is full of squatters, but it's not in the byways. It's still part of the outside. But that one . . ." He pointed to a tidy-looking place that looked like an old-fashioned department store. "That one is. It's also full of people," he continued. "An otter clan. They don't like trespassers much."

"Um . . . noted," she said, wondering if there was a river in that department store.

"Anyway, there *are* people out there who know about the byways." He shrugged. "But really, what are they supposed to do about it?"

CeeCee tried to picture cops mobilizing to go after the slug man or a charity group holding a benefit food drive. In her head, she could see them stumbling around for an entrance or an exit and knew it would never work, if anyone could even convince them the byways were really here. "Yeah, I guess you're right," she said. "But why did it pull me?"

"It must have had something to do with how you felt or what you were thinking about. What did you expect, what were you seeing? Something like that."

CeeCee racked her memory, but all that came to mind was

the swirling nausea and being squished flat. She had a growing sense of screwing up because she couldn't even remember *how* she had screwed up.

"I just don't know," she said, frowning. "What about you? Why is it so easy for you to travel the byways?"

"It's because I don't expect anything and I see all!" he said grandly.

She snorted.

They passed two more halfway places that Jesse knew. Both had people blocking the way. It was getting so late, she doubted anyone would be there to open the door anyway. The air was quickly turning cold, and she shivered in her hoodie, missing that tank top. Her chest ached with disappointment—she was still in the byways after all.

Jesse noticed. "There's another place we can try, but we'll have to get off the roofs."

She nodded. There was more risk, but she had to keep trying.

"Put your hood up," he suggested.

She knew he meant more for disguise than the cold, so she looped her hair in a loose knot and pulled the hood over her ears. Then they climbed down to the street.

They strode purposely, like they had somewhere to go. Not like they were running from anything, CeeCee reminded herself, and forcibly stopped looking over her shoulder. Jesse seemed to see farther in the dark than she did. They occasionally saw people at a distance, and he put his hand on her elbow to either steer her in a new direction or to let her know to keep going. They passed an old woman humming to herself, and she smiled vaguely at them. It made CeeCee twitchy, not knowing who worked for Doc M and who didn't.

They stepped past the old woman into a new corridor, and

far down the alley, four young men lounged near the corner. They looked different than the other people of the byways. They wore fancy uniform jackets, but the clothes underneath still looked ratty. They held themselves like they owned the street. It was an attitude she hadn't seen in anyone except Doc M, but where his authority had seemed credible, these men seemed like street punks trying too hard.

"Who are those guys?" She pointed.

"They work for the Queen."

"Oh, can they take me to her? Should we ask?"

"Not them. They weren't good even before they were given a uniform." He scowled in their direction, and CeeCee was surprised at his degree of dislike. "They walk patrols around the byways and run whatever errands she needs. I'm surprised you haven't run into any of the Queen's men before," he said.

"I was thinking about being alone a lot. Would that do it? Like when you think where you want to go, and the alleys take you there?" She'd been mulling over the question of how she got there.

"It doesn't work with people; otherwise, Doc M would have found you right away," he said thoughtfully. "But it might work for solitude. Maybe you were just lucky."

"Well, I do have lucky magic," she joked, deadpan, thinking about Trudy. She felt a pang when she remembered their fight. It seemed so stupid now.

His eyebrows quirked up. "Do you? That will be useful."

Before she could say she was kidding, the youngest man at the corner turned and caught sight of them. He stared at her hard, and there was something ugly in the look. His buddies noticed and started to turn as well.

"Shit," Jesse said.

Without him saying anything else, she turned and walked down the alley.

"Not too fast," he whispered next to her.

They turned at a corner, and as one, they both picked up speed. With a shudder, CeeCee thought she was getting the hang of this place.

They turned again, and a number of doors appeared. Cracks of light beamed from several of them, casting shallow shadows across the pavement.

He grabbed her hand, and a jolt zinged through her.

"Quick, in here." He tugged her through a door.

They were in a club. CeeCee stood stunned and disoriented at the change in volume; she hadn't heard a thing while in the alley. Sound was always one of her bigger sensory triggers. It took her a moment to adjust. The crowd was large, but it felt furtive, as if everyone was underage and trying to get a drink. Jesse took her hand and pulled her gently away from the entrance until a knot of people blocked them from view. The callouses on his hand were round pads and rougher than she expected. They stood next to a stage where a man was busy setting up a drum kit.

"They probably won't come in," Jesse said, watching the entrance. "They shouldn't, as long as they don't know who's playing."

"Why? Who's playing?" she asked. As soon as she felt like she understood something, something else popped up. "And why does that matter?"

Instead of answering, Jesse leaned over to the man on stage. "Hey, there were Queen's men outside a moment ago."

"Thanks." The man nodded at him. "We don't start for another fifteen minutes; the patrol should be gone by then."

Jesse turned to her. "We can stay here for a while."

CeeCee realized she was still holding his hand. She dropped it and immediately felt awkward. She pulled her hood down and shook out her hair, just to have something to do.

The club was a tiny little square of a place, with towering ceilings and exposed rafters. The walls were papered in concert posters from bands she had never heard of. Two sets of thin wooden balconies circled the room one over the other, with rickety-looking ladders built to reach them. A bar was squashed into a corner. There were only a few tables and chairs, but no one seemed to mind.

The crowd was mixed, like the marketplace, but with a lot more young people than she had seen before. A few mad ones from the park were having drinks, but no obvious drugged-out clients of Doc M's were around. She didn't see anyone in a uniform, either. A lot of the crowd were changed ones, even though she knew that wasn't an accurate description anymore. The club was packed and getting more so by the minute. CeeCee was astonished at the numbers and the diversity in the room. It made her realize she had only seen a tiny portion of what the byways held. A group clustered by the door had skin as green as vines. A flash of violet caught her eye, and CeeCee craned her neck to see a woman two feet taller than everyone around her. The woman's hair showered purple sparks every time she laughed. People's clothes, although often far from new, were worn with a creativity she didn't see in the regular world. A very few wore fashions as fresh as Taylor's, and they reeked of money. One man, standing in a corner, looked human, but somehow he reminded her of a dragon. When he turned to meet her stare, she saw he had flames in his eyes. The man on stage finished setting up and taped a paper sign across the bass drum that read DEAD HEARTS DOWN.

Despite everything that had happened, CeeCee felt a thrill grab her. She had never been in a club before. The place smelled like beer and sweat and the joy of freedom. She was too young to get in anywhere on the outside, and no matter what people said about her, she just didn't have the criminal connections to get a fake ID. It was especially irksome to have the reputation and none of the benefits because she loved music. Just for that, she would have bought a fake ID, rules be damned. Her mom had promised to save up and take her to a concert this summer, so she'd had to content herself with that.

The band started up. They played mainly rock but threw in a wild fusion of styles. They opened their set with a punk rock song with anthem overtones and followed it with a folk-inspired tune. They kept the pace fast and danceable, and the lead singer sang with committed intensity. The crowd obviously knew the band because they sang along with lyrics or cheered in between verses.

She bopped her head in time to the music. She couldn't catch the lyrics, but the tunes were catchy. She knew she was grinning ear to ear. Jesse laughed beside her and caught her hand. He twirled her around, then dropped her hand and started dancing. After a breath, she danced too.

For a time, CeeCee felt only the music. She wasn't lost or running away or trying to make up for anything. She was only dancing in a club with a boy. It was even more fun than going to a dance at school. Jesse danced just as gracefully as he walked. She closed her eyes for a moment and swayed closer to him, until his heat felt like it was leaping from his skin to hers. When she opened them again, he was gazing down at her face.

"Why have you been helping me?" The question burst out of her without planning.

"I'm not doing much." He pretended nonchalance and looked away, scanning the club for nothing.

CeeCee's hand shot out impulsively and brushed his chin. She froze, and he did too. Then he turned to face her, his eyes staring unconcerned over her shoulder.

"Yes, you are," she said softly. "You could have pointed out a halfway spot and left me to figure it out. You could have given up after the mirrors or when those guys chased us, but you've stuck with me. I know this could make trouble for you. Doc M and the others aren't going to let it go, are they?"

"Maybe I'm just sick of the way things work around here."

She had questions, so many questions, but something deep inside told her to wait. She wasn't good at waiting, but she watched him look at the people, the room, the bar, at everything except her.

He shrugged off his indifference like a cloak and met her eyes. "There's something about you."

Her breath caught. *Too loud, too surly, too much*, beat in her head. But the beat didn't sound quite as loud as it used to. Maybe the music was drowning it out. Or maybe all that just didn't matter as much here. "Something . . . good?" she asked.

He smiled that surprised smile again—brief, then gone. "Yeah."

Her breath went out in a quiet whoosh. She struggled to think of something casual to say. Instead, she let her hand drift down to his arm, took his hand, and kept dancing. It felt like sparks were crackling along her skin, dancing with them. It was weird to think that Jesse took her exactly as she was and liked her anyway. It wasn't a feeling she was used to. Even her best friends wanted her to settle down sometimes.

The pace picked up on the next song, and she couldn't help jumping up and down and throwing her hair around until Jesse laughed.

When the band took a break, a couple of people circled the room, handing out fliers. A lot of the club goers broke into huddled groups. A charge was suddenly in the air. Or maybe it had always been there, and she was just noticing it now. People talked excitedly to each other, their eyes shining and fierce. A fox man, who looked like he could be the coffee guy's cousin, handed her a flier. At the top of the flier, it read "We Deserve Access."

Underneath that, it said things like "free distribution" and "no more locks." She realized that this gathering was as much about politics as it was about the music. She wondered if this had anything to do with Jesse being "sick of the way things worked."

The club was suddenly roasting hot, and she took off her hoodie, shoving it into her backpack. Her shirt was sticking to her skin. Jesse leaned over, looking just as sweaty. He said, "Let's get something to drink."

She followed him to the tiny bar. The crowd around it was huge, so she waited while Jesse waded in. At a nearby table was the tiny mouse lady she'd seen earlier that day. The lady was waving her hands around just as enthusiastically as she had that morning. She sat with a man who was so pale, he was almost colorless. He blinked constantly while they talked, like he was trying to bring her into focus. CeeCee edged closer.

"Hello," she said politely. "I saw you at the market. You were selling baskets."

"That's me!" The mouse lady smiled proudly. "I make them all myself. I'm Eugenia, and this is Horace."

"I'm CeeCee." She held up the flier. "Please, I'm new here. Can you tell me about this?"

"Oh, it's terrible! The whole byways have changed. They're just not the way they used to be," said Eugenia.

"What have you seen so far?" Horace asked.

"Well . . ." CeeCee wasn't sure what was important and what wasn't. "I've been to the park and to the market and a few other places. But mainly it's been just the alleys."

"The market isn't what it was," Eugenia said sadly. "You should have seen it before! It stretched out over streets! We all went. You could get practically anything."

"Yes, the market has taken the biggest hit because of the new rules," agreed her friend.

"I sold there, but I used to take my baskets to a halfway shop too," continued Eugenia, "and the owner would sell them to the outside. Then I could take pay in food or money or materials. I did well for my family, but then the Queen started instituting all the locks! Now I only make a portion of what I used to!"

"She was always mercurial, you see," said pale Horace. "But she used to leave most of us alone."

"And the shopkeepers were okay with the locks?" CeeCee asked. She thought of the sawn-off lock that Jesse had shown her and all of the doors she'd tried that wouldn't open.

"Some tried to resist, but they've been falling one by one. Only a few are holding out now."

"You see, she's halfway herself," said Horace. "She sits in between, and if they don't agree, she can make things hard on them out there."

CeeCee thought about that, being halfway and using it to her advantage. "Someone told me she likes to make deals." If the Queen was that involved with the outside, maybe she was Cee-Cee's best chance to get home. There must be something the Queen was willing to trade for.

"Yes, and she's been making them with people who only think about themselves. The rest of us have been suffering ever since."

"Like Doc M?"

"Oh yes, he's one of them! Terrible person! Trying to control supply and demand!"

"There used to be a lot more gardens, more places that were self-sufficient," said Horace.

"The Queen took over some of the bigger ones. She always did love her plants. But he's the one that put that whole warehouse nonsense in her head! You can't even get the essentials." Eugenia threw her arms out in exasperation. "We can't continue like this!"

"Do you sell things too?" she asked Horace.

"No. Things aren't so bad for me. I just go underground. But it's the principle of the thing, you see. If we don't stop it now, who knows where it'll end?"

"Do we want our kids to live like this? No!" Eugenia said.

Jesse walked up beside CeeCee and handed her water in a plastic cup. She took it, grateful it wasn't alcohol, and gulped it down. Eugenia and Horace stilled as Jesse stood there. He stared at them, unblinking, but for once he didn't look teasing or smug. CeeCee stared from him to the other two, feeling the sudden tension. She wondered if this was the result of one of Jesse's cons or jokes gone wrong. Tito hadn't been exactly friendly to him either.

Horace cleared his throat. "I expect we're all here for the same thing."

"I just came for the music." Jesse shrugged.

"Don't try any of that nonsense with me!" snapped Eugenia. "She said she was new." She leaned closer and focused a fierce look at Jesse. "I've heard things about you, despite you playing neutral. You're trying to get her out, aren't you? So get her out!"

"I'm working on it," he said and bared his teeth at her in a sham of a smile. He put his hand on the small of CeeCee's back and steered her away from the table.

A tingle ran all the way up her spine. "Thank you! It was nice talking to you," she called over her shoulder. Then she spun on Jesse. "What was that all about?" They had seemed nice enough to her.

"There's some history there, is all." He saw her arched eyebrows and threw up his hands in defense. "Not personal—I didn't do anything! It goes way back, more of a family thing."

He looked so rueful, she couldn't help but laugh. "There seems to be a lot you aren't telling me." She said it half teasing, half challenging.

"Actually, there's something I should tell you."

"Really? The vault is opening?"

He smiled his mischievous smile, but she could see wariness behind it, and it faded quickly. Her smile faded as well. He didn't seem to know where to begin.

"I'll tell you a secret," he said instead. "I've been with you longer than you know."

"When?" She was astonished. Even if she wasn't paying attention, she didn't think she could have missed him.

"This morning, before the market."

"I didn't see anyone this morning before the market. Just Kelly."

"You saw someone else." His stare was intense. "Someone you talked to about this place."

CeeCee took half a step back and stared at him. Something clicked in her brain and something else crumbled. "All I saw was a cat."

He held perfectly still. "I told you some of us just were." He sounded nervous.

"Show me," she demanded.

He heard the challenge in her voice. "Okay." He started to reach for her hand, then stopped himself.

He walked to a corner of the room that was draped in shadow. But it wasn't shadow, just a curtain blocking a narrow and cramped hallway. The walls were covered in graffiti, flyers, and want ads scribbled on scraps of torn notepaper. They had messages on them like, "Batteries Wanted," or "Shipment of tea in trade for spores," or "Missing: 27 blue hats." There was even an old pay phone, and CeeCee automatically picked up the receiver and held it to her ear. It was so quiet, it was almost like someone was listening.

At the end of the hall were two doors. Jesse knocked on one

and then opened it and waved her in. A bare bulb hung from the ceiling of a single stall bathroom. It was dingy with grime, years and years of it. The chipped white tile was covered in graffiti. It had one toilet stained dark with time and a sink with a hole smashed in the bottom. The bucket underneath it to catch the drops was almost full.

"Okay, I'm waiting!" She didn't know which of them was more tense.

"Be patient," he said. "And, um . . . don't hit me."

She didn't know how to describe what she was seeing. It was another impossible thing, in this place of impossible things. His body didn't transform, like a werewolf's; he didn't change in a sparkle of magic. The edges of him blurred a teeny bit, and then he faded—except for his eyes, except the part that was just him, physical or not, like when you know who walked up behind you without seeing them. That part stayed in front of her, but the rest faded. It was like he was there and he wasn't at the same time. It was all Schrödinger and nothing about boxes. And then Jesse was something else.

It was the brown cat she had talked to earlier that day when she tried to smash the window—the same glossy fur and head tilted just so and golden eyes blinking at her slowly. *Why didn't I see it before?* she thought. The cat was so completely Jesse. Of course, she hadn't gotten to know the cat yet. For a moment, everything went fuzzy and she reeled. Not because he was a cat, but because she couldn't fathom how she had gotten here in the first place, where a cat and a man made perfect sense. *In the drop of blue, everything had been fine*, she thought. *Everything had been fine.*

Jesse, in his human shape, grabbed her arms before she fell. His eyes had gone squinty with worry, and she could barely see the gold. "It's that bad, huh?"

"No," she said and stepped close. "Not bad. Not bad at all."

She rested her head against his chest, and he stiffened. She felt the warmth against her cheek like a hearth fire, and she listened to his heart pounding. It was reassuring, how all hearts beat the same.

"It's you," she whispered. "It just takes some adjusting."

He relaxed a little and put his arms lightly around her back. They stood there a minute while the rest of the wall inside her brain fell completely down. She swayed and caught her balance. "I'm okay now," she finally said, and they awkwardly disengaged.

"What now?"

"What now . . ." she said slowly. "Well, I'm ridiculously glad to see this toilet, so I'm going to use it, and then I'll meet you back outside."

Jesse took a deep breath. "Okay."

Normally, she would have half crouched over the dirty toilet and tried not to touch the seat. Now she collapsed onto it gratefully. She stared at the broken sink while she peed. She saw patterns in the grime that she wanted to follow with her fingers. She thought about cats and people and how much she would like another cup of coffee about now. She thought about home and the strangeness of perspective. Then she thought about how much you can think about while you pee.

Her mind was scattered, unfocused, too fast, and yet everything was clearer than she had felt in a long time.

She left the bathroom, walked down the tiny hall, and found Jesse at the edge of the dance floor waiting for her. The light caught in his hair, and he grinned ruefully at her as she stood next to him. "Not what you expected, huh?"

"Oh, stop." She banged her shoulder against his, and he looked relieved. "So I think my next step is to visit the Queen."

It hurt a little as she said it. She already liked Jesse; he was funny and infuriating and different. Now she wanted to know this man-slash-cat person even more. She wanted to know everything. But she felt that unknown deadline dangling like a noose.

He was silent a moment. "It's probably better to wait until morning to decide. We can't reach her now anyway."

"Yeah, okay," she agreed quickly. She couldn't quite keep the smile off her face.

FOURTEEN

All Our Own Words

The band came back on stage, playing fast and frenetic, and the feel of the club amped up, the charge becoming a current. If she wasn't leaving until the morning, she might as well enjoy being in a club. She pulled Jesse to the floor. A million thoughts flew through her mind, and she danced wildly, until the strangeness was just a new buzz under her skin. Weirdly, it was more fun than she'd had in a long time.

They left after the band's second set. People in the club were forming into groups again, and it seemed more serious this time. Jesse saw something in the room and said they should go.

He paused outside the door, scanning up and down the alley and then looking up at the sky. "It's gotten really dark tonight. We should hurry."

She wasn't done teasing him. "Can't cats see in the dark?"

"Yes, but so can other things."

Well, that was an unsettling tidbit. "So . . . where are we going exactly?" she asked dubiously. "We're not just going to walk around all night, are we?" She could probably go back to Kelly's, if she had to, or maybe up on the roofs.

"Oh no," he said. "I know someplace we can crash for a bit. Get some sleep, get some food. Sorry, I should have mentioned that."

"Someplace warm?" She struggled into her hoodie again, still high from the club.

"Yes." He laughed.

"Sounds great to me."

They made a game out of it, walking the quiet alleys. They were still wary of strangers, still scanning ahead, but it was so late, they assumed most of Doc M's clients would be sleeping off their medications of choice by now. They became silly, making each other laugh with exaggerated sneaking motions and dramatic pauses. They swung on the ends of fire escapes and half walked, half danced down the paths. One long stretch smelled like alcohol—before they saw the drunks.

Jesse stopped and assessed the passage. CeeCee squinted too; it was darker than most, but she could still see a path between the bodies slumped on the ground. Not one of them stirred. She wondered how many of them might be helping Doc M. *I'm standing right here*, she thought, smirking into the dark.

Jesse interrupted her thoughts. "We can go around, but this is faster," he said. "Where we're going isn't far beyond this."

"Do you think they're asleep?"

"Probably."

"Race, then?" she challenged.

His teeth flashed in the dark, and he was off, dodging and weaving around the sleeping men with the grace of a dancer. Not all of them were asleep. One or two sluggishly raised hands or jumped, startled after he passed. CeeCee sprinted after him, knowing she wasn't half as graceful, but she'd always been fast— like a runaway train to his cheetah.

He still beat her, though, laughing at the end of the alley, barely visible in the dim.

She was almost out when she tripped over one of the drunks. She hit the pavement hard, sprawled halfway over the drunk's legs. The sick smell of urine washed over her, and she felt him move. She spun around so she was facing him, before he could grab her. But the man wasn't going to do anything. He was slumped, sitting against the wall. His eyes were rolled back into his head, and spittle gathered at his mouth, foaming and sticky looking. He had started twitching all over. She stared at him in horror. Had she done that, by landing on him? The shaking got more intense, and the man slid down the wall, until his head was banging violently against the ground.

He was OD'ing, CeeCee realized. It was awful to watch. The dead man had been peaceful compared to this.

She scurried backward and smacked a pile of bottles. They echoed loudly in the small space.

Down the alley, something moved, and she jerked her eyes away from the twitching man. Far down in the dark, blocks of color were moving in their direction—colors that she recognized but still couldn't name. A chill washed over her. She didn't know what the colors meant, but now she knew the byways enough to know it was bad.

The other drunks were scrambling up in ones and twos, buddies helping their friends stagger down the alley. They hurried past her.

She grabbed the twitching addict's arm and tried to drag him away. He was a large man, heavier than she thought, and he kept jerking out of her grasp. She'd only managed to move him a foot.

"Help me," she said to the fleeing drunks. "Help me!"

"CeeCee!" Jesse rushed back and pulled her arm. "We've got to go! The jib jab is coming."

Every other drunk in the alley had fled.

"We can't just leave him!" What would happen if those colors reached them?

He took a good look at the man spasming on the ground. "I don't think he's going to wake up."

"We've got to try."

The look on Jesse's face was strange, sorrowful, and alarmed at once, but he hooked a hand under one shoulder, and CeeCee took the other. They walked backward, yanking the man across bottles and litter, but with every heave and new rattle, the colors jumped faster.

They were just as beautiful as they were before. She watched them as she heaved on the limp body. A pulsing not-peach color caught her attention. It had sparkles in the very center. They winked prettily at her.

"Don't look at them!" Jesse barked.

She tore her eyes away and looked down at the man's slack, drooling face. They had managed to pull him only a few feet down the alley. She grit her teeth in frustration. The colors were jumping faster than they could move.

The first color had reached the man's feet. The not-peach glow jumped to his leg and seemed to attach itself, sinking into the man's pants. The fabric melted away, like the color was made of acid. Despite being completely unconscious, the man let out a gurgling scream and jerked out of CeeCee's grip, dropping to the pavement. She reached for him again as a peacock block and a red swirly one joined the first color on the man's leg. The man's shaking got even worse. He screamed and choked on the ground.

Jesse dropped his arm.

"It's too late. We've got to go now." He pulled on her arm. "CeeCee!"

One of the colors jumped to the man's torso, just inches away from her hands. She jerked back but kept staring at the pulsing, gorgeous block. Jesse grabbed her around the waist and spun her until the colors were out of her line of sight. It was like a spell had broken. She sucked in air in a great gasp. He seized her hand, and they ran frantically down the alley.

Five blocks later, they finally slowed. They stopped, gasping, in an alley full of garbage and castoffs, dimly lit from a window above them.

"What the fuck are they?" she choked out.

"No one is really sure. Something old. We call it the jib jab." He sounded hollow.

Her hands were trembling from adrenaline and from the knowledge she had seen two dead men in the space of one night. Just a moment ago they were dancing! The world twisted around and settled heavy in her throat. It felt like her fault the second man had died. She should have tried harder.

"Didn't you run through them before?"

"I did, but"—she whispered, horrified—"that was when I first got here. I thought they were reflections. I didn't know they did that. I just knew you shouldn't stop."

"They stay in the dark. It's better hunting for them."

With a blinding and furious insight, she understood Trudy's compulsion to organize, to fix things, to make order. She wanted to fix this. She wanted to undo what had just happened, the man OD'ing, the jib jab, her being there in the first place . . . and she just couldn't. Shock and frustration and despair threatened to drown her. What if she was stuck in the byways for good? What if she changed? What if she ended up as another strange, forgotten resident?

The horrid, wretched voice inside her whispered that it might be easier. Sure, she wouldn't have to try to fit in anymore or follow rules or curb her temper. She wouldn't have to think too hard about her future, beyond finding food or the next place to sleep. She wouldn't be a burden on anyone.

But most of it would be a whole lot harder—like trying not to die.

She screamed. Jesse jumped next to her. She grabbed an empty bottle and hurled it back the way they came, as if she could hit the jib jab from there. It wasn't enough, so she picked up a broken board and smacked it against the brick wall. The edge of it splintered, and pieces flew out in a satisfying explosion. She hit the board over and over against the brick; a chunk of it disintegrated with each smack. The jarring impact felt good. It centered her in her body, connected her to the ground, slowed her swirling thoughts. She could feel herself calming as she burned out her frustration. When she had run down enough and the board was just a short stub, she kicked the wall for good measure.

She hung her head and stared at her feet, trying to steady her breathing. There was a film on her hands, grimy from the man's dirty coat, and she kept trying to wipe it off on her jeans. She was acutely aware that Jesse was watching her. He was a still figure in the corner of her eye, standing back against the wall. A sick feeling crawled inside her stomach. She waited for him to make some excuse and wander off into the night without her. "I'm sorry," she said.

"Why are you apologizing?"

"I know I was out of control again."

"You tried to do something. You tried, and it didn't work. I know it's frustrating."

He didn't seem to be looking for an apology, or a fight. She looked up anxiously and met his eyes. His face was smudged in the dim light, but she could still see him. He looked sympathetic but not like he felt pity or was embarrassed for her. It was like maybe, just maybe, he understood.

"I don't freak you out?"

"You surprise me sometimes." He shrugged. "You feel the life you're living. You don't just stand by and watch."

She had never thought about it like that.

"I've seen other people come through, ones like you. It's too strange for most of them. You're strong. You're handling this place better than most."

"*That* was handling it well?" The instinct to argue, to defend herself, had nowhere to go.

"That was an understandable response to a whole lot of shit."

The validation hit her hard. It was so unexpected to feel good when she felt so awful. Guilt rose and hung in the background like a soundtrack. She was so confused. She never thought she was being unreasonable, but if everyone else said she was unreasonable, how were they all wrong? Probably she overreacted at times or maybe her emotional response to the world was over the top compared to other people, but it wasn't like she was reacting to *nothing*. She had reasons to feel the way she did.

"Thank you," she said, faltering. Part of her didn't think she deserved to be called strong. She was just reacting, like she always did, bulling through one situation after another. And the man had still died. "You've seen that before, haven't you?"

He nodded. "A lot of the people who come here, they can't wait to go running to Doc M or someone like him. There are a lot of addicts." He paused. "The jib jab only gets some if they're being foolish. Or if they've stopped caring."

He sounded calm, but she heard a tired anger just under the surface.

"There are other dangers here. Those men were stupid, passing out drunk in the open," he said.

CeeCee looked at him, stricken. "Did you lose someone?"

"We've all lost someone."

"I haven't lost anyone."

He looked away. "Yeah, well, it sucks."

The silence stretched out, but it wasn't awkward for once, just kind of sad and thick with the words they weren't speaking. After a moment, he broke it.

"Let's get going. We'll need some sleep if we're going to get you home in the morning."

The rest of the walk was subdued. But with Jesse, it also felt strangely comfortable to just walk in silence and think, and gradually the heavy mood lightened. It didn't go away completely—CeeCee didn't think any of this would ever go away completely—but her fears didn't drag her down quite so much.

"We're almost there." Jesse stopped at a set of metal stairs on the side of a building. He patted the rail distractedly. "So . . ." he said, hesitating. "Just act like being there is no big deal, and it'll be fine."

"What?"

"I mean . . . it's safe. You don't have to be scared. But try not to punch anyone. That will get us kicked out."

"I don't just randomly punch people, you know!" CeeCee wanted to feel offended, but he had seen her about to belt someone with a garbage can earlier.

"I know." He met her eyes. "But the people here take fights pretty seriously."

"You mean, they don't believe in violence?" She squinted at him. He was acting almost . . . nervous.

"Oh no, they fight all the time. It just means something serious when they do fight." As if it just occurred to him, he added, "Although sometimes they're actually playing when they look like they're fighting, so just stay out of the way." He shook his head. "You'll be fine."

CeeCee hoped that "fine" in his world meant the same as "confused" in hers.

He climbed up the stairs to the roof and crossed to the other side, where a wooden ladder led back down. From the roof, she could see the alley they were climbing into was very short, almost a square, hedged in on all sides by the backs of buildings. Most of the buildings looked in good repair and had lights on, like they were still part of the outside. There were ladders and tall stacks of wood boxes braced against almost all of them.

Squished into the short alley was an old building. Really old. It was small, with plain clapboard siding and generations of old paint chipping off around the windowsills. All the glass was missing, and someone had pinned paper and cardboard loosely in place over the gaps. The whole sagging structure reminded Cee-Cee of a saloon or a seedy bordello out of the Old West. It looked like it was about to fall down, but dim light came from within.

Jesse knocked in a quick and precise pattern, and an older man opened the door. He stepped back to let them in, then returned to lounge in an overstuffed chair. It gave him a perfect view of the outside through a slit in the paper covering the window. Someone had begun remodeling the small front hall, adding partitions. The drywall contrasted sharply with the original wood. Bizarre holes were punched in the walls and in the ceiling to the second story. CeeCee took a few cautious steps across the floor, expecting to fall through at any moment, but beside a few creaks, it felt solid. In fact, the inside seemed structurally sound, the holes neatly made, the lines plumb, like it was meant to look more dilapidated on the outside than it actually was.

Jesse crossed the floor, and it didn't make a sound. Her footsteps echoed loudly, and the floorboard creaks were even noisier.

The next room was large and crowded with old couches. A set of stairs led to the second floor. A man and woman sat watching a movie on a tiny, ancient TV with the sound turned down. An elderly man dozed, sprawled on a couch. Despite the overabundance of furniture, the place was clean and cozy. Someone came in behind them and hurried through the room to a door at the back. Not one floorboard creaked as he passed. A teenage girl came down the stairs. Partway down, the girl jumped neatly over the banister and padded into the kitchen. Everyone moved with uncanny grace and balance. They were, she realized, all people like Jesse—cats.

Suddenly his comments about fighting made a lot more sense.

Everyone turned and looked at them as they passed, curious. She tensed up self-consciously. No one said a word. Jesse walked into the kitchen and opened up an avocado-green fridge. A middle-aged man sat at a battered folding table, eating chipped beef on toast.

"You hungry?" Jesse asked her.

"Yes," she said, relieved. It had been forever since they had the hamburgers.

He pulled out a block of cheese and fished a knife out of a drawer. CeeCee was aware the man was giving her the eye. It was the kind of no-nonsense, strict look she might expect from a teacher, but he looked throw-down street tough. It was intimidating as hell. Remembering Jesse's warning, she kept her back straight and pretended unconcern, but her hand was unconsciously rubbing her arm, just like in school.

The man suddenly growled, "Who's this, then?"

"This is my friend CeeCee," Jesse told him. "She's going to crash here tonight."

"Is she the one everyone is looking for?"

Jesse said nonchalantly, "Maybe." He stared at the man and waited for him to say something.

The man seemed to think about it, staring back unblinking. Then he nodded and continued eating.

Jesse handed her a thick chunk of cheese. "Come on. Let's find someplace to sleep."

They walked up the stairs, and the next floor was obviously all bedrooms. She was suddenly terribly nervous. He poked his head in two rooms before he found one he liked. She followed him hesitantly and saw a couch, a bunk bed, and another bed in the room. All of them held people except for one. Almost everyone was asleep or nearly so, but a girl on the couch was still up reading a book. There were two cats curled up next to her, and a minute later, another one shot through a hole in the wall on silent feet. CeeCee hovered by the door while Jesse sat down on the bed.

At least there were lots of people in the room. That should have made her feel better.

Jesse ate cheese and smiled at her, rakish and silly and charming.

Nope, she was still nervous. Why was she so nervous? He was cute, sure. But it wasn't like she had never been around a cute boy before. She'd even kissed a few. CeeCee shook herself. This was ridiculous; she wasn't planning on kissing him anyway!

She crossed the floor and sat down gingerly, facing him. It was a surprisingly comfy bed, and her limbs suddenly turned to heavy goo. She sighed and sagged into herself, then gave up and stretched out on her back and felt her bones melt into the worn comforter. Jesse scooched over to sit cross-legged against the wall so she would have room. She nibbled her cheese and thought she might never get up again.

"You can go to sleep; it'll be okay," he said quietly.

"I'm tired, but I'm too wound up to sleep yet. There's too much in my head." She spoke softly so she wouldn't wake anyone. "This place is so confusing. Can you explain some things to me?"

"I can try. Like what?"

"Like . . . did you grow up here?" She waved her cheese at the room.

"No. This is just a house that my people share. A place to sleep or meet or hang out."

"What happens if someone in an outside building goes into an alley?"

"You mean an alley in the byways?"

"Yeah, like there's a door in that office building across the street from here. If someone comes out, aren't they going to see this house?"

"They have to be halfway themselves or know how to cross. Otherwise, the byways redirect them."

"What do you mean?"

"I think they see an alley that's just . . . normal. I don't know if they're taken to a different alley or they just see what they need to see. I know they don't see the byway. Just like they didn't see you yelling at them outside their windows." He paused. "I'm not completely sure how it works. All my people are halfway, so I've always walked into the byway alley that's really there."

That was a strange thought: Which alley was real, and which one was not? Or could two exist at the same time? It was kind of like Jesse being a man and cat at the same time and how cats ended up in boxes by theoretical sadists.

"Can all cats change into humans?" she asked.

"No, not all. But all cats can go where they want to go."

She'd never had a pet—their apartment was too small. But she thought about the cats she had met. "It's probably that irritating confidence you all have," she mused.

He guffawed and quickly smothered it. When he laughed, his knees brushed the side of her leg.

"Did you go to school?" she asked.

"Not traditionally. I learned math and how to read and write. Most of the families here just teach their own kids. And there are a few teachers floating around. Not all of my people live in the byways, and my parents could have sent me to school out there. But my family has always been here, and there are other skills that are more important."

She could well imagine more useful skills than the ones learned in school. The mirror trick—that would be useful.

"I used to think about leaving and never coming back. Plenty of my people stay on the outside." He sounded very sad when he said it. Again, CeeCee had the sense of something lost.

"Why didn't you?" she asked softly. Her heart ached at his sorrow, but she didn't want to push and make it worse.

He shifted in his seat. "There are things I would miss. There are things here you can't see anywhere else. I don't really like the idea of leaving something completely. I like to have my options open." He said that last part in a cocky and teasing way.

She could tell he was steering the conversation away from whatever had made him sad, cheering himself up. She imagined he'd seen a lot of crap growing up here.

"What was all that back at the club, with Eugenia and Horace?" she asked instead. *Could it be a cat-versus-rodent thing?* she wondered. Wait, did she just racially profile them? She sure hoped not. It was bad enough she had called people monsters when she first got here.

"They're political. Most of us try not to get involved in that sort of thing; it's not really in our nature. Although, I can't say I disagree with their concerns. However, some of our people have started working for the Queen. There was already bad blood, and that just made it worse. People are getting paranoid or angry." He shook his head. "It's not going to end well."

CeeCee thought about the people she had met in the byways.

The ones who wandered in from her side brought their own level of illness or strange. And the ones who had lived here for generations had no place else to go. It was not a great combination for added pressure; it was like tinder floating in the air around them, waiting to spark at any moment.

"Is that why you wanted to help me get out? Because you knew what I was walking into?"

"I felt bad for you. You didn't seem like the usual type."

She cocked her head at him. "I remember you said that, actually."

He switched gears. "Although . . . you *are* a little mad. You know that, right? Not *that* different from the people at the park, now that I know you better."

She laughed despite herself.

"Can I ask you some questions now?" he teased.

She felt a flutter of anxiety but mock groaned, "Okay."

"Tell me about your life."

"That's not a question."

"Come on." He poked her shoulder. Every time he moved, it grabbed her attention.

"I live with my mom. I go to school. I like music and history." She paused and thought about it. "Actually, I love music. I like having the apartment all to myself and listening to songs. I mean really listening to them, out loud on the speakers, not just in my headphones. Studying the lyrics and reading the band's history. The stories about them. There's almost always drama behind every band, and out of that comes music. It's kind of amazing, really."

"I like music too. Especially blues."

"Huh. Really?"

He poked her again, refusing to change the subject. "What else?"

She shrugged awkwardly, lying on her back. "At school, I get in trouble a lot. I don't mean to, but I kind of lose track of what I'm supposed to be doing, and then it happens. I try to keep my head down, but I'm not very good at it." She took a deep breath. "I have to take medication because I'm so . . ." She waved her hands in the air. "You probably figured that out already. I don't usually tell people. I don't usually have to."

"That's my favorite thing about you."

"Shut up."

"I'm serious. You have so much passion. You're a force."

"That's a nice way to put it." She stretched and rubbed her fingers slowly across the nubby comforter.

"What else?"

She tried to think of a story that didn't end in disaster, and failed. "I don't know . . . just normal stuff . . ." Her voice trailed away.

"You don't like talking about yourself, do you?"

She sighed. "Every time I'm asked to talk, it's when something went wrong. I always feel like I'm explaining myself."

"Like how?" He looked at her expectantly but not like he was ready to condemn her.

"Like . . ." she started slowly. "I have this friend Sam, and he's autistic. He's really smart, but he gets caught up in details. One time, this older kid Greg—he's a real dick—he started making fun of Sam at lunch. He kept asking him questions that required really long explanations, and then he'd repeat something back to Sammy, but the detail would be wrong. So then Sam would try to explain that, and Greg just kept him going and going, laughing at him. Everyone knew what he was doing. Everyone except Sam. I got so mad, I threw mashed potatoes at his head."

Jesse laughed loudly, and one of the sleepers propped himself up on an elbow and glared at them. They hushed until the man rolled back over and went to sleep.

"Mashed potatoes?" he whispered.

"Well, they were right there, and I couldn't think what to say without hurting Sam's feelings." Another girl had tried, she remembered that, and Greg had steamrolled over her, insisting he wanted to talk to Sam. "It turned into this huge food fight, and, of course, I got the blame for starting it. Then I end up in the office explaining myself, and I hear all the same lectures I always hear about self-control and positive choices, and it goes on and on. But Greg was still a dick, and he didn't get in trouble." In retrospect though, she remembered a lot of food being aimed at Greg's head. It hadn't just been her who was pissed. He looked like he had bathed in food by the time it was over.

"I bet that was fun, even if you did get in trouble. And satisfying. You probably should have just punched him, though."

"That's even more against the rules."

"See, here you would have gotten in trouble for wasting food, not for fighting."

That made a lot of sense. Her cheese was all gone, but she was still hungry. What if she had been alone and ran out of granola bars? She sighed, heavy with all that had happened in the last two days. "I always felt different, felt wrong, but not . . . not like it is here. It seems kind of silly now. Actually, a lot of things seem silly."

He studied her closely. "You know, the passion you have, it's not just about getting angry."

"What do you mean?"

"I mean, when you're sad, you're really sad. When you laugh at something, you're really laughing. It's infectious. It's fun to be around you because nothing is fake."

Her whole body warmed. The anxiety fluttering inside her got better and worse at the same time.

"I'm not used to being startled," he continued. "You're unexpected, and you catch me off guard."

"Do I scare you?" CeeCee said, half teasing and half jangly nerves.

"In the best of all possible ways."

A thought came to her, and she said delicately, "You said something else earlier. You said I don't stand by and watch life. You don't think that about yourself, do you?"

"No, not really. Well . . . maybe sometimes. I don't always go charging toward it, either." He sounded regretful.

"I've seen you do some pretty daring stuff," she said quietly. She patted his knee as if that would reassure him. It felt awkward, and she let her hand fall.

"Yes, but that's after careful assessment and planning. Lots of planning."

"That's a good thing. I'm always trying to work on my impulse control. Patience and planning aren't my forte."

He caught her hand and gave it a quick squeeze before letting go. "Trust me, quick reaction time isn't a bad thing."

Her air went out of her in a little puff. She felt warm again. "Well, maybe we make a good team then," she teased shyly.

His teeth flashed in the dusky room.

"What do you want to do? When you grow up?" she asked him.

"How offensive. I'm grown up now."

"You know what I mean."

"I don't know. Sometimes around here, it's just about getting through the day." He continued, "I know I don't like the idea of being stuck in one place. There are too many stuck here already. Don't get me wrong—it's not all bad. If it weren't for the byways, some of the people here wouldn't have survived at all. The byways saved them. But . . . no one should be trapped."

She knew he was talking about her as much as he was talking about himself. "Well, you're good at planning, right? Make a plan."

He laughed quietly. "What about you?"

"Well . . ." she confided, hushed and hesitating. "I think I'd like to do something with music. But not performing. Everyone expects that if you like music, you'll sing, or write, or kill yourself trying to get on a competition show. But there are loads of jobs without doing any of that. I looked them up—sound engineers, producers, stage crew."

Jesse's eyes shined. "Wouldn't it be cool to travel with a band?"

"Yes! I'm not completely sure what I want to do yet, but that's where I'm leaning." She smiled ruefully. "But don't tell anyone; you'll ruin my reputation."

"I have absolutely no doubt," he said, "that when you figure it out, you'll be surer than the rest of us."

He moved away from the wall and stretched out flat on his back next to her. He stared at the ceiling. The ceiling had cracks in it and a hole in the corner, perfect for a cat to pop its head through. She felt like she did when she spent the night at Trudy's, sleepy and warm but unwilling to go to sleep because she wanted to know what he would say next—like they had been lying on beds talking for years, like they were just continuing the most important conversation ever. But it also felt brand-new, and whenever he shifted, a line of fire sprang up where his body touched hers.

She was desperately tired, but she didn't want to miss anything.

He shifted so he was facing her, on his side. She turned her head so she could see him, and hair fell across her face.

"You should sleep," he said. Very softly he brushed her hair back.

"You should too," she whispered, her heart racing.

His eyes were shimmery and gold and sleepy looking.

"What if I can't get out?" she asked.

"You will."

"How do you know?" He seemed so sure. He couldn't have that much confidence in her, could he?

"Do you remember what I said about flying?"

She nodded, and her cheek caressed his palm. "You have to know it, like it never occurred to you to be anything else," she said.

"It's the trick to everything," he said.

"Tell me about when you were a kid."

"I'll tell you mine if you tell me yours."

"Deal."

"I was rotten." He smiled sleepily and launched into a tale about stealing eggs.

In the end, she didn't remember falling asleep at all.

FiFTEEN

Still by My Side?

Her face was on fire. She cracked one eye open and immediately shut it. A beam of light slanted from a corner of the window directly into her eyes. Despite being burned alive, she was extremely comfortable and didn't remember where she was for a minute. This wasn't her bed, but in her half-asleep state, she decided it didn't matter. She flipped onto her side to escape the death ray, her eyelids fluttering, and came face-to-face with Jesse.

Now she was fully awake.

She lay in bed and watched him sleep. The sun was full in his face, and he had the most contented expression because of it. He looked exactly like a cat in sunshine. His cheekbones were high, and a narrow scar peeked out from the hairline near his ear. The light caught in his hair and played in the chocolate colors and rich shadows. Her fingers itched to pet it. *Wow, that's condescending*, she berated herself. Why did she always want to pet people?

He smiled suddenly and opened his eyes with a knowing, delighted look in them. Her face flushed as though she had been caught at something. She waited for him to say something, but he just looked at her with that smart-ass grin.

"What?" she finally demanded.

"Nothing." He shrugged.

"Okay, then," she grumbled.

It was kind of cozy lying there, not doing or saying anything. Jesse had a really nice smile, and after a minute, she smiled too. The night before played over in her head. Then her mom's worried face flashed through her mind.

"I've been missing for two days," she said softly.

"Has it only been two? It seems like I've known you longer than that."

"I know. It feels like forever." Or maybe she had just been waiting forever and didn't know it.

His hand crept over and lightly took hers. Her heart made a funny flip in her chest.

"I suppose we should get going," she said slowly.

She didn't want to move, not really. It made her feel terribly selfish and guilty, and, way in the back of her mind, a teensy bit worried.

Jesse looked very serious for a minute. He opened his mouth, and her breath caught. Then he said, "I don't think you should go to the Queen. We can find another way."

She frowned. "You said I couldn't wait too long. She's the fastest way out, right?"

"Maybe. If she helps you. But she's . . . unpredictable." He squeezed her hand. "I think you have time. You don't seem like . . . you're not getting that . . ."

"Strange byways look?" she filled in for him.

He laughed silently. "It's hard to describe, but yeah. Besides, the Queen won't even be available for a few hours."

She pretended to think it over while he watched her

worriedly. "I guess getting breakfast won't make a difference one way or the other." She grinned. "You've got food, right?"

He beamed, pleased and grand as he popped up and off the bed. "Of course."

She sat up and groaned. It was going to be one of those days. Everything was always blissful until she actually got out of bed. She felt rested but still a little fried at the same time. That usually turned into being unfocused and frazzled, with too much energy and no way to burn it off. These were always the days where she got in trouble at school, despite her best efforts.

"Any chance we can get coffee somewhere?" she grumped.

He looked sympathetic but irritatingly chipper.

"Sorry, they usually don't have any here."

"I have two cups waiting with that coffee guy at the market, but we'll be seen by Doc M's stupid minions."

"Huh," he said, and she could practically see the wheels turning in his mind.

She waited, as patiently as she could without coffee, which wasn't much, while he mulled over whatever it was he was thinking.

"Maybe not." He grinned mischievously. "We might be able to do it without being seen."

They made their way downstairs and scrounged in the kitchen for food. Jesse cut more slices of cheese and found half a can of tuna and some crackers. They washed it down with water, but CeeCee couldn't wait to get some caffeine. She jittered from foot to foot, until Jesse noticed and led the way out of the house. They passed two men sitting in the front hallway. One was telling a lively story about a hunt, and the other laughed along, but she had no doubt they were keeping careful track of who was coming and going.

"Hey, wait up!" a voice called behind them.

The teenage girl they had seen the night before was loping toward them. She stopped and posed nonchalantly like she hadn't just been running. Up close, she appeared a year or two younger than CeeCee. Her black hair was cropped short, and her clothes edged toward punk, with ripped jeans and clunky boots.

"Hey," said Jesse.

"Hey," she said, "whatcha guys doing?"

"We're going to liberate some coffee. Want to help?"

She shrugged. "I have time to kill."

"This is Mikayla," he told CeeCee. "She'll be useful."

"Hi, I'm CeeCee."

"Yeah, I know. I heard about the whole Doc M thing." She shrugged again. "He's a jerk." She walked along with them, scuffing her boots slowly as if she didn't really want to be there. CeeCee noticed, though, that she kept up just fine.

Jesse said to Mikayla, "You still look bored. You're supposed to look inscrutable."

"Well maybe I *am* bored," she shot back. At CeeCee's look, she added, "I'm still in training."

"Training for what?"

Her face went shifty and nervous. "Um . . . stuff."

CeeCee looked at Jesse, and he made an exaggerated show of pretending ignorance. Normally that would have pissed her off, but he looked so cute doing it, she let it drop for the time being. She could dig it out of him later.

"Anyway," CeeCee said, rolling her eyes, "how are we going to do this?"

"There is a hole in the market roof."

Mikayla blinked at him. "Really?" If her ears had been showing, they would have perked up.

Jesse smiled smugly. "Yep, and if we travel by rooftop, I think we can get there without running into anyone."

CeeCee asked him, "How are we going to get coffee from the roof?"

He clapped his hands together like a delighted evildoer. "Mikayla will get us a basket from Eugenia. Make it big enough for two cups . . ."

"Three," said Mikayla.

"Three cups of coffee."

"How am I gonna pay?" Mikayla thrust her hand out, palm flat.

Jesse pursed his lips and looked questioningly at CeeCee. She slipped off her backpack and dug around in it.

"How about this?" She held out a bottle of painkillers. She always kept a bottle of Aleve and Tylenol with her for headaches. "Didn't she say she couldn't get the essentials?"

He took the bottle and popped off the lid. It was about three-quarters full.

"That'll work, and we'll get change." He turned back to Mikayla. "Okay. You'll get the basket, then walk around back and toss it up on the roof."

"Yes sir!" She mock saluted him.

"Why don't we just ask Mikayla to get the coffee for us too?" said CeeCee.

Jesse and Mikayla turned to her with matching raised eyebrows.

"Where's the fun in that?" said Jesse.

"Every route should be explored," intoned Mikayla solemnly, as if it were an oft-repeated phrase.

CeeCee laughed in spite of the lack of logic. "Wow, you guys are going to be a real bad influence on me, aren't you?"

"Yes," said Jesse gleefully.

"Whatever." Mikayla shrugged.

"Don't you know by now that I shouldn't be indulged?" Cee-Cee asked.

"I think you should be indulged every day," he told her gallantly.

Her heart warmed, and she couldn't help but grin goofily. Mikayla's eyes went back and forth between the two of them, and suddenly she was smiling too—a bratty, shit-eating grin.

It made CeeCee feel caught out and squirrely.

"Lead on!" she said and turned her back on them.

They traveled over the roofs and only saw people at a distance. It was nice being out in the morning sun with people close to her own age. Mikayla practiced at being cool, but Jesse teased her mercilessly every time she did, like she was his little sister. Despite the bratty grin earlier, CeeCee liked her immediately. She was naturally observant and had a dry wit that was more than a match for Jesse's needling. Their banter made CeeCee laugh more than once. The frazzled head she had woken up with was quickly clearing. She probably didn't need coffee after all, but she wasn't about to beg out of the adventure. For the first time, she didn't feel so freaked out by the byways. She was getting the hang of being here, at least a little, and having fun. *A small delay before going home won't make a difference*, she thought with a guilty twinge.

When they were one rooftop over from the bowling alley, Jesse handed the bottle of painkillers to Mikayla.

"Okay, get the basket," he told her. "Tell her it's for CeeCee, if that will help negotiations. Then toss it up. Come up when you know we have it."

"Hell no, I'm getting a front row seat for this." Mikayla stepped onto the fire escape. "If it works, you can show me later."

"That will mean taking point. Stay near the entrance!"

"I'll be fine." She grinned, wicked and excited, all nonchalance dropped.

They watched Mikayla climb down to the alley and walk casually around the corner to the market entrance. The building they were on faced the back of the bowling alley and was close enough to jump to the roof. Jesse went first. When CeeCee jumped off the edge, for a brief moment, she felt like she was flying. He caught her for balance, even though he didn't have to, and she found herself grinning at him, elated. His eyes sparkled, smiling back, and for a moment they didn't do anything but breathe.

Then a basket sailed up and over the edge of the roof. CeeCee ran to pick it up. It was the perfect size, tightly woven, flat on the bottom with high sides. Tied to the handle was a small skein of colorful yarn, which must have been their change.

In a corner of the roof was the hole. Water had pooled there, and the stucco was stained around the edges. Someone had put a piece of corrugated metal over the hole, but it was a half-hearted fix at best, too short and rusty itself. Jesse grasped the corner and shifted the metal over. He lay flat on his stomach to poke his head in.

"I think this will work, but we'll have to be careful." Then, as if it had just occurred to him, he asked, "How's your balance?"

"Pretty damn good when I'm paying attention. But aren't they going to hear us?"

"Yeah, but it's always pretty loud in there, and we should have enough time to get our drinks before too many people notice us."

He lowered himself into the hole, feet first. She saw him bounce slightly as he tested his weight on whatever he was standing on. He must have been satisfied because he waved, then ducked down out of sight.

CeeCee's pulse raced. She was excited, but misgivings were stirring guiltily. She wasn't sure coffee was worth this much effort and the potential of falling. She'd feel horrible if something went wrong and they got hurt. *Holy crap*, she thought to herself, *am I becoming responsible?*

However, that wasn't the right question. She already knew she was responsible for the important stuff: schoolwork, checking in with her mom, and so on. It was the little moments, when she got distracted by impulse, that got her in trouble.

She peered into the hole. Directly below her was a thick wooden support beam. Below, that light seeped up through suspended ceiling tiles. The tiles were pretty ratty from age, full of holes where cracks had formed and chunks had fallen in. There was no way the metal grid holding the tiles was going to support her weight. But as she looked around for Jesse, she saw a heavy-duty A/C duct running the length of the building, intersecting the wood beams. From the ductwork, one could move to any section of the bowling alley. Jesse crawled across the support beam to the ductwork, the basket hanging from the crook in his elbow, like he was going on a picnic.

The sight was silly and charming and weird, and a sudden thrill washed away her doubt. She scooched into the hole and balanced on the dusty beam on her hands and knees. It felt reassuringly solid. She took a moment to center her gravity and make sure her backpack wouldn't slide and yank her to her death. She crawled along the beam to where Jesse was waiting.

The ceiling tiles were so damaged that it was easy to see where to go. The coffee cart was close to a cross section of the A/C duct and a support beam. Red's distinctive hair was a beacon, and the smell of coffee called out like a siren. CeeCee's mouth watered, like a good little addict.

They crawled to the area above the coffee cart, and Jesse reached down and slid the ceiling tile to the side. It left them a clear view of a quarter of the market. If they leaned, they could see up and down several aisles. Red was directly below them. He was brewing a new pot and chatting with the booth owners on either side. They could even see Mikayla slouching near the entrance, looking cool and detached and like she was working hard at it.

Jesse settled himself comfortably on the beam and fished a small roll of twine out of his pocket. Using paper from her notebook, CeeCee wrote a note and placed it, the skein of yarn, and her travel mug in the basket. He tied the twine around the handle and lowered it slowly down.

Red looked so surprised when the basket swung in front of his face that CeeCee and Jesse burst into stifled giggles. He looked up, and they waved to him, grins huge, their legs dangling beneath them on the beam. Red scanned the note and inspected the skein of yarn before giving them a thumbs up. He poured coffee into the travel mug, and Jesse pulled it up.

He handed CeeCee the mug. "You first—I know you're dying for it."

She took it gratefully and slurped a huge mouthful, scorching her tongue a bit. It was just as good as it had been the day before. Was that really only yesterday?

Mikayla was suddenly in front of the cart. They clearly heard her say, "I'm the third cup," before she retreated back to the entrance with her coffee.

CeeCee handed the coffee back to Jesse. He took a sip, and they were suddenly both smothering their laughter behind dust-covered hands. She couldn't believe they had pulled it off! Only a few people near the coffee cart had noticed anything. They sat hidden, high above the market, watching people come and go, passing the cup between them. It was a delicious sort of secret.

When they sent the basket back down for their second cup, they caught more attention. A couple of people nudged their neighbors and pointed, laughing at the two of them on the beam. One booth owner scowled at them, as if they were somehow going to shoplift from there, armed only with a basket. Soon you could see the gossip wave move outward, with the coffee cart at its center.

Mikayla, still near the door, suddenly stretched her arms up way high, then scratched her head.

"Uh-oh," said Jesse. He scanned the market. He pointed out two men who had just come in. One was wearing carpenter pants with a couple of heavy, ugly-looking hammers hanging from the loops in his belt. The other one looked more like a park resident. He wore an odd assembly of jackets layered over each other and had the twitchy look of a meth user. The two men stood inside the entrance and surveyed the market like they owned it.

"That guy with the hammers—he works for Doc M," said Jesse. "It's time to get moving."

CeeCee took one last gulp before twisting the lid tightly on the travel mug and putting it in her bag. As she turned, her backpack knocked the basket sitting between them off the beam. It popped through the ceiling tile and dangled halfway to the floor before Jesse caught the string and reeled it back in.

More people were pointing now. That caught the attention of the burly man with the hammers, and he squinted through the holes to see what was going on. She could see the exact moment he recognized her sitting in the ceiling. His hand shot out and grabbed the twitchy guy by the shoulder. He whispered urgently in his ear, and the man hurried out the entrance.

Her blood pressure spiked, and she felt exasperated at the same time. "Well, that was obvious," she said.

"Let's beat him to the roof. We can handle that guy."

They started crawling. The man kept pace on the floor beneath them. When he passed a metal vendor, he grabbed a long pole from the scrap pile and poked it into the ceiling at them. Jesse swiped it away when it came close. They were gaining attention by the second now, and two other men walked up to Hammers. When he directed one of them outside and one to the market corner where the hole was, Jesse froze on the duct. He looked at CeeCee, alarmed.

"Shit," she summed up.

"We could wait them out. Or see if Mikayla can stir up a distraction."

"Four is still too damn many." She frowned, her mind racing through options. Even if they could jump to another roof, those men would be too close. Doc M was really starting to irritate her.

The pole jabbed through the ceiling, and CeeCee reared back out of its way.

"Knock it off!" she hollered. There was simply no point in trying to be quiet anymore.

"Oh, CeeCee," said Jesse. "I fucked up."

She got mad then because she hated the stricken look on his face. "This isn't over," she insisted hotly.

A rumbling below caught their attention. Hammers was trying to aim the pole at them again, but several market goers were yelling and pulling his arm. He swatted them away, his attention torn between watching the crowd and the ceiling. The pole jerked in his hand and knocked a man backward, causing even more of a scene around him.

"This way," she growled and flipped around to go in the opposite direction. She crawled as fast as she could. "Do you see those other guys?" she called over her shoulder. "Are they near us?"

"No, I think most of them are outside," he said.

She doubled her speed, slipping precariously on the dusty metal. She could hear the man arguing with the crowd that was yelling at him. She came to a wood beam and scrambled onto it. Jesse paused at the duct, confused.

"Get ready," she said.

"What?"

She grabbed the beam with both arms and lay on her stomach across it. Then she swung her legs hard at the ceiling tile below her and punched right through. It popped off the metal track and crashed to the ground. A cloud of disintegrating tile material billowed up where it landed. Before she could think about it too much, she dropped to hang from her hands and then let herself plummet to the floor.

She crouched low when she landed, to absorb the impact, her arms splayed wide for balance, and then jumped out of the way. Jesse landed a second after she did, graceful as always.

They were right near the entrance. Mikayla was gaping at them by the door. Hammers was still three aisles away. They dashed outside while the crowd shouted behind them. CeeCee threw one last look backward, but there were too many people for her to see anything but the pole sticking up.

Several blocks later, they finally slowed their run when it was clear no one was following them. They scrambled up a fire escape to the roof to catch their breath.

"I can't believe you did that!" Mikayla was goggling at her, all pretense at cool completely gone. "You were like a fucking ninja!"

"That was a ten-foot drop, CeeCee." Jesse looked equally concerned and impressed. "That's not too bad for one of us, but I didn't think you'd try a jump like that."

"Well, I got mad." She was still mad, actually. Her hands clenched and unclenched with leftover adrenaline. She was fully sick of people chasing her, let alone poking her with sticks. And she'd thought the way people tried to control her in the outside world was bad!

"Yes, you did. You should have seen the steam coming out of your ears. It was beautiful!"

He was so gleeful, her anger melted away, and she laughed along with him.

Then his face fell. He said seriously, "I'm so sorry I got you into that."

"You didn't get me into anything. I wanted to go. It was just bad luck that guy walked in."

"I shouldn't have gone in there without planning. I should have had a backup route."

"Really, it's okay, Jesse."

"We both should have known better," Mikayla joined in. "It's one of the first things we're taught."

"It's just, we usually run with cats, so sometimes we can go in with only a little planning, and it's still all right." He clawed agitatedly at his hair. "But we shouldn't have taken you in."

He was getting a bit worked up. She hadn't seen this side of him before. "You could have gotten hurt or taken or . . ."

"Oh, that would have been bad," said Mikayla, going pale. "Really bad!"

"Okay, you both need to stop right now! It all turned out fine!" CeeCee knew she had barked at them, but she couldn't help herself. It was hard enough dealing with her own emotions without dealing with theirs too.

Oh, said a very small voice inside her, *that's why people tell me to settle down.*

Jesse took several deep breaths, visibly trying to calm himself. Mikayla put on her bored face. "Yeah, you're right, it worked out." She shrugged.

"Damn right it did," CeeCee blustered. "We completely handled it."

Jesse still looked tense, but he gave her a wry look. "You really do have lucky magic, you know that?"

"You have lucky magic?" Mikayla asked, cocking her head to one side. "Cool."

"No, I . . ."

"I never would have thought of punching through the ceiling!" Her cool dropped away again as she gushed.

CeeCee fidgeted awkwardly. "I was just being impulsive—again." It was just like all the other times she got in trouble.

"No, that was instinct and quick thinking. That can't be taught," said Jesse.

"Yeah, making your own opening!" Mikayla agreed. "I'm totally remembering that move."

CeeCee didn't want to go over it again, so she tried brushing it off. "What? As one of desperation?"

Mikayla ignored her. "We're taught to be as quiet as possible, but that exit was worth the noise!"

"Taught for what exactly?" she asked purposely. It was embarrassing the way Mikayla was going on. CeeCee knew the cats had secrets, and she bet questioning Mikayla would get her to stop gushing. Plus, maybe she'd learn about the mystery—win-win.

"Oh, um . . ." Mikayla stammered right on cue. "So, I gotta get going. Catch you guys later." She shot to the side of the roof. "It was fun!" she threw back over her shoulder.

CeeCee and Jesse were left, one bemused and one distracted, as Mikayla disappeared down a fire escape.

SIXTEEN

Play Me
Like a Mannequin

They stood awkwardly for a moment. She could tell Jesse was still upset. She fished her coffee mug out and took a swallow with an exaggerated, "*Mmm,*" then handed it to him. "Totally worth it," she said firmly.

He smiled sheepishly, another new look for him. "Sorry, I . . ." He shook his head. "We spend so much time planning, it's hard not to obsess over what can go wrong. I still shouldn't have taken you there."

She tried on his confidence. "I think I handled it marvelously, thank you," she said grandly.

"You did, actually."

"We're pretty badass," she continued, cajoling.

The tension in his face eased. "Yeah, we are!"

They beamed at each other, in triumph and amusement and spent stress. They kept grinning, standing like goofballs on the roof. It was long enough for her to think about how nice his smile was and how fun he was and how he was more interesting than anyone she had ever met. And she was just starting to get to know him. She wanted to hang out with him more. Like, if she could see him every day, she'd be pretty happy. If she got stuck here, at least it would be with him. In fact, maybe he would be a good reason to never leave.

The thought cascaded over her like cold water down her back.

"Oh," she said. She stepped away and looked out over the edge of the building, at torn paper blowing down the alley. Her face felt as rigid as stone.

"Are you okay?"

He looked at her questioningly, but that grin still hung around his lips, like they'd be laughing again at any moment.

She couldn't like him . . . not this much. She couldn't fall for someone in this strange, mad, forgotten place! What was wrong with her?

"I need to go see the Queen now," she said, firm and hollow. Would Doc M start chasing him, too, now that they'd been seen together? She stifled a shiver as the cold coursed over her again.

His face fell, and a moment of panic crawled across it again. "I really don't think you should. We can find another way."

"We've tried the other ways."

"There are still options. Maybe we can bribe someone. It might take some time, but . . ."

"With what money? You said it yourself; I can't wait too long." She sounded so reasonable, it was like it wasn't even hurting her to argue with him.

"But, CeeCee!" He grabbed her by the shoulders. "She's dangerous! I didn't want to say it before, but she is. If you catch her at the wrong time, people go . . ."

She interrupted him with a shout. "It's dangerous here! Jesse, we saw two dead men last night!"

"I know, but . . ."

"I think she's my best bet. I can handle her."

He dropped his hands to his sides.

"You said you would take me to her."

"I never said that." He crossed his arms and for a moment looked ugly stubborn.

"Jesse!" She stared at him until he went from mad to guilty.

"Fine."

They walked, silent and resigned, by rooftop before descending to the street. It wasn't far, and it went by too quickly.

Jesse escorted her to a door. This alley was just like all the other alleys, but the door was different. They were double stainless steel ones, and there was an exaggerated heart etched into each side like a logo. Not a speck of dirt was on or around the entrance.

"This is it?" she asked.

"This is it." He didn't seem angry. Just withdrawn.

"Do I knock, or do I need one of those keys?"

"No, you just walk in."

She blinked slowly at him. It scared her, how easy it was all of a sudden.

"You can't go in with me, can you?"

"It's probably better if I stay here." He took a deep breath and let it out shakily. "Sometimes she likes me, and sometimes"—he shrugged—"she likes no one. I don't want to give her a reason not to help you."

"If she doesn't help me . . ."

"Then I'll be waiting."

CeeCee's heart was ripping. She could feel it. Ceiling-tile dust was still in Jesse's hair, and his confidence seemed to have disappeared. She leaned up and kissed him very softly on the cheek. His eyes were hard to look at as she turned away. "Okay."

She opened the door and found a brightly clean, long corridor. Her boots echoed loudly off the tile as she walked down it. At the end, she found an upscale waiting room with a reception desk hulking authoritatively next to an elevator. A large version of the heart logo from the door took up one wall. Cushioned chairs and end tables were scattered around the room. Everything was coordinated in sleek gray and silver, with pops of vibrant red.

A silver mirror hung behind the reception desk. CeeCee caught a vivid look at herself. Her lank hair needed a wash. Her clothes were dirty and smeared with grime, and one of her jean pockets had gotten caught on something somewhere and was hanging down, trailing threads. A gray swipe of dust from the market was all down one side of her hoodie. She slid her backpack off her shoulder and saw dirt under her nails.

She knew suddenly that she looked like she belonged to the byways, and that scared her more than the slug man or Doc M or anything the Queen could throw at her.

She stood uncertainly in front of the desk.

The receptionist had bright, candy-apple red hair in a model's bob. She stared at her with arched eyebrows, crisp and efficient.

"Yes, I'd like to see the Queen?" CeeCee tried to be firm, but she heard the anxiety in her own voice.

"Write your name and take a seat, please." The lady pushed a pen and clipboard toward her.

She rolled the pen between her hands nervously. Under "reason for visit" CeeCee wrote "key." Other people sat waiting, reading magazines, and she joined them, a little stunned. After two nights in the alleys, she felt awkward and dirty and out of place in the high-end room. The man next to her had grayish skin and a head that was rather shaped like a rhino's, but he was wearing a smart sports coat and looked like he had taken some care to clean up.

She stood up abruptly. "Excuse me, is there a bathroom I could use?"

The receptionist looked at her with knowing eyes. "Right over there." She pointed to a corner door tastefully hidden by a potted tree.

In the bathroom, there was actual soap and everything was sparkling clean. CeeCee washed her face and hands and wiped down her backpack and jeans with damp paper towels. She shook her hoodie out vigorously and managed to get off most of the dust. Then she ran a wet towel around her neck and under her armpits. She stared at herself in the mirror. Just in case, she touched the mirror with her outstretched fingers and pushed. It held firm. Her eyes were beginning to form shadows from lack of sleep, but all in all, she looked . . . not her best, but better, like she had made an effort.

She had a feeling that looking like she tried would make a difference. The fancy lobby, the comment Jesse had made about the Queen's hair . . . this Queen seemed to care a lot about appearances.

In the waiting room, she sat back down next to a woman with worry lines etched around her mouth and tissues poking out of pockets. The lady's hands kept clenching together in her lap, but she gave CeeCee an automatic mom smile as she sat down, tiredly welcoming.

The receptionist chirped out a name, and the lady hopped up and hurried to the elevator. CeeCee sat alone and fretted.

It was just like sitting outside of the principal's office—except at least after that, she knew she could go home. Now that she was here, she realized she didn't know what to say. Should she talk about Doc M chasing her? No, Suspenders had made it sound like the Queen and Doc M were friends. If she started bashing him, the Queen might not like it. Anxiety rose up sharp as a knife inside her. Better not to mention him at all. What then? To calm her nerves, she pulled out her notebook and started writing lyrics on a fresh page. Even though her hand was moving, she didn't know what she wrote.

God, how the waiting killed her.

"CeeCee Harper?" The candy red hair nodded in her direction.

She stood up, and the receptionist pushed a button for the elevator. It was at her desk, not on the wall next to the door, so not just anyone could go up. With a queasy feeling, CeeCee stepped into the too-small booth. The air felt staticky and unpleasant. Only one button was inside the elevator, too, and no floors listed—one way in and one way out.

The elevator pinged, and the doors slid open. She faced a floor-to-ceiling window in another slick waiting room. This lobby followed the same decor theme as the one downstairs, except it felt more moneyed, more exclusive, more . . . everything.

Regal, CeeCee thought. It was a stark contrast to the people she had seen living in the alleys.

She stepped gingerly out of the elevator. The carpet was rich and plush and white, except for a red runner that cut a bloody swath across it to a set of towering double doors. At a sleek, modern desk, a lady with auburn hair looked up. She was just as sharply dressed as the receptionist downstairs, but she seemed more harried and had piles of paperwork and a laptop on her desk.

"Hi, I'm here to see the Queen."

The assistant looked CeeCee over carefully, but her manner was warmer than the lady below. "Are you applying to the service? You look a little young," she asked kindly.

"The service? I'm not sure. I'm here about a . . . key? You see, I . . . I stumbled into the byways by accident, and it was all just a terrible mistake, and I tried the halfway shops and the mirrors, but those didn't work, so I'm really, really hoping that the Queen can help me get home." Her pitch wasn't coming out as strong as she'd hoped. "Because I heard she's really nice like that," CeeCee finished faintly.

The assistant's eyes narrowed worriedly at her, and she said in a low voice, "She's not in a good mood."

CeeCee bit her lip. That invisible deadline loomed again, especially now that she knew she looked halfway to homeless. She had made it all the way here; she couldn't give up now. "I've been gone for two days. My mom will be really worried."

The woman sighed and jotted a note down on a clipboard. "It'll be a few moments." She nodded toward a chair.

The chair was pristinely white and CeeCee was afraid she'd smudge it, so she stepped up to the window and looked out. She tried to come up with a better speech for the Queen in her head. The view here was the same as from the rooftops, but somehow she knew she wasn't in the byways anymore. Home was really— she pressed her hand against the glass—only an inch away.

It was an agonizingly long time before the assistant waved her over. The woman shot her a look, then opened the door, bobbed in a curtsy, and announced, "Your Grace, this is CeeCee Harper. She is here to request a key."

Luxury, CeeCee realized, made her twitchy. The Queen's room was even fancier than the rest of the building. There were art pieces on pedestals, and crystal decanters, and beautiful flower arrangements in glass vases. She stepped into the room warily, as if she could break something just by looking at it. The floor-to-ceiling windows continued, but the carpet melded from white to crimson red. A massive white desk dominated the room, all carved wood and gold gilt, chilly in its supremacy, with a chair that easily could have been called a throne.

There was also a private elevator in the office. Hope sounded like a bell inside CeeCee. She bet, she just bet, that was the one that led out. Her feet itched to run to it, but she stayed frozen by the door.

Behind the desk sat the Queen. She frowned at a laptop while simultaneously scrolling through her phone. She was extremely polished, like an aging model or high-powered executive. Her dark hair was cut at a chic shoulder length, and she wore a designer black-and-gray leather jacket over a white blouse, impeccably tailored red velvet pants, and strappy peephole pumps. Even though the clothes were modern, she looked every inch like royalty.

When she finally looked up, her eyes were sharp and black and voracious in an undefined way, like she was waiting to see what was on offer before she decided if she was hungry.

CeeCee stood stunned a moment before dropping into an awkward curtsy.

"Your Grace, I . . . I'm here to ask for your help . . ."

"You may approach." The Queen waved impatiently.

When CeeCee reached the front of the desk, she curtsied again, rattled. She hadn't *really* thought the woman would be an actual queen, but now that she was in front of her, she couldn't think of her as anything else. She wasn't sure who was supposed to speak first. After a moment, the Queen raised her eyebrows at her and sighed heavily.

"Excuse me, Your Grace," CeeCee launched into her speech. "I've heard about your generosity, and I'm hoping you can help me. You see, two days ago, I was walking home from school when I accidentally got lost, and I'm not quite sure how it happened, but I . . ."

"So you would like a key, would you?" the Queen interrupted.

"Yes! Yes, Your Grace." She paused awkwardly. "Or just passage out of the byways. I don't need a key, per se. I really just want to go home. I don't need to come back in again." Jesse flashed through her mind and her heart hurt as she said it, but she pushed on. "I mean, if that's easier."

"I only give keys." The Queen measured CeeCee with her eyes.

"Oh, okay."

"If they've been earned."

"Oh," she said faintly, "I see," even though she didn't. Having to "earn" the key had never occurred to her, but maybe that was part of working the deal. So she waited. Because her speech was shot, and she knew this was another part where you waited. Her stomach clenched as she did it.

"Do you? I'm a businesswoman, after all."

That caught her attention. She forced interest into her voice. "Really? What kind of business?"

"I run an online relationship service, HeartsAlight.com. I'm sure you've heard of it; we're one of the top services."

"You mean a dating site?" CeeCee asked carefully because part of her thought "relationship service" sounded a lot like prostitution. The same wariness she had felt with the washer woman was creeping down her spine. But why would she be getting that feeling from the Queen? It's not like she was brandishing a knife!

The Queen smiled sharply. "That's a very small-minded view of what we do. Dating sites are for people who want to hook up— once, twice, move on. They are for people who don't understand commitment. We specialize in helping people find long-term and meaningful relationships. It's a very hard road for a lot of people. We help them."

"Wow," said CeeCee. "That's great. I'm sure you've helped lots of people." She hadn't heard of the site, top service or not, but she'd take the Queen's word for it. At least she had remembered to kiss ass—that was progress. She laced her fingers in front of her to stop them from fidgeting.

"Of course, you're still quite young." Condescension dripped off the Queen's lips. "You have all your youth to waste before you appreciate what's important. The young are so reckless; they don't understand the work it takes. It's very difficult to find love in this world. Sometimes, you have to make your own." There was a knock at her office door. "What?"

The assistant's head peeked around the crack in the door. "It's time for your treatment, Your Grace."

The queen waved her away. She opened a desk drawer and pulled out a ready-to-go syringe, alcohol wipes, and cotton pads. She hiked up her shirt and used one of the alcohol wipes on her belly. She leaned against the desk as she unwrapped the syringe from its sterilized plastic wrap. It was strangely intimate, and CeeCee forced herself to look away from the Queen's stomach and back at her face.

The Queen's eyes glittered, bitter and dark.

"I hope you don't mind," she said in a tone that meant anything but that. "I'm on day three of my cycle. Fertility treatments have to stay on schedule. I have an IUI round coming up!" she changed to an overly cheerful singsong. "But you wouldn't know about that, would you?" She pinched skin and inserted the needle into her white belly, coaxing the plunger down with a practiced motion. "*You'll* probably get pregnant without even realizing it—drunk and partying and knocked up behind the bleachers one night, like a little tramp." She smiled viciously. "Kidding."

It was the kind of comment Taylor and her cronies would make, but it was a smoother venom. CeeCee's heart sank. The Queen already disliked her, that was obvious, but she hoped she would still be open to a deal . . . if she could think of something to offer. "I'm just trying to get home. Your Grace, I . . . humbly . . . request your assistance."

"Have you seen the keys? Shall I show you?" Without

waiting for an answer, the Queen tossed the used needle in the trash and pushed an intercom button on her phone. "Michelle, come in here."

The assistant popped her head in instantly. "Yes, Your Grace?"

"Show the girl your key." She said the word "girl" like it was dirty.

Michelle turned back the cuff of her sleeve and held her palm up to CeeCee. On her wrist was a stylized heart tattoo, the same heart that was on the logo. CeeCee remembered, suddenly, the rhino man's Hokey Pokey dance in front of the door with the heart scratched in it. He must have had a tattoo.

"So you see, it's not something I hand out willy-nilly," the Queen said smugly. "You'll have to undergo a couple of hours with my corporate tattoo alchemist, and then the finished product is subject to my approval afterward. And, of course, it can only be removed by my approval as well. I've had supplicants go through the process several times before getting it just right. You'll be representing me out in the world. I can't have my brand bastardized."

CeeCee's heart dropped all the way to her stomach. She didn't want anything permanent or painful or to be a toy doll for the Queen's amusement! Jesse had warned her. He had warned her, and she hadn't listened. She didn't have anything against tattoos per se, but she always thought that if she got one, it would be her own idea. But . . . if that were the way out, wouldn't it be worth it? It would be just a little pain and then home. She just had to negotiate.

Her mom was going to kill her.

"So . . . why should I give it to you?"

"I could work for you after school." CeeCee tried sounding chipper and industrious. "Run errands or any help you need. I learn fast. Free labor is cost-effective for a company."

"Oh, I think not. I'm tired of pretty young things cluttering up my court."

"It doesn't have to be in the office—I could work online! Then I wouldn't be in the way. I'm a whiz at social media, and all my friends are too. I could network, bring you new clients."

"Please. The people you know are hardly my target audience."

Crap, those were her best ideas. "Maybe help in another capacity? Like dog sitting or . . ." she trailed off.

The Queen managed to look bored and sneer at the same time.

"I can pay you," CeeCee offered, even though she knew she couldn't. She'd figure something out. She just hoped the Queen would take a payment plan.

"Do I look like I need money?" The Queen actually looked offended. Her dislike seemed to increase.

CeeCee squared her shoulders and faced her head-on. "You could just let me walk out a door. You won't ever have to see me again."

"I could." She smiled cruelly. "But why should I?"

CeeCee racked her brain for a better offer. Maybe the Queen wanted something from the outside? Maybe something her mom could help with? "What do you want?" she asked finally.

The Queen tapped her fingers on her lips and considered it. She looked CeeCee up and down, assessing her with a little frown. It made CeeCee feel small, and her temper started to fray at the edges.

"You look healthy, and none too worse for wear for being in the byways a few days, so you must be strong." She breathed in deeply. "I don't smell any addiction on you."

The wariness screamed at her, and CeeCee's heart beat hard in her ears. She didn't know if she was more alarmed by the Queen's tone or the fact that the woman had just *smelled* her.

"I could use a healthy young woman in my back pocket—just for shits and giggles, you understand. I highly doubt that *your* chances would be better than mine, however much you commoners breed."

"I . . . don't know what you mean."

"I'd like some insurance if the fertility treatments fail. I'm proposing two contracts: First, you would act as my surrogate, if for some reason I'm not able to implant and carry to term. Second, I'd like you to be tested for egg viability, and if it ever came down to it, your eggs can be either donated or you would be inseminated with a donor of my choosing. Of course, this would be an open-ended contract. I'd need at least ten years to exercise my options, if not more."

CeeCee's mind, usually racing, came to a standstill. It took her a moment to work through the Queen's words. "You want me to have a baby? If you can't get pregnant?" she asked slowly. This situation couldn't be happening.

"I highly doubt I'll need it," the Queen spat out. "But just in case, it's good to have a contingency plan."

Her blood went cold. She'd learned that "just in case" happened a lot in the byways.

"What I'm really offering you," said the Queen, brisk and patronizing, "is the chance to set yourself up nicely. You'd be well taken care of while you gestate, and then you can go on with your little life. Just think: a nice payoff and none of the responsibility of a child. You can go right back to partying. Motherhood is wasted on the young anyway."

It would be ridiculously funny if it wasn't so horrifying. CeeCee had never even had a regular boyfriend, and this woman wanted her to have a baby! What's more, she knew on a gut level that this woman would hate her intensely if she even agreed, whether she had the baby or not. Stay in the byways on her own or be subject to the angry whims of this woman for ten years. That wasn't even a choice.

"I'm sorry, but I can't do that," she gasped.

"Now don't be stupid. The plan I've laid out is quite generous for one of your class."

"One of my class," she repeated. *They'll stick you, hoity-toity-like.* Anger flared, but for once was buried under her shock. Really, this was just unbelievable—too impossible to even touch her.

"I'm sure you have your little dreams and goals, but really, what are you going to amount to out there? Clearly the byways have already marked you. That says something about a person. You'll probably finish school, get a dead-end job, pop out a couple of kids—if you don't get knocked up earlier." The envy dripping off that last part was clear. "Then it'll be a life of bad decisions and alcohol or some other nonsense, and eventually you'll just wander back in here again. It's only a matter of time."

She sounded a bit like Doc M.

The Queen leaned forward and pierced CeeCee with disdain sharpened to a fine point. "At least my way, you can be useful, instead of just a waste. But you know that, don't you?" she purred.

CeeCee's brain kicked back into high gear again. With a start, she realized she did know. She knew who she was. And it wasn't anything the Queen thought.

"I'm not who you think I am, Your Grace," she said. She smiled prettily. It felt good to say it out loud. Really good. She hadn't recognized how terribly tired she was of hearing about herself from other people, making their beliefs her own.

The Queen's voice became perilously soft and slinky. "I do hope you're not under the delusion that you're too good to carry a royal child." Her eyes went even darker, and a tiny chilling smile played around her lips. "Maybe you should be detained until you learn not to insult your betters."

There was the trap. Fear and anger crackled through CeeCee's head and chest and swirled down to her fists. The trap was there the whole time—no matter how CeeCee answered, the Queen would have someone to abuse. That's what Jesse had been trying to tell her. That's why she had that creepy feeling. The Queen had just been waiting to pounce. Holy shit. She could be in real danger of never leaving this building, much less the byways! Time seemed to freeze for an instant. Her hands twitched, but she forced them to stay relaxed and open while her mind raced. This woman was not the bullies at school or some random street thug. But now she understood why Jesse could make a trade on compliments. Now she knew what the Queen wanted. CeeCee stood up straight and thought about flying.

Then she flew in a completely new direction.

"Anyone would be honored to carry your child, Your Grace," she declared, "but I know that you won't need me. You'll have a baby and very soon."

"How would you possibly know that?"

"I have lucky magic," she said boldly, putting all her belief into it, like it had never been anything different.

The Queen cocked her head to the side and gave her a look of stone. "Really."

"How do you think I survived two days in the byways?"

"I think you had help. Or you're full of bullshit." The Queen's tone was flat, but a snip of interest was hiding behind it.

"Or I was very lucky. A dumb kid like me, I wouldn't have made it otherwise. I ran into the jib jab twice." She channeled all her power and emotion into making it true. She wasn't going to be bullied into that horrible deal, but she couldn't go to jail, either, or whatever the equivalent was here. That would make her belong to the byways for sure. "You know magic is real. You live in it every day."

The Queen's eyebrows had shot up when CeeCee mentioned the jib jab. "Maybe," she said. "What's your luck have to do with me?"

"I can make a wish for you, and my lucky magic will make it happen."

"That's not worth a key," the Queen scoffed, but there was a glimmer of hope in her eyes underneath the bitterness and desperation. She stood taller, too, mimicking CeeCee's stance. "It *might* be worth a key nine months from now."

"It's a gift, Your Grace, for seeing me." She stood eye to eye with the Queen now. They were almost the same height.

"Oh, you're giving me a gift? How special."

"Royalty deserves the best, Your Grace. And you are every inch royalty. It's an honor to share my luck with you, and my magic gets even stronger when it's *freely* given." She let the hint hang in the air.

The Queen glowered at her. She wanted the wish, no matter how unlikely it was to work. She wanted the wish and she hated her for it, especially since CeeCee had neatly taken away the threat of detainment. CeeCee stood ramrod straight, in agonizing silence, as the Queen angrily mulled it over.

"Make the wish, then," the Queen snarled finally. "Make it, and we'll see. Leave now."

"Thank you, Your Grace. I hope you'll remember me favorably when everything works out." She knew she was pushing it, but she had to convince this woman. She dropped into a deep curtsy before turning to leave. She heard the Queen push the intercom.

"Girl!" the Queen called.

CeeCee paused just outside the door.

"You better watch your step. I will remember you. And you don't want me remembering you."

With that threat, the door closed in her face.

SEVENTEEN

Voices Are Calling Me

CeeCee's legs shook all the way down in the elevator. She forced herself to march stiffly past the receptionist at a normal pace before rushing through the door into the empty alley. For a brief, horrible moment, she thought Jesse had left. She'd been inside a lot longer than she'd planned; maybe he thought she went home. Then a small noise alerted her, and she saw a brown cat sitting attentively on top of a wall. He'd found a sunny spot only a few yards away.

"Jesse!" The sound of her own fear made tears rush to the surface.

He jumped, turning from a cat to a man before he hit the ground. He swept her up in a ferocious hug. She clung to him.

"I'm sorry," she whispered. "I'm sorry."

"I know it's selfish, but I'm really glad you're still here," he said in her ear.

"I almost didn't get out," she babbled back. "I pissed her off.

I didn't mean to, but I did." She thought back over the conversation. "Or maybe she was mad before I got there. She threatened to jail me. I managed to get out of it."

He pulled back, looking scared and angry. "How?"

"I told her I had lucky magic and I'd make a wish for her." She drew in a shaky breath. "I told her it would only work if I was free. She's trying to have a baby. Did you know that?"

He laughed out loud, relief showing in his face. Then he leaned forward and kissed her.

It was a revelation, and not one at all. She fell into his kiss. His lips were so warm and so were his arms. The whole world blinked out, out of their lives, out of that moment. There was nothing but breath and soft skin. She kissed him back until her teeth hurt.

When they finally pulled back, she wasn't sure what her face looked like, but she suspected she looked like a goof. And she absolutely didn't care because he looked marvelous. His eyes were very gold and very solemn, and they had a light that glinted in the sun. She wanted to look at that light forever.

He put his hands up to her face and brushed his thumbs across her cheekbones very gently, until she couldn't stand it any longer. She reached up and kissed him again.

"Okay, then," he said very quietly.

It was stupid to be afraid of this, especially to run to the Queen.

She looked back at the Queen's door and decided she was still too close to her for comfort. "Let's get the fuck out of here."

He kept his arm across the small of her back as they walked away. She leaned into him as much as she could without breaking their hurried stride down a path bordered by wood fences. Trees and lush vegetation could be glimpsed just on the other side, backyard gardens creeping over the edges.

"What did she say? She wouldn't negotiate with you at all?" Jesse asked.

"No, she wanted to negotiate. It's just . . . you know when someone is setting you up for a deal that's going to screw you? No matter what you did?"

"Yeah. She was in a bad mood, then."

She should have listened to that and come back another time. Probably . . . she should start listening to her gut instincts too. Rushing to the Queen when she got scared by her feelings for Jesse—that was impulsive, dumb. But her wariness of the Queen was right on the mark. "She was horrible! But she wasn't . . . it wasn't like. . . ." She sighed heavily. "I've run into that before. She basically said the same shitty things that other people have said to me. She's just more intense and a lot better at it than most people I've met."

"I'm sorry she was like that. She has to spit venom because otherwise she'd have to swallow it herself."

That was an interesting way to look at it. The Queen's source of misery was obvious. CeeCee thought about Beauchamp and Taylor and suddenly wondered what their venom was about. Maybe it didn't have anything to do with her, and she just got caught in their bad moods—not that CeeCee forgave any of them, especially the Queen. "Yeah, well, she said I wasn't going to amount to anything, so I might as well be useful and have a *baby* for her! That was her price for a key out."

Jesse stopped dead and sputtered for a full minute, which was so un-catlike, she looked at him with real concern. Then, even though some of his speech was still hard to understand, he went on a full-scale rant. She decided not to tell him about the ten-year clause.

She didn't feel as devastated as she thought she would after the Queen's games—freaked out, yes, but not hurt. The Queen's words kept replaying in her mind, but instead of stinging or making her fall into a shame cycle, it was like she could hold the comments up and analyze them from a distance. Could she have changed that much in her short time here? She had managed two days in the byways, and she realized now that that was an accomplishment. Even the Queen had said she must be strong—strong enough to know who she was, despite what anyone said.

She still needed to get home, though.

When Jesse finally caught his breath, she asked him, "What do we do now? Bribe someone at a halfway shop? We'll have to figure out how to make some money."

"I think we should try the mirrors again first. If you practice, I think it'll work eventually."

"Okay," she said slowly.

"Have you thought any more about how you got stuck?"

She flashed back to the impossibly skinny alley two days before and tried to think it through, tried to hold the events at a distance and analyze them. "Maybe my frustration? I was so sick of school that day. I have this teacher who hates me, and they want me to take his class again." Something the Queen said was niggling at the back of her mind, but she couldn't quite catch it. "I wanted to be anywhere but there," she continued. "Then I had a fight with my best friend. I was really mad, and I ran out of school."

"What was the fight about?" he asked.

"It feels stupid now. We had plans, and she canceled on me. She's on all these committees, and there was a mix-up with money. She said the others might think I took it because of my reputation. I know she didn't mean it the way it came out, but I got so pissed." The hurt had faded since their fight, but she still felt the frustration. "Do you know that I've never actually gotten in trouble with the law? But somehow they all keep waiting for it to happen, like it's inevitable because it's me. Like I was pre-disposed to be a criminal. That's why I took the rabbit—because I just had to go and prove everyone right!" Even to her own ears, she sounded exasperated at herself.

"The rabbit?" He sounded confused and skeptical at the same time.

"Yeah, the rabbit," she said distantly. "I stole a rabbit key chain."

"I still don't think stealing would do it . . ." Jesse was saying, but she hardly heard him.

Make yourself useful. That's what the Queen had said, and she'd done the exact opposite. But it wasn't in the Queen's office that she'd felt that way—it was right before the skinny alley.

"Holy crap." She looked at him with wondering eyes. "I felt useless. I was mad at myself and thought I couldn't do anything right. That's when I got stuck. I made this happen; I made myself useless." Her mind whirred.

Jesse stopped and held her by the shoulders. His eyes were intense with belief. She expected him to start flying at any min-ute. "You are the least useless person I know."

Her breath went out in a rush. She hadn't realized she'd been holding it. It felt like she'd been holding it her whole life. "I know. I finally figured that out." She knew she made mistakes some-times, but she wasn't useless. She had talents, even if they weren't traditional. She was damn good at thinking on her feet, for one. She stared at him, and her throat grew hot and tight. It wasn't just that she liked him, that he made her laugh or thought she was cool. He wasn't just a really cute guy. It went deeper than that. "You actually see me, don't you?"

His brows furrowed. "That is a strange question."

She swallowed hard. "Maybe in here it is, but out there? Peo-ple don't always see a lot out there."

"Yes, I see you. Don't you see me?"

This man, this cat, who was entirely himself; who looked puzzled right now; who took her exactly as she was, always; who knew who he was in the world around him; who knew the trick to everything, even when he didn't—she saw him.

"Yes," she said, flabbergasted.

He still looked perplexed, but he drew her into a hug. "I don't want you to ever feel useless."

"Thank you," she said sincerely. "After being here, I don't think it's going to happen that often anymore."

"Good," he said. "This helps us, though! Once you know why the byways took you, it'll help you master the mirrors."

He smiled and leaned against the fence, pulling her with him until the wood groaned behind them. An apple tree had grown over the backyard fence. It was studded with late-season fruit at the top, but on their side of the alley, the apples had been picked clean.

"Once you master the mirrors," he said, smug and pleased, "you can go back and forth anytime you want." His grin was the widest she'd seen yet. Then he leaned in and whispered, "But I would have visited you anyway."

She smiled back so hard, it hurt.

They made their way slowly through the alleys. Now that they knew they were heading back to the mirrors, they dragged their feet in silent agreement, enjoying the afternoon together. The visit with the Queen was behind them, and they hadn't seen any of Doc M's men for hours. CeeCee tangled her fingers with his, and Jesse took her on a long circuitous route, pointing out new landmarks. Every time they passed a place she knew, she told him what had happened there, and they would stop and lean, wrapped against each other on a convenient wall.

They walked near the shopping cart sculpture and around a corner was a parking lot of unbroken carts. The carts were embellished with fancy wheels and ornate metal, cracked gems and fancy ribbons—far more interesting than the ones outside the byways. While she admired them, a small man came by with three brooms, put them in one of the carts, and wheeled it away.

They passed a three-story brick building completely overgrown with ivy. It looked like a giant leafy square. At the windows, faces looked out at them, and they all looked furry or feathery, mousy brown or brightly colored. An older woman with brilliant blue hair shouted something unintelligible as they walked by.

CeeCee looked at Jesse, and he shrugged with a wry grin.

"Some people just don't like cats," he said. "I have no idea why."

"Could it be that she's"—she widened her eyes in sardonic innocence—"a bird person? And cats eat birds?"

"Yes," Jesse answered and laughed. "Yeah, that might have something to do with it."

There were places that Jesse steered her away from completely: an aging Victorian that looked like it would collapse at any moment; a straight shot of an alley that looked like it was an easy walk to the next street but gave her vertigo when she looked down it. She knew instinctively there was something wrong with it. "What's in there?" she asked.

"Didn't you say you ran into the caterpillar?"

"You mean that pervert slug man who was into child porn?"

"Yes. There are others who are dangerous in the byways. Some of them lay traps to lure people in."

She shuddered. "Is that what the slug man was doing, trying to lure me in?"

Jesse made a face. "He's actually too lazy to set a trap, but I'm sure he was delighted when you wandered in anyway."

She was getting a better idea of the byways, but it was still so much larger than she thought could possibly fit in the alleys of her city.

They walked down a twisting lane with a low wall. CeeCee recognized it as the one near the mushroom alley. Maybe they could peek their heads around the corner again. She smiled, remembering how cocky and irritating she thought Jesse had been. She turned to tease him, when something caught the corner of her eye.

A man wavered indecisively at the entrance, half-camouflaged by shadow. The alley of mushrooms looked like a gaping maw ready to swallow him. With a start, CeeCee realized it was Apple Cheeks. "Jesse, look!"

"What?"

But she was already running to the entrance, and she grabbed him by the shoulder. "What are you doing?"

Apple Cheeks jumped and stared at her. "Oh! Hello, dear. I ...I'm ..."

"You can't go in there!" She peered into his face. He looked shaken and more rumpled than usual. A dark smear was streaked across his forehead. She thought it might be blood. "Oh my god! What happened?" she asked, breathless, as Jesse caught up to her.

"Oh, my dear, my things were taken! And my little house torn down," he said. Anger suffused his features in a pale wash. "They broke my house!"

"Who did?" Now she was angry too.

"Oh, men, men. Scoundrels, all of them." He looked down instead of meeting her eyes.

With a sick certainty, CeeCee knew it was her fault. They were men looking for her, either Doc M himself or men working for him. She'd been having so much fun with Jesse, she'd forgotten for a moment. They had attacked Apple Cheeks to get to her! She looked at Jesse, appalled.

"Don't," he said. "Don't—it wasn't you."

But guilt clawed at her throat. "What are you doing here?" she asked Apple Cheeks.

"I was just . . . so hungry. I thought maybe only until things turn around," he said sadly. "And no one looks for you here. I mean, if they came back."

"You can't go in there; you know that," she said gently.

He shook himself. "But of course you're right, my dear. I was just having a moment."

"We'll get you some food." She turned to Jesse. "Won't we?"

"Yes," Jesse said.

She raised her eyebrows at him in a silent question, and he jerked his chin in the direction they should go. When she took a step away from the alley entrance, Apple Cheeks followed. She breathed a sigh of relief.

Jesse asked him, "When did this happen?"

"Yesterday evening. I was just setting to make dinner."

"We can go to the gathering then," said Jesse, pointing the way.

"But I don't have anything to bring!" Apple Cheeks looked up, dismayed and agitated. "They took everything!"

"Don't worry," Jesse said soothingly. "We'll take care of it."

As they walked, she noticed Apple Cheeks had a few new tears in his grubby clothes, but he didn't smell quite so much like urine as he had before—or maybe she'd gotten used to it. He seemed smaller, if that was possible. All the sparkle that had buoyed him up was gone. He looked very glum in a way that was beyond hunger.

"Are you okay? I promise we'll get you something to eat." CeeCee patted him on the arm, feeling how inadequate her words were.

"They took some of my things . . . some things that were important to me, from when I lived out there."

"What did they take?"

"An old photo. I had a little boy once, before the byways. He's all grown up now, but I like to remember when he was little. I promised that I would always keep it." He sounded so terribly heartbroken. "These are the letpasses and the letdowns," he whispered.

She looked at Jesse, stricken.

"They probably would have taken it to the warehouse, if it was Doc M's men," Jesse explained. "They do that sometimes."

CeeCee felt sick. If it weren't for her, he never would have been attacked. Even worse, what would he do when she was gone? Sure, they could take care of him right now, but Apple Cheeks didn't have anything to trade for his next meal. She flailed around for a solution.

"Do you know Kelly? She has a garden," she suggested. "If you're running low on food, you could ask her. She doesn't eat much."

"Do you mean the grave dirt girl? Oh dear, I hear she doesn't like visitors much. Visiting her is like visiting your own grave!" said Apple Cheeks.

"Oh no! She's really very nice."

"I heard the same thing," said Jesse. "You can see your death in her garden."

"You can't really believe that. She helped me! I'm surprised you haven't met her," she said, thinking how much Jesse would laugh at Kelly's jokes.

"I don't know if I believe it, but I know what she can do. She chases everyone away, especially men. I've been by as a cat." He shrugged. "I wouldn't go like this. She doesn't seem to want the company, and she has the power to keep it that way."

It occurred to CeeCee that Kelly might still be hiding in her room, even here. A wave of sadness crashed over her. These are the byways and the bypassed. "Actually, I think she's a little lonely," she said softly.

She found Jesse's hand and held it so hard that she was sure she hurt him, but he never made a sound.

Jesse stopped at a fork in the path and looked keenly at Apple Cheeks. "We have to make a stop before we go. Why don't you meet us at the gathering?"

Apple Cheeks looked anxious, like he thought they would ditch him. "Don't you think I should stay with you?" he asked quickly. "I can help, my dear."

CeeCee put a hand on his arm. She looked at Jesse for an explanation.

"They're still looking for her," he said. "It's probably safer if you're not seen with us right now. We'll meet you there."

"Promise," she added, forcing cheer into her voice.

"Such a sweet dear!" he said, before walking down one branch of the path.

Jesse urged her down the other.

"Do you think he'll be all right?" she asked.

"I doubt they'll bother him again. Most of the men who are Doc's clients are only organized in short bursts. If he doesn't keep dangling a reward in front of them, they'll go back to their own business. And if they don't see you for a while, they'll get bored and give up."

That made sense, considering what she had seen of the men at the park. "What about the others?" she asked. "The ones who work for him? Like that guy with the hammers."

He looked her in the eyes, steady and true. "They're a problem," he admitted, "but there aren't as many of them, and none of them are welcome at the gathering. Even if they dared to show up, they wouldn't be allowed in."

Jesse turned down a snaking dirt trail. It wove in between buildings and behind fences, the dirt packed hard under their feet. Then the trail opened into a hidden back lot. A wrought iron fence guarded a courtyard full of sunny light, and men in uniform lounged in front of the gate. Tall rose bushes and sunflowers bobbed their heads above the railing.

"That's one of the Queen's gardens," said Jesse. "You used to be able to walk through it."

"Eugenia said she had been taking over the gardens."

"She has her own, but most of the gardens were planted by the people here over time, in strips of alleys and open lots. Little spaces that were left behind while the city grew. They shared the work and the crops. The Queen started setting guards in front of them a while ago."

"Why?"

"She's the Queen. It's all hers anyway."

CeeCee thought that was both unfair and unenforceable. Her chin set stubbornly. She wanted to argue, but she knew she was arguing from a democratic point of view. Suddenly, Eugenia's comment about not getting the essentials took on more weight. CeeCee had thought she was talking about items like Band-Aids or Tupperware. She knew food was hard to come by in the byways. She didn't realize food was available and the Queen was actively blocking access to it!

"Let's see if we can get in," Jesse said.

Before she could say anything, he walked up to the guards on duty. CeeCee's shoulders tensed. When she edged closer, she noticed one of the guards was lean and graceful and smirking smugly at Jesse. She thought he might be another cat, but older than Jesse by a decade. The other guard just looked bored.

"We're going by the gathering," Jesse was saying. "Is there anything that won't be missed?"

"Everything is missed eventually but no inspections today that I know of. You?" He nodded to his partner.

"They just did a count last week. I doubt there will be another soon." He narrowed his eyes at Jesse. "What will you give me to let you in?"

"A favor."

"What type of favor? Labor?"

"Merchandise only," Jesse countered.

"Unlimited limit?"

"Hmm." Jesse mulled it over. "No limit on merchandise within reason for a one-man gig, one job only. You supply extra components if needed."

"Deal," the man said and smiled wolfishly.

The smug guard looked surprised. CeeCee had the alarmed feeling that Jesse had gotten the bad end of that bargain. What was he getting into? The guard stepped away from the arched entrance and waved them in.

It was a very pretty little garden. There were rows of snap peas trellised on cast-off bed frames. Roses hedged in the vegetables like an old schoolmarm. None of the flowers or plants were as big as Kelly's, but she was a special talent in her own right. An orange tree was on the far side, shedding late fruit all over the ground. Jesse pointed at it. "That will work. Let me have your backpack."

She opened the top and rearranged things to make room. "What was that about a favor?"

"Oh, since I can go back and forth, it's easy for me to get stuff."

"Like what kind of stuff?"

"All sorts of stuff. Fancy stuff, a lot of the time."

"What's the other type of favor?"

"Hmm?" He pretended not to hear her as he squeezed oranges to find the best ones.

She touched his shoulder so he would look at her. "He asked about labor. What does that mean?"

He tried to look nonchalant. "Oh, sometimes people give their skills as favors, when people are trying to put together crews."

She could imagine that Jesse had some very desirable skills. "What do the crews do?" She knew, but she wanted him to say it.

He sighed before answering. "All types of jobs. Burglary and raids mostly, but sometimes vendettas spring up or special projects." He nodded toward the gate. "I told you some of the guards were bad before they got their uniforms. Some of them didn't improve with it."

"But it's not just guards, is it?"

"No, all sorts of people run jobs here, and skills are a good way to trade." He shrugged. "But it doesn't matter. I don't get sucked into those type of favors anymore."

With sudden insight, she asked, "Is that why you've had run-ins with the Queen?"

"Yeah, that's why I've negotiated with her. I took a couple of jobs that landed me on the wrong side of her notice. I'm careful, but not everyone is."

Another piece fell into place. "That's what Mikayla is training for, isn't she?"

"My kind of people are very good crew members." He fell quiet and then confessed, "That's one of the reasons people like Eugenia get worked up around us. It's not just that we're different peoples. It's because they want us to take sides."

She mulled that over. Raid skills could be very useful in politics. "But aren't some of you already taking sides if they're working for the Queen?"

"Yeah, but most of us just stay clear of it all, and sometimes that makes people just as mad as when you get involved."

They packed as many oranges as they could into the backpack. CeeCee spotted some mint, too, growing rampant over a smaller plant. She snaked long stems of it into the top of her bag. There was lettuce ready to harvest, almost gone to seed, but she ignored it. Clearly, the Queen wasn't eating it, but CeeCee bet it was something that would be "inventoried." She frowned. Apple Cheeks was hungry, and here was food just going to waste!

They nodded to the guards on their way out. Now the bored one looked smug and the other guard looked concerned as they walked away.

CeeCee was starting to worry too.

"Do you like being on crews?" she asked Jesse, carefully. She wasn't judging, but her feelings were strangely mixed. On the one hand, she thought he'd be good on a crew—she'd seen him avoid trouble like a pro. On the other, she didn't like the idea of him doing *anything* dangerous. The thought made her stomach hurt. She especially didn't want him doing anything because of her.

"Sometimes it's fun, like at the market," he said offhandedly. When she scowled at him, he sighed. "Not particularly, but it was what I was raised to do. I'm good at it, and I like the skills I have. But I get tired of it too. It's just another way of being stuck. Ironic, isn't it? People expect you to be a criminal, and here I am, an actual one."

She stopped then and kissed him. "You're not anything like a criminal," she said. "Be careful on that job."

"I always am," he said, full of bravado. "Besides, he'll probably take forever to cash it in. Most of the guards aren't that organized."

"Hmm." The more people she met in the byways, the more volatile the place seemed. She had been sure there had been rules before; she just didn't know them. Now it felt more and more as if the rules were kind of arbitrary and inconsistent—definitely inconsistent.

They reached an older section of byways—buildings that didn't look like they belonged to this century or the last, crumbling away. Plants were reclaiming the land. The path worked its way through the shells of disintegrating corridors, and they walked through a tunnel of trumpet vine, the flowers pulsing with life. CeeCee was charmed by it instantly. Under the cool, shady light, she squeezed in next to Jesse to fit, her chin grazing his shoulder. Her hand drifted down, and he twined his fingers in hers. He smiled at her expression. At the end of the green tunnel, they stepped through the gaping wall of a building.

CeeCee blinked at the sudden brightness. The roof had fallen in on the long, low barn made of unfinished wood and old corrugated metal. Ivy and trumpet vine spilled over the wall they had passed through. Grass grew across the floor, and scattered flowers had taken root. There were even a few small trees, but most of the area was open and sunny. A small stream crept under a wall, stole across one corner, and disappeared again under the other side.

The room was lined with picnic tables. People milled around, and there were quite a few families with children, which Cee-Cee hadn't seen much of before. People sat at tables or visited with neighbors or fussed with food. Small kids sat with their parents, and the older ones ran around the area, playing. She saw a fox child trying to sneak something to eat before having his hand slapped away. One long table in the center held all the food. Everyone coming in had a dish or something to drink. The assortment was odd, but it fit the people of the byways. There were hard loaves of flat bread, roasted nuts, unrecognizable stewed meat, packaged food that looked slightly beat up, pitchers of strange-colored drinks, and even bowls that looked to be filled with grubs or insects. It was a little like the market but out in the sun.

She spotted Apple Cheeks sitting off by himself. He looked longingly and guiltily at the food, like he didn't want to get too close for fear of devouring it all. It was clear that the unspoken rule was that to eat, you needed to share something. CeeCee had the sense that this was a gathering that had been going on a long time. It felt like tradition. She suddenly knew she was seeing a very true part of the byways—the real byways, where people lived and worked and died, raised their families, and never ventured out into the world she lived in.

Just because they're forgotten doesn't mean they stop living, she thought.

She stood on her toes and waved to Apple Cheeks. He perked up at the sight of them and hurried over when she and Jesse walked to the food table. She opened her backpack and unloaded the oranges and the stems of mint onto the table. A few people held politely back, but their eyes gleamed when they saw the fruit. A young teenage girl who looked a bit like a bat, with pointed ears and charcoal-gray hair, gave her the biggest grin when Cee-Cee offered her an orange.

A small stack of unmatched plates were at one end of the table. Apple Cheeks grabbed one first and loaded food onto his plate. Jesse and CeeCee each took one as well. She was famished again, she realized. There just never seemed to be enough to eat. She piled bread and nuts on her plate. After carefully watching what other people served themselves, she chose some stewed meat, too, but not the one the bird people ate because there was something in it that looked a bit like worms or maybe mouse tails. Either way, it seemed much worse than anything her cafeteria cooked up, and she was going to politely pass, thank you very much.

She sat in a patch of sunshine with Jesse and Apple Cheeks. The family of foxes shared the table with them. Jesse knew another man, and they talked in undertones as they ate. Apple Cheeks urged her to try a cookie someone had made, and it melted into a sweet buttery taste in her mouth. The fox mother chatted with her about her favorite books. It was wonderfully warm. CeeCee felt muscles relax that she didn't know were tense. All the horrible periods of the last two days fell away, and there was only that moment, full of nice people and good food.

Jesse kept glancing at her while he talked with his friend. He finally turned toward her with a troubled expression.

"What is it?"

"You look . . . comfortable." His brow furrowed more. "I think we're running out of time."

A pulse of fear shot through her, but she squeezed his hand. "I won't forget home, and I won't be forgotten," she said stubbornly.

"Of course you won't," he said and leaned in to kiss her.

"Oh my! Hello, dear!" Apple Cheeks grinned at her hugely from across the table and gave her an exaggerated wink.

After eating, people roamed from table to table, talking and catching up on news. Apple Cheeks's story spread quickly. Now that the dam had broken, he couldn't stop talking about his son and the picture he had lost. Then other people spoke up.

"They took a whole bundle of letters I had, from a girl long ago when I was in the war."

"I used to write poems from time to time. I kept them in a little notebook."

"I had a locket from my mother."

CeeCee felt her heart squeeze with every story, and underneath, that anger flared higher and higher. "This is bullshit!" she said to Jesse. "So many people have had their things stolen!"

He looked just as mad as she felt. "It almost sounds like it's a regular occurrence," he said slowly. "Like maybe they're targeting people."

"But why?" she demanded. "Just because they can?"

"Because they can," said Jesse's friend on the other side of the table. "And because sad people are easier to control."

Her vision turned red. It made sense, in an ugly, ghastly way. She thought back on her conversations with Doc M. They were sprinkled with compliments and flattery, sure, but in the end, all she did was doubt herself. All she had felt was useless and out of options. This was how the Queen had tried to make her feel, too, so she'd take that horrible deal.

When it came right down to it, they were just another type of bully, a horrifying type. Because as bad as Taylor or Mr. Beauchamp could be, neither of them were stealing personal items or stopping people from getting food. These were people's lives they were messing with!

"That Doc M has had a spike in business since the Queen let him use the warehouse," the man said, too casually.

A little girl had come up behind him, half hiding behind his arm. She shyly peeked past her father at CeeCee. Her hair was so fair it was almost white, and her eyes were huge. She turned her face away, ruffling her hair, and CeeCee realized that it was actually very fine feathers. She couldn't have been more than five.

"And he's hooking more young people. Did you know that?" the man continued.

CeeCee knew all her triggers were being pushed. She knew, and she didn't care. She just wanted to make it right. She turned to Jesse with a snarling determination and a slim hope. "Can we steal them back from the warehouse? We can be sneaky, like we were at the market."

He looked thoughtful and intrigued. "It hasn't been done before. That doesn't mean it can't be done."

"Do what?" asked Apple Cheeks.

"Break into the warehouse," she said.

"Oh, my dear! They say there's no way to break in. And even if you did, you'd never come out," he said.

"Who's 'they'?"

"Everyone," said Jesse's friend, now looking alarmed. "They say something terrible is guarding it."

CeeCee was tired of everything *they* said. She was sick of all the "theys" in the whole world, actually. They said she was too twitchy and too loud and too out of control. They said she was a delinquent, and a troublemaker, and a tramp, and she wasn't going to amount to anything. Doc M and the Queen were just the latest in a long line. And they never, ever stopped talking.

They also never expected anyone to fight back.

"They say a lot of things," she said.

She exchanged a glance with Jesse. He looked deadly serious and smiled ferociously.

"But just because they say it doesn't make it true. So the 'they-sayers' can kiss my ass," she said.

The moment she said it, she felt better. She felt certain and purposeful, and it sang in her veins. They couldn't fix all the problems of the byways, but they could do this.

"We've got to get you out, though," Jesse murmured so only she could hear. He looked determined, too, but also worried. "I was serious when I said you shouldn't stay too long. If the byways decide you really belong here, if you fit in, then you won't be able to get out—not without a key."

Her heart squeezed again, but this time for her mom, who must be frantic by now. Her mom would have called Trudy and school and probably the cops. She could picture her circling the city in her beat-up Honda. But then she thought about being stuck in the byways, like Apple Cheeks. She didn't even have a

picture of her mom in her wallet, just a slip of paper with important numbers, such as her mom's work and the doctor's office and
her drunk grandmother, if things got really bad. If she stayed
trapped here, would she pull that piece of paper out and stare at
her mom's handwriting and think of her?

Then what if somebody stole it?

It was all so very wrong.

"I can stay a little longer. If I master the mirrors, it won't be a
problem," she insisted.

He kissed her hand. "We've got some planning to do, then."

Jesse's friend leaned across the table with a light in his eyes.
"They'll be glad to have you," the man said eagerly to Jesse.

"I'm not joining anything," he shot back, heatedly. "And I'd
appreciate it if you don't spread that around. This is a one-time
thing, just to see if it can be done."

The man threw his hands in the air, acknowledging defeat.

Jesse turned back to CeeCee and lowered his voice. "Are you
sure? I don't want to put you in danger again."

"It'll be fine. Like you said, this time we'll do more planning."

"There's something else . . ." he said. "We'll be going right
into the heart of Doc M's territory."

EIGHTEEN

Hitched a Ride

"To get to the warehouse, we have to go by the park."

After they said goodbye at the gathering, they hurried away to discuss the job in private. Apple Cheeks had fussed and fretted, much to their embarrassment, vacillating between wanting to go with them and wanting to talk them out of it. They finally got him to quiet down by promising to meet him after it was done.

"I walked through that whole area. I didn't see a big warehouse near the park," said CeeCee.

Of course, it was dark, and it probably wasn't obvious. It's not like she knew exactly where she was or how the byways worked back then.

"It's not off one of the alleys," he said. "You know that big hole in the wall across from the park? It's in there."

"Oh." She remembered the murmuring sound coming from the hole. "The people at the park said they didn't go in there."

"Well, now you know why." He grinned ruefully. "If we're going to do this, we'll need some things first."

They sped down the alley, an unspoken sense of urgency filling their footsteps. Underneath the urgency, a heady thrill of excitement was building. They were going to stick it to one of the biggest bullies!

"Like what? Burglary tools?"

"Nothing too fancy. Equipment will be the easy part."

"What's the hard part?"

"People."

She gave him a curious look.

"Ones who won't talk or sell us out. You've seen how fast news travels. People who can help, if we can talk them into it. We won't get anyone to go with us, but we might get some support along the way."

"What about your friend at the gathering? Will he talk?"

"Nah, he'll keep his mouth shut. He does enough crew work himself to know better."

CeeCee had her doubts, but she kept them to herself. She trusted Jesse to know what he was doing.

The alley made a left turn where two buildings kitty-cornered. Where another path would have branched off to the right, someone had nailed a short section of fence, blocking the way. "This is our first stop," he said.

He squeezed through a swinging gap in the wood fence. She followed, and they walked down a cement chute before the path opened up. A section of freeway overpass arched above them, just a sliver of it, with parking garages built unsafely against the concrete. Traffic zoomed by overhead, but CeeCee didn't remember a part of the freeway that looked like this. She wondered which parts were in the byways—the overpass or the garages? Or was it thin slices of each of them? Whichever it was, they now stood sandwiched by concrete, and on the other side of the underpass was a wide culvert. An angry green man face had been painted around the tunnel, its snarling mouth as the opening. Unlike the rest of the byways, not a speck of graffiti was anywhere else.

CeeCee tilted her head at the clean concrete sweeping around them. "That's . . . odd."

Jesse approached the tunnel entrance slowly, with his hands open and loose.

Two men appeared like ghosts from the gloom. They didn't have anything in their hands, but they carried themselves like they were used to handling trouble.

Right now, Jesse and CeeCee were the trouble.

One of the men raised his hand, and Jesse halted ten feet away. The man wrinkled his nose as he looked them over.

"Yeah?" the man said. He was tall and broad, but he walked with a slight stoop. His hands were very large and stained with dirt or oil. His companion was shorter and still wide but more compactly built, like a rugby player. They were both very pale, like they spent a lot of time in the tunnel.

"We need to arrange passage," Jesse called to them.

"Passage isn't cheap, and not all requests are granted. Where do you need to go?"

"To the park."

The man scowled. "You can walk to the park. That's not even a real request."

"It's important we get there without being seen."

"If you're bringing trouble to our door, you can leave right now." His companion took an aggressive step forward.

"Wait!" CeeCee stepped in front of Jesse. "Can we talk to Horace?"

"How do you know Horace?"

"I met him last night when the band was playing. Dead Hearts Down—you know them?"

The man stared at her while he deliberated. He nodded to his buddy, and the guy disappeared into the tunnel.

It took a long time before the man came back with Horace, enough time for CeeCee to wonder how big that tunnel really was. Horace followed the man out, blinking at her in the light.

"CeeCee?" he said.

"Yes! You remember me," she said, relieved. "Do you remember what we talked about last night?"

"Yes, you asked Eugenia and me about what had changed in the byways. But what"—he blinked at her—"are you doing here?"

She took a deep breath and really hoped her hunch was right. "We're going to break into the warehouse."

All three men blinked at them.

"Why?" Horace asked and cast a sidelong look at Jesse. "You're awful new here to be a revolutionary. Aren't you trying to get home?"

"Yes, I'm still doing that. But Doc M and his men have been taking things from people. They took something from a friend of mine. We're going to get it back."

"So it's personal."

"It's unfair! They're doing it on purpose, to hurt people." CeeCee thought about Apple Cheek's face, and her fists clenched. "We'll try to get as much of it out as we can."

"Personal or not, it'll send a message," said Jesse.

"They say you can't break into the warehouse," said the tall man.

"We think we can." Jesse looked at her, and she nodded. He said, "That will also send a message."

"Why do you think you can, when others haven't?"

"I don't think anyone has really tried," said Jesse. "Everyone has been afraid."

"We can do it," said CeeCee with absolute confidence. "He's clever and sneaky, and I'm brute force and luck."

They grinned matching grins, full of determination and ferocity, and the men looked taken aback.

"Well, you've got balls, I'll give you that much," said the tall man. "What are you asking for exactly?"

"We just need to get to the park without being seen," said Jesse. "And back out again. There's too many of Doc M's lackeys in that area. Once we get to the park, we doubt anyone will follow us through the hole."

"Doc M has been chasing me ever since I got here," CeeCee explained. She was going to get him back for that, and everything else.

Horace looked affronted, and the other two men looked distantly sympathetic. "When are you planning on doing this?"

"Tonight," Jesse answered.

"If they do this, it might bring heat down on us," the shorter man spoke for the first time.

"If they do it and succeed, it might be worth it," said Horace. "It can't go on the way it has been. This could be a start, you see."

"We'll have to talk to the others," said the tall man. "Come back in an hour, and we'll have an answer for you."

Horace and the two men turned without another word, into the tunnel. Jesse and CeeCee walked back to the gap in the wood and squeezed through.

"What do we do for an hour?" she asked him.

He grinned wickedly. She was really starting to love that look.

His bolt-hole was in an empty building only a couple of blocks away. If the building had been apartments at one point, they probably belonged to a slumlord. Peeling paint and mold bloomed across the walls. The rooms were tiny and countless. Large apartments had been subdivided into new rooms that could never have met safety codes, like a tenement from the Victorian era.

However, Jesse navigated the maze like a pro. In one little room, right near a window and a rickety fire escape, was a cozy pile of blankets. Next to it, an apple crate held a couple of books, a bottle of water, and a metal tin.

CeeCee was impressed and saddened by the practicality of it. The floor had been swept clean, and it was very tidy in comparison to the rest of the building. There were two exits, and except for the books, there was no indication of who had been here. It was very private.

"How many of these do you have around the city?" she asked.

He gave his usual shrug. "A few. I try to pick places that no one goes to, but eventually they get found, and I find a new place."

He sat down on the nest of blankets and looked at her expectantly. "You look tired. I thought we could use the rest."

Suddenly she felt both shy and insatiable. Her feelings were so intense, it rattled her. She wanted the intimacy they had the night before. She wanted to kiss him constantly. She wanted to never stop talking. She wanted nothing more than to climb into his skin and stay there, but she thought that would sound really creepy out loud.

Instead, she sat down shakily facing him, her knees brushing his.

He must have sensed how she was feeling because he didn't move. He smiled playfully and simply said, "Kiss me?"

She leaned forward and did, tentatively, and then harder. Without even realizing it, she had climbed into his lap. His hands were tangled in her hair, and she kept rubbing her cheek against his skin in between kisses. His skin was very, very warm, and hers was burning. She didn't think there had ever been anything other than the two of them kissing.

When they finally pulled back, she buried her face in his collarbone. Her eyes were burning too. He held her tightly against his chest, like someone was going to snatch her away if he didn't take care.

It was quiet, but it was hardly peaceful. Images spun through her mind like a tornado: her mom, Trudy, the jib jab, Apple Cheeks after the attack, the first time she'd seen Jesse. She had to go home. She couldn't bear the idea of being away from him.

She lifted her head to look at him. His eyes were very gold this close; they practically glowed.

"I live in that big apartment complex on Fifth Street. Do you know where that is?" It was suddenly important to tell him. "It's not too far from the library and Lincoln High School. That's where I go."

He nodded. "I go to that library all the time," he said, his voice rough.

"You do?" she asked, and it was too much because she burst into tears. "I'm sorry," she said automatically.

"Don't," he whispered. "Don't." He brushed the tears off her cheeks.

"I just found you."

"I know. I just found you too. I didn't even know I was look-ing." His arms tightened around her.

"We can meet at the library. I always get kicked out for being too loud, but I'll learn to be quiet if it kills me."

He snorted. "I'll teach you how to steal books."

She looked at him for a beat, appalled. "That is just awful," she said.

He burst out laughing. "That's it? That's the thing that bugs you?"

"Those books are for everyone," she said primly.

"You know we're planning on stealing things tonight, right?"

"That's different." But she grinned sheepishly at him as she said it. "What do you do with stolen books anyway?"

Now he looked offended. "I read them!"

"Why don't you just get a library card?"

"I don't have an address. I told you . . . I belong nowhere."

"That's not true," she said quietly. Then she said it: "You belong with me."

A slice of afternoon sun cut the air around them. She leaned her head against his chest. He was so easy to be with, even when he was being irritating or outrageous. She smiled to herself— even when *she* was being irritating or outrageous. She didn't think that had ever happened before.

"Where would you go," he asked, "if you could go anywhere?"

"Well, I kind of have this list. Historical places mostly . . ." she trailed off.

"Oh good—then we can compare lists." He smiled. "Want to travel with me?"

"Yes." But she didn't want to move at all.

They had barely made it down the concrete chute before men emerged from the tunnel entrance. The tall man stepped forward, but he didn't seem quite as defensive as he had earlier that day. He nodded briskly and waved them forward. A moment later, Horace was at the entrance.

"You have passage," he said. "If you come back tonight, we'll take you through."

"How much?" Jesse asked.

Horace pursed his lips and glanced at the tall man. They exchanged a long look.

He said slowly, "We've decided . . . given the nature of your errand, you see, that we'll forgo payment for this trip."

"That stays between us—you understand?" the tall man barked.

Jesse looked uncharacteristically surprised, but he recovered quickly. CeeCee felt a surge of satisfaction. These men didn't seem like they normally gave free trips. But if they were helping them, she took that as proof that their mission was important! Or . . . it was highly dangerous and they felt bad charging a couple of kids before they got hurt. She bit her lip. Hopefully, it was the former.

"Would an hour before sundown give us enough time?" Jesse asked.

"That should do it."

"Then we'll be here."

"Thank you," said CeeCee sincerely. They turned to leave.

"Don't tell anyone about this," said the tall man behind them. "If we hear about it before you come back, the deal is off."

NINETEEN

I Took the Path

They left the green-man tunnel behind and hugged in relief once they were out of sight.

"I wasn't sure how we were going to get there without them," confessed Jesse. "Even the roofs are occupied in that area."

"I noticed we haven't gone anywhere close to the park lately."

"Ha, you're learning your way around!" he crowed. His brow furrowed in concern a moment later. She knew his fear, but she pushed it away. She couldn't think about that right now. They had to plan.

"Don't worry," she said, "we'll find a way out. It'll be easier now that I know how I got stuck."

He let it go. "We have a few hours yet," he said instead. "We need to make a few more stops."

They walked beside a stone wall. CeeCee trailed her hand along it absently. It took her a moment to realize that something about the wall bothered her. She turned to look at it and stopped slowly. It was fitted stone, the edges of it soft and crumbling. Graffiti covered it, just like everything in the alleys, but not with ink or paint. It was carved. The oldest and most faded carvings looked almost like pictographs. Then more had been cut on top of those and around the edges—other symbols, animal faces and plants carved into the surface, languages she didn't know. The most recent were small messages in English or something close, sliced and scratched and squeezed in where they could fit. They looked like prayers. *The wall must be ancient,* she thought. *Probably had been standing there forever and would stand for hundreds of years more.* There was just a short length of it. It broke off into the side of a building on one side and a tiny strip of meadow grass on the other.

She put her hand out again and felt the grooves against her skin. The stones were warm, warmer than the sun warranted, like it had its own blood singing through it. People had left bits of candles on top and at its base; years and years of candles and little stubs melted down until the wax ran between the stones.

Jesse stopped at the end of the wall and looked back at her. "It's amazing, isn't it?" he said.

"Yeah," she said, before catching up with him. It felt like magic.

The byways were horrible, but they were beautiful too. The profound extremes of it were hard to comprehend. She wasn't sure, wasn't sure at all . . . if she could go back in time and erase ever coming here, would she?

Jesse smiled at her gently then. He looked so tender and sweet, she knew her heart would be crumbling into a million pieces if the bubble of happiness inside her wasn't holding them together.

A street later, they walked up to a house. It was one of those very skinny Victorians, squashed in between two much wider buildings. The builders had compensated for the lack of space by cramming in as much ornamentation as they could. It had dormer windows and gingerbread woodwork and a round tower room with a witch's cap roof high above the rest.

"Just follow me in quietly," said Jesse. He knocked loudly three times and then carefully opened the door.

He stepped in and stood attentively in the front hall. The air felt hushed and heavy. She tensed up automatically, hovering at his shoulder until he kissed the top of her head in reassurance. A deep voice floated down the stairs: "Come up."

They climbed all the way to the tower, the stairs creaking like portents under their feet. The Victorian felt like a church or a courthouse—someplace important. The woodwork in the house was immaculate, with not a speck of dust on the banister or railings. Even the wainscoting gleamed in the afternoon light, but the house was cluttered even while it was clean. It took CeeCee a moment to register what she was looking at. Then, as she passed a landing and a room full of paint and canvases, it clicked. This was all arts and crafts supplies. There were stacks of paper and balls of yarn and jars of beads. There were origami animals gracing shelves and tapestries on walls and small wooden sculptures. Half-finished projects laid in nooks and crannies. It should have been a mess, but it was meticulously organized.

She just never knew what to expect in the byways. It wasn't a church—it was like a giant craft room.

They reached the top landing. The door before them was beautiful, with blue-and-yellow stained glass in a pattern all around the frame and a round window in the center that looked like a clock. Jesse knocked again, very politely, and the door swung open on silent hinges.

In the round room, a man sat on a papasan chair. The chair was turned slightly away, and as they came in, he swiveled toward them. He had very long arms and very long legs, and his skin was dark and glistening. His clothes were dark and narrow too. He held his arms up as if he were about to play an imaginary piano. He seemed too big for the room, perched as he was in the too-small chair, his knees sticking up on either side. There were windows all around, which looked out farther than she expected. Some books were stacked tidily on the floor near him, and a small table held an electric kettle and a cup of tea. The blue painted walls were faded, but as dust-free as the rest of the house.

The man reminded CeeCee of an absentminded spider, but when he finally met her eyes, his own were piercing and clear and deep.

"Jesse," he said. "And CeeCee. What can I help you with today?"

A shiver ran down her spine at the sound of her name. She supposed word from Doc M could have traveled to this man, but her gut whispered it wasn't that. What were they doing here? Jesse had said they were getting supplies. Did this man have something that could help them?

"Hello, Gideon." Jesse extended his head in a nod. "We're planning on breaking into the warehouse."

"I see," said Gideon. He stared absently into space as if he were seeing something only he could see. His fingers plucked unconsciously at the air.

"I thought we couldn't tell anyone?" she murmured in Jesse's ear.

"He never tells anyone anything, unless someone asks him directly, and he is usually quite clever about avoiding even that."

The man smiled faintly. "What are you planning to do at the warehouse?" he asked.

"I think you already know."

"I must hear it." His deep voice tolled through her like a bell.

"We're going to take back people's memories. The ones that

were stolen," CeeCee burst in and then wondered why she had phrased it like that.

"Yes, I see." His hand lifted and strummed through the air like it was a harp. He turned his head sharply away, eyes narrowed, then back to them. "If you do this, you're going to have to stay out of sight for a bit," he continued. "Perhaps a visit to the outside?"

"We must be successful, if I go visiting," said Jesse happily.

Gideon frowned and cocked his head. "Perhaps."

Jesse's smile faltered. "There are lots of people to visit there," he tried instead.

"But only one of importance."

Jesse reached out and squeezed CeeCee's hand. "She's with me now."

The funny thing about falling in love is that it never occurs to you that there was ever anything else.

Gideon stayed silent, and Jesse's head furrowed in thought. Then he breathed an anxious sigh. "Thank you, Gideon. I look forward to visiting you soon."

Gideon dropped his hands then and smiled fondly. "Not too soon."

Jesse took her hand and started drifting toward the stairs. He looked troubled.

"What was that about?" she asked him in a hushed voice.

"It never hurts to check in with him. We'll have to be careful." Seeing her confusion, he said, "He knows things."

"Like a psychic?" She thought about how he knew her name. A psychic could be helpful. She'd never really given them much thought, but she wasn't going to close the door on anything—not in this place. "It didn't sound like you asked him anything."

"I didn't. Questions have a price, but statements cost nothing. I figured that out when I was very young, and he likes me for it." He smiled faintly. "And I bring him stuff."

"For answers?"

"Nah, I just like him too."

"Wait!" Gideon called after them. He was staring into space again, one hand strumming the air. "I think CeeCee has a question."

"She does?" Jesse asked, startled.

"I do?"

"She needs to ask."

Jesse stiffened and stared at her with wide eyes.

A thrill ran through her, curiosity and dread mixed together. "I don't know what I'm supposed to ask, and I don't have anything to pay for a question." Yet even as she said it, she knew he was right.

"You have beautiful hair, young lady. Might I have a strand?"

"My hair?" It was thick and blonde and fell to the middle of her back. She'd been complimented on it before but always by guys leering at her. Gideon's request didn't feel like that. He looked patient and still, like time didn't mean the same thing to him that it did to the rest of the world.

She pulled a strand loose and handed it to him. It lay on his long palm and gleamed in the light.

She should ask something about their mission, something Jesse hadn't said, but what? Would they be safe? Did they need special equipment? There were too many variables, and she couldn't focus. A million other thoughts swirled through her . . . would she get out, was her mom worried, what should they do next, was Trudy still her friend?

The question that popped out surprised her more than anyone. "Why does Doc M want me so badly?"

Gideon frowned thoughtfully, his hand strumming the air. After a long pause, he said, "Not everything is eye to eye. Remember to look up."

"Look up?" she asked. Bewildered, she looked at Jesse, then back at Gideon. "What does that have to do with Doc M?" She glanced at the ceiling as if the answer would be written there. Gideon stayed silent.

Jesse stared at him for a long moment, then squeezed her arm. "It wasn't the right question, but he's giving you an answer anyway."

She wanted to kick herself. She'd screwed up their chance to ask a question that could help! Would he let her try again? She fumbled for another strand of hair, and Gideon stopped her with a hand. He said gently, "Perhaps seeing what is in yourself will allow you to see what is in others. Or not."

She shivered at his words. She'd felt, strangely, more comfortable with herself in the byways than she had in her regular life. But deep inside a voice whispered spitefully, *What if I look, and I don't like what I see?*

"Thank you," she said politely to Gideon.

They walked back downstairs while her head spun that around. She was unnerved, but she didn't want to add anything to Jesse's worry. *"Look up."* What could that mean? She frowned behind his back.

Behind the Victorian, they climbed up onto a brick wall. It was only eight inches or so across, but it was solid enough. Along the top, they twisted and turned between buildings, squeezing through tight spots until Jesse hopped down into a side lot. Next to it sat a squat building and a set of stairs leading down to a sub-level room. The alley looked dusty and unused, but it felt like camouflage. There were a couple of cardboard boxes in the mouth of the alley and a row of battered cans in a crooked diagonal line near the stairs. But everything seemed carefully set rather than abandoned, like if you tripped over those cans, whoever was near would know you weren't in the right place.

As if to prove her theory, Jesse stepped precisely over the cans, and she followed his lead. They went down the stairs, opened a heavy door, and walked into a square concrete block of a basement. In front of the door was a U-shaped wooden counter that barricaded most of the room. Full shelves and bins filled up the rest of the bunker. Voices floated from behind a curtain-covered doorway in the back. A simple old-fashioned desk bell sat on top of the counter, which Jesse rang before leaning against the wooden surface. She recognized his studiously nonchalant look. That meant business, and she swiftly adopted, she hoped, an equally casual stance.

The curtain parted, and she caught a quick, shadowy glimpse of two large individuals before a woman stepped into the room.

She rolled in on a formidable wave of personality. The woman was tall and blonde, her hair caught up in a French twist. Her clothes, a pair of plain slacks and a fitted coat over a knit shirt, were made in simple lines but were incredibly well cut. She took them in at a glance and, with a no-nonsense attitude, stepped up to the counter. The air seemed to crackle around her. She was the type of woman who could transition from a boardroom to a military conclave without changing her shoes.

"Hello, Duchess," Jesse said almost warmly.

"Hello, kitty dear," she said, snarky and efficient. "What do you need to deal with today?"

"Locks," said Jesse, "and maybe heights."

"Hmm," murmured the Duchess. She pulled various items from the shelves and plopped them on the counter. CeeCee didn't recognize some of them, but most were straightforward tools. The Duchess also pulled out several coils of rope, everything from thin nylon to thick and heavy cable. She even hoisted a heavy-duty chain onto the table, one so thick that CeeCee didn't think she could lift it, but the Duchess didn't break a sweat. While Jesse picked over the items, checking the quality or size, hefting the weight in his hands, CeeCee let her thoughts drift back to what Gideon had said.

What was inside her? *Someone who doesn't fit in*, the mean little voice piped up again, *a troublemaker*. *Stop*, she told herself firmly. Those were the type of things the bullies would say, but that didn't mean she had to say them too. Still, she kept her face blank while she squirmed inside—the fear was there all the same. Gideon had thought it was important, though—important enough to answer, even though it wasn't the right question. Maybe it was time to put on her big-girl panties and look anyway.

"Do you have packs?" Jesse asked.

The Duchess nodded and displayed several duffels and backpacks in different sizes. He set off to the side a small pile of items.

Okay, what was different between her and Doc M? Well, she didn't have any ulterior motives for one. She was pretty relentless once she set her mind to something, but that sounded like it applied to Doc M too. She could be impulsive, but she was learning she also had good instincts. She'd like to say she was a nice person, but since she *was* prone to punching, she just wasn't sure.

She wasn't used to praise, either, especially from herself.

She watched Jesse sort the piles on the counter. According to him, she "felt" her life—she wasn't fake about it. She wasn't sure how that helped her, though.

"The Queen's been a right bitch of late," said the Duchess conversationally.

Hearing the Queen's name shocked CeeCee back to the present. She still didn't always pay attention.

"Has she now?" asked Jesse.

"I hear she's in quite a snit—denying requests, arresting people, generally being a pain in the ass." She looked at CeeCee for confirmation.

CeeCee raised an eyebrow at her, deadpan.

Jesse said, "Duchess, you know I don't get involved in politics."

"Oh, neither do I. You know that," she said. "We're all mum and confidence here." The Duchess drummed her fingers on the table as he inspected the merchandise. "Is this on credit?" she asked.

"If you don't mind."

"You better bring me something good."

He smirked at her, cocksure and unconcerned.

"So, a little birdie told me," she probed, "that the Queen was in a particular snit this very morning. I heard someone gave it to her good." She paused and smiled tightly. "Serves her right."

She didn't mean *her* meeting with the Queen, did she? Cee-Cee made a small sound, somewhere in between the beginnings of a gulp and a laugh.

The Duchess pinned her with her stare. She looked her up one way and down the other. The gleam of discovery in her eyes looked delighted in a severe way. "You're quite the commodity right now, girly," she said.

CeeCee shrugged, offhand and elaborate. "So I heard."

"Did you? It's not just the good doctor asking around. It seems her royal bitchiness wants a word now as well."

CeeCee felt herself blanch. Jesse stiffened and stared at the Duchess, hard and unblinking.

"Oh ho!" she said. "I thought you would bring me news, and instead, I've brought you some. Well! Apparently, my dearest cousin would like to keep this one close. You know her . . . whatever she wants, immediately, and damn everyone else." She stared back at Jesse, unblinking as well. "Politics are starting to sound nice, aren't they?"

With an effort, he looked down and went back to his sorting. "Politics are never nice."

Her eyes went back and forth between them. "Sometimes people are stirred to passion."

She said "cousin," thought CeeCee—cousin. *That means she's related to the Queen.* She didn't look much like the Queen, besides a taste in good tailoring, but they both had some of the same . . . sharpness about them. Did that mean they were on the same side? She felt herself tensing, coiling like a snake ready to defend herself. She still tried to look casual though, like she didn't have a care in the world that this woman might try to turn her in or call to whoever those shadowy shapes were in the back of her shop.

"Oh, don't worry yourself, girly," said the Duchess. "I have no love for the Queen, as your beau here very well knows. In fact"— she smirked at him—"I'm not going to ask what you plan to do, but I hope it's all mischief and mayhem."

Jesse continued to set tools aside and then reduced his small pile to a select few. "This will be it," he said.

She looked over his selection, pursing her lips, clearly disappointed. "Well, that's not that big of a splash, is it?"

Jesse suddenly dropped his inscrutable face. He smiled, but it looked harder than CeeCee had ever seen it, dangerous even. "You of all people should know that plenty of mischief can be made with very little."

It was an innocuous statement, simple conversation really, but menace oozed out of him.

She realized he was sending a message . . . if anyone messed with CeeCee, he'd be there too, protecting her. CeeCee squared her shoulders, stood by his side, and glowered at the Duchess. They were in this together.

The Duchess looked between Jesse and CeeCee again. If anything, her eyes gleamed even more.

"Well, then," she said, "if that mischief is aimed at pains

in the asses, so much the better." She took out a notepad and marked down his supplies. "Goodbye, kitty dear," she said almost sweetly.

Jesse loaded his items into a backpack, and they turned to leave. As they walked through the door, the Duchess sang out after them, "I hope you know what you're dealing with."

TWENTY

Out of the Red, into the Fire

Outside, Jesse immediately turned toward the alley mouth. He warily looked up and down the street before heading toward a fire escape, clutching CeeCee's hand protectively.

Once on the roof, she stood stunned as it sank in, her head spinning. Jesse prowled back and forth in agitation.

"They're both after me now." CeeCee felt nauseated. Anger was burning, as always, but it was a small ember compared to her growing alarm. Doc M was relentless, but he was still just one man with a few flaky thugs. She and Jesse hadn't even seen any of his men since breakfast. But the Queen had organized guards. CeeCee thought she'd taken care of her, but she was wrong. She shouldn't have dismissed either of them.

"We have to get you out," Jesse said. "No more delays; as soon as tonight's done, we'll go for the mirrors."

They were putting out a lot of effort for one teenager, just because they could—just because they were in power.

"We should get some other supplies," Jesse fretted. "I should have thought about it at the shop!"

And there was nothing she could do about it. She couldn't go back and change anything. Even if she had been all sweetness and light to both of them, it probably wouldn't have made a difference. She stared at her hands. This was normally about the time she wanted to hit something. But that would cause a racket.

Jesse said, "We'll need to go back. Of all the stupid mistakes!"

And if she went charging around, she'd probably get them both caught. She had to be smart about this. Jesse wouldn't even be in this mess if she hadn't shown up.

Jesse.

He had stopped pacing and was clawing through the pack, cursing under his breath. He was getting worked up again.

"Stop—it's too late," she said.

"It's not too late," he muttered.

"It is, and this won't help."

"No, no," he shook his head. "If we can just . . ."

"Hey, I'm the one they're after, so I'm the only one allowed to freak out!" It was supposed to be funny, but it came out wrong.

He froze with his head down, and she could see him getting ahold of himself. He looked up. His cocky grin stretched a wall across his face. He beamed at her like he was trying to be reassuring. It was much, much worse than the panic. It was brittle at the edges, and for once, she could see how much he had practiced it.

Her heart seized in her chest. "Don't do that," she whispered.

"Everything will be fine," he said. "We'll just plan for some extra contingencies . . ."

"Don't. Do. That!" she yelled.

She grabbed him in a fierce hug. He clung to her. The tension didn't go away, but it eased slowly out of his shoulders.

"It's okay to be worried. We don't have to plan more. We don't have to hit anything. We'll just be worried together," she whispered. "And we'll be very, very careful."

"I don't want you to get hurt." There was old pain in his voice.

It would kill her to make it worse. She thought about Apple Cheeks and the others and all the things they had lost. She wondered how much people brought with them when they came to the byways. "We don't have to do it," she said reluctantly.

"What?" He blinked at her, surprised.

"It was my idea, and it's going to paint a target on your back." Her throat tightened.

He shook his head. "People get targeted every day. Look at you." Rage crept into his eyes, and it took the edge off his fear. "I'm tired of the way things work around here."

When she saw his anger, hers flared up, too, like it had been waiting. "They'll think you took sides."

"I did take a side. I took yours. It's the only one I want to be on." He studied her intently. "But if you want to stop, we'll stop."

She thought about how little she really had in her backpack from home. Her mom's handwriting on that slip of paper—it wasn't important to anyone but her. But they were using those things to hurt people. Her spine stiffened. "No, I don't want to stop. If they're after me anyway, I'd rather make it worth it."

He smiled grimly, "Okay, then. Let's make them pay."

They traveled the rooftops back to his bolt-hole, watching over the sides the whole time. Everything suddenly felt treacherous. They saw a guard patrol and ducked down as they passed. An old woman sweeping the walk seemed to spy after them. A group of men milling in an alley looked like they were laying a trap.

CeeCee shook her head sharply. There was no point in getting paranoid. It wasn't like everyone was on the Queen's side.

It was hard, so hard, to still her nerves, though.

Jesse showed her another path to his hidden spot, down a fire escape, across an empty floor and up again. In the bolt-hole, Cee-Cee sat down on the pile of blankets next to the window. The afternoon shadows had lengthened, so the sun no longer lit the room. She shivered and looked for strangers.

"We probably have another hour," Jesse said. "We might as well get some rest, if we can."

He didn't seem to know what to do with himself. He opened the metal tin and revealed beef jerky and a packet of saltines. She dug into her backpack and pulled out an orange she had saved and the last granola bar, half-mushed and crumbling. He tidied his meager belongings as they ate, but he left the pack of supplies alone.

"Let's go over it again," she said, despite what she had told him earlier. She didn't think she could sleep.

"Okay," he said, relieved. "I went once, just to check the ware-house out. I didn't break in, though. I made it to the dock and looked in a window."

He explained the layout, and they roughly sketched their plans, drawing in the dust on the floor. Her thoughts swirled faster and faster. There was only so much they could strategize for, but it was enough. They weren't going in completely blind. This crusade had always meant something, but now it was a lot more important that it go right. If they could sneak in and out undetected, they could head to the mirrors after, with no one the wiser. Hopefully, they'd be long gone from the byways before an alarm was raised. The break-in might even provide a distraction. Why would anyone look for her when they had a crime to solve?

But deep down, she had a feeling Doc M would know it was her.

The butterflies beat themselves to death in her stomach.

When they couldn't go over it anymore, they leaned against each other and watched the sky. For a brief luscious moment, it felt like she melted into his skin. Her breath matched his exactly, like it was always supposed to be so.

She jerked up with a start, alarmed for no reason. She hadn't slept, but she hadn't been awake, either.

"CeeCee, it's time to go."

They trekked through the cement chute once more and met Horace and the short man at the tunnel entrance. Horace looked alert and friendly, but the short man had a thick length of pipe hanging from his utility belt.

"Glad to see you again. Now remember," Horace said, "we hope you're successful on your venture, but word of how you got there doesn't go anywhere." He smiled amiably. "Or there will be consequences, you see."

The shorter man scowled at them.

"We understand," said Jesse.

The short man waved them brusquely inside. CeeCee stepped forward, but Jesse wavered at the entrance, peering in, curious and wary. She looked at him a second before it clicked. This was unknown territory for him. As much as he knew the byways, this was one place he hadn't traveled before.

She reached out and squeezed his hand. He squeezed back; with a deep breath, he stepped inside, and they walked into another world.

The tunnel was dry, and the walls looked a little crumbly, but it was swept clean. Horace led the way, and the short man took up the rear. As they moved farther in, the light faded, and a glow took its place.

Emergency light sockets, probably meant for city work-ers—even though CeeCee doubted anyone came down here anymore—held burning bulbs. The pipes containing the wiring had been cracked open, and other wires and electrical outlets were spliced from the system. A man as pale as Horace was working at an electrical panel. He had a sunlamp set up at his feet for additional light.

Moss grew on the walls where there were lights. The moss looked cultivated; different colors were arranged on the wall in patterns, and some air plants were mixed in as well. Every inch that could take advantage of the light was used. While the man worked, he pinched off a small piece of moss and popped it into his mouth as they passed.

Soon, the tunnel branched, and other lights were reflected down passages and at crossroads. Every once in a while, a light bulb was out, and they walked briefly in darkness until the next lamp. Sometimes, a crossing path was completely, utterly dark.

"Does the jib jab come down here?" Jesse asked suddenly.

"Yes, during the day, but it stays away from the light, you see. Some of us go up during the day and down again at night, but most just rely on the light system."

CeeCee shuddered. The jib jab was something she didn't want to think about down here.

As they traveled, the air changed—sometimes damp, sometimes dry. The tunnel evolved as well. At times, water ran down the middle of the path or dribbled down the walls. Basins had been added to catch it where it ran clear, and small filtration systems added where it was not. There were sections where the tunnel walls had been worn away completely, and gnarled roots were meticulously pruned to form the wall instead.

"What are these?" CeeCee asked, laying a hand on one of the roots. It was thicker than her hand. Except for the twins' place and the alley gardens, she hadn't seen any plants large enough to warrant the huge roots. "There aren't trees above us, are there?"

"They're underground forests," explained Horace. "Above, you might see a few leaves or twigs growing in cracks, but most of the plant is under here. They evolved to grow this way, you see. It lets them take advantage of limited resources."

It was very quiet as they walked. The tunnels seemed to swallow sound, and it didn't encourage anyone to chat much. CeeCee clutched Jesse's hand, but she was left alone with her racing thoughts. In a dark patch between bulbs, the face of the man overdosing suddenly swam up in her memory. Her breath caught, and tears prickled at the backs of her eyes. She could tell the last couple of days were catching up with her. Fatigue hovered at her edges, waiting for her strength to wane just a little more so it could pounce. That non-nap didn't help, although it was her own fault she didn't get enough sleep the night before. She shook her head stubbornly. She could push through a little longer.

One thought wouldn't go away, the one she wouldn't say to Jesse. What if she couldn't master the mirrors? What if it took too much time? She knew the longer she stayed, the harder it would be to escape. The byways would try to save her, just like everyone else who was forgotten or didn't fit on the outside. She didn't want to be saved that way. *I don't want to leave him*, she thought guiltily, *but I don't want to be trapped here*. The darkness crept in around her, and her anxiety ratcheted up another notch.

They passed a side tunnel where the ceiling had collapsed a few feet in. Someone had set up a small floodlight so that the rubble and broken stones were visible, and a wooden brace had been built against what was left of the cracked ceiling. It occurred to her that there could be tunnels and manholes that led back home. It was all so organized. There must be a way for them to get all the electrical and building materials they needed.

"Horace," she asked slowly, "are there halfway places down here? Ways to get back to the outside?"

"I think you know we guard our secrets pretty closely."

"Yes, but . . ." She tried to come up with a compelling reason for him to tell her and failed. "Are there?"

He looked her in the face, and she knew all the desperation and fatigue of the last few days was showing in her eyes. She could practically feel it leaking out.

"We're going to try the mirrors. I just don't know if they'll work," she explained.

"If you do this—break into the warehouse—I might be able to share a secret with you," he said, measured and soft. "Come back here after, if you need to."

Now she really was going to cry. It was a small thing—not even a promise, just an almost promise. But it felt like a weight lifted off her. She was so tired. She wanted to go home. "Thank you."

"But all must be kept quiet."

"I understand."

She knew Jesse had heard, but she also knew he would never betray her. When Horace turned away, she smiled at Jesse, and the relief she felt was reflected in his face.

If felt like they had traveled miles before Horace finally slowed to a halt. She expected another tunnel entrance, but Horace led them to an iron ladder set in the wall. They climbed up until the three of them were crowded into a tiny closet, which was mostly taken up by the square hole they had crawled through. They perched on the narrow ledge around the missing grate. The short man stayed below, still scowling.

Horace looked through a peephole in the closet wall. He felt around, his exact movements hidden, until a dim crack of light appeared. He pushed it open.

They stepped out of a hidden alcove built inside an old factory building. The false wall was cunningly made, the cubbyhole positioned next to an office so it blended into the original brickwork. CeeCee would never have spotted it if she didn't know it was there. The factory was full of moldering equipment, large chemical vats and runoff pipes, all cast iron and grimy steel, providing shelter from view for their secret entrance. The sharp smell of old chemicals and oil hung in the dusty air. Dim light came in from a line of high windows, but it was fading fast.

"This is as close as we can take you," said Horace. He led them past a vat to the side of the factory. "You're half a block from the park. If you take that door"—he pointed—"then circle around to the left of the building, you'll find the gap."

"Thank you, Horace," said CeeCee. "Really."

He looked at them with measuring eyes and only nodded.

They waited at the door while night fell, another stolen moment to stop and lean against each other, arms wrapped around like shields. CeeCee kissed Jesse's collarbone and breathed in his scent. She could feel her skin buzzing, jangling with nerves and excitement, dread and anticipation. It was almost like when she stole the rabbit, except she didn't think she was going to feel bad after.

Not bad at all, unless they got caught, of course.

When the shadows were deep enough to hide in, they eased around the corner until they could see the park. Every detail jumped out at her—the cracked brick, the knife-edge of light, the cooling air—and she knew she was hyper focusing. It was the opposite of the frazzled ADHD feeling, and while it was helpful right now, sometimes the rebound crash was awful. She concentrated on the other side of the alley. A trash-can fire was burning on the loading dock like before, but there was only one old man staring vacantly into the flames. A long one hundred feet lay between them and the gaping maw of the hole.

Sticking to skittish shadows, they crept to the edge of the light. Voices echoed noisily from inside the park. It sounded crowded. Someone could come out at any minute, and there was still a twenty-foot run to the gap. The old man had his back to the hole, but he stood directly across from it. He only had to turn his head for a full view of the alley. He gazed into the fire, humming softly and swaying on his feet.

"He looks kind of out of it," CeeCee whispered hopefully. She remembered how many of the park residents had stared into nothing, drugged or drunk or just plain mad.

"Let's make sure." Jesse picked up a can and tossed it past the man. It rattled down the alley. The man didn't flinch. But then, very slowly, he turned his head toward the sound.

Without hesitation, Jesse dashed over and zipped through the wall. CeeCee was right behind him, but she misjudged how high the hole was. She had to boost herself up a second time and had a moment of panic before catching the edge of the broken brick and swinging herself over.

She landed on sand with a grunt. The air rushed out of her. Jesse waited just off to the side, ducked low behind a rock. She scrambled over to join him, taking her bearings as she regained her breath.

A beach stretched out beyond the jagged teeth of the hole, a narrow strip of white sand running along the water. Boulders were piled at the base of the wall, and when she craned her neck, she could see an edge to it, way up high. Who built a wall on a beach? CeeCee wasn't sure where in the world this shore came from, but she knew it wasn't anywhere near her city. It was colder here, and the light was strange, painted red and blue and pink by the late afternoon sun. It had already been dark on the other side of the wall but not here, not yet. Everything stood in stark relief, shadow figures against the slant of the light. Down the beach was a dock with a long squat building built over the water. There were lights on in the warehouse, and they burned cheerily, as if anyone were welcome to walk right up. She wondered why nobody had.

Dark clumps threw shadows on the sand between them and the dock, just at the water's edge. It wasn't until one moved that she realized they were alive and not more rocks scattered on the shore.

"We'll keep close to the wall," Jesse said quietly. "It'll be slow, but we can't be seen."

They stayed low, ducking behind big boulders when they could, flattening themselves against smaller ones when they couldn't, pretending to be just another pair of evening shadows. It was a lot of crawling. The barnacle shells scraped her skin and caught at her clothes. Clamshells littered the ground, some still with meat clinging inside. They smelled, but she tried to ignore it. The gritty sand wasn't wet at least, but it quickly filled up her boots.

"This doesn't seem too bad," she whispered to him.

"People used to come to the beach. It's pretty during the day. I used to play on that dock as a kid. It was a kind of a dare to climb the beams underneath during high tide and not get wet. The water is freezing."

"Did you ever make it?"

His grin flashed in the fading light. "Not dry."

She laughed quietly, despite her nerves. She could just picture him as his cat self . . . cocky and sopping wet, clinging onto a wood beam.

Their crawl brought them parallel to the strange, dark shapes at the shoreline. Jesse put his finger to his lips. Her muscles tense, she moved as quietly as she could. Now that they were closer, she could see more movement. The humped shapes huddled together, occasionally rolling or scooching to reposition themselves in the sand. There had to be fifty or sixty of them. She squinted in the fading light, trying to figure out if they were seals or some new byway animal. They seemed very large, but it was hard to tell with them all piled up against each other. One finally reared its whiskery head. It had the huge tusks of a walrus.

Then the creature stood up.

CeeCee froze, paralyzed. Jesse grabbed her arm and yanked her behind a large boulder. She stared through a crack in the rocks. It felt like seeing the slug man all over again.

He was more walrus than he was man, but he pushed himself up with flippers that were more like arms, until he stood on flippers that were more like legs. Upright, he towered more than twice her height. His tusks were longer than her arms. He surveyed the beach, eyeing the boulders and the dock commandingly. Then he turned to gaze at the sea. He grunted loudly, and five other heads popped up. He nodded and walked to the shore's edge before disappearing into the water. Some of the walruses stood and walked, and some simply crawled on their flippers over the sand, but the others followed him into the ocean and swam toward large, flat shapes that looked like ice or floating docks. Several were positioned around the warehouse.

The walruses swam far enough from shore that they looked dim and blurry, and only then did Jesse move again. It was slow going, crawling along the rocks, but she understood his caution, and her anxiety shared it. Walruses were a lot bigger in real life than they looked in pictures—a *lot* bigger. If they were guards for Doc M, they could be a problem.

They were two-thirds of the way to the warehouse when the boulders tapered off into small rocks. An open stretch of white sand lay between them and their next shelter. The wind kicked up and howled along the shore, tossing silt. CeeCee hovered behind the last big stone and looked at Jesse doubtfully. The dock was so close—could they run for it without being seen? How did he get there last time?

Jesse lay down flat on the sand. He crawled a little way and then went still as stone, but he watched her over one shoulder. Then he slowly crawled again, keeping his movements as low as possible. When he froze again, he looked like another row of rocks on the sand.

She nodded to him. When he had made it all the way across, she lay down too. *It's funny*, CeeCee thought, *how sand always looks warm*. Sand made you think of sunny days and deserts. But when she stretched out on it, a chill seeped up from the ground and stole her body warmth away in an instant. She clamped down on the impulse to jump up out of the cold. Instead, she pictured Doc M gloating over his stolen photos. She gritted her teeth and moved like an inchworm across, the sand spilling like cold rivulets through her fingers.

On the other side of the gap, she stood up behind a rock, and the wind howled ice through her bones. She had new respect for Jesse clinging to the dock, trying not to get wet. She rubbed a hand over her face and tasted salt as she shivered.

It wasn't much farther to the dock. There was a staircase midway between the water and the rocks. Jesse ignored it and scrambled up the boulders instead, piled high near the base of the dock against the wall. The wall was starting to crumble here, too, and they pulled themselves up over rocks and loose chips of brick as quick as they could, sending small pieces skittering down. They were exposed, but not as much as if they had used the stairs. She was glad for the wind now because it covered the sounds they made. At the top of the rocks, it was only a short stretch to hoist themselves onto the dock.

Relief coursed through her. They were almost there. And the wood dock was easier to navigate than the beach, by far. They bent low and scurried to the warehouse, quick and straight across the planks. The warehouse wall was cast in shadow. It took a moment for her eyes to adjust to find the entrance.

The door that faced them was completely ordinary, made of plain seaworn wood. It had a regular padlock on the handle, just like the one she used on her locker at school. After the trip through the tunnels and crawling painstakingly across the sand, it seemed rather anticlimactic.

Of course, they still had to get inside and back out again.

But they *had* just managed the beach, no problem! A giddy thrill worked its way inside her, and she wanted to jump in glee. She bounced on her heels instead, stretching her calves.

"See that?" Jesse pointed to the lock. "Not one of the Queen's. It's not in Doc M to trust someone else." He slid his backpack off and opened the top. "How big a message do we want to send?" he asked her.

"Hmm . . . what are our choices?" She threw her hands wide.

He grinned and pulled a strange-looking key and a hammer from his backpack.

"What is that?"

"A bump key."

He slid the key in the lock and tapped it gently with the hammer until the lock sprang open.

"This is how you get merchandise on the outside, isn't it?" she whispered.

He only smiled. Carefully he opened the door an inch and listened. Then he dipped into his backpack again for a rag. He wrapped the lock in it, set it on the dock, and offered her the hammer with a flourish and a bow.

With savage delight, CeeCee banged the hammer down on the rag. The wind helped here, too, drowning out her enthusiastic destruction. When they unwrapped it, the lock was mangled bits of broken metal and a cracked shackle. She smacked a kiss on the remains, and Jesse hung it, teetering and unbalanced, back on the latch.

He eased inside the door, bright light spilling out like a spotlight. She followed quickly, closing the door behind them, and turned to the left. A stair led up to a platform and a small office with windows to oversee the floor. The office was locked, but they crept up and crouched on the edge of the platform to scope out the warehouse.

She had expected, somehow, something that looked like one of those big-box grocery outlets, with orderly rows full of goods and probably a refrigerated section. Pallets would be stacked above, and maybe one of the more lucid inhabitants of the park would be driving a forklift around. She had no idea why she kept expecting things to have a certain normalcy. She held on to expectation like a bad habit, even though in the byways it had no relevancy at all.

The warehouse was not only stuffed full of strange, but it was also laid out in a logic she couldn't fathom. The building was much bigger than it looked from the beach, but it had a peaked roof that started low, so the shelves weren't very high. Electric lights hung suspended from the ceiling, burning bright and orderly, but the rest of the space was chaos. A series of thin walls with shelves partitioned the warehouse into small sections, but there weren't always doorways leading in and out of the rooms. Shelving of every style and size and material had been commandeered to hold the warehouse contents, but sometimes there weren't even aisles. CeeCee was at a loss as to how you would get to anything. She remembered finding her file in Mr. Reyes's office, how she could always find her file when he had lost it. Maybe she really did have lucky magic. Maybe that would help her here.

She hoped.

Scattered windows along the roof's highest point let in natural light. As well as shelves, the warehouse had platforms suspended from the roof under each window, holding plants to catch the sunshine during the day. The plants drooped down over the tops of shelves like a watchful jungle. Skinny ladders led up to the platforms.

"We'll have to split up," said Jesse. "It's too much to search."

She agreed. "What if we each take one side and meet at the other end, in the middle?" She pointed.

"Okay. I'll go left, you go right." He pulled her into a quick hug. "Be careful."

She walked down the stairs and along the back wall. On the far side was a gap between one shelf and another. She started down the narrow aisle, searching, but the shelves were full of nothing but empty cardboard boxes and packing materials. The aisle dead-ended, and she huffed in frustration. All that effort getting here, and she couldn't even get to the next section! She thumped one of the walls, and it jerked away, dropping an empty box on her head. The wall was built on wheels! With a triumphant grin, she grabbed the wall and pulled, opening a skinny gap into the next room.

Now she was with the real merchandise. She passed a long, deep shelf full of prescription bottles and pills. The pungent scent of marijuana hung heavy in the air. She wrinkled her nose and searched carefully among the drugs, then moved to a new section. And then another. The warehouse held a dizzying array of items, enough to keep the byways in merchandise for a long time, enough to keep people clothed and fed without struggling so hard. Bolts of fancy fabric and piles of old clothes, machine parts, and cans of food were stacked haphazardly. There was a whole room of hats and another full of Tupperware.

It was overwhelming and distracting and threw her sensory issues into overdrive. For a brief, horrible moment, she forgot what she was looking for. She spun in a circle and then stared at a vase until her mind refocused—Apple Cheek's photo, that was it, and everyone else's memories, too, as much as they could find. Could she possibly find them in this mess? Some of the aisles were clean, evidence that they were used often, and others were coated in dusty grime. She pictured the mementos tossed on a forgotten shelf, and anger coursed through her again. She opened boxes and containers as she went. She doubted Doc M would have done something as respectful as pinning photos to a bulletin board. But maybe he liked to gloat over them. It was a ghastly thought, but finding a photo board would certainly be convenient.

There were also stranger things in the warehouse: tanks of worms and giant chess pieces, plants that were the wrong color, and bottles that glowed eerily in the dim light. She walked past a freaky collection of full-size stuffed animals, and she nervously wondered if they were toys or actual dead animals. But she really didn't want to check. There were statues of people in odd clothes and of creatures she had never seen before. One aisle was crammed full of heart paraphernalia, like the world's worst valentine collection. This warehouse definitely belonged to the Queen.

CeeCee wasn't sure how long she had been searching. It felt like a long time, and she wasn't making much progress. They should hurry. The longer they were in the warehouse, the more likely they could get caught. However, she had to be getting close to the middle, right? She'd lost track of how many aisles she'd searched, but it couldn't be that big. She half-heartedly jumped, as if she could hop high enough to see over the shelves. They had forgotten to discuss a signal for when they found the photos, but she figured if Jesse found anything, he would whistle or something.

There was a faint scuffling sound a few aisles over. She sighed in relief. There was Jesse. They'd be done soon.

She opened an old chest and found it full of dolls. Most of them were missing their heads.

She shuddered and slid open another shelf. The aisle held cages on one side and murky terrariums on the other, catching light from the window above. This place was so creepy. She peered into the cages warily.

"Ah, there you are, poppet," crooned a voice.

Her body flashed ice cold and then hot. She turned slowly. Behind her, under one of the spotlights, loomed Doc M.

His velvet coat caught the light like before, gleaming with authority. He didn't have his doctor's bag, but his too-gray eyes pinned her in place, and she flushed. Every detail was in hyper focus again, piercing and implacable. The cages next to her rattled, like the animals were running for cover. Then they fell silent.

Her heart beat loud in her ears. She couldn't understand what he was doing there. It was time for his usual rounds.

"A little bird told me you would be visiting. They didn't mean to, of course, but I have my ways. I couldn't believe anyone would be so audacious as to attack the Queen's property, but here you are."

He smiled, and it shook her from her frozen state. Menace rolled off of him from twenty feet away. But she still had a whole aisle behind her. She ghosted a foot backward.

"Did you really think you could accomplish . . . whatever it was you were trying to accomplish here? Tsk-tsk. No matter, your stupidity is fortuitous."

Defiance raged in her, and she crept back another step. "Stay away from me."

"Oh now, now." His eyes were hard and sharp as steel. "We have things to discuss, you and I."

He took a long step toward her. He was still smiling, but the jovial mask had dropped completely. For the first time, she was seeing the real man underneath, and it was even more chilling because of the grimace stretched across his face.

"You've ruined everything, haven't you, poppet?" He snarled,

"I had such plans for you. But you made a mistake—the Queen will be after you now, and after her ire, there won't be any of you left."

He stalked her efficiently, matching every step she made with a longer stride of his own. With dismay, she realized he was catching up and that he knew this place much better than she ever could.

"I heard about the promise you made to her. Risky, to be sure. But now that you broke in here . . ." He waved a hand at the shelves around him. "You probably won't live long enough to see whether it worked. She can be very possessive about the things she thinks are hers."

CeeCee risked a quick glance behind her. When she looked back, Doc M had gained ground. Her hands curled into fists.

"It's really quite a shame. She's especially vicious and not very nuanced about it when she's angry," he taunted. "At least you know it'll be brutal and quick. The people who make her angry don't *always* die, but they usually do. I've counseled a slower approach for years but to no avail. There are other means that are just as effective, but she feels most of them are too messy."

His brows furrowed thoughtfully as he watched her.

"Of course, that's only if she gets to you first," he mused. "I suppose I'll have to squirrel you away for a rainy day. A bother, but it must be done. I have just the spot, too—quiet, secluded, and quite horrid."

A very real horror raced through CeeCee. Of all his responses, she hadn't expected that. She had thought he was a pimp, someone who would slap her around, try to prostitute her, if she gave him half a chance. That had been naive, so dreadfully naive. Now she knew he was much worse than that. He would hurt her, torture her, without a second thought. He would enjoy it too. She knew it bone-deep.

"I'm not worth that kind of bother," she tried. "The Queen will still be mad, no matter how long you hide me. And then she'll be mad at you too."

"Oh, poppet, I've known the Queen for years, and you've only just met. She'll be all spit and fury for a while—it's quite terrible to see—and then some distraction or new project will capture her focus, and poof, it'll be over. A distraction I'll provide, perhaps. No, you're mine now." He smiled wide when he saw her face pale. "And I'm quite discreet; no one will ever suspect the good doctor or know where you disappeared to. Then I can show you my own methodology. It's really very effective, and when we're all done, you'll be a model employee."

He was enjoying rattling her. As angry as he was, he didn't let it get in the way of a little entertainment. Her own rage rose to match his. But the terror was rising too, which was exactly what he wanted. Her breath came fast and hard, and she shuffled backward to keep him out of arm's reach.

She couldn't talk her way out of this one. Doc M was different from the Queen and the other bullies. The Queen had thought she knew CeeCee and tagged her with convenient labels so she could dismiss her, treat her as a lesser person. Doc M didn't care who she was. He didn't care that she was a person at all. She might as well be another item in the warehouse. She flashed back to the people at the picnic, all their stories. Fury rushed through her like wildfire, bolstering her against the fear. Doc M didn't care about any of them.

"Don't worry, poppet. We might have gotten off to a rocky start, but in the end, you shall be very grateful for my assistance. I promise."

Her fists clenched. She wasn't anybody's poppet. "Damn, you are fucking creepy."

He smiled even wider, just to prove her point.

She leaped backward. Her legs were strong, and she cleared three or four feet before he knew it. He quickened his pace. One of the ladders to the plant platforms was close behind her, and she retreated toward it. She was tall, but Doc M was taller. He lunged at her, and she instinctively scrambled backward up the first few rungs. He swooped again and caught hold of her arm. She wrapped her other arm around a rung and kicked him hard in the side.

He grunted, but he was smiling around his snarl. CeeCee could see the victory in his eyes. He grabbed at her leg and tried dragging her down. She hung on with one arm and fought furiously, screaming and kicking out again and again to dislodge his hands. She knew she was hurting him, even saw blood on his hand where she had kicked it, trying to scrape him off of her, but he wouldn't release his grip. The skinny ladder rocked, jostling the platform. She refused to let go. Bits of plants started falling from above them, white and startling as ghosts. Her eyes jerked up. The platform held the same white mushrooms as that awful alley.

She was outraged in a distant part of her mind. She knew he wasn't anything remotely like a doctor. She knew he was a drug dealer and that he wasn't helping anyone, but growing those horrible mushrooms was just taking it too far.

He managed to pin her free leg with his forearm and elbow so she couldn't kick anymore. CeeCee twisted her whole body back and forth so he was jerking from side to side. He looked startled by the tactic, and she flushed with fresh anger. Did he think she would just give up? The ladder wrenched from side to side with her, and the platform shook violently. Doc M couldn't get the leverage to pull her off completely. Her arm holding the rung was slipping. She knew it was only a matter of time, but she didn't have to make it easy.

She gave another violent heave, and the ladder went up on one leg, overbalancing. They tumbled to the floor, the ladder knocking the back of her head before clattering to the side. His breath went out in a great whoosh. She was dazed, but not so much that she didn't realize she had landed on him. She had to make the first move.

He'd finally let go of her, but she saw him trying to bring a fist around. She pinned his throat with one arm while he was still trying to get air. He gagged, and his hand slapped her face instead. She leaned on him harder. His silver gray eyes bugged out, mad and inhuman and frightening. His other arm was partially blocked by her body, but he twisted his fingers into her clothing, trying to dig into flesh. She knew he was stronger. She could feel it. But she wanted it more. She was desperate and angry and sick of his shit. Before he could buck her off, she scrabbled around for something to hit him with. There wasn't anything heavy or solid or useful, just plants. So she grabbed a mushroom and stuffed it into his mouth instead.

CeeCee had really just been hoping that he would choke on it, but the effect was infinitely stronger.

He gagged again and tried to spit it out. Panic tempered the hate in his eyes. She held her hand over his mouth, and his struggling became frantic as he was forced to swallow. She grabbed another mushroom and shoved it at him, but he turned his head sharply and she only got part in his mouth, smearing the rest across his face. He gave a great heave with his legs, and she flew off, rolling into a shelf.

He lurched upright. He looked furious but confused. She scrambled on hands and knees away from him. He tried to follow her, but the different parts of his body didn't seem to be working together. His eyes looked funny, too, alternating between being out of focus and then blazing mad. When he stumbled and fell over, she started crying in sheer relief. The ugly sob hurt her throat, tears and snot mixing together to coat her face. Doc M's body writhed uselessly on the floor. But he stared at her the whole time.

Her legs wobbled as she got up. She pushed on the first wall she came to without looking back.

She wiped her hands across her eyes, trying to clear the muck away. Her breath kept coming in great gasps, fear and anger and a weird sense of guilt swirling together. She searched for photos in the miles of shelving, pushing walls out of the way as she left Doc M behind. She felt relieved that he couldn't hurt her. They would have time now, she thought dazedly, to find what they needed and get out. She really wanted to get out. Her head hurt where the ladder and then Doc M had hit her. Her fingers tingled and shook.

It wasn't until her sight went funny that she thought about the mushrooms. Then she realized her mistake.

The passage twisted one way and then the other, corkscrewing in front of her. Her head stopped hurting, and so did her heart. Everything went very blue, lush as velvet, and something flew past and all around her, sparkling. CeeCee thought they might be stars. Yes, this aisle was full of stars. She wondered how Doc M had gotten a whole universe in here. Her body felt funny, like it was further away from her than normal, but she was too interested in looking around to pay attention to it much. There was a mirror there, at the end of the aisle, a mirror just out of reach, just ahead, in no time at all. She walked up to herself, and it was like she was seeing CeeCee for the first time.

There was a faint outline behind her; it glowed in time with her pulse. The outline got stronger and brighter, or maybe her perspective changed, because it was in front of her now. No, it was all around her. It was all of her, bright and shining. She thought the light outline ended, but it didn't—it just went on and on. She was much bigger than she thought. She spun around and watched herself whirl in the velvet galaxy. It was beautiful, and she fit exactly.

She had something to do, though, so she turned away from the mirror. *What was it again?* She pushed the walls and pushed them again. They opened into galaxies and nebulas and her heart. She knocked backward into a shelf, and it started raining stars.

She picked up one of the stars. It shone and shone in the light. It looked exactly like a little boy. She picked up another, and it was a love letter on faded, torn paper. The halos were so bright around them.

A wall shivered, and Jesse pushed into the room.

"Look! I found stars," she cried out.

"CeeCee!" He threw himself down next to her and gathered her face in his hands. "Are you okay? I heard you scream, and I got stuck behind one of the shelves. What happened?"

"Look!" she said again and pushed them at him.

He took the handful of photos and papers and looked at the rest on the floor where they were sitting. "You found them," he said. "I didn't think there would be so many."

She danced her hands in the air in front of her and sent the galaxies spinning. "We'll have to give everyone their stars back."

"Are you okay?" He narrowed his eyes at her. He touched the bright red spot on her cheek.

"Was I not supposed to touch the mushrooms?" she asked him vaguely.

"Holy shit, did you eat them?!"

She shook her head and pointed at her eyes. *Look up*, she remembered suddenly. Those mushrooms had saved her. "Everything is rich now. It's just like swimming. I knew it would be."

"You just touched them?"

She nodded and petted his hair when he leaned close to her. "You are all gold and orange, did you know that?"

"It should wear off soon. You promise you didn't eat any?"

"I promise." She leaned forward to kiss him. His warmth seeped into her skin, all the way to her center. She closed her eyes and felt a profound peace. "I kicked Doc M's ass," she whispered into his shoulder. "It was kind of an accident on purpose. He said he was going to hide me away."

His arms tightened around her, and he kissed her hair. "Well, that's just ridiculous," he said very tenderly. "No one can hide you away."

He leaned back and looked at the photos again. A large cardboard box lay on the floor next to her, probably the one she had knocked down. It was too big to easily sneak across the beach.

"We should take everything," he said and rummaged along the shelves until he found two smaller boxes. "Can you walk? Do you think you can carry one?"

The mushroom was already starting to wear off. The halos around the photos and letters diminished as she watched. She was sad to see them go, but part of her knew they were still there. Her body felt a little floaty, but everything else was coming into focus.

Jesse hurriedly scooped up papers where they had fallen and closed them up tight in the boxes. He searched the shelf behind her and found another box of jewelry and trinkets. He slipped it into his backpack, then helped her stand. She was surprisingly steady, but the universe still played at the edge of her vision. She thought the light might stay forever.

"We should get out of here. Are you ready?" he asked.

She nodded. He handed her a box, and she carried the stars down the aisle. She hoped she had the picture that belonged to Apple Cheeks.

The tide had come in while they were inside, and the narrow strip of sand was even narrower. The humped shapes had shifted closer to the water, but there were still just as many as before. A crescent moon had risen, and it lit a path straight down the beach. It glittered to CeeCee's eyes as if it had been waiting for her.

Jesse said, "It's going to be slow going with the boxes, but we'll go the same way we came in."

"No," she said. "Doc M is here. I think we should run."

"What?"

Instead of answering, she bolted down the stairs. When she reached the bottom, she took off running right down the moonlit path. She clutched the box, and her long legs ate up the sand. She felt larger than she had before.

Jesse caught up to her, and they ran side by side. They passed the first of the sleeping walruses, and a head popped up with a grunt. Then more stirred, and more heads lifted. A massive walrus in the center bellowed and started pushing himself up. That must have been a signal because the entire group shifted and called each other and humped along in their direction, faster than one would think.

But CeeCee and Jesse were faster at a full run, by far. They blew past the angry walruses. The far end of the herd maneuvered to cut them off, but it was too late. CeeCee heaved in great breaths of cold, brisk air, and it cleared the last of the mushroom from her head. They bolted for the wall, scrambling over the rocks and through the hole.

She stood gasping in front of the wall. Now that the mushrooms had worn off, she couldn't quite believe she had done that.

Actually, yes, she could. That run made her feel more like herself than tiptoeing around ever did.

Leave It All Behind

They stood on the other side of the gap, expecting to see park residents hanging out in front of the bay doors, expecting to have to scurry run past a few of Doc M's lackeys, expecting the night to feel the same as when they went through the hole.

Instead, the air felt electric. She didn't need to say anything; she knew he felt it too.

Jesse swiveled his head around, trying to locate the change. Shouting echoed from inside the park. No one was on the loading dock, but the fire still burned, roaring high above the edge of the trash can. He twisted back toward the wall, and CeeCee spun with him. Had they been followed? No. But all around the jagged edge of the hole, someone had spray-painted "Dead Hearts Down" in red paint. It glared bright as a beacon.

"Holy crap, that's how Doc M found me!" CeeCee gasped. "I thought they were going to be quiet. After all those threats to keep our mouths shut!"

"Yeah, well." Jesse looked angry. "I think someone decided to use it instead. To use us."

Down the alley, the Queen's guards came around a corner. They milled in front of the factory and other buildings, poking at grates and opening doors. Their tunnel escape was out.

CeeCee instinctively pressed back into shadow and moved in the opposite direction, Jesse on her heels. She started to use the nonchalant, unworried pace that Jesse used with such good results. But he hurried her faster. The boxes they carried made them too conspicuous. As they barreled away from the park, they realized there was more going on than incriminating graffiti.

It was a protest, maybe even a revolution. They had organized quickly. Or maybe they had been organizing for months, and Jesse and CeeCee had just given them an opportunity. It was a different type of protest than she expected. Outside, when a rally got out of hand, troublemakers started fires or looted and destroyed business areas before people went safely back to their homes. Here, setting fire to anything was setting fire to everything they had, so the revolt was quieter and sneakier, all sabotage and messages that rang loudly in the silence. New spray-painted tags had popped up everywhere. Slogans and artwork had been embellished or changed. CeeCee realized that some of the strange graffiti marks she had seen must have been political messages all along.

Groups of men and women ran down the alleys or huddled in doors. She recognized some of them from the club the night before. Guards moved in squadrons and challenged people in loud commanding voices, or pushed people up against walls. Anxiety tightened her stomach painfully. While she cheered the protesters on silently, there were too many people out now. She and Jesse couldn't get caught. They shouldn't even be seen.

Now that the mushrooms had worn off, all the peace of the stars had dissipated.

They slunk from dark corner to shadowed spot and picked any empty alleyway they found. The plan had been to take the mementos back to Jesse's bolt-hole, then head for the mirrors. The photos could be stored there until the next gathering, where Jesse could spread the word quietly. But without the tunnels, it was a long way to that part of the byways. And they couldn't climb to the rooftops without being seen, not with the boxes.

"What are we going to do?" She crouched next to a dumpster and scanned the street.

"We're going to have to stash these." His anxiety showed in the tense lines of his jaw.

"Can we find someone to give these to? Maybe one of the protesters?"

A bottle crashed on a street near them, followed by ugly voices. The sounds pinged through her like bullets.

Jesse flinched. "I don't know if they're a good idea, either."

"They wouldn't turn us in, would they?"

"No, but they might stop us from leaving. We're useful to them now."

The hair on her neck stood up. That had never occurred to her. No wonder Jesse never wanted to join the revolution.

"Listen," he said urgently, "if anything happens, drop the box and just go for the mirrors."

She leaned forward until her forehead could touch his, even with the boxes in the way. He breathed in deeply as they looked at each other. His gold eyes glowed in the dim light. She smiled faintly before they got up, as one, to keep going.

The alleys were a mess. Spray paint and garbage and worse were everywhere. Dodging people was hard. You would think people would go into hiding until it blew over, but it seemed like more of them were walking the byways.

They turned a corner and almost smacked into two guards. A scream caught and died in her throat. She would have started swinging if she hadn't been holding a box.

Jesse pushed in front of her. He challenged them with his stare. She didn't understand what he was doing for a minute. But the guards were both uncannily graceful, and they had matching sour looks on their faces, like they wanted to be anywhere but there.

It was a tense moment before one of the guards nodded.

Jesse glanced at her quickly before veering around them. She gingerly scooted between the guards.

"You've got to get out of sight," one of them hissed as they hurried away.

A block down, a figure hovered anxiously at a corner, peeking at the guards around the building's edge. CeeCee recognized his frame and sped up toward him.

"Apple Cheeks!" she cried out.

"Oh, my dear, I was so worried! Everyone went crazy a while ago! I was at the park watching, and Doc M left in the middle of his rounds. He never does that." He wrung his hands fretfully.

She pushed the box she was holding at him. "We got the photos. Can you make sure these go to the right people?"

"Oh, my dear, of course, of course!"

"There are more," said Jesse. "But we've got to hide these for now."

Apple Cheeks turned and scurried alongside a building. He kicked at a basement window at just the right place, and it popped open.

"This window is always very agreeable," he said. "And no one knows her like I do."

He pushed the box in and then crawled through the window. Jesse looked slightly impressed.

"Okay then," he said.

CeeCee crawled in next, and Jesse passed his box through to her. It was dark as pitch until Apple Cheeks lit a candle. Inside was a cluttered space, just one small room of unfinished drywall, like someone had started to remodel the basement but abandoned the project. Another window faced the adjacent street. It smelled like urine and Apple Cheeks and Darjeeling tea. Boxes, tins, and old blankets were piled up next to a lone apple crate—anything small enough to fit through the window. There was no door.

"It gets lonely here, but it'll do," Apple Cheeks said in answer to their unspoken question.

CeeCee set the other box down. "We haven't had time to look, but we think your photo might be in here somewhere," she said gently.

"You did it. You really did it," he said, eyes shining. He reverently opened the top of the box. "Such a dear."

He looked at them, and his face was full of something like wonder. It hit her harder than she expected. Her throat tightened and burned. She cared about people, unlike Doc M. She *liked* people, even when they weren't always nice to her. People were interesting and always different, and their lives meant something, no matter what anyone said. She just spent so much time alone, she hadn't known how deeply she cared, until now.

"Thank you," he said simply.

She nodded at Apple Cheeks. Without her saying a thing, Jesse wrapped his arms around her. How did he know her so well in such a short time? She leaned heavily against him.

"Do you want to rest?" he asked. "We can hole up here until morning."

"It'll be harder to sneak past people during the day. I think we should keep going."

"And get you out," he whispered.

"We should both get out," she said back, her voice rough. "You can stay with me. I'll figure out something with my mom."

He laughed quietly. She suspected he was giving her that look when she was being naive.

They peered through one window then another. When the way looked clear, they crawled to the street. She paused just outside and gazed back at Apple Cheeks. "Thank you for everything," she said.

His face broke into the cheeriest smile yet.

In the alleys, it was getting louder; it was getting worse. Cee-Cee hunched her shoulders instinctively. It was as if the byways had boiled over. More people were in the streets. The quiet, sneaky attacks were done. Jesse grabbed her hand. They ducked their heads down and ran. There was no point trying to look inconspicuous anymore. Everyone was running.

They passed tiny Eugenia, with a sledgehammer that seemed much too big for her, smashing a doorknob clean off a door. She shouted orders to revolutionists, and a group split off down an alley. A second later, a squadron of guards waving nightsticks made a beeline for her. Eugenia brandished the sledgehammer at them.

CeeCee and Jesse dove into a side passage before they were spotted.

"They're breaking the locks," he gasped.

She bet they were dismantling the gates at the gardens too. "Then we can try a halfway shop," she said, "if we can get there."

Jesse looked fierce and determined, even more so than when they decided to break into the warehouse. "We'll get there," he said.

They crossed to the next alley, but there was nowhere to go. Shopping carts had been lined up at each end of the passage, filled with trash, and set on fire. Jesse went to push one away, and the metal blazed hot. CeeCee kicked at one with her boot, but it was tied to the other carts and only sparks moved, shooting out at them. She couldn't tell if someone was trying to protect their space or lay a trap.

They turned down another path, and a crowd was standing off against an uneasy squadron of Queen's men. No one really wanted to engage. The protesters outnumbered the guards three to one. And even the guards realized that they themselves were more professional bullies than they were professional soldiers. CeeCee and Jesse backed up quickly. Someone roared, and a bottle exploded behind them.

They ran past an office building, and a late-night worker stared, oblivious, at his computer while the revolution raged outside. Jesse and CeeCee couldn't get out of the area. The byways seemed to be responding to the chaos by being even more confusing than usual. Or maybe too many residents were pulling on it at once, making demands the byways couldn't fill. They finally got to an area Jesse was happy with. "Yes! It's a straight shot down here." He hurried down a side path.

He pulled up short at the mouth of the alley, and CeeCee ran into his back. She looked over his shoulder. Hammers and some of the scarier-looking park residents were bunched together, blocking the next street. They weren't alone. Hammers spoke urgently to a large group of Queen's guards. Whatever he was saying, the guards were nodding in agreement, their faces hard and aggressive. Most of them carried clubs or knives. There were no cats in the group to let them slip through.

"Shit," she said very quietly.

Jesse turned toward her, and his face was terrible. It was part ferocity and part that fear she had seen when he thought she was caught at the market. "I'll lead them off," he said. "Get to the half-way shops. If the locks have been broken, you should be able to get through."

CeeCee's heart was in her throat, and she choked on it.

"No! No way!" She clutched at him in rising panic. He had said it before, to just drop everything and run, but she hadn't really thought they would be separated.

"You have to." He held her face in his hands and said urgently, "They're organizing—if we wait too long, they'll start blocking the routes, and that's too many men to get by. I'll make a distraction. They know my face more than they know you, and by now, Doc M knows I'm helping you. Head that direction." He waved to the right. "And concentrate on the halfway shops."

"What if you get caught?" Her vision was blurring.

"I won't." He shrugged and smirked his old cocky grin. "I'll work it out."

She knew the act was for her benefit, but that didn't mean he couldn't do it. He was amazing, after all.

That didn't make her feel any better.

"What if the byways won't let me go?"

"Remember—where do you belong?"

"I belong there." She started crying; she couldn't help it. "The only part of me that belongs here is the part that belongs with you."

"Well, that's okay then," he said and kissed her fiercely. When they broke apart, his eyes were shiny and wet and too large. He walked backward away from her, toward those horrible men. "I'll find you no matter where you are," he promised. Then he turned and ran.

Her brain didn't work for a minute. It just blanked out, probably to stop her from screaming. But when she heard the first yell and a faint laugh she recognized, she spun on her heel.

"It's time to go," she said ferociously to herself, to the alley, to where she needed to go. She took a firm step forward and thought of home.

TWENTY-TWO

Breathe

The byways didn't take her anyplace near home. It was chaos in the alleys. Crashes and shouts echoed loudly through the streets. People were running back and forth. Some were protesters, some were guards, some were fleeing the chaos, but others were taking advantage where they could. A large man with a rhino horn ducked out of a doorway to look down the block, and an old woman snuck into the room behind him. She came creeping out a moment later with an armful of cloth. A young man sang quietly on a roof, and rocks floated up from the alley floor to hover around his head. When a guard yelled at him, he pelted the man with the stones. Fights were breaking out everywhere. CeeCee ducked behind a garbage can, wrapped her hair tightly in a bun, and pulled her hoodie over her head.

There were other things traveling the alleys too. Something that looked like a six-foot plant crept toward people gathered at a crossroad. The way it moved looked predatory. She yelled and threw a loose brick in its direction. The people spun around, and a man pulled out a lighter and set a stick on fire—primitive, but it worked. He waved it at the plant, and it cringed back.

CeeCee kept moving, no matter who or what she saw. She ran past the same building three times, turning down a new alley every time. She doggedly veered back to the right direction. She couldn't stop; otherwise, Jesse would have left for nothing. She gritted her teeth stubbornly, refusing to give in. She could feel that exhaustion again, nibbling at her edges.

She ran and walked and hid for a long time. It was very early in the morning again and just as cold as that first night.

Her legs burned with fatigue, so she slowed to a stop. She hadn't seen anyone in a while, but she could hear them. She leaned against her knees and tried gauging where she was. It felt like when she had first entered the byways, one endless alley after another.

Her hands shook as she gulped the last of her water. A vague thought fussed at the back of her mind. Something was familiar—another time she had been going nowhere. If she weren't so wrung out, she could probably figure out what it was.

She crouched down to put the bottle away, and on the ground was a gray-and-white feather, half-matted in the garbage. It reminded her of the birds when Jesse found her. She straightened up slowly. That was after she had run into Doc M again and was trying not to be seen. That was when she kept walking in circles. The byways had taken her to empty alleys. It had tried, in its own way, to help her stay out of sight.

Maybe . . . she had been approaching this wrong. She had been trying to do two things at once: avoid people and find a way out. Maybe she couldn't do both; maybe the byways knew that. "No more hiding," she whispered.

She concentrated on how it felt to listen to music in her

room, then laughing with her mom, the sense of belonging that she hadn't fully comprehended until she missed it. She didn't think about the alleys or Doc M or the Queen's guards. She didn't think about hiding. She thought about her friends at school and the crowded halls. She thought about opening doors and walking right through.

She took a step, and her leg buckled. She staggered until she caught her balance. The alley stretched out in front of her as she moved doggedly onward, her muscles quivering. She imagined having breakfast with her mom, pancakes at their kitchen table. The bricks blurred and wavered.

Suddenly, there were a lot more doors in front of her. She knew they weren't there before. She clutched at each doorknob, willing them to be unlocked. "These aren't open," she said to the byways. "These aren't home."

Down a side alley, she glimpsed a furtive group of men tearing apart a wooden crate. A rabbit woman stood at a doorway, looking out worriedly. CeeCee ignored them all. She turned down a path full of doors. The passage grew dark, hemmed in by towering buildings. The doors were shadowy and hard to see in the dimness.

But there was a light.

A mirror was there, down at the end of the alley. It was far away, but she knew it down to her bones. Through it, she could see a spot of brightness and the clutter of a room. The brightness called to her like a ringing bell.

CeeCee ran. She was so tired, she was clumsy—clumsy and too loud and not very fast, but she kept her eyes on the mirror, willing it to be true. She crashed into garbage cans and stumbled against a door, stopping to catch her breath while she stared in painful hope. She knew she was making a racket. Something flickered in the corner of her eye, but she was concentrating too hard to pay attention. If it were a guard, he would have shouted by now. She pushed herself off the doorframe and saw the flicker again. She turned her head, just a little.

From a side path, jumping toward her, were blocks of gorgeous, vicious colors. The jib jab was down there.

Icy horror cascaded through her. With a pulse of adrenaline, she pounded down the alley. She kicked a bottle, and it echoed loudly. The urge to look behind her, to see how close the colors were, screamed at her. But she was afraid, so afraid, that if she looked away, if she looked back into the byways, the mirror would vanish. She had to stay focused.

Now she was close enough to see through the mirror clearly. There were racks of clothes and little toys and miniature teapots. They looked . . . strangely . . . familiar, like she had been there before. It was familiar . . . but not. Then it clicked. She was seeing it from the wrong angle. She knew this place! She couldn't believe it—it was the import shop! The place where she'd stolen the rabbit.

She stumbled the last few feet, reaching forward and nearly falling. The cool glass pressed against her fingertips. A great sob tore out of her. She floundered a moment, trying to organize her thoughts. She needed to be there, on the other side, not this side with the colors coming, with that horrible gurgling scream the man had made when the colors touched him. Her hands scrabbled at the glass.

"Don't do that!" she shouted at herself, and pushed the man out of her mind.

She took a deep breath and stared through the mirror. She concentrated on the way the shop smelled, of rice cooking just out of sight, and how the dust made tornadoes in the afternoon light. CeeCee remembered being there with Trudy and how delighted she felt when she found the right T-shirt. She focused on how it felt to be standing *there* on the carpeted floor instead of *here*. She pushed at the mirror, and it wasn't quite so solid. A fuzzy tingle ran through her hands.

A color jumped on her arm, pearly green and beautiful. It burned like acid, right through her hoodie. CeeCee tried to scream, and it came out a strangled hiss instead. She wanted to bat it away, but she knew it wouldn't work, and she kept her hands crushed to the mirror. The pain clawed at her. She could feel the edges of the color probing her skin, sharp and corrosive, teeth and fire at once. It was eating its way down, prying to get to the heart of her.

Through the agony, something funny happened in her brain, different than what had happened with the mushrooms, and more alarming. Emotions swirled up inside her, random and abrupt. The color burrowed into her arm, and it wasn't just eating flesh and bone. It was eating all that she was, everything she felt and believed and hoped. It took not just terror and pain but, absurdly, pride and joy and laughter; embarrassment and triumph; shame and compassion; everything she hated, and everything she loved. And as she struggled to control her panic, her feelings were held up for judgment. It was as if the color were saying, "See? You're not good enough to have this," and then it devoured each one. It was an attack on her soul.

It was a funny thing, though, the color's voice, the one judging her—it sounded an awful lot like her own.

Her energy sapped as if siphoned away. The voice whispered at her to give up. She struggled to concentrate, to keep pushing through the glass. The other colors would catch up soon. Her body trembled violently. She felt the color stripping her away.

But as it peeled her piece by piece, in the obscene intimacy of its attack, a little of its camouflage stripped away as well. She got a glimpse of it beneath the surface. The color, the beauty of it, was nothing but a disguise, a thin, pretty veneer to pull victims in. Underneath, it was only a gray mass and gristle and gaping maw, nothing but hunger and horrible need. And under that, she sensed the absolute assurance of a predator who knows it has you.

Anger rushed in, and she felt that judged as unworthy as well. But her anger was always stronger than her fear. The judgment made her furious, fighting mad, and her hand closed into a fist on the mirror. "You can't have any of me," she snarled.

She held her rage to her as if it were a precious thing. It was hers, after all. They were all hers: all her intense feelings, her exuberant reactions, her strength. Her fury focused into sharp will. She gathered up all the emotions swirling inside her and shoved at the glass.

CeeCee thought about her mom. She thought about the sweet, dusty scent of the shop. She recalled the sign that always hung crooked and how she wanted to straighten it. She remembered the way the clothes felt on the rack under her hands and her mom laughing at her quirky finds. She flashed to the lucky-cat jar full of pens on her desk in her room. She had bought it here— right here, standing at the register and resting her elbows on the countertop while the tiny shopkeeper swore at the machine for sticking again. She remembered it like it was still happening.

She fell through the mirror, the jib jab color falling away from her arm as if it had been scraped off. CeeCee sprawled on the floor. She cried helplessly into the musty carpet.

Suddenly, the shopkeeper was there, coming around a stack of boxes with her dark hair sticking out all over, like she had been unpacking merchandise.

"Oh!" she said. "You came through the mirror? Are you all right?"

"I got lost," she gasped without thinking. "I got stuck."

"Yeah," the woman grunted. "That's always a pain in the ass."

CeeCee sat up slowly. The shopkeeper's lack of surprise would be shocking if she wasn't so exhausted. The woman gently took her arm and looked at the ugly, open wound through the ruined hoodie. It felt like her arm was on fire. CeeCee couldn't seem to stop crying.

"You're lucky I came in early," the woman said. "I heard there was trouble starting." She nodded at the mirror. "I wanted to check the store, listen for news, you know."

CeeCee could only nod shakily, and the shop owner grunted again.

"You got someone you can call to pick you up?"

"Yes! Yes, thank you," she said, another wave of relief flooding her. The clock on the wall showed it was five in the morning, and she didn't think she could manage the walk home. She didn't think she could manage much of anything at the moment. Then she remembered. "Wait!" she cried, and fumbled in her pockets. "This is yours." She thrust the rabbit into the woman's hands. "I've had it the whole time. I'm so sorry."

The shopkeeper looked at the key chain and then met her eyes with a sharp nod.

"You're a good girl."

Her mom was frantic, of course, and furious, and very, very happy. She rushed CeeCee to the emergency room, and in between the crying and the yelling, there was an endless embarrassing conversation about whether she needed a rape kit. Besides the wound on her arm, she had a sizable knot on her head where the ladder had hit her, and several bruises.

Despite her injuries, the cops thought she had run away to party. She insisted she got lost and a man had been chasing her.

The younger cop kept peppering her with questions. Under the cold, sterile lights of the emergency room, she sounded sketchy even to her own ears. It was hard to know what to leave out, until she realized that everybody she had met was a regular person. It didn't matter what they looked like or what they could do or where they lived.

"Why didn't you borrow a phone?" the young cop kept asking.

"I tried," she said for the hundredth time. "They looked right through me. No one would help. Wait, that's not right. There *were* some people who helped me." Her heart tightened painfully. "But none of them had a phone. They were all street people."

Like Jesse—he was all she could think about. Did he make it past those men?

The cop sighed. She stared dully at the dirt caked under her nails. She knew he didn't believe her. Before the byways, that would have really pissed her off. Now it hardly mattered. Sometimes the impossible things are the ones that are most truly real.

"That guy who was chasing you—what did he look like?"

When she described Doc M, the older cop started and looked at her with a blank, knowing stare. "She's back now," he interrupted his partner. "That's the important thing."

When she finally, *finally* got home to her room, she walked up to her closet mirror and pressed her forehead to the glass.

"Are you there?" she whispered. "Are you okay?"

Trudy ditched school as soon as she heard CeeCee was home. Trudy never ditched school. Then she sat in her room doing homework, while CeeCee slept like the dead or grieving.

CeeCee didn't *want* to sneak out—that would break both their hearts—but she was starting to get desperate. Her mom wouldn't let her leave the apartment. She took off days from work she couldn't afford, mainly to lecture and hug her a lot. As happy as CeeCee was to be home, she couldn't sit in her room any longer. All she did was worry. Was Jesse all right? Did the protest manage to break the locks, or did it turn into a full-out revolution? Did anyone get caught? Every night, she had a nightmare about her friends lined up on the shelves of the warehouse, like those creepy stuffed animals. If she didn't move, she was going to scream. After looking up city maps online, she was pretty certain of at least two areas with halfway points. She wasn't ready to get too close yet, but she could throw notes in bottles down the alleys.

Finally, on Thursday, she convinced her mom that she would never catch up in class if she didn't go back to school. Her mom bought her a new phone with a lot of tracking software on it, but CeeCee was okay with that. In the end, she had to promise to text practically every five minutes.

That morning, she found herself dressing extra carefully, like it was the first day of school. Her favorite hoodie was ruined, of course, and she didn't want to wear another one. She didn't want to wear anything that suggested "homeless" or fed the rumors. It was silly, she knew, but still. She picked out a super-soft midnight-blue sweater that she usually saved for going out to dinner. Her backpack was also the worse for wear, but underneath the grime, it still smelled like oranges and mint. She hung it reverently on the back of a chair, and decided to just carry her folders and a pencil case that fit her phone. Catching a glimpse of herself in the mirror was startling. Even with a bulky bandage on her arm and the bruise shadowing her forehead, she looked suddenly, inexplicably, older.

Stepping into school, the hallway was just as loud as it always was. She walked slowly, almost floating in place, as she adjusted to the noise crashing into her senses. She pulled out her fuzzy pencil and rolled it between her fingers, grounding herself. She could feel people staring. Maybe they were staring because of the rumors, maybe because of the way she was acting. But, for the first time ever, she was excruciatingly glad to be visible. She knew what she was doing and why, even if no one else did.

Science was first period. The day stretched out strange and familiar in front of her. She knew it would be hard to concentrate, but if she could make up her homework, she'd have more time to find a way to contact Jesse.

"Hey, CeeCee!" Her lab partner, Gwen, was waiting outside their classroom door. "Are you all right? I heard you were missing for three days!"

"Yeah, I got lost. Like, really lost." She had decided it was the easiest answer to give most people, the ones cruising for gossip anyway. But Gwen, although she was lost in her own world sometimes, was also super smart and creative and, most importantly, not judgy. "It was really scary," she confided. "I'm glad it's over."

"I bet!" Gwen gave her a sympathetic look. "People are saying you joined a biker gang."

CeeCee barked a laugh. That rumor was kind of awesome, actually. "Yeah, let's go with that one," she said. "Next I'll be the leader of the biker gang!"

Gwen laughed. "Right? And then . . ." A tense look crossed her face, and she fell quiet.

"Morning, trailer," a voice sang smugly. "I heard you had another incident. What did you do? Get in a bar fight? End up in juvie? Shack up with some loser trailer trash boy for the weekend?"

"Maybe they'll have some trailer babies," piped someone else.

CeeCee turned halfway. It was the usual squad. They stood in a loose semicircle, blocking the hall. They were striking poses and showing their best sides and smirking venomously. But it was the venom of overly groomed poodles. Despite her bright designer clothes, somehow Taylor looked washed out and smaller and suddenly very . . .

"Boring," said CeeCee, surprised. She turned back to Gwen. "So do you think you can help me catch up in science?"

"Um." Gwen's eyes darted between CeeCee and the girls behind her. "Yeah, sure. Do you need help in math too? Mr. Beauchamp is always picking on you."

CeeCee threw her up hands. "Finally! Someone notices!"

"Hey!" A finger stabbed her in the back. "We're talking to you!"

She looked over her shoulder. Ashley looked imperious, her hand raised for another stab. CeeCee stared hard at her, face blank with just a touch of menace laced in. She hated to borrow a move from Doc M, but it was certainly effective. Ashley faltered and withdrew the hand. CeeCee continued staring until Ashley looked distinctly uncomfortable and wavered back a step. Out of the corner of her eye, she saw Taylor start to puff up. CeeCee pointedly turned her back on her before she could bluster any more bullshit.

There was a pause before she heard the footsteps edging away. She grinned wickedly.

Gwen goggled at her. "Wow, CeeCee! That was amazing!"

She shrugged. "I don't have time for it, you know?"

"I'm glad you're back. Class is way more fun with you there."

She cranked through her work as if she were on fire, staying behind after every class. It was never a question of whether she could *do* the work; that had never been the issue. It was just a matter of letting distractions or drama get in the way. She still couldn't control the sensory overload, but the emotions—those were entirely her own. At lunch, she met up with Trudy, who blew off the Committee Crew. Their fight seemed to have dissipated in the face of . . . well . . . perspective. And it turned out it was the caterer who had misplaced the money after all.

"The girls are still being bitchy about it, though," Trudy confessed over sandwiches. "Always doing half the work but pointing all their fingers."

"Ugh." CeeCee rolled her eyes. "That would drive me nuts."

But as much as she had missed Trudy, her mind kept going back to the byways. In CeeCee's spare moments, she yanked on unused doors and checked out forgotten spots on campus. You could never be sure what might turn out to be a halfway place. They could be anywhere. At one point, a dark head of hair slipped gracefully around a corner. She hurried after him, only to find a senior from the track team scowling at his locker. All day, people stared and they whispered, but she had other things to think about. Wondering what happened after she left was driving her crazy. She really wanted to talk to Jesse. Missing him was an ache that wouldn't stop.

By the end of the day, she felt as taut as a wire. The library was next on her list, and hope beat like a wild, caged thing as she hurried down the front steps of school. If the library didn't work, she would go back to the import shop and ask for news. Maybe the shopkeeper would be willing to send a message. She swallowed. She still didn't know who worked for the Queen and who didn't. It was a risk she'd have to take.

The weather was turning, and the cement kicked up heat. She thought about a long summer sitting in her apartment. It sounded almost as unappealing as summer school. She could get a job or volunteer somewhere, but she knew her mind would always be in the same place.

She was never good at waiting.

The library was only a few streets away. It called to her, and she broke into a jog, eating up the distance. Her urgency grew with every step. When the library materialized at the end of the block, she practically flew to it. She pushed through the doors and stopped, panting, just inside. The need to find him pressed on her, but she didn't know where to start. One of the librarians gave her a wide-eyed stare. CeeCee could feel static buzzing along her skin. She took a breath and tried to look a little less frantic.

"Excuse me." She approached the checkout desk. "I'm looking for someone—a young man, dark hair, about this tall. He's graceful and . . . um . . . cute. Have you seen him come in?"

The librarian gave her a sour look. "Do you need help finding a book?"

CeeCee sighed. "No, thanks. I'll just look around."

The stacks of shelves seemed smaller than she remembered. She poked through the half-hidden reading nooks and made a circuit of the tables twice. There was a bulletin board, and she scrutinized it for messages, coded or otherwise. She even lurked next to the men's bathroom until a librarian scowled at her. Finally she flopped, defeated, into a chair.

He wasn't there. She hadn't realized how much she had expected to find him until now. Her face flushed hot, and she swallowed around the burning lump in her throat. She studied the room to distract herself. Ordinary high school students worked at tables. In front of her, a young mother sat in the story-time circle, trying to teach her unimpressed toddler to read. A low bank of shelves held librarian recommendations and "books of the week." The ceiling was tall and vaulted, with high windows and an equally tall sliver of mercury glass above the shelves reflecting the afternoon light. It was all lofty and impressive, which is probably why she got in trouble here so often. That stupid ceiling really bounced back sound.

She glared at it to stop the tears. What if he had gotten caught? What would she do if she never saw him again—pretend that the byways had never happened? That was almost tempting . . . push it down, pretend it was all a dream. But she didn't think she could; the outside world wasn't the same anymore. Part of her knew she'd always be looking. *Maybe the Queen was right*, she thought. Maybe the byways had marked her after all.

No matter how tempting it was, she could never, *would never*, forget Jesse.

I can't give up. Her jaw clenched, stubborn and aching. I'll just have to wait, and come every day if I have to. She probably had an hour before her mom got home and freaked out. CeeCee texted her to let her know she was studying and then pulled out her homework. She tried to pretend everything was normal, like anything could ever be normal again. The words on the page danced around blurrily. She forced them into stillness through sheer will and doggedly started on homework.

After a while, the toddler began fussing, and the mother packed her up and left. Students cleared out in ones and twos. Eventually, even the librarians disappeared into the depths of back rooms. The sudden quiet reminded CeeCee of the alleys, like someone was listening.

There was a tiny sound—maybe not even a sound. It was so tiny, she shouldn't have noticed it. Her head jerked up. She could swear it came from the wall. She heard it again, like a fingernail scrape, somewhere far away . . . no, near that skinny slice of glass! CeeCee's book clattered to the floor. She hadn't considered it before—it wasn't a real mirror, more decorative than functional. Someone would have to squeeze sideways to get through, and not everyone would fit even then. But as she stared, the silver glass rippled like water.

She was running toward the wall before she thought about it. A hand appeared. Just a hand, brown and scraped up, hanging in the air. Then it yanked back out of sight.

She forgot to breathe. The shelf below the mirror wasn't high; it only came to her shoulder. She dragged a chair over and scrambled onto the shelf.

Fingers pushed through again, tense and reaching. She grabbed them and tugged, hauling an arm out up to the elbow. The hand held onto hers tightly, but she felt resistance. CeeCee planted a foot against the wall and the edge of the shelf, precariously balancing her weight. She heaved backward and a shoulder came through, wedged between the sides of the glass. It was going to be a tight fit.

Then the hand jerked back, and she almost lost her grip. Someone was pulling from the other side for sure.

She grabbed his hand in both of hers, let go of all balance, and threw her whole weight back. In the split second before her feet slipped, she felt the hand disappear. "No!" she screamed, scrabbling at the empty air.

Then she saw eyes, golden and gleaming. As she fell, a cat leaped through the mirror, gracefully launching himself to the side so he wouldn't land on top of her when she hit the floor. The carpet was very hard, and she skidded a bit. The cat changed mid-leap, and Jesse collapsed next to her while she writhed on the floor. An ugly bruise colored his cheek purple, his clothes were ripped, and he was missing a shoe. He panted and grinned his crazy grin, the one he wore when he was getting away with something. But underneath it, there was a haunted relief, and he reached over and tightly clasped her hand.

"You're hurt," she said, when she got her wind back. "What happened to your shoe?"

"Guard has it now," he said, breathless and cocky.

She knew getting out had cost something, but she couldn't seem to stop smiling. She could take him to the mall and buy him a pair of Vans. "I know it's selfish, but I'm so glad you're here."

"Good," he said, scooching closer. "Because I can't go back for a while. Hope you meant that stuff about your mom."

She laughed so loudly, a few tears leaked out. "Worth it?" she whispered, leaning in.

"Totally worth it," he said.

She kissed him for three whole minutes before a librarian kicked them out.

Acknowledgments

First of all, a huge, giant thank-you to all my ladies who never stopped encouraging me: Christy Bulan, Jeanne Diaz-Kleiboer, Jeanne Rupprecht, Darcy Ogle, Thuy-anh Do, Sonja Jeter, Monica Pulizzi, Kira White, Jamie Do, Isabel Salcido, Diana Stanley, and Adri Samaniego. Let's go get some tea.

Big hugs and thank you to my parents, Dave and Kitty Pascual, for raising me around so many loved and rescued books. Your enthusiasm when I wrote anything was very much appreciated. (And thank you for being a little weird. That is super helpful when you want to be a writer.) To my family and my extended family, thank you for being too loud, exuberant, and a bunch of characters. (Also helpful.)

Another big thank-you to Brooke Warner and Shannon Green and everyone at SparkPress! Your direction and patience has been amazing. My sincere gratitude to Andrea Chebeleu at A Work of Heart and everyone from the Creative Entrepreneurs group: You were just what I needed at the most perfect time. To Lorraine Haataia, Maya Carlyle, Keiko O'Leary, and the entire Prolific Writers crew, thank you for your never-ending spirit. And I have to send my fondest gratitude to all those early bloggers, writers, and authors who still pop up as cheerleaders.

Thank you to my son, Chance, who has to put up with an awful lot of smartassery. (Good thing he's a smartass, too.) I love you, kiddo. And to my dear husband, Brian . . . you know that feeling when your emotions are so big they fill up your throat and your head and your spirit until they push all the words away? Yeah, that. I'm so, so glad you got to see this with me. Meow, babe.

I'm going to forget someone, I hope you will forgive me, but please know that you are in my heart. More importantly, a bit of you is spinning around in my brain—some look, or gesture, or thing you said, or secret you whispered, or laugh-cry-snort we shared in the car. That little bit is morphing and changing and worming its way into a story or a painting or a batch of cookies. It sounds like theft, but I mean it in honor. It is the way I say, "Thank you, I love you."

So . . . thank you. I love you.

About the Author

Mary Pascual is a writer and artist who believes finding magic is only a matter of perspective. She loves stories about characters with heart and fantastical settings that are more than meets the eye. She grew up in California and enjoys reading, art, traveling, exploring outside, and building elaborate stage sets for Halloween. Writing has taken her on a number of unexpected adventures, including working in high tech, meeting psychics, interviewing rock bands, and even once attending a press conference for Bigfoot. She got hooked on reading adult science fiction and fantasy in the fifth grade— so in retrospect, much of her reading material was completely inappropriate (which probably explains a few things). She lives with her husband, son, and assorted demanding cats in San Jose, California.

SELECTED TITLES FROM SPARKPRESS

SparkPress is an independent boutique publisher delivering high-quality, entertaining, and engaging content that enhances readers' lives, with a special focus on female-driven work.
www.gosparkpress.com

Caley Cross and the Hadeon Drop, J. S. Rosen, $16.95, 978-1-68463-053-0. When thirteen-year-old Caley Cross, an orphan with a dark power, is guided by a jumpsuit-wearing mole into another world—Erinath—she finds a place deeply rooted in nature where the people have animal-like powers and she is a Crown Princess—but she soon learns that the most powerful evil being in *any* world is waiting for her there.

The Goddess Twins: A Novel, Yodassa Williams. $16.95, 978-1-68463-032-5. Days before their eighteenth birthday, Arden and Aurora's mother goes missing and they discover they belong to a family of Caribbean deities. Can these goddess twins uncover their evil grandfather's plot in time to save their mother, themselves, and the free world?

Above the Star: The 8th Island Trilogy, Book 1, Alexis Chute. $16.95, 978-1-943006-56-4. *Above the Star* is an epic fantasy adventure experienced through the eyes of three unlikely heroes transported to a new world: senior citizen Archie; his daughter-in-law, Tessa; and his fourteen-year-old granddaughter, Ella. In this otherworldly realm, all interests are at war, all love is unrequited, and everyone is left to unravel the truth of who they really are.

Below the Moon: The 8th Island Trilogy, Book 2, Alexis Marie Chute. $16.95, 978-1-68463-004-2. Cancer has left Ella mute, but not powerless. When she finds herself in a parallel dimension, she must paint to communicate, fight alongside fearsome warrior-creatures, and—along with her mom, Tessa, and grandpa Archie—overcome the Wellsley family's past in order to ensure a future for everyone.

The Blue Witch: The Witches of Orkney, Book One, Alane Adams. $12.95, 978-1-943006-77-9. Nine-year-old Abigail Tarkana has a problem: her witch magic has finally come in, but it's *different*—and being different is a problem at the Tarkana Witch Academy. Together with her scientist-friend Hugo, she faces off against sneevils, shreeks, and vikens in a race to discover the secrets about her mysterious magic.

Wendy Darling: Volume 1, Stars, Colleen Oakes. $17, 978-1-94071-6-96-4. Loved by two men—a steady and handsome bookseller's son from London, and Peter Pan, a dashing and dangerous charmer—Wendy realizes that Neverland, like her heart, is a wild place, teeming with dark secrets and dangerous obsessions.